THE PRIVILEGE OF DARKNESS

a novel by
Bert Underwood

MALCOLM HOUSE

The characters of the book are purely fictional; therefore, any connection between them and prominent people of the times mentioned is also purely fictional.

Chester House

P.O. Box 1469

New York, New York 10163

ALSO BY BERT UNDERWOOD
A BRANCH OF VELVET

Library of Congress Catalog Card No. 85-72808

ISBN—Hard: 0-935763-00-7 $13.95

ISBN—Soft: 0-935763-01-5 $5.95

Jacket/Cover design by: C. Hutchins

Printed in the United States of America by
BOOKMASTERS—Ashland, Ohio, and BOOKCRAFTERS—Chelsea, Michigan

Publisher
CHESTER HOUSE   PO Box 1469   New York, N.Y. 10163

First Printing, 1985

To dear Rebecca,
    who bravely fought off the thieves and hypocrites,
    the politics of race,
    in the battle for life and dignity.

The Privilege
of Darkness

PART ONE

1859-1861

Chapter 1

That Sunday morning before breakfast Marg had a dish of strawberries and whipped cream. Just a little of those big red gems. Not enough to hurt. For relaxation. She knew religiously that one week's ups and downs could deter a good person. The Christian thing was to persevere, rewarding each day, ready for that mystery of duty. Margery Malcolm Spence was to begin that first week of October 1859 by giving a little party of three favorite old friends. Lydia Farley Smith was down from Lancaster, Pennsylvania, back in the beloved Georgia of her childhood. Louise Johnson, a second cousin, was visiting from Washington, D.C., the nation's capital. The third lady of the party would be a lovely local person, Sue Barrows, a dear young first cousin, who had long enraptured Marg with her beautiful piano-playing. Sue had just finished two years at Oberlin College up North. Blond Margery loved these three handsome and correct ladies more than life itself. She considered it almost a miracle that she could have the older two together once again with Sue. The house would be joyous, like old times. Or was God sending her a warning? He had often intervened this way with something magnificent as a beginning, then before long a terrible devilish consequence would happen. And so it happened that first week of October.

On Thursday morning, when the last of the party things was being put away, a sombre black carriage pulled up before Margery's stately white house on Plum Avenue. An equally sombre black man came knocking at the door. He announced that the Malcolm family was summoning Marg to her father's house. Immediately her good mood fell apart. The Malcolm family had never asked for her before. It had to be a crisis. And sure enough, it was. Her beloved father, Judge Edward Malcolm, had had a stroke. Like the humble, well-bred, God-fearing young woman she was, tall, erect Margery went dutifully to the big house in their perfect carriage.

Pale white faces with tense turned-down lips greeted her in the temple-like house. She and her father had a peaceful few minutes together. Then she exited over thick carpets, saying a cheerful good-bye that was not returned. Then on Friday she came among them again; she and her father had a good talk. Then that Saturday morning, they sent another plush carriage. He was dying. She had to be there with all the rest.

He died quietly, as the week finished. Margery then had to endure the sad faces of the servants fussing over her so that she'd be dressed perfectly for the Monday funeral. She went alone. Among all those strangers, all those prominent people. Had anyone else died she could have taken it. Now her strength wavered among the too-proud Malcolms, the remaining fortress, yet, none having that tender guiding voice of authority which had been with her every year of her life. She'd miss that single strong warm face, with its side whiskers, its justice, its gentle smile. And that little encouraging tap on the shoulder. Stoically she watched with owl eyes and thin pink lips as the earth swallowed his bronze casket. Mountains of flowers in her favorite shades went pressing him into the ground. She had always feared what his death would do to her. Some wise one among the persecuted had whispered that it would make her a new person. But Marg, now alone and independent, knew she could perhaps wind up also a bitter person.

A cool breeze stirred that last moment with him, all life seemed to stand still. Some daisies and roses remained above, to watch her. Still fresh and erect, while she was trembling. Her lips quivered; something sour like lemon juice, a mandibular oozing, seemed to dissolve sweet memories. A reality came to mind: that great man who had been her father had also been her connecting link to everything. With him gone, there'd be no magic god-like person to guard her way. Now she could only speak to God. "Lord, have mercy, please."

***** ***** *****

That beginning October week had blossomed so beautifully. Marg greeted warm breezy days admiring her tall red dahlias which had always won prizes at the Maple Fair. She had no reason to feel herself a stranger in this beautiful place. Maple, Georgia was a thriving river-town nestled on the Chattahoochee at arm's length from Alabama. It was a cultural outpost. A prosperous, tuneful place. Maple citizens enjoyed walking its wide avenues lined with oak and maple trees. Like

4

Savannah, it had been a planned town, and its citizens were proud and at ease in that neat beauty. Visitors too liked its vitality, and that look of style and comfort all around. Almost everyone's spirits were lightened by the well-kept yards and good solid houses, especially on Plum Avenue, the wealthy enclave just off the heart of town. In the beginning days, it had been the best street. Some sea captains had come down from New England in the 1820's, trying their luck American-style. They had built fine New England-type houses on Plum Avenue. And the next generation becoming southerners continued the art. Among them was imposing, handsome Malcolm House, with its mossy green lawn, colorful garden, its four white columns, Georgian or Greek Revival, nobody knew for sure. Standing big at the corner of Spruce, it mingled with giant oaks, and gingko leaves caught the sunlight and shade making a perfect spidery picture of good living.

Originally the Malcolm family had had this as their principle residence; then, in 1845 they built a bigger place out on Peachtree Drive. Judge Edward Malcolm had decided to greet retirement seeking newness. The old house, his prized heirloom, he readily gave to his favorite daughter, Margery. He knew it would help her to leave spinsterhood. And in 1847 when she married Charles Spence the judge was happy, and willingly made all the papers over in Charles' name. The town's scions frowned. Others whispered about it. Most passed it with a quick stare, still calling it Malcolm House, defiantly.

Indeed it remained a grand house in every way. Its white clapboard stretches gleamed elegantly, as its crown of white Victorian garlands. A black captain's eagle stretched over the doorway, and black shutters beckoned as well as matched the spiked iron fence that surrounded the property. Inside, the foyer's high ceiling made it cool and inviting. On the right, a double sitting room had a rare pastel-colored ceiling fresco of angels and cupids done by an Italian artist. On the left, the drawing room paneled in rich pecan trimmed in mahogany and spruce served also as library. There were six magnificent fireplaces done in green granite, topped by beveled bronzed mirrors of the highest quality. The six upper bedrooms were all airy and huge. Parquet floors downstairs glistened as did the solid oak plank floor upstairs. The two staircases had always been carpeted; some people talked about this as an example of the way Judge Edward felt about his servants. They could use either stairs!

One peculiar thing about this grand house, its young master now, Charles Parker Spence, was only a vegetable man. True, he was a prosperous vegetable man, surely the richest one in town and perhaps in all of central Georgia. His matched team of four handsome straw-berry roans proudly pulled his big wagon all over town. This attractive aloof man was gentle to his customers, rich and poor alike. He had a slight body of good proportions, soft curly brown hair, hazel eyes flecked with grey, a face showing Scotch-Irish ancestry foremost. Most people liked that he showed good manners and some breeding. Style, said some!

Those townspeople who knew Margery were happy for her; she could not have done better. Her dreamy-eyed Charles was calm, peace-ful and diligent. Furthermore, he sometimes went to church, and that was all a woman like Marg needed. Her father never criticized her for selecting Charles, for Judge Edward knew that they'd have beautiful smart children to carry on. Others felt a vegetable man living in one of Maple's finest town mansions had to be an imposter. Charles' sup-porters said he went about his chores properly and was never uppity about his station or luck. While the uniqueness of his peculiar position was a growing subject in town, everybody knew that the big fish in Maple were the plantation owners, the bankers, some merchants and officeholders. Charles Spence could be none of these, because he was the wrong caste. Yes, America in the 1850's had rigid and definite castes. Judge Edward belonged to one, and his daughter Margery belonged to quite another. And his son-in-law Charles belonged to still another.

They were a family and yet not a family. Social customs and wealth held everything together. Mainly, the family name was the true crown. Judge Edward scoffed at the plantation scions for making that rule. But he was as strong as any of them, and defiantly kept his New England accent. Often he had told Marg that politics alone could break the entire society apart.

Maple, like the rest of Georgia and the country, in 1859, believed strongly in politics and in the castes. Survival meant the class structure which had been growing for two hundred years. People knew the ranks of life through custom and through their senses. When you hear names and see faces, you quickly classify them, and act accordingly. A respected way of life. A bond as strong as the money people carried in their pockets. Margery had discussed this often with her father. She couldn't believe that all America was so glued to this tainted ritual, this unChristian fashion. The Judge always avoided the direct subject. He taught his pleasant-faced blond daughter to be wise about life and not to expect too much of people. If you had money and class, the charlatans and bigots would go on respecting you. And when he died she wondered immediately how far money, class and family name would protect her future in this place.

***** ***** *****

On that last Sunday of his life, after she had had her strawberries, Marg was feeling glorious. As usual, he came early to Plum Avenue to have breakfast with her. And they had talked about the party she was having that afternoon for her three childhood friends. He was proud that fair Margery loved people and respected the ties that bind. Praising her biscuits, he left as usual as the eight-thirty sunlight hit the fig tree outside the dining room window. Then she scurried about, rushing to get to St. James Methodist on time. She was Baptist, but she went there because her Cousin Donald was its simple and correct minister. That morning she had been up too early, setting rolls and making pies. She couldn't relax during the service.

Maybe it was something her father had said. As usual, he was discussing property and the behavior of her half-brothers and half-sister. In spite of the caste system, he made the Malcolms respect each other through his grants. Those with the pure-white mother wanted everything. And she never discussed things with those people. Alas, Judge Edward knew that the system itself was tricky. The courts were tricky. With all the devils at work, he had put a lot of little things in Margery's hands, hoping she'd see his true aim. She was annoyed to get little things while others got big things. Mainly she worried because she did not have the power in this town of 8,500 to do half of the things he thought she could do.

After benediction, she greeted church friends half in a daze. Matilda and Elias would take the children home in the wagon. She was to stay and pour tea, but Marg didn't feel like such ritual this day. She wanted to get away. Yet, with special company coming home for dinner at three o'clock she knew she had to transform herself to a good mood. Matilda had tried to cheer her up, but this was something between herself and God. She went back to the pews, got on her knees, with heaving chest, and prayed, imitating her sweet mother, with closed eyes and deep concentration. Right away she felt better. The emotions of Man were truly connected to the Spirit World. And belief in the Spirit World could take away the qualms and bad body feelings. Sighing, she vowed she'd always believe that. Getting up, she felt wonderful.

With tingling pink cheeks, she drove her gelding and buggy back to her solid pretty house, feeling refreshed. Her cherrywood piano greeted her with sunlight in its smooth shiny veins. Humming a tune,

7

she polished the wood one more time, and the ivories, knowing that talented fingers would soon make the air alive with cultured music. She draped over the instrument a silk shawl from China. A gift from Aunt Bess. God didn't want her too fussy about material things, but recognizing the beauties of man was culture, a big part of life. Respecting the good taste of her North European forebears, she felt her house looked beautiful. And, her guests would know that it took a caring person with the love of God to make it so. Then cheerfully she joined the black girls in the cookhouse, making sure the prime roast beef was correct, the escalloped potatoes, and the green beans and beets from Charles' wagon.

The meal would be followed by a magnificent peach cobbler she had learned to cook from her grandmother, Margery Lyons, on her mother's side. Her dear grandmother and mother, Alice, had both died in the yellow fever epidemic during the winter of 1844. In this house. In its comfortable attic rooms, now closed. That whole life was now just a memory. It had taken Marg a long time to get over those customs and those deaths. With every death her life changed. Her father called it growing up. She knew the whole concept of her life in Maple was like a delicately-woven fabric. Every thread had its place, and to remove one or two disturbed the pattern terribly. And some outside never had liked the pattern, beautiful as it was. She tried to smile like her mother when thinking such thoughts. Those dear, sterling women could not have possibly lived life without examining its fabric! But it was a silent observation. Nobody would dare discuss the real thing.

The fair, proper Lyons family were property people from Alabama, with Creek Indian blood, and 800 acres. They had had to fight constantly to stay in close with the pure whites, and to stay as rich as they were. Grandfather Shep Lyons had been killed by an erratic neighbor who kept moving fences, stealing land. Marg didn't want to think about those trials this beautiful Sunday afternoon. Cousin Sue would appreciate the cobbler so much, as Grandmother Margery Lyons was her grandmother too. Matilda, who helped out in the kitchen, had wanted to make the pies but Marg insisted on doing them herself. That flaky crust which was Grandmother's made all the difference, as did sweet, meaty peaches. Marg had done every preparation before church, except the baking. Now the tangy cinnamon odor was everywhere.

Just as Marg placed the six pies on the windowsill to cool, Sue arrived, pink-cheeked and smiling, with curly blond hair, white curly ruffles starched perfectly. Wringing her hands quickly in her apron, Marg hugged Cousin Sue, genuinely.

"Oh-h, they smell simply divine," screamed Sue, kissing Marg, then reaching for smiling black Matilda as well. "I told Mama I'd bring her a piece of yo' pie. I knew for sure you'd have it. Bless you, Margery!"

"You can take a whole pie home," said Marg proudly. "I made one for yo' mama, Albert and Mitchell." She loved Sue's younger brothers because they were so correct and handsome. It was a beautiful family, with blond women and red-topped men. All had flawless complexions. And in an age where looks mattered as much as money, those closely-knit, good-looking mulatto families could be proud. Everyone, including the pure whites, appreciated their pleasant features and manners. Most ivory-colored adults could be proud and thankful for God's blessings: the great duty was children, and usually they were diligent and correct, ready to serve the world with gladness.

Margery often thought alone of the fact that her little family had been half-white for several hundred years. They were Malcolms and they were not Malcolms. Tucked on the side, like a fine garment's gold trim. Their little touch of Negro, from the earliest days of America, had not been a curse. The mixture meant everything good. And she had never had reason to think of herself as a black person. They had not been raised that way. The marriages had not produced any brown persons yet. Her father had told her they could be exactly what their looks made them to be. And they really looked the same as the pure-white portions of the family. But the people controlling things knew of the dash of salt, that little Negro in her mother's blood, and the service status of that family. Keeping them down was an art, and politics. Whenever a touch of Africa showed in a man's background, fight it like a bucket of snakes, and this continuous war consumed the American southland, especially among rednecks hating old-rich families.

The near-whites calmly considered that most pure whites were greedy and selfish by nature. The system made them manufacture racial distance where there was none. And they'd court racial ignorance. Only few knew that historically the South had supplied a bevy of beautiful correct young ladies of mixed blood, for years, as proper brides for respectable young Army officers even in the days of the British crown. It was not uncommon for such half-caste women to marry into the best American families. Some were taken up North where there would be no marks on their heritage. Yet, it was not a subject anybody raised: *to be mixed with Negro blood.* And the institution of slavery continued to produce them. Aggressive southern gentlemen, thinking ownership, did fancy the beautiful half-caste girls with their cupid-doll faces. Others fostered a second society to improve on life, as well as to glean a dessert. Yet, as proper society grew, it scorned the mulatto caste, never accepting its ladies, in the sense the pure white wife was a lady. And for generations the fair comely colored women knew that they had to be quiet, charming, dignified and lady-like. Always. In that way, they survived very well.

The mulatto boys were bound to have more problems in life. Whereas many were skilled after excellent apprenticeships, and their works were in demand, there was danger in their lives. Pure white men were jealous of their looks and their skills. They had to be packed and ready. A mobile few searched America well-supported by their aristocratic white fathers, and some could do well in business situations far from home. In secret, for the toll of identity was great. The scorn was in the North as well. Those who stayed home, often errand boys in big houses, remained calm and pleasant, careful never to act like loud-laughing black people. They could be charming and faithful to their own women, but the main thing in life was Duty, a need to work hard, in service or with a skill. Very few could ever move above service class, because so-called pure whites of lesser wit and station made a life of talking them down. Being sons and grandsons of the most-respected white men in town, they were disliked by the poor white trash. But city people were careful not to treat those with money too badly. As Margery's father had said, the South would change as it grew. He wanted his boys to keep on being their dignified selves. Marg, with soul, was his surprise general, waiting in the wings, ready to defend them all. Looking at a near-perfect Sue, with all her Anglo-Saxon beauty, Marg thought: pretty soon politics could make bad times for all of us so-called fair colored people. *We need to enjoy each other more!*

Sue offered yellow chrysanthemums. "Oh, thank you," cried Marg. "These are gorgeous. I have a vase in the conservatory, then let's sit in the parlor till the others come. Maybe you'll play that nice Beethoven tune for me."

"Later," laughed Sue, big-chestedly. "I know Charles will ask me an' I don't want to repeat myself. Hah! Where is he?"

Marg frowned. "Out to the barn. One of his horses got sick last night. Let's not talk about problems. Sue, I'd rather hear about your exciting life at Oberlin. Oh, these mums are so pretty!"

Sue beamed. "I knew you'd like them. Mitchell has a garden full. He wants Charles to sell them with his vegetables. They've been talkin' this for weeks. Marg, how pretty everything looks! You've certainly done wonders to this house. It looks like a millionaire's place."

Marg led the way into the huge, bright conservatory. "Oh, don't exaggerate. We feel very poor, the way prices are going up."

"That's why I didn't go back to Oberlin. Do you think there'll be a war?"

"Sue, let's not talk that way! Here, smell my new herb garden. Isn't it divine? I wanted it indoors to last the winter months. Nice, huh?"

"Everything you do is beautiful! I like these leaded-glass windows. Aren't they one of your changes?"

"No-o," said Marg, clipping chrysanthemum stems. "This was Jane's special room, an' we haven't changed a thing."

"How is Jane?" asked Sue, with a little downward twist to her pink lips.

"No, no. We won't talk about *them*. Not today. Sue, I do believe the world is full of nice people who make you feel good. You are one of them! Come, we'll take these to the parlor. Louise was so worried that rain might ruin my day, she came yesterday from the country, an' stayed overnight with a cousin in town. She wants *me* to call her Cousin Louise, but we're only distant kin. And, without obligations. Ha-ha! Isn't it wonderful to have cousins?" Arm in arm, they went to the front of the palatial house.

Passing through the sunlit foyer, Sue marveled at the deep burgundy drapes catching the light. "Yes, those are mine," confessed Marg, contentedly. "I think of Charles when I decorate. Poor man works so hard out there in the world. This is his only refuge, an' that's his favorite color. I told him he has to run you back to the farm. Did Jeeter bring you?"

"Yes," sighed Sue. "Still proposin' marriage every step of the way."

"Why don't you say 'yes', Sue? The two of you have been close since you were babies . . ."

"I don't love Jeeter," whined Sue, getting a chocolate from the crystal bowl. "Mama says I've got time. I'm only twenty-two."

"But, dear, in this town all the best men are taken by twenty. You don't want to wait too long!"

"It doesn't have to be a man in this town."

Marg whipped around, staring at her cousin. Whenever her ivory-colored face registered surprise, it looked long and angular. What gave her half-beauty was a good complexion and by all means her long "stringy" yellow hair perfectly-groomed. "Dear, what are you sayin'? Come, out with it. Some man up North? At Oberlin?"

"Well," Sue blushed. Red splotches appeared in her peaches-and-cream cheeks. "Like a fool, I told Mama all about it. That's the real reason she doesn't want me goin' back this year."

"What's his name? Is he somebody nice?"

"Joseph Kelly. From Cincinnati. A minister, an' musician too. I reckon my po' family thinks we'll starve together. His folks are quite without means. His father works on the railroad. They're from Ireland."

"Oh, Sue! T-then he's *white*?"

Sue smiled, with raised, delicate hand. "Marg, you know I don't go for these racial classifications. He knows precisely what we are. I've met his mother an' she likes me very much."

"Then it's serious. My dear, I'm sorry, but perhaps your mother is right."

Sue stood up, irritated. "Oh, you said we weren't goin' to discuss serious things today. You used to be understandin'. Now that you've got Charles an' yo' children, you talk just like others. The idea of my goin' North was to broaden myself." She sat down at the piano, playing a flourish of scale exercises.

Marg sat back listening to the music. When finally Sue paused, she said: "You must consider, marriage is important. It becomes yo' whole life. Everything else disappears. All this choosey life, gone."

"With Jeeter it would certainly be this drab Maple sameness. All predictable!"

"Honey, that's what you want!"

"No, no." Sue was playing again. This time from Beethoven's *Sonata in C*. After some minutes she stopped and came back to the deep burgundy velvet chair, and the chocolates. "I can't imagine every girl has to go through the turmoil I've gone through."

"I know, I know," said Marg, sympathetically. She came over and hugged Sue's shoulder. "With yo' father passin' on early, an' you havin' to do so much out at the farm. I know, it's been rough. But God will bless you, Sue. Just think it all out an' do what you know is right."

Sue took a handkerchief to her tears. Then she smiled. "Mama thinks like you. Maple is life, an' we have to live by the rules of this town. But I learned one thing up North, Marg. There's a different truth. It's refreshing in a way. You don't have the sins of moneymakers pushed at you like golden parables. This society here is wicked."

"Oh, Sue, it's home. It's been good to us."

Just then, the doorbell rang. Marg rushed into her wide foyer, and a servant came forward as well, to greet the arriving guests. This time it was menfolks. Marg's tall and handsome brother, Gregory, and his friend, Lou Simpson. Like the ladies they too were fair-skinned; almost white. Gregory had an Italian's look, with straight brown hair. His friend, Lou, with dark curly locks, looked like an Egyptian or Turk. Lou's father Vincent had been around the world as a cook on a ship; he had told them at earlier dinners that the Free colored people of Maple could be proud since most of the world's people looked like them.

Gregory kissed his sister and cousin. On Sue his bright eyes glowed like a suitor's. He and Sue had always teased. "You do look lovely, or should I say 'In love'?"

"How dare you, Gregory. Introduce yo' friend, sir!"

"You haven't met Lou? I thought everybody knew Dr. Lou Simpson. He's graduated from Augusta. Has had his dental practice here in town for nearly one year. Isn't that right, Lou?"

"That's right," grinned the good-looking, fat-faced man. "And I've certainly heard of charmin' Miss Sue Barrows. You're the musician, mam?"

She blushed deeply. "Who's been talkin'?" If he were single she'd love this man as a husband, she thought.

"Oh, surely you know Lou," said Marg, standing between them. "When Bradley's Cotton Mill moved from Front Street they left a beautiful li'l office that Lou's wife transformed into a darling place. An' there he serves the best families in town."

"Well," said Sue quietly, trying to hide her disappointment. "I live out in the country. I don't know everything happenin' in town."

"And she's been away up North," grinned Gregory. "Play us a love tune from Ohio, Sue."

She slapped his shoulder. Then reached for another chocolate.

"No, no," said Gregory taking it away. "We don't want you fat until you're well-married. Besides, this is no good for yo' teeth. Isn't that right, Dr. Lou?"

"That's right," sang Dr. Lou. He really was a full-fledged doctor, but Maple whites told him when he came there that they wanted him to stick to dentistry. And he did, with his white patients. "I'm havin' my wife restrict our baby from sweets. If animals can have good teeth, we humans can too. By bein' moderate in how we live."

"Amen," said Marg, sitting again. "Lou, for an unchurched man you impress me with yo' spirituality. I keep tellin' Lilian to bring you to our church, but she says you love yo' freedom too much."

"Well," cried Lou, sitting too, "I work so hard, on Sundays I like to rest. Besides, the Bible says we're to do no work on the Sabbath, an' gettin' to church for me is like work. Ha-ha!"

"I do believe you're gettin' fat and lazy. Lilian is feedin' you too well! Hah! Sue, his wife is Lilian Tibbs. They used to live in that pink cottage up by Daddy's li'l rental houses, on Rose Hill. When you were a tot, I'd walk you up there. Remember, Sue?"

"Marg, I have a terrible memory of this town. It's growin' and changed so, I can't remember a thing how it used to be. Was Lilian Tibbs that thin girl with reddish hair, an' freckles, who always wore shoes?"

"That's the one," chirped Marg. "In those days we went bare-footed in summer. Shoes were only for church and school."

"Did the colored people have a school here in Maple?" asked Dr. Lou.

Gregory and Marg exchanged quick glances. "We went to the white school. It was our father's insistence. All four of us."

"Any problems?" asked the dentist, sober now.

"No," continued Marg, defensively. "None that I remember. Of course, there are always people complainin', but Daddy hates this caste business and I'm fully with him on that."

"Well," sighed Lou, "you have to have yo' own people. You can't be in close with everybody—"

"Daddy says New England was the country's first melting pot. Down here people make iron rules to keep other people out . . . to steal and get rich themselves."

"True," said Lou. "Nevertheless, as small as this town is we should know each other. Sue here should have known me and my wife."

"We're twelve miles out," cried Sue. "It's almost a separate little town. An' I'm bored with the white politics around these parts."

"More reason why we should start our own," said Gregory taking a chocolate.

"Yes," put in Lou. "We need solidarity. Christian closeness. Right, Marg?"

"Absolutely," she chirped.

"But the colored in town could never support yo' business," Sue told him. "They can't make you rich."

The doorbell rang again. Margery was on her toes. Her out-of-town guests had finally arrived. Lydia Farley Smith strode in laughing through peacock feathers and perfume. As she and Marg kissed, Gregory came out and put himself in the arms of his chic cousin Louise Johnson, who wore white gloves and a full taffeta skirt of midnight blue. It was a gay reunion. The ladies were brought into the parlor to meet the others. Then black Matilda came out from the pantry to participate in the greetings. She was smartly dressed in a starched outfit, a uniform.

"Miz Farley you sho looks good," cried Matilda taking her hug. "Not a day older. How long it's been? Ten years?"

"Longer than that," laughed the charming Lydia Farley Smith. "Marg knows, but I dare her to tell it. That would reveal how many years we've been on this earth. Whew, I'm winded! Somebody be kind enough to get me a lemonade."

Matilda dutifully went to the kitchen while the ladies got out of their wraps, and Elias came out to take them away. A punch was served and Lydia got her lemonade in a tall beautiful crystal glass.

"Oh, this is lovely," said Lydia. "I knew in comin' back to Maple an' this house I'd be surrounded in elegance. Margery and Gregory, you have no idea how much this lovely place is in my dreams up North."

"We've heard you live well in Pennsylvania," exclaimed Marg taking the compliment.

"Oh, it's a nice little house. My husband's a barber; we have two children to raise. Socially there is no need of luxuries like here. Ours is just a simple solid life. And, Margery dear, I'm working!"

"Working? Oh, how nice. You heah that, Gregory? She's working. Just what do you do, Lydia? It must be exciting."

"Well, there's a bachelor lawyer, actually he was a schoolteacher when we met. I take care of his house. It's just in front of ours. He's a wonderful man. He's in government. As we live comfortably by my husband's wages, I've been investin' my li'l money in various business things."

"You were always a smart one," chirped Marg. "Gregory, ask Lydia how it's done up North. Ask her some questions so we can get rich too!"

The dinner started and there was conversation all around. Marg was a little worried over Charles' absence, but he had told her of his hectic life and never to wait for him. She had invited her brother and

15

his friend to balance the table, but this group found so much in common to talk about that it didn't matter who was male or female. The one thing the mulatto aristocrats did that was unique, the ladies and gentlemen stayed together for coffee, not dividing up in British fashion. Charles came in just at that time, with two of his beautiful rust-colored German retrievers dancing at his heels. He got them out of Marg's house, then came back with a weary forlorn look. Marg rushed to get him something to eat while he sat in his workclothes making charming conversation with their guests. Soon Dr. Lou offered to visit the spavin-ailing horse and Gregory decided to come along. The four ladies were alone for the first time.

"Tell us about Washington, D.C.," Marg asked Louise who was the shy one.

"Oh, what is there to tell? Like Lydia, I'm a working girl too. I'm in charge of chambermaids at the Willard Hotel. It's good pay and I get to see quite a number of the big shots in government. Once at a banquet I even had a chance to chat with the President—"

"The President of the United States?" chirped Sue excitedly, having a second piece of peach cobbler.

"The very man . . . Mr. James Buchanan. Well, like President Pierce he is for the pro-slavery faction. He wants the people and not Congress to decide on slavery in the Territories. I wanted so much to talk to him about that terrible Dred Scott decision and about the flaws of the Kansas-Nebraska Bill, but being' a woman, I just fluttered and fell apart at his presence."

"In other words," said Lydia tartly, "nothin' was gained by God bringing the two of you together?"

"Oh, I think he'll remember me. I voluntarily told him I have an uncle in Kansas an' that I thought it should be admitted to the Union as a free state."

"He's not really pro-slavery," Lydia spoke up. "Remember, he's from Lancaster. He's a friend of my boss; I've been right in the house with him. In that political front they vacillate, but he's really opposed to slavery. I know his niece Harriet Lane who serves as his mistress in the Executive Mansion—"

"He's not married?" asked Sue.

"A bachelor. I understand there was a rich girl, Ann Coleman, some thirty years ago but her father disapproved of the marriage. He was an ironmaster but felt himself better than the fledgling po' young lawyer. Hah! These people kill me always bein' betters, but you know somethin'? It got Buchanan the presidency. You see, his friends felt sorry for him then, and saw to it he got elected to Congress. Been at it ever since—"

"He sounds like a good man," smiled Marg. "Tell us, Louise, what did he say to your suggestion about Kansas?"

"He laughed an' said it was none of his business, that Congress would decide."

Sue had a question. "Did he talk to you like a lady? Or, well, did he know you're colored?"

"Of course he knew. Remember, my family has never been like yours. While we're fair, we've always been Negro. My voice, my hair. I want people to know."

"Exactly," said Lydia Smith. "I married a black man. We fit in as Afro-Americans. An' my children are brownskinned colored."

Margery frowned. "What difference does color matter," she snapped, turning red.

"A lot," Lydia snapped back. "You see, this whole fight begins with treatment by sight and an interpretation of the Constitution that says any man who is white can own a poor black slave, treat him like dirt. Also the rest of the colored too are inferior."

Marg figgeted. "You're forgetting that one of the country's founders and constitution-maker was a colored man . . . Alexander Hamilton."

"The rest of the country forgets," shouted Lydia. "These white people will rewrite history a thousand times to keep every identifiable Negro out. Look at the voting situation. You can't vote. In the old days Free Negroes could vote all over the country. Then Georgia and South Carolina said no, then slowly other states even in the North said no. Some things today are not improvements. Our rights are slidin' back. And Marg, you might consider, the day for yo' privileged class has passed."

"What do you mean," Marg asked, still flushed.

Lydia was serious. "I mean, this country is reshaping. Two years ago we had a crash. It's all money now. An' with that cotton gin, a two hundred dollah slave is now worth two thousand. An' the South ain't lettin' go four million slaves, the backbone of this place. An' there'll be no more blond, blue-eyed people with a touch of Negro blood. Either you're on the ruling side, or you're property! Dear, how can you teach your children to survive?"

Marg was quiet for a while, then after sipping coffee she said: "Charles and I think the Christian life will prevail. Also we've learned through our parents how to be industrious. We're frugal and comfortable by our own labors. Such feelings and accomplishments guide our children more than anything—"

Louise decided to talk. "What Lydia is saying, the whites will not let you survive in yo' present unnamed position with comfort and possibilities. They mean to separate people, if a fight comes."

"Yes," snorted Lydia. "Northerners wantin' freed slaves don't realize how it will upset the roots of this society. People like my boss won't rest until slaves are free and equal. Yet, new machines will make their labor obsolete. So what's a freed darky to do? Roam about competin' with whites for the same jobs? If so, a race war will certainly go on and on—"

Marg's frown deepened. "This talk frightens me. Lydia, how do you know these things?"

"I told you, the white man I work for is right in the middle of it. He was a Whig leader who served three terms in Pennsylvania's legislature. Now he's in the House of Representatives in Washington, an' very big in shaping the new Republican Party. He's tryin' to get me and my husband to move to Washington to do things for him there."

"Why don't you go," cried Sue Barrows, "if it means a rich new life for you?"

Lydia sighed. "My man's not interested in movin' to D.C. for money or a new life. My Mr. Smith's a good barber but I tell him maybe Jesus is callin' us to new duties. Hah! If he came he'd be followin' me . . ."

Louise laughed. "In some families a woman can lead the way. Maybe yo' white man will become president, then just think how important you'd be!"

"We don't want that," scoffed Lydia. "Just to do our duty. With the mess we've got now between North an' South, nobody knows what will happen!"

"You're absolutely right, girl," said Judge Edward from the doorway where he had been listening for some time.

"Daddy!" screamed Marg. She was surprised and glad to see him. This was the first time he had come twice in the same day. She felt sure he had done it to meet her friends. Actually Judge Edward had met the two before, as children. Now he saw them for the little brown coloring they had. So he was frowning a bit as he walked into the room. He had heard one of them talk "molasses-tongued" like the slaves, and the other had that lazy owl-eyed look of blacks. He had always been precise in his racial feelings. He was completely for the "elite mulattoes", those who were Scandinavian blonds or perfect white people in looks and manners.

"I hope I'm not interruptin'," was his pleasant greeting. "Thought I'd say hello to your ladyfriends from up North."

"Oh-h how nice," cooed Marg, grabbing his arm. "Daddy, this is Lydia Farley Smith who used to live next door to the Baileys on Front Street. She's now in Pennsylvania working for a congressman. And this is Louise Johnson, whose mother was Mama's cousin Prudence from North Carolina. Louise now has an important hotel job in Washington, D.C."

"Nice to meet you ladies," said Judge Edward sitting down. Immediately Matilda came out and asked him if he had eaten, or if he wanted any dessert and coffee, and he waved his hand at her, finally agreeing to a glass of brandy. At that time Gregory and Lou came back from the barn. Three sparkling crystal goblets were brought out. The women continued to sit around the gas lamps and the round cherrywood table at the bay windows. The men sat with their brandy in dark upholstered chairs. Finally Judge Edward said, "I agree with some of what you were sayin'. Yes, the nigra people will be free. It'll create confusion an' all, but I think it'll be done without war. The thing is, how to do it? Since people confuse slaves with money, Government could buy them, first order. Then free them. Hah! People are nevah goin' to give up money voluntarily, No-suh!"

"Judge Edward," said Lou Simpson with great respect, "it all depends, sir, on whether government allows slavery to gain a foothold in the Territories. Congress can't go on representin' only the interest of a few Americans. If we're a Christian nation we have to stand by—"

"Bosh!" yelled the Judge. "The Bible tells you they had slaves from the beginning of time. There is no sacred ideology to justify the acts of man. Conscience is rational only where the power thirst is satisfied. Evil or not, chattel slavery stands as somethin' the states have to agree on, somethin' they *all* want! Right now it's the *division* amongst them that hurts. That Lincoln fellow said that. A house can't be divided. Law is to be the bindin' force, but tangent selfish interests can have men separated by interpretations of the law—"

Lou got a bit more courage this time. "Judge Edward, sir, my people came to Georgia as Free Negroes in 1765 when the colony begged them to come because they were havin' trouble with hostile Indians and Spaniards. Soon, my ancestors were told they could do anything here but vote and hold office. Earlier rights were taken away, following Virginia and Carolina. As I hear it, wherever Free Negroes live, in a society of black slaves, the white man's not sure of our loyalty. He kept changin' the rules governin' our lives, and soon he wanted to treat us just like slaves."

"That's right," barked Lydia. "In a racist South the brown-faced Free colored were made to suffer like slaves. Nowadays real freedom in this land hangs on whether a colored man, any color, can have his rights! Naw, you call 'em fugitives from justice. An' treatment, Judge Edward, that's the main thing. Black men are gettin' lynched and killed everywhere! The Government, the law, turns its head."

Judge Edward looked at this half-black yellow woman and smiled. "My dear, if you want the courts into every bad situation, we can't lock up half the country! I personally think mistreatment by race, color or class is wrong. An' I don't go along with legalities like the Dred Scott decision. Where thinking's clouded by hatred, class can made the difference. In these specific times, race means inferior treatment, even in interpretations of the law. We have to live through this to get to something better."

"Daddy started the school for slaves at Edgewater Plantation," exclaimed Marg, proudly. "Now it's caught on an' there are slave schools at the nine biggest plantations in the county. I for one think that's progress."

Just then, Matilda brought in three beautiful white-faced children. A bright-eyed blond boy of ten was attractive, pleasant and correct. He was dressed meticulously in tan suit with white starched collar. The two little cupid girls, one six and the other one three, were gorgeous in ruffles, pink satin, and Irish linen. One was blond and the other, brunette.

"These are my children," said Marg proudly. "John, say hello to our guests, and give Grandpa a hug. You too, girls."

"Oh, my, my," exclaimed Judge Edward, beaming as the fully white children clamored over him. Now Lydia Smith wore a scowl. Marg and Gregory noticed it. The smaller girl began picking at a pie-crumb from the table and her mother was embarrassed.

"Now you children have eaten," she said. "Kiss everyone goodnight and off you go!"

When they had left the room she asked Lydia, "What do you think of my children?"

"They're darlings," sighed Lydia with knitted brow. "But I was just thinking, what on earth will happen to them!"

"What do you mean?" asked Marg, and Judge Edward too, raising his eyebrows at Lydia.

"Well, Judge Edward, sir, they *are* colored children!"

"What are you talking about?" he bellowed.

The room was silent. Nobody dared to speak. "Young lady, you explain what you mean."

It was an order. Lydia knew she had to say something. "Well, I suppose, in a way, life in Maple can go on as it has gone on for decades. In the North we know who we are and I think it is a little easier that way. When I lived here I was always petrified when people spoke to me . . . you had to know how to answer . . . if they were a judge, that required one kind of answer, a schoolteacher, another . . . if they were white—"

"You're talkin' about my family," he said in a strong voice.

"Daddy, don't explain," cut in Margery. "Lydia was only—"

"I want to explain," was his sharp reply. "She feels she has a right to question me as a father. As an intelligent Christian contributing man. I know what's behind such stupid remarks people make. Well, young lady, my white-faced grandchildren will be themselves. They can fit the labels if they have to, or they can avoid them. They will be decent, respectable, upstanding citizens, if I know my Margery—"

"Daddy—"

"An' furthermore, the country will accept them. Exactly as they are. They're not paupers or criminals. They are aristocrats, exactly as my family were in Massachusetts, and now here in Georgia. They have a legacy—"

Lydia rared back. "But you never married her mother—"

"Lydia," screamed Marg, jumping to her feet.

The room was deathly quiet for another second. "I'm sorry," said Lydia Smith, scurrying up. "I just had to say it. Now I'll leave. I had a wonderful time, Marg. Simply wonderful. I hope my honesty has not hurt anyone."

The red-faced judge finished his brandy, then had another. Remorsefully he sat staring at the table. He was back to thinking the thoughts he had when he had entered this room. This half-nigger woman was psychic. She knew deeply that his curiosity had brought him here, hating her African blood. It was really her manners that upset him.

"Just a moment, young lady," he called to her. "My daughter welcomed you here as her guest, so I'm not goin' to chew you out for

21

yo' impertinence or ignorance. One can excuse curiosity, and show-off tendencies, but a tactful guest would leave devilment home, givin' due respect to the host's house. Well, it's true I never married Margery's mother, but my dear Alice knew that my energy and love were hers. And, my wife Gloria has known completely my love and energy. I don't expect you to understand the class I belong to. It tends to respect manmade institutions, no matter how imperfect. I didn't invent slavery, but I've had to live with it. With my concepts of honor and responsibility. Another thing, educated people, white people, know to choose words to avoid hurt to innocent souls. We love our children too much to damage them by words, or labels." With this, he kissed his daughter and left the room.

Marg almost swooned. Gregory came and offered her brandy. Sue took brandy as well. Also Louise Johnson. A tense Lydia stood majestically, and ambled to the foyer, ready to leave. Judge Edward bolted past her, banging the door. The servants were whispering, and Lydia felt she was being upstaged. The carriage meant for her had now gone off with Judge Edward, so she cooled her heels on the front porch while other arrangements were being made. Like that morning in church, Marg closed her eyes for a moment of silent prayer. Then with a forgiving smile, she came out on her porch, made a few words about the weather, then showed Lydia all the exotic flowers she was growing.

"I'm sorry if I said the wrong thing," said Lydia, finally and quietly.

"Oh, think nothing of it! Daddy doesn't care. He's like a turtle. He's had to answer many others before you. And I forgive you, too. My children are secure, Lydia. Very secure. And I hope that yours are equally secure."

With this, the two women kissed and parted. Margery went back into the glimmer of the evening lanterns thinking that she had kept a friend, and that it had been a wonderfully human day.

Chapter 2

Margery's best friend was Phyllis Potter Korner, a fair and proper housewife like herself who lived in a big and beautiful old white house. Phyllis, a pretty blanched-almond-colored white, represented a certain unrealized security because neither of her parents were pure whites. However, the Potter mixture, an ancient thing, had been preserved over years, so equally there were no pure Negroes in the immediate family. Her husband Frank, the best photographer in Muscogee County, was recognized as a white man, just as his father Otto had been, and his German grandfather Helmut. But even the Korner family knew a touch of Negro blood. It went back to the seventeenth century. Phyllis and Frank considered it miraculous that they had found each other. God's work, she called it. And they lived as all people have to live, peacefully within their abode.

The two near-white girls had been friends since teen years, having met at a social function. For Margery there was no more beautiful face on earth than the bright, round, healthy and cheerful face of Phyllis Potter. Even her father agreed that this smart and charming mixed-blood girl with the excellent disposition was fairer than most pure whites, rich or poor. Judge Edward encouraged the friendship because he thought his Margery could marry Phyllis's handsome older brother Clyde. But Clyde went to New York. After a couple years he returned home and was killed in a property dispute just like Marg's Grandfather Shep Lyons.

That had happened in 1849 the same year that Margery's older brother Paul went to California. Phyllis, brokenhearted, cried a lot. She had not yet married Frank. Marg and young Charles invited the lonely and distressed maiden to live with them on Plum Avenue. Marg was a young mother with her son John barely three-months old. The two girls became so excited about their friendship in the same house that for a time it kind of put a knot in Marg's marriage. But Charles had a big heart. He could understand the joy of like souls as well as his wife's friend's grief. And Margery herself learned how to take grief and mold it away. Daily she administered comfort to Phyllis who did not want to think of the Maple nightmare as one of race or color. Soon, the memory of the seizure and loss of her brother moved into oblivion. Now that they both were settled and hitting middle age the girls' friendship was deepening. Just as Marg could not live without Charles, she also could not live without Phyllis. The two planned their lives so that they would meet almost every day if only for a short while. On Sundays they did not see each other; this was agreed to please the husbands. So early that Monday morning Marg was preparing a breakfast cake and tea for her friend when by surprise here again was her father at the door.

"Daddy, what a surprise," she beamed, really wanting to see him alone. "Come right in."

"I didn't know if you'd be an early riser today," he said, kissing her cheek. Usually they met about six times a month, never more. "Did yo' friends take leave okay?"

"Oh yes. It ended well. Thanks to the brandy."

"I was surprised seein' you take it. Well, what better than brandy to soothe the doings of that black witch . . . I mean, your friend, what's-her-name?"

"Lydia. Now don't think badly, Daddy. You know very well that others have cornered you the same way."

"I'm a judge! What right has that mouthy black devil to corner me?"

"Daddy!"

"You're right," he sighed, taking his tea straight. "Everything is relative. But others have never brought my grandchildren into it. That I disliked very much. It was cruel."

"Well, I'm glad Lydia got it out of her system. Frankly I think she's jealous. My children looked like little angels last night. I must thank Matilda for dressin' them so carefully."

"That could be it . . . jealousy. But I must warn you, I know a bit more about black people than you do. They can be poignantly vicious. Can cut out the heart of a best friend."

"Now, now, Daddy, aren't you bein' prejudiced?"

"Truthful, lady! Remember, throughout my years in the courthouse, I got an education about blacks. An' you know I'm not a biased man racially. I say there's wickedness in the blood, an' that is what I want to talk to you about today."

"I knew there had to be a reason for your visit," she smiled. "You're spoilin' me."

He was frowning. "Margery, I don't know how much longer I'll be here. You know I've tried very hard to bring you kids together. Where it hasn't worked it may work in the next generation. That gal was right about one thing: we're headed for a war. An' the South won't win. Since all this nonsense has race at the bottom of it, I think you and Charles should pack up yo' belongings an' go North—"

"Daddy, why on earth should we do that?"

He got out a cigar and chewed its tip off. "Because, I think, you should completely raise yo' children as white."

"Oh, Daddy." She came and kissed his cheek. "Why can't we be who we are, like we've been, forever?"

"Because the world won't let you. Now, sit down. I'm talkin' serious. Here's a draft for three thousand dollars. You can go to my home, Concord, Mass., or some other place. Maybe Charles and you ought to go off on a holiday an' look at it first. You two have never been outside of Georgia . . ."

"I know. Isn't that terrible? An' what happens to my children?"

"I'll take 'em in. Don't worry, the servants will keep 'em away from Jane. They'll be happy there until you get back. Or, maybe you could leave 'em with your friend Phyllis."

"Daddy! You're serious. Here, take this check. Charles wouldn't hear of it."

"Don't you be so sure about that. Your Charles has been havin' troubles, didn't you know?"

She frowned. "What kind of troubles?"

Judge Edward lit his cigar. "Well, for one thing, the wholesalers won't sell to him. He has to buy up everything by goin' to separate farmers."

She became pale. "I figured somethin' like that had happened. Every mornin' now he's out of here by four-thirty. It used to be six o'clock, now four-thirty. He's not gettin' enough rest. An' he's worried. Daddy, isn't there something you can do?"

"I've done all I can. Don't have much pull left at Town Hall. Here, take this check." He stood up. "If you put it to Charles in the right way, he'll see what I'm talking about . . . be glad to go."

"And what happens to Malcolm House? We love it here. This is home."

Judge Edward stood in the doorway trying not to look pitiful. "If war comes nobody can put all their love in a house. You tell him that too."

She watched his big body cross the lawn to his carriage. Phyllis's carriage was just pulling up. Her father got out and had a word with Phyllis, then he was on his way. She waved at him but he was too engrossed to notice.

"Mornin', honey, yo' father looks fine."

"Mornin', Phyllis. Come in. I suppose he told you what we talked about."

"No. He merely asked me why I wasn't at the party yesterday. How did it go?"

"Then you don't know?" Marg sat her friend down and told her everything while they ate cinnamon cakes and chocolate muffins.

"That Lydia sounds terrible—"

"Phyllis, you don't know the worst of it. Somebody I know has been to Lancaster. They say she's livin' in sin with Mr. Thaddeus Stevens."

"Mercy! An' with her husband right there?"

"Right there under his nose. An' she professes to be a devout Catholic."

"Yo' father said right, Margery. That woman has no tact, no respect. An honorable person could never treat a spouse that way."

"The way she looked at my children hers is jealousy mixed with race rage. An' I'd guess you'd have to say an inferior feeling. Many half-Negroes have that."

"Honey, people have everything if their religion isn't strong enough. I thank God for knowin' you because you're one of the strongest Christians I know."

Marg smiled, fanning herself with her father's check. "An' you know somethin' else? Tomorrow mornin', lookin' pretty, I'm goin' out in yo' wagon, Uptown to buy myself a new Sunday-go-to-meetin' hat!"

On Tuesday morning Margery didn't go any place. Charles' horse had died and systematic as he was, he tried looking everywhere for a brown and white to match his other three. The horse could not be found. The wagon couldn't go out with three nor would Charles take an unmatched horse for the fourth. The wagon was too heavy for two horses, so he had a quandary. A neighbor helped by loaning his smaller and lighterweight wagon. Charles was not satisfied. He drove out to the horse mart at the county line, and to his surprise was chased away. He had not realized that he was unpopular or that racial feelings had mounted so. Marg preferred to think of it again as a case of over-wrought jealousy. The Malcolm name was big in town and a lot of little people looked for ways to spit at it. This never would have happened in the old days, but times were changing.

Marg kept some respect for the Spence name as well. In fact, the whole decor of her sunlit foyer was built around her husband's family. Ezra Spence, his father, had been a much-sought-after cabinetmaker. He was famous in the South for his round gate-leg maple dinner table. And a cherrywood chest with satinwood veneer. All the rich homes in Maple had something by Ezra Spence. Marg only had an English walnut lowboy, Queen Anne style. She kept it under her big rectangular foyer mirror, always highly polished and attracting attention. Mr. Spence had died of tuberculosis as he reached his prime in his mid-forties. His wife, Pearl, died of grief soon after. Their only other child was a daughter Margaret who married a doctor and moved to Baltimore. She passed away childless. All the good things in the family had gone up to Baltimore, and Charles never asked about them after her death. So, to honor him and his family, Marg kept her huge family Bible on that table. It was a special gift her father had presented to her mother: a Bible weighing more than twenty pounds, more than a foot wide and nearly two feet in length, of expensive red and gold tooled Moroccan leather. It had been a source of wonder in their childhood. The beautiful color lithographs of Jesus and His world made lasting impressions. Alice taught her children from this giant book of life. And Marg respected it as much as she did anything of the world. So, the two things, the shining Queen Anne table and the open Bible with gold-leaf pages, greeted each day and each visitor to Malcolm House.

Late that afternoon Phyllis dropped by, and her aristocratic hands touched that magnificent Bible as she smiled and took off her wrap. She came digging in her purse and Marg knew that there was another letter to share. Appreciating their ability to read, one of the greatest joys for these young ladies was receiving mail. This time Phyllis had a letter from her cousin, Angela Baker, who lived up North. Marg always enjoyed Angela's letters. "She's havin' wonderful times," cried Phyllis. "Travelin' again!" Still in hat and scarf, she began to read:

October 3, 1859

My dear Cousin Phyllis,

Forgive me for ten long silent months. I am no longer with the girls' school in Massachusetts. First I went home to Palmyra, New York. I was delighted to be back there. It's grown so, with many beautiful shops and hotels facing the Erie Canal. I found myself wandering down to watch the gay-colored boats pass by, then realized I was wasting my life. Well, you remember the Hall sisters, cousins on my mother's side? They both married well. Two brothers, relatives of Mr. Hiram Jerome, our lawyer. They live now in Rochester, and Catherine invited me to her fine house to watch over her two boys, Lovell and Bill, frisky teenagers. I mainly cook for them while

27

their mother helps her husband, Lawrence, with his financial business.

      The Jerome Brothers also have a newspaper in which they are very successful. Mr. Leonard Jerome, married to Clara, is very clever. He teases, promising to get me into the business, but I know that all I'll ever have is my dowry money, since it seems unlikely I'll ever marry. So the brave side of me says to invest with these gentlemen. Wish me well.

      I was really fearful of writing, with so much talk of war, and slavery. Let's not discuss it. I enjoy hearing so much about your warm family life in Maple.

Love,

Angela.

"She sounds lonesome," said Marg, getting the tea things.

"Poor Angela," sighed Phyllis. "She's been lookin' so hard for a man. I told Frank we should invite her down here. He says she's already too old. Thirty-two. But I'm sure there's somebody around!"

"Now, Phyllis, you've told me she's very particular," exclaimed Marg, setting the table.

"That's true. She's never admitted to Negro blood. That part of the family tells people their brunette and black hair comes from Indian blood. Hah! Well, I'll answer her in a religious vein, like you've taught me. Brighten her life with a suggestion of truth and a feeling of hope. That should help solve her problems. An' again I thank God for knowin' you, from whom I learn so much about strength and joy."

Pouring tea, Marg only smiled. She began sipping quietly. At peace.

Wednesday was an uneventful day filled with steady, gloomy rain. Lydia Smith left Georgia, taking her train back North. Louise too was on her way back to Washington via Charleston. Marg had wanted to give the three thousand dollars to one of them, to bank up North. She really didn't trust local banks any more. Her brother Paul could have used it out West. Clever as Paul was, she could not trust him with money. Pride and gold fever were in his blood; he had been ten years getting nowhere. Her brother Anthony had connections with northern people. He was sweet and friendly, but a little naive. Poor Gregory was anxious but she didn't like his politics. Finding a person you could trust was getting to be a problem. She had always left things to her father but something deep inside told her that this habit needed altering. Then Thursday morning the sad news came. The stroke.

Friday found her puttering around listlessly in a steaming backyard. Around noon Phyllis came with a pretty white box tied in ribbon.

28

It was a little bonnet she had picked out, in honor of Margery's dead mother's birthday. Marg was so grateful she couldn't hold back the tears. It was a kind of modern bonnet, for younger girls who wore curls, or exposed their pink ears. Marg's flaxen hair was too straight for curls. And she felt her ears were not perfect enough to expose. Yet, she didn't want to look like an old woman before her time. "It's lovely," she told her good friend. "So fresh and dainty-looking."

"You're goin' to wear it for a beautiful portrait my husband will do of you. I told Frank we need one of you alone, one with me, and one with yo' dear father."

"My goodness," laughed Marg. "You sound as if I'm going away!" She was thinking death at that moment but fought it out of her brain.

Then on Saturday it all happened. She had to go there again. She had to enter that door, see Jane, Edward and Jack, Sybil, Ursula and Odella, and Miss Gloria and Mr. Tom, and Miss Wanda. The family. These sour people who had surrounded her father and kept him in chains. Phyllis rode along in the carriage holding her icy-cold hands. And, after an hour the ceremonial visit was done. She came out shivering. None of them had any heartfelt sympathy for that great man who had made them all, in breath, sinew and class. He had given them that step above other whites which had made them so proud. Now as his face turned to wax they'd think like other southerners, scorning his mistakes and not needing him any longer.

Phyllis sat with her until evening. Talking silly girlish talk, but it was nice. And at church Sunday Cousin Donald looking like a tan version of her father kissed her cold cheek, and gave a little confidence tap, that so familiar too. Then on Monday, wearing Phyllis's lovely bonnet, and curls, she went to Daddy's funeral, alone in thoughts and body. When she got home sunlight possessed the foyer, illuminating the rich gold tones of her father's Bible. The rest of the house was bathed in bright light as well. It all felt holy and she was glad.

Quickly she took up her favorite spot in Malcolm House—the big bay window on the front stairs, and breathed several relaxing sighs. Then all of a sudden, like rain, the tears began to flow. So vividly he came back to her: it was Friday afternoon again. Frank and Phyllis were with her, entering the sainted Peachtree Drive house. And the nine white ones with equal mean stares eyed the three of them, equally white. Frank quickly got his picture over Jane's strong protests. Then, at her father's insistence Margery was allowed to have a moment alone with him. By instinct she knew that she was entering that big flowery bedroom for a last time. He was smiling a bit as she came closer to his magnificent rosewood bed. "Marg," he whispered hoarsely. Then there was a long silence. She allowed a finger to touch his white flannels. He looked so peaceful and subdued in his deathbed, she couldn't utter a word.

"Marg," he whispered again, "when you spend a life d-defendin' something, it can slap you in the face. Two years ago when Chief Justice Taney's Court ruled against poor Dred Scott, I was horrified. As a slave h-he had traveled to free soil with his master, an army surgeon. First into the free state of Illinois, then into the f-free Territory of Minnesota. Well, day came they had to go back to Missouri. C-Court says he's a slave again. Never a free man! C-Constitution didn't say that. W-white men can be fools. It's greed. Taney's is the highest court in the land, with men actin' same bitterness and spite you see here. Be brave, daughter. Christ knows you're fighting. Now yo' mother she was g-good to me. An' I would have married her had the s-system allowed. I've always been a c-conscientious man of the law. Even those f-few I didn't like. M-my job was to get men to respect them. The c-country's laws. Now I wonder, m-my weakness, I should of fought for better laws. Yo' mother was my angel, if not my wife . . ."

That was the last she heard of his voice. Thinking it that burying Monday drew a sigh from great depths in her bosom. Her composure broke like a cloud of rain; she cried for fifteen minutes, letting the quiet of Malcolm House soothe her. Slowly she rose with the chiming clock; with God on her mind she returned to her usual endless chores.

A week passed and she was still crying a few minutes each day, and drinking tea alone. One day her brother Gregory came. She took a deep breath before speaking to him. "They missed you at the funeral," she said rather sharply.

"I reckon," he sighed, pulling up a chair. "When the staging of the performance was explained to me, I wanted no part of it."

She lost her sad little-girl sentimental look. "Gregory, I know you're a proud man, but one day, one hour, you could have done it—"

"No, Marg, not me. They had lines and files. The pure whites all around close. As if they were the only ones. An' we'd stand in back . . . with the servants."

She laughed. "Oh, Gregory, under God, we're all servants! That shouldn't have stopped you from seein' yo' father one last time . . . payin' yo' respects." As cheer left her voice she looked away, and cleared her throat.

"Manmade conventions," he said taking the tea Matilda brought him. "Dad always knew how I felt about him. He had my full respect. He never asked me to be another person . . . to act how I didn't feel."

"A man can be too proud. An' I'm certain it's made you some enemies in the family."

"How can you say 'family'? I don't fear *them*. Besides, Paul wasn't there, nor Anthony. Are they also to be regarded as enemies of the *family*?"

"They're up North an' out West. No way they could have gotten here. But I wrote them just the same. That's the only thing Jane said to me . . . givin' orders for me to write them. Hah!"

Gregory laughed too. "That Jane is somethin'. You'd think she was the pearl mother of the family, rather than just another daughter. Marg, the four of us have to separate ourselves."

"We've always been apart."

"I mean we should forget the connections with the others. Announce it after the will is read."

"Yes. Perhaps we should."

"Jane will start her fighting anyway, you watch an' see."

"I'm not goin' to think about it," said Marg standing to clear away the dishes. "Already Lawyer Perkins was by here askin' me questions."

"Really? Jane probably sent him. Does she know about the three thousand Dad gave you and Charles?"

"Nobody knows that but you, an' Gregory, I've told you not to repeat it. I've decided . . . well, I've already sent it all to Anthony."

"Marg, I thought you were going to help me with my problems."

"No, no. You and Valerie have plenty of assets. You don't need my help."

Gregory frowned. "But what can a college boy do with all that money?"

"Put in away safely. Now, the subject's closed. At least you and I are not goin' to fight about money. Not ever." She kissed his forehead, then took a string off Gregory's jacket. He was a tailor and there were always threads on his clothing.

"We'll be left out. You wanna bet?"

"Oh, I'm not worried about it!"

"You can say that. They'll be dishonest, Marg, an' the law will let them do it."

"Gregory," said Marg with a frown. "This Perkins man asked me something. Tell me, do you have any papers?"

31

"What kind of papers?"

"Birth certificate."

"Oh, I think it's down at the courthouse."

"Well, you go an' check. No. Not openly. We must get Elias's brother to check. He cleans up there at night. Lawyer Perkins says without papers they can declare us colored an' we would be entitled to nothing from Daddy's—"

"Declare us colored?"

"Freedmen, Gregory. Ex-slaves."

"That's impossible! Mother was free. She had papers."

"I still have her papers. But we're another generation. Nobody thought that we'd need them. Gregory, the more I think about it, you and I, we'll have to go to the courthouse at night an' thoroughly check on all this ourselves."

"We could never do that! People would find out. We'd be in trouble."

"We're already in trouble," she told her brother. "I'll go alone."

Whenever Marg had serious business with the servant Elias she'd first talk it over with his mate, Matilda. This short and plump good-natured black woman was in many ways like a friend. They had an arrangement of respect. Matilda would do most things without any grumbling. And Marg would listen patiently to Matilda's views about house matters. Then she'd usually manage to get her way by bringing the Lord into the picture. Matilda did not profess to know as much as Miss Margery. She was only a slave. Margery would frown profusely whenever the dark woman used this word. She had never thought of Matilda and Elias and the others as slaves. They were just there serving in the house on her father's orders. This was their home. Now that he was gone she had to consider legalities and ownership, and here again she had to see papers.

"I'll let them all go free," she told Gregory. "I'm sure they would serve me just as well."

"You know that can no longer be done in Georgia," Gregory replied. "Did you hear what just happened?" He then told her the news that came clickety-clack into Maple via the telegraph key at the railroad station.

Up North, almost North, in Harpers Ferry, Va. a man named John Brown had started trouble. In 1849 he had settled in a Negro community in North Elba, New York and grew to take sympathy with Negro causes. In the spring of 1858 he went over to Chatham, Ontario and

32

told the people he'd be starting a stronghold for escaping slaves. So, in the summer of 1859 he rented a house in Harpers Ferry and had himself sixteen white men and five blacks. They attacked on 16th October and took the armory. Got sixty hostages of leading white men. The local militia fought them, then the U.S. marines came in. After two days it was all over. John Brown was wounded, ten of his followers were killed including two sons.

"Oh, it's dreadful," scoffed Margery. "Why can't men live in peace? Did they say what happened to this Mr. Brown?"

"Oh, he's jailed," said Gregory. "Bein' tried for slave insurrection an' treason against the state. All the whites in town are talkin' about it."

"Hm. Which means I have to be very careful with my plans."

His light-brown eyes grew big. "What are you plannin', Marg?"

"Not so much. I'm goin' on a learnin' expedition, and that's not desperate. Haven't you noticed, Gregory, whenever there is trouble, people always claim everything you did was against the law? Law is their golden word! To me it means a lot of secrets in the courthouse. Rules to control men. Practically every poor man can be made a slave by manipulating those laws. Now that was Daddy's life. That's how he got powerful. He had the iron of laws all around him, but we are completely naked."

"Really? Well, I own my tailorshop. They can't take that away from me. An' Valerie's proud because we own our house—"

"Daddy told me not to put any trust in a house. He said in war I might even lose Malcolm House."

"Really? What did he want you to do, Marg?"

"Go North."

"Sure enough?" Gregory finished his tea. "Seems like with what happened at Harpers Ferry, they're no better off. At least the steaming hatred in the minds of people is the same."

"That's people actin' out laws of control. An' Cousin Don said it Sunday: 'What's lackin' is religion'."

Soon the day came when Margery decided to tell Matilda her plan. She had thought it all over carefully. She knew the blacks had a way of talking too much amongst themselves. She imagined most of the house's secrets were known by many people, including some ignorant slaves out in the country. Marg needed Matilda's cooperation to get Elias to talk to his brother Humphrey at the courthouse. And she had to be strict. It was a very serious matter.

"Matilda, we've got to talk this mornin'," Marg told her on that last day of October. "Things are changin' so fast we have to be prepared."

Matilda's fat cheeks dimpled in a knowing smile. "You worried about dat Mistah Brown in Charlestown jail? Dey'll hang him, Miss Margery. For sho!"

"It'll be history repeatin' itself," said Marg, taking to her knitting. "Back in 1831, Nat Turner, a colored man, had been used to life on a rich plantation. Then, they sold him. Two times. He and seven black men killed Joseph Travis, his new owner, and all his family. Then they marched on town killing 51 whites in two days. State militia of 3,000 stopped him. Yes, he was hanged. But the part that worries me, many innocent slaves were massacred. The whites get very mad when you do not obey their laws."

"Dat's de truth!" laughed Matilda, busily washing windows. "I'm so glad, Miss Margery, I don' work in one of those places."

"What places, Matilda?"

Their eyes met, Matilda's cold blackish ones and Margery's soft grey ones. "Oh, I mean a pure white house. I couldn't stand it."

"Matilda, remembah our religious discussions? I told you God puts tribulations out there for us to trifle with. While none of us is perfect, trials make us stronger."

"Shonuff," called Matilda, wise in her singsong.

"An' remembah too, when I gave you those six dresses, it was because I wanted to do something nice for you. Then you got impertinent with me an' asked for yet another dress, for some church meetin'—"

Matilda didn't say anything, just kept on with her work.

Marg was watching her. "An', angel dearest, you never realized the joy of my small gift-giving, because this vanity of man was possessin' you. We always want more to show off—"

"Dat's the truth," chimed in Matilda again, knowing the bosslady was leading up to something.

"—Well, I told you, Matilda, how much that hurt me, because I had given with joy what I thought was nice for you to have. But you expected more of me! Then I stopped givin' gifts. Just stopped cold. An' you got mad an' stopped workin' so hard. That was a war, baby, an' the South an' North are about to come up on somethin' like it. Only thing, this is a shootin' war. Many will be killed."

Sweat began popping from Matilda's deep brown brow. Her little fat fingers began moving faster across the windowpanes. Margery kept

34

talking in her calm, sanctified manner. "—The Lord knows good people will die. An' the bad won't get no better. But somehow in it all, some of the blessed will see Glory an' work that much harder to help the rest of mankind realize his sinful ways. I've come to that road, Matilda."

"Lawd, hav' mercy," was Matilda's singsong shout.

"When my dear father passed I decided I wanted to exert myself to get Christian things done. Of course, I'll always have my children to think about. I can't harm them in what I do—"

Just then Matilda dropped a drinking glass. It shattered on the hard floor. She began running around, grabbing at her wooly hair, looking nervous.

"What on earth is the matter?" asked Margery.

Matilda pointed towards the window. "It's Miss Jane. She's comin', she's comin'!"

Marg looked out of the window and spied a big handsome black brougham standing at the curb. The horses were calm, as if they knew where they were. Full fluffy skirts with a light print pattern swished across the lawn. Then Margery spied a second wagon, a work wagon standing behind the first. "Oh goodness, she's come to take away my plants." cried Marg, rushing for the conservatory. Just as she hit the front foyer Jane sallied in.

"Margery, what kind of housekeeper are you? These same curtains were at the window the last time I was here, an' that was four years ago!"

"Come in," called Marg. Then feebly, "Do they look so bad?"

"Terrible! All yellow! Maybe you should wash them in lye soap. The smoke from the fire can be deadly."

"Have you had tea?" asked Marg, leading her half-sister into the parlor.

Tall and erect Jane, with similar blond face, became all serious-faced. "This is not a social call. I'll only be here minutes. Where can I sit down?" With nose turned up as far as it would go she acted as if the chairs too were dirty.

"Oh, that's fine," said Marg, as the pure white woman found herself a place in the green velvet Chippendale. "I'm so glad to see you."

Jane's straight nose was regal now; her rigid mean lips could have been set in clay. "I'm here about the slaves. You've got six of them and Father never meant for you to keep them."

Marg stood up trembling for all she was worth. "My goodness, Jane, what on earth are you talkin' about?"

"I mean to take them back with me. This mornin'!"

"You can't do that! I-I mean they're mine. No, what I want to say is that this is their home. I can't let you take them. That would be a crude ungodly act."

Jane figgetted in her purse. "I knew you'd try to fight me. Margery, it's about time you realized you're half a slave yourself!"

Marg brushed a stray blond hair from her pale cheeks. "It was you who sent Mr. Perkins here. Starting trouble an' he's barely in the ground—"

"Don't be impertinent. Judge Barlow has already signed the order. Here it is. You are to turn them over to me."

"I'm not turnin' anybody over! They can come and get me. Lock me up, or kill me. Daddy never would do any business with Judge Barlow."

"It's not his business, it's my business. I'm in charge now. These slaves were bought and paid for by Father, for the Malcolm family. They're not yours—"

"When is the reading of Daddy's will?"

"None of your business. And you're not to call him that. *Judge Edward*, that's what you're to say. Margery, you do not seem to realize your own precarious position—"

"If the flesh of my body was made by Judge Edward, an' I'm free in that body and mind, you don't tell me what to call him. You can do none of your terrible unChristian acts to belittle me. I do wonder, Jane, how a person can be as evil as you!"

"I'm *Miss Jane* to you. Understand? And what evil do you mean?" Jane's rigid cheeks had flushed pink.

"You know what I mean. The South has a lot of two-bit judges who will make any evil ruling or law, but people here also have religion, and truth. If you choose to go down the unChristian road of greed and false pretendin', it will keep leadin' you into more and more trouble—"

"Don't you lecture me! Don't you *dare* lecture me, you half-black hussey! You go an' tell those slaves that they're mine an' to get ready this instance. I'm takin' them back."

"Anybody you take will be over my dead body. You will *never* take Matilda or Elias! An' when the townspeople hear about this you'll have lots of new enemies. An' others in sympathy will fire on yo' house on Peachtree Drive. An' slaves at Edgewater will stop working; no cotton will be sold, an'—"

"An' they'll all die! Don't you dare talk insurrection to me, young lady. You forget who you are talking to! I swear I'll have you behind bars—"

"No, Jane, I'll have *you* behind bars. I'll go to Judge McKnight, the federal judge, an' he'll set you right."

Jane came and pushed Marg, then blew steam into her face. Margery bit her lips and stood firm. "Well, you can keep Matilda and Elias," said Jane calmly. "They're old an' half-able, but the other four will go with me. Immediately! An' I'm takin' my piano!"

Heat rushed to Margery's cheeks. Her heart was pounding. The room was swaying. She felt very weak. Jane now went into the foyer, clapped her hands loudly, and began shouting orders outdoors, then at Matilda and Elias who moved off smartly. There was movement at the back of the house, then screaming in the kitchen. The four young black girls, mortified, went down on their knees asking Jesus to deliver them. At that moment the two huge black drivers Jane had brought came into the house with whips. The slick, menacing cat-o-nine-tails looked like vicious snakes.

As the four screaming young girls were brought forward with ropes on their wrists Marg fought off the two men with trembling scratching fingers. They kept pushing her back in a rough manner. Then Matilda tried to help her mistress, and Jane grabbed a whip and hit her hard across the buttocks. Elias just buried his grey head in the curtains and wept. Soon it was all over. The subdued black girls were pushed through the door and out on the lawn, as neighborhood children were already lined up to watch. As Marg reached the screen door the two huge black men came busting their way back into the house. A vase smashed as they threw off the Chinese silk scarf and began wrestling with Marg's beautiful cherrywood piano. The groaning heavy piece went through the door reluctantly, like another slave.

Marg stayed indoors. She watched as her piano was wedged between the writhing slaves in the dusty back wagon. A burgundy drape ripped from her parlor window now protected the purloined instrument. Now Jane strutted across the porch like a reigning princess. She even spoke to one of the grinning young white boys at the curb. There was boisterous laughter as they drove off. The devil in Maple! Marg fought her tears, remembering some school days when they had to learn about the French Revolution and the terrible behavior of ungodly people in power.

Chapter 3

For days, Margery sat in her silent parlor which had been whipped by Jane and by a hot autumn sun which made the red and white Oriental carpet a stifling living thing. There was a big bursting tiger spot where the piano had been, and an ugly tear in her Irish curtains where the drapes had been ripped away. Charles had told her to forget it. She could, the material things, but there still was Fanny with her missing front tooth, acrid Coogie, tall and lanky, who always had a pleasant word, perspiring Johnnie Mae, so strong and determined, and smiling brown Wanda with her brave fighting spirit. Marg regarded these purloined black women as part of her family. To be truthful, not as relatives, but as obedient loved ones. Students, perhaps, and of course, servants. Their feelings of attachment, she was sure, were as deep as her own. Her responsibility was exactly that same charge God gave to every saved person to care for their children and to be good guardians. Yes, those four lost girls were her children. Now she could cry. She had straightened out the attachment in her mind.

The pure whites, iron-faced, went to their Bibles, ready to stretch words to cover greed, and to justify their power over blacks. Such ownership was blatant sinning, thought Marg. She didn't want to own anything. She merely wanted to share and teach, and the Good Lord gave this duty to every Christian. But some churchgoers just couldn't live sweetly in a town's humble territory. They had to be showoffs, with joy from wickedness justified. A sick joy.

Leaving the parlor, she tidied up in their drab grey bedroom at the back of the house. There were treasured pencils, hairpins, and smells. African smells. Charles had told her she'd get used to being without them, that she herself would get sick if she worried. Marg physically felt okay as she examined everything, trying really to connect them to herself. She had to discover how much she loved them, if at all. How far would she go to rescue them?

"This is the sad state of affairs in Georgia," said Lilian Tibbs Simpson, with a flip negroid manner. "Miss Jane can get away with it because she's regarded as white. You're just as white an' you can't dare do such a thing."

"I know," sighed Marg, playing with her little white cat, Tabby.

Cashew-colored Lilian took a coconut candy. "They come to Lou's office puttin' on airs an' talkin' politics all the time. And they're vicious, Marg. They want *everything* for themselves!"

"I've tried to think out the end of this, but I can't, Lilian. We're *all* livin' in sin. Maybe it's best that I've lost my four girls."

"Yes, Marg, that's a healthy way to think of it. Lou and I only have one, an' if it were left to us she'd be set free. Just consider, most of the slaves are held by just ten per cent of the population, the rich planters. Three-fourths of the pure whites own no slaves, but they are livid with hatred of the black man."

"Yes, Lilian, we own them to satisfy feelings of importance, to be like the 'best people', we say. Listen, I have a letter from Louise. Would you like to hear what it's like in South Carolina?" Marg took a thick folded paper from her breast. It read:

November 8, 1859

My dear Margery,

     Yes, I did get home safely, but it was nerve-wracking. Many boisterous whites are riding the trains and all they do is drink, gamble and talk politics. That John Brown business has upset everybody. As they can see I'm colored I don't feel safe riding around. Luckily there were two of us together.

     I enjoyed my brief stay in Charleston. It's such a pretty town. Our mutual cousins were glad to see me. Ruth gave me a splendid little party. Then somebody threw a rock through her window. They had seen a congressman come in, all elegant and refined. Now everybody is thinking racial, and we are not to have pure white friends any longer. The congressman told us all the talk of secession started with the representatives of Georgia and South Carolina. He says it's all race hatred and money-making, and they're trying to make an inferior slot for all colored to fit into!

     Whether or not there is war there is certainly a need for us to be more careful. I felt so depressed I didn't stop in Raleigh. My home now is Washington. Here we Free-colored are in such great numbers (over ten thousand) that the pure whites dare treat us with disrespect, but I do see shenanigans out on the streets. The poor white man is vile and he will ruin this country. The gentleman class had kept him in check, but now they're careless and we have to watch out for ourselves. This is my way of telling you to stay well and take care. We're praying for you all the time. It was certainly a pleasure for me to visit with you in your beautiful mansion, Malcolm House. What saddened me was not seeing your sweet mother once again with her magnificent smiling, godly face. Cousin Alice had the strength of Moses, and that's what we all need now! More later. I must get back to my hotel chores.

With love,
Louise.

"That's a nice letter," said Lilian. "I'm sorry I didn't get to meet Louise. That was my week doing nursin' duties. Hah! I thought Ole Mr. Traynor would die an' leave me somethin'. Not a cent! Rich ole devil. Ha-ha-a! Marg, what happened to yo' father's will?"

"Rumors, that's all. I'm sure Jane has got some crooked judge changin' things. Lilian, I have a plan. See what you think of it. I told you they're plottin' to squeeze us out, an' Mr. Perkins threatened us with slavery unless we can find some proof of freedom."

"Margery, angel, you were never a slave!"

"Exactly. But these poor whites runnin' things now will do any devilish trick. His was a serious warning. It prepared Gregory and me for the fact that Jane and her family will get everything. But it also made me mad, and bold. You know Humphrey, Elias's brother? Well, he cleans up at the courthouse. In fact, he bosses a team of ten nightworkers. I want him to get me on that team, an' I'll find out everything in the records of this town."

"Wonderful idea, but how could you fit in with a black team of workers?"

"Lilian, what I have in mind, I'll blacken my face, wear old clothes, an' go over there every night with the gang, until I find out what I want to know."

"It could work, but you mustn't speak of this to another soul. People talk, you know."

"Yes, yes. But I trust you, Lilian."

"Don't trust too many. In times like these, you can be betrayed by anybody, even yo' own kin!"

"I'm workin' for the Lord. He is my strength."

"Yes, honey, an' you could destroy any bad papers. Understand?"

"Jesus wouldn't want me actin' too devilish."

"No, angel, there's nothin' wrong. Once you get in there, create the security you need. You can sign yo' father's name if necessary."

"Hm, if I find the right forms, and the place. Oh, Lilian, it's fascinatin' and daring! I wish you could come with me."

"No, angel, this Maple white man is too rough for me. I'll work with you, though. I can write like any of 'em. Just gimme anything you want to copy. Okay?"

"How sweet of you!" They shook hands, and had a spot of brandy too, to celebrate their agreement to conspire.

It was just about Christmas time when the officials got around to reading Judge Edward Malcolm's will. Sure enough, everything of value went to Jack, Edward, Jane, Sybil, Ursula and Odella, Miss Gloria and Mr. Tom, and Miss Wanda. The pure white ones. Over a million dollars, and Edgewater Plantation. Margery, Gregory, Paul and Anthony simply got the drab gunshot rental houses that mostly had ditchdiggers and colored people in them. It was a racial decision. Marg suspected her father didn't make it. The only thing that sounded like him: Charles was to share with a white cousin, Ned Malcolm, the ownership of the three biggest blacksmith shops in town. Judge Edward had bought them all up in the last year of his life. Ned wasn't exactly a redneck, but he was poor, the only congenial one in the bunch. Marg felt her father knew that Ned could be trusted to cooperate across racial lines. And she was sure this was her father's way of punishing the vegetable people and the horse people who had set themselves against Charles. And it was his way of keeping the whole family together.

"We'll make it as partners," said Ned pleasantly, looking pinkish-red, with his hat on his knee, as he visited with Margery and Charles one night soon after the announcement. "It oughta make us rich."

"At least I shouldn't have any more trouble with produce or horses," said cashew-colored Charles, lightly.

"That's for shore," chimed in Ned in the language of the poorer whites, which was different from that of the aristocratic Malcolms and of the half-whites around them. "If'n you wanted to, we could straighten out all the Maple bigots. Keep 'em from shoeing their horses unless they behave an' sell you everything you need."

Charles looked glum. "I wouldn't want to chastise any of them. No, I believe in the Lord's way, turn the other cheek."

"I'm mighty glad you said that," cried Ned, touching Charles' shoulder. "You know, I've been gettin' all kinds of advice about you. Only reason those papers stayed in tact, Jane doesn't like me too well. She doesn't care if I have to work with a—"

Charles smiled broadly and looked at his wife's cousin in his weatherbeaten face.

"I-I was goin' to say 'colored man', but drat it, we're the same, Charlie! I know that!" They shook hands, and the pure white man left by the same back door he had come through.

When Margery finally finished telling Matilda her plan to secretly look at papers at the courthouse, Matilda was frightened, then supportive. "But, Lawd-a-mercy, I can't bring Humphrey here to talk it, Miss Margery. You forgets he ain't a free man. He only gets holidays off, an' if'n he came here people would know it."

"How true," said Marg, remembering too Lilian's caution about talking this to too many. Matilda she could trust but news had a way of going from one to another in the black community. "If you and I make this a first-class secret, Matilda, nobody would evah know. Bring Humphrey here after dark. Christmas day."

And so it happened. Margery's handsome children and their father were up in the front of the house having a great time laughing and sharing stories among tinsel and little toys, while Margery sat with brown Matilda, Elias and his brother, Humphrey, in the dimly-lit servants' room in the back of the house. "I got Dr. Simpson to make me a concoction with walnut juice," she explained over wine and cakes, "but it's strong enough to stain my face permanently. Since I only want blackness for a few working hours, I've decided on something I've made myself. It's a mud-mix of tar gel and lampblack. I've also added shoe coloring so its brown looks quite natural."

"Ain't you afraid for yo' complexion," asked Humphrey.

"I've tried it," she smiled. "I use bees' wax first. Afterwards, it's taken off with oils. Does no damage. Main thing, I want yo' group to accept me as one of them—"

"Nawsuh," said Humphrey. "the way you talks an' look, an' acts, dey'd know! Besides, all dem blacks belong to Judge Barlow like me. Dey certainly knows if'n a stranger jains in."

"Then we'll simply have to tell them."

"No, no, Miss Margery. You can't trust people like dat."

"Even if it's a noble life and death matter? With a reward?"

"Nawsuh! Too exciting, especially if'n dere's money on de table. An' dat only lasts a short time—"

"I guess you're right, Humphrey. Well, why not just let me in with the group, an' I go on alone in the building?"

"Better I gives you a key," grinned Humphrey, proud of his sudden idea. "You come an' go as you pleases. Mainthing, you wear dat black face in case ob emergency. If'n you bumps into somebody!"

"Great idea! When can I start?"

Humphrey explained that he had to go that same night, but he'd be alone, that the other slaves had the holiday off. Marg thought it excellent for her first time. So on Christmas night, thinking of God, she began her big mission.

The huge marble and wood building had creaky floors. And it was drafty. Cold air kept hitting Marg's raggedy shirt as she stealthily snooped around. It seemed her squeaking feet could be heard all down the hall. Humphrey with a low-lit lamp showed her where all the papers were, and he even took her to a damp cellar where older papers were stored. Marg was fascinated. Only thing, she was not cautious enough. He showed her how to cross in front of windows. There could be a buzzard out there in a tree, or a mean and wicked white man. Marg began to take more care. And when he let her out she was to scramble under bushes on her stomach until she reached the patch of elms down the road. Cross the street, follow the ditch to Gould's pasture. That was the only way to avoid humans, and to be safe. Humphrey knew.

Along about eleven-thirty Charles grew irritated. It had been Christmas and he felt she should have been with the children who kept asking for her. He had had a time getting them to bed. Marg came in at 12:20. All glowing with excitement. By one, her face and body had been cleansed, and perfumed. After an orange and a cup of tea, she got all warm in bed, talking calmly, explaining to her husband the great importance and the danger involved. Yes, she'd continue other evenings, and he had to engage the children with stories. Her vital work was not to cease. When he asked specifics of what she had discovered, she told him hers was a mission of mystery, that some day she might be able to tell him some things, but not everything. He noticed that the gloom of her father's recent death seemed to pass her up this night. Her voice had a light air. It matched his holiday mood, and for this he was grateful.

It was winter now and Charles' vegetable business suddenly gave up. He simply couldn't get any more the things he wanted from the white people in the middle. After eight prosperous years he was forced to quit. Thanks to Judge Edward there was luckily the blacksmith business with Ned. All three shops had Negroes doing the heavy work and a white man supervising and making contacts with white customers. It was agreed that white-faced Charles could do the carpentry, the painting and fixing. A step above black work, and the Malcolms knew he was pretty good at this. So he came in medium-good clothes, and happily took on the chores of keeping the buildings up. Ned didn't let him talk to the managers but Charles didn't mind that. He was sharing equally as silent partner and the profits seemed huge. As much as he got from his vegetables. He told Marg she'd be able to buy a new piano soon.

Charles began looking happier in his new work. His handsome ivory face lifted, and took on youth again. He had for years worked alone, now he had a friend. His assistant carpenter was a tall and big Free-colored man called Mel Young. Mel was brownskinned. Married, with a couple of kids, he lived in a shack near the railroad junction. He couldn't read or write but had a great sense of humor. He kept Charles laughing. Charles became a new man after years of wearing a serious expression. Mel became a special friend because he was the first brownskinned person Charles had ever known intimately. Marg was happy for Charles. She listened to the stories (Those he would tell her) and was enlightened to learn how the Negro group, the brown people, lived in Maple.

*****   *****   *****

The year 1860 started with dark clouds, a freeze and a few snowflakes. Again the enslaved black people had a day off and Margery went again to the courthouse at ten p.m. This time she carried a notebook and wrote down many things she did not want to forget. The famous *Giles vs Miller* trial had been dishonest. Where sworn testimony said Penelope Giles had heard George the Blackman enter through the side window to rob them and beat up Miss Carrie, it turned out that Miss Penelope Giles was deaf. She could hear nothing more than a foot away. Notes in the judge's handwriting said so. Yet, poor George the Blackman was hanged for his crime. Another thing, the Malcolms had paid off a blackmailer. Somebody named Smoot who claimed Judge Edward's brother, Paul, was wanted for murder up in Illinois. Marg had never heard about this before. Uncle Paul died suddenly. That too needed investigation.

There was so much Marg wanted to know that she had to force herself to be quick and systematic. The first thing, she had to get to the business of births. She had to find out how her own birth was recorded. The searching would take more than one night.

Along towards the end of that first week in January a letter arrived from Lydia Farley Smith. Marg was surprised to see that it was postmarked at Washington, D.C.

December 29, 1859

Dear Margery,

Seasons greetings, honey. I'm ashamed not having written you earlier. You see I'm happy here in Washington and Louise has told me she's written and I felt awful. I'm glad to learn you are well. I was really worried about you. What I said with my big mouth may have caused your father's stroke. I'm sorry for that. Well, he had lived a good life and I think he wanted to make that confession about your mother. God made him surrender from dedication to the wicked laws of this land. My Mr. Thaddeus Stevens has a similar dedication to what he calls America's chewy strength. He claims dedicated legal men can keep us out of war. He asked me to come down here and manage his D.C. house for him. A congressman is too busy, and being that he doesn't have a wife, I agreed.

I must tell you, my poor husband passed away with grippe soon after I returned. The children are in school in Lancaster. I'm always there when Congress isn't in session, and even when it is, I get back fortnightly, since we have good railroads between Lancaster and Washington. Nothing like those sordid southern lines! Aren't these new inventions wonderful? So far, I like Washington, I do my job, and he doesn't make me feel like a nigger.

All good wishes for a healthy and prosperous 1860.

Your friend,

Lydia.

Marg was quick to write a condolence note to Lydia, but with the modern tone of her letter, Marg didn't say too much. Working and alone in a strange town! Abandoned children! Well, with what she herself was doing at Maple's courthouse she had to rethink her own christianity. If she got into trouble and landed in jail, she could not ask the Lord to overlook her sins. Or could she? The abolitionists had so clearly explained how slavery is the crime, and how the risks to abate it were noble, and that the sin of slavery makes so many more. Thank God she could read and learn so much about the ugly happenings in the country, in the South. It was really God's work at the courthouse, her secret way of becoming a special soldier for Christ.

Phyllis Potter Korner frowned profusely upon hearing of Marg's undertaking. She could not understand a Christian woman behaving in that manner and she told her friend so. She agreed there were evil officials in Maple but there was absolutely no need to break into the courthouse. The town also had many upstanding Christian officials, some who would be as kind to slaves as they were to their own kin. She felt Marg's motivation was a bit of anxiety or greed about her father's estate. Phyllis kept reminding her friend how comfortable they were. And she feigned not to be interested in Marg's legal finds until told that her own mother, Beth Potter, was listed as a pure white. Everybody knew Mrs. Beth Sycamore Potter was part-Creek Indian like the Lyons, Margery's people. Yet it seemed what went on in the court-house depended largely on who was in power at that time. The judges weren't the only power forces. There was a County Clerk named Vincent Pyles who served for ten years, and he listed all the part-Indian women as pure whites. He did so because one of them was his own mother, Naomi Smith Pyles. Margery's mother's papers said she was "part-Indian". It didn't say what the other parts were. Marg decided to leave it that way. She like the scrawly writing somebody had done.

Now she began looking for the records of her grandmother; there would be no birth certificate because Grandmother Margery came from Alabama. Maybe she could find some other document. She was sure it would say part-Negro. Actually the court records never said that. "Colored" was the popular way of taking care of broad mixtures. One clerk marked "White + Colored". Another simply put a dash under race. Marg liked that. God never marked humans with these horrible man-made tabs.

One record that she found very interesting was the listing of Free-colored by states. It showed that the state of Georgia had 2,931 such people in 1850. Maryland had the most with 74,723, followed by Virginia with 54,333 and Pennsylvania with 53,626. New York had 49,069 which she regarded as not so big considering its population. But Louise had been absolutely right; the record showed Washington at 10,059, which was a lot of mixed people considering its small size. Actually she realized that wasn't a record of mixed-bloods, only of Free-colored. There were plenty of free brown people, but in the South they were usually the Nearly-whites. She had heard that brown people really had to be on their toes, even up North, not to get sold back into slavery. It could happen for small things like owing someone a dollar.

While she did not care for these records so much, knowing they were full of mistakes like the listing on Phyllis's people, the important thing was that these were the official records by which the white man ruled the society. Whether true or false, he'd make death or life by these records. That was the cruel truth, and right there in the court-house she got down on her knees and prayed to Jesus while some tears stained her lampblackened face, making terrible smudges.

One cold wintry night she almost got caught. A white judge or court official came in very late, red faced, blowing and stomping, and he asked her something. Luckily she had her cleaning pail nearby and she mumbled an answer pointing to the others down the hall. Humphrey saved her by talking to the white man. Then he cautioned Miss Margery to be more careful. She had no business in that judge's room, but she had discovered her father's will there, and this was very important.

For weeks she went into that room, opening his oak drawer and taking that precious will into her hands. During the first week of Lent it disappeared. Marg almost panicked. But she found it, after three long hours, in a file cabinet. Now, every week she'd sit down and read it each time. It was mostly about Edgewater Plantation. He wanted Edward and Jack to run it together. The day-to-day business would fall to Edward who lived out there. The plantation house would belong to him, and the eighty-two slaves. Jack, the older brother and lawyer, had never been interested in farming, but Judge Edward made him joint-owner with Edward of the one thousand five hundred acres of Edgewater. The Malcolm ladies would share in the profits of two hundred cotton-producing acres, plus joint-ownership of the Peachtree Drive mansion and the seven business buildings in the heart of town. The big red brick building on Broad Street, called County National Bank Building, where Jack had his office, would go to him alone. Judge Edward had planned it so he would be respected as the older brother, and eventually upon becoming a judge, he could carry the family name on to new heights.

Marg now remembered how her father used to put her and Edward in his buggy and take them out to Edgewater Plantation at a fast gallop. She would scream with glee when they went over bumpy roads. They were younger than ten years and Edward would hug her like a real brother. She also remembered how that big smoky house would suddenly come into view through moss-covered trees. She thought of it as a palace. Maybe a spooky palace. Its wide columned veranda was always in shade, and the chimneys were always smoking. And there would be black women always coming and going through its doors like on a busy city street. The ones in the house had white kerchieves wrapped tightly on their heads. The others who went out into the fields, they wore plaid or gingham turbans. She had asked her father why nobody could ever see their hair. She hated those turbans. They made her think of work-bees and work-ants.

And she remembered that red-faced white man, Mr. Fred Thurston, who was always there, explaining things to her father in a loud voice. As overseer he had full control over the blacks while the

Malcolm young men gave gentle orders to the few white men working there. Marg also remembered the white-faced and yellow-faced house servants at Edgewater. They were neat and good-looking, and always treated her warmly. Mr. Thurston couldn't say anything to them. He had no control in the house ruled by Miss Gloria and Miss Wanda. Marg was glad of that because he was a man she didn't like.

Thurston had to act respectful to her father but at the conclusion of their visits, he would bring bushels of fruit and vegetables and place them in the carriage. He'd offer handfuls to Edward but never anything to Marg. She couldn't understand his scorn. His wicked eyes would dart up at her constantly. Her father never saw that. And whenever she'd complain about Thurston to her father, Judge Edward would just laugh, saying he'd give Marg a piece of Edgewater one day. But that day never came. Now she remembered there was a piece of land in town that he did give her on a whim for her fourteenth birthday! It was a large sandy lot uptown where the circus was held. She had told him her wish for music and the horses more than once a year, and he had said she could have them any time, since he owned the land. Marg now realized she had never taken possession of that Broad Street lot. Part of it had become part of the town's Week-end Market, and the circus still came to the vacant part. Never had she been given any papers of ownership. This became a new item to search for in the courthouse.

As grey February faded into greenish March, there were a few balmy days, followed by more wet ones. On those dark days when steady rains made it difficult to get about, Matilda would look at her mistress to see if she had a message to get to Humphrey. It was on Friday nights that Marg generally went to the courthouse. Even in rain. Like an exercise of faith, she had to do it, even if it meant getting soaking wet. On one late April evening heavy thunder made Matilda suggest that she not go. But Marg was cocky this evening. At ten p.m. wearing a thick sweater and rags, she blackened her face and walked out into the brisk threatening weather. That was the night she found the deed to the Broad Street circus land! Her father had indeed left it to her! While there was no mention of it in that official will, here was a deed dated 1842 with her name clearly designated as owner. Marg now knew the importance of this paper. It could mean that the will filed at his death was a forgery. Rushing back to that judge's office she got out her father's will and read it one more time. Then it suddenly came to her to let Lilian Simpson copy these documents. She'd need her own copy if she'd ever go into court.

While lightning was striking all around the quiet room, she gathered up the documents in her scarf. At the big door she met a warm angry wind. She ran all the way to Lilac Street, to Lilian's darkened house. The dog barked as Marg laid on the knocker. Then Lilian came in nightclothes. The exciting story woke her up completely, and together they worked at the documents while raindrops pattered on the roof. They finished at four a.m., and Margery had a frightful time getting back to the courthouse, for now there was a steady downpour. As the original papers were somewhat wet, she had to blot them on the carpet before returning them to their official places. As she started home, daybreak was breaking. This time she really had to follow Humphrey's advice and shimmy along the highway on her stomach. After the crossover by the elms she stood up and ran. She was a mess.

The muddy rags kept separating from her body. Luckily she had some decent clothes on under the rags which she literally ripped off in the streets. The rain washed nearly all of the black from her face. She made a towel of her white shirt and finished the job in the streets. Soon she entered Plum Avenue. This time, sure enough, at dawning, somebody was walking along the sandy path. She kept her head down and covered her face until she got home. She told Charles if any questions arose to say she had had a tooth pulled. Charles scolded her, thinking all this detective business was too much. If she wanted a copy of the will, or the other paper, he said, all she had to do was to ask Jane for it. His naivety she excused.

As spring came, bathing the courthouse in sprinkles of golden light, the building became more a jumble of papers. It seems the Government was taking the census again and the issue of slavery was very important to a lot of people. She found masses of papers on runaway slaves. She read the drastic laws for apprehending absconding slaves. It seemed the Federal marshals and their deputies were in charge. Citizens were expected to help capture the Negro. She read literature showing that vast numbers were being moved from Virginia and the Carolinas into Alabama, Mississippi, Louisiana and Texas. Over 200,000 were moved that way during the decade 1840-1850. She saw where they were now getting a minimum $800 per slave and often as high as $1,500, and $2,500 for a few. Flipping over the pages about the profits made, she read that some areas of the country had very few slaves, like the highlands of the Appalachian Mountains, from Pennsylvania down to Alabama. Her brother Anthony would be coming home in early May from college, and she'd ask him now many questions about slavery in the rest of the country. Actually she was more interested in the movements of Free-colored because in Georgia many of the officials treated every brown one as if he were still in bondage. Thank God, she could be a white woman when she wanted to, and a black one too!

"The Quakers are helping the runaways," Anthony told her as he proudly sipped his madera like a southern gentleman. He also had acquired an air in the North, and a beautiful ruby birthstone ring. "Only a few hundreds are getting away, but Government makes it a big issue because slave holdings have become a major part of documented wealth. Frankly it's all a mess, an' it surely has brought dollars to the North as well. I like those who see the demon in men bigger than their religion. Those who press to have it legally in the West are certainly dollar-hungry men without feeling. And like Dad said, interpretation of the law makes all the difference. Do you realize when the first Negroes arrived at Jamestown in the 1600's they were not slaves at all, because the slave laws did not exist? They were indentured people just like the whites, who could buy their freedom in time. Today this is forgotten. Now every white is an angel and every dark man is the tool and fool. There are so many laws pushin' him down, if and when he's free and there's a budding in his life, laws and evil men may crush him again . . . they may even crush us one day."

"You really believe that, Anthony?" asked Marg, trying a cake Phyllis had brought over.

"I certainly do. It's a bold money game operatin' within the law. And with any such game there are shifts of interest from time to time. Momentarily we fair-skinned are not recognized as blacks or as former high-priced slaves. The white man says we have risen genetically to freedom. While you and I know we were never inferiors, never as bad off as the average pure white, jealousy will stigmatize us. We'll be labeled as inferiors. Nobody will remember our rich aristocratic fathers. When they die off, alas, some profit-minded officials will review it and propagandize against us. Enough of it and the profit feature will be reintroduced to our lives. To keep power we must stay colorless. And we need representation. Otherwise, we'll go back to the mill."

"Gracious, don't talk that way! You speak as if there is no morality."

"Very little, my dear. Say, about your three thousand dollars, you know I took it out of the bank. I have a knowledgeable friend. He advised investment. So on my way home from Michigan I went through New York, meeting our broker. I must say, I was very impressed."

"Has he made us rich?" she smiled.

Anthony's pinkish eyes looked weary. "Not really," he replied. "He thinks southern people don't know things. But really, the suggestions have to come from us. We must know the trends. He's inclined to want to invest only in New York things. I want you to see New York. Maybe you can tell whether the future is here or there."

"Anthony, what are you saying? Do you want me to travel up North?"

"Why not? We'll only be gone for two weeks. Can't Matilda watch over the children?"

"Mercy, you're serious. Well, I wouldn't worry about the children. I was thinking of Charles. He needs me so."

Anthony came over and rested a hand on his sister's shoulder. "My dear, husbands always need their wives. You're more than a wife, now that Dad's gone. I saw the Suffragettes. What's so frightening about their plea, an enlightened woman really is the sharper mind for society as well as for good men. I don't put you in that category but you can't go on livin' by books alone. Your role in the family demands that you see something of the world."

Now she became excited. Under her father's guidance she had been raised a homebody like all the women of their family. Cousin Sue had told her something of what it was like outside their world. Now so easily she felt a sudden joy with the idea of traveling. Could it be that the courthouse reading had opened her mind? Or was she really getting tired of it? In a way she felt like a crook needing a holiday. "Well, Anthony, I'm willing to go, since you've made me realize my responsibilities straddle two families. But I want you to explain the matter to Charles. I don't want it to come as my proposal."

"Leave it to me," he said, kissing her cheek. "Charles likes money too."

Chapter 4

Margery had been on railroads before. Her father had taken her several times to Augusta and Savannah. However, Anthony made sure that her trip North would be something special. He booked seats on a reserved train that only rich people rode. It had the new Pullman service, all elegant and clean. They even had a plush dining car attended to by well-trained black slaves. The North had gone money-mad and Anthony used this trip to explain it all to his sister. First he told her about John D. Rockefeller, Jay Cooke, Oakes Ames, Jim Fisk and Jay Gould, and how the riches they were making involved deals and people in the middle. Such prosperous people came from their class.

Marg could see that at their very fancy hotel, the new Fifth Avenue Hotel. Theirs was a three-room suite, beautifully decorated, looking much like home. She marveled at the new moving box some called "elevator". She also marveled at the exquisite food and the lively and colorful dining rooms. Anthony was anxious to show her Wall Street and everything else in New York. The newspapers however were all full of Chicago where the Republicans were having their national convention. It seemed the two most popular candidates for the nomination were Senator William H. Seward of New York and Governor Salmon P. Chase of Ohio. But in their long careers they had made enemies. Also neither one could carry Pennsylvania, New Jersey, Indiana or Illinois. Republicans needed to carry all the free states to win. So, on the third ballot, on 18th May, Abraham Lincoln was nominated.

There were banner headlines. Marg shared in all the excitement in New York. Straightaway she wanted to go down and see Cooper Union where Lincoln had spoken so eloquently on 27th February that year. Anthony showed it to her on their way to Wall Street.

Their broker, Mr. Thomas Haney, was waiting for them with an Irish pleasantness and a sharing of her political mood. He really wanted to talk more about southern life and about slavery rather than about money. When Marg pressed the issue of their investments he delivered a prepared little sermon about the Erie Railroad and the Copp Steamship Line. He talked as if Margery and her brother had more dollars to invest. Whereas he behaved a bit like a rogue, she could trust him. In fact, to Anthony's surprise, she had brought along an extra three thousand which could be invested. First she let the young man do all his talking then she told him quietly what she wanted. It had to be put in Sparks Textiles, Inc. whom she heard were making business uniforms and soldier uniforms. Haney's eyebrows lifted. He slyly suggested the duPont Company of Delaware, who were making munitions. Marg flatly said no. She wanted no part of killing.

"Surely, Mrs. Spence, you don't believe there'll be a war," he asked, with bright blue eyes, picking up his cigar again.

"Enough of politics," she laughed. "I'm only here to satisfy my family's need to invest, and a desire to help industrial development. I think we could have a continuing dividend outside of war implements. Now, in case there is a war, God forbid, I've opened an account at the New York Savings Bank. You can have our dividends go there rather than sending them to Georgia."

Haney laughed. "And you don't trust southern banks?"

She simply smiled. "We're one nation, Mr. Haney. There shouldn't be all this pullin' back and forth."

The big surprise of the day, Haney took them to lunch at fashionable Delmonico's. Margery had never seen such a fanciful display of food. This busy, bountiful luxury haven had a parade of proper people: elegant men and dainty ladies in beautiful gowns. She realized her drab practical wardrobe needed some attention. Haney knew just the shoppes for a conservative well-bred woman. The shopping took the entire afternoon. At dusk, he accompanied them on a carriage ride back to their hotel. Marg found New York fascinating. She couldn't get over the hustle and bustle. They stopped at brass-shining Scribner's where she bought a few books. When Haney offered to call for her the next day she had to refuse. She had to go to Brooklyn to look up Phyllis's relative, Angela. So she said goodnight to the flirting Irishman, sending warm regards to his wife and children.

That evening she and Anthony had scented hot baths then dressed to attend a soprano's recital. Afterwards, at midnight, they had a candlelight snack in the hotel's lounge, and she marveled over the chic ladies arriving in jewels and magnificent costumes. It was like a show in itself. The next morning after breakfast Marg got her brother to spend two final hours shopping. Remaining frugal and conservative, she bought herself a few more dresses.

"Yo' husband never has to worry about your spending," Anthony told her. "At least, not in the shoppes."

"You're worried about my investments, aren't you? Well, I'll admit I acted on a hunch. With Dad dead we'll never have such gifts of money again. I had to be brave. If we lose, we chalk it up to experience. It really depends on whether we can trust your Mr. Haney."

"Yes, we can," he replied. "He's a fraternity brother of mine. He finished Michigan last year. His family live up the Hudson. They're very wealthy—"

"I would expect that he'd be studying medicine, like you are."

"No, Marg. That's the thing about northerners; they're not planters, colonels, or judges. Their interests are very wide, but they certainly know how to be comfortable. I've been up to the Haney mansion—"

"Did you tell them you're colored?"

Anthony frowned. "No, Marg. I don't believe that much in race. Remember what Daddy told us: we should aim to be accepted as cultured people, without any tabs."

"You know I'm proud to be who I am. In your business world there is a coy language of omission. Men are so moved by impressions alone. I don't want them thinkin' me Scottish or British. Mr. Haney should know I'm a Christian who had a lovely mixed mother. You university men who shape the truth, I find some of your views fickle, like Cousin Sue's. Lord, look what that trip North's done to her. The dear thing's talkin' marriage with a northern young Irishman!"

"An' what's so bad about that?"

"She certainly can't bring him to Georgia!"

"Well, maybe not now. She could have, a few years ago. Marg, these new powerbrokers should not rule our lives. Or, maybe we *all* should be out of Georgia!"

Marg's trip to Brooklyn was postponed to Thursday. She felt better after receiving Angela Baker's note. Now she'd have another day to get ready. She'd read up on Lincoln's victory and she'd practice moving about in her new finery. That morning, she got up bright and early. They were sending a big brougham carriage for her at noon. While Angela was really only a servant in the Jerome mansion, Phyllis had emphasized that her cousin worked for wealthy kin. So Margery had to be ready to be observed by the lady of the house. Angela had said frankly in her note that she'd only have one hour free. That was enough time to chat and give her the little present Phyllis had sent up. After so many years sharing Angela's letters Marg did feel a bit nervous about the visit. She never liked going among strangers. And Anthony who was good at it had an appointment of his own. He did see the fine carriage that came promptly for her. Marg felt wonderful in its plush comfortable interior.

Soon they arrived in Henry Street Brooklyn Heights. The Jerome mansion was a large square brownstone with flowers lining every window. The black iron fencing had been newly-painted and was shining in the sunlight. Marg wondered whether she should enter by the front or back door. The chauffeur was not very helpful; he merely opened the carriage door for her. So she looked him right in the eye for guidance. He pointed to the sidedoor on the lower level. And there among glistening green bushes she rang a brass bell, over which a neat sign read: "Deliveries".

A young male servant (white) opened up smiling at Marg. Actually he was eyeing her bonnet and flowing pink satin gown. Now she worried whether she was overdressed. Suddenly from the darkness came a gushing sigh of welcome; a pale ivory-colored Angela appeared, plainly attractive, hugging Marg as if she were her own kin. The guest was led into a little green sitting room on the lower level. The cook, a huge white woman with a wicked knit in her brow, moved around beyond the thick glass wall. She behaved as if she knew a few things about Margery. Nevertheless, Angela made her comfortable, giving the best chair and sitting stiffly in front of her. Admiring her. Marg felt better. Angela indeed looked just as white as the rest of them but there was that little glint of recognition in her eyes. And she was very pleased that Margery had turned up as white as the rest of them!

"I thought it would be a little awkward," she explained quietly after opening the gift of handkerchieves. "I seldom have guests. While I'm related to Mrs. Jerome, the others here forget that and treat me like a real servant. Hah! But I don't really mind. I'm quite happy here with my sewing and fixing things. Tell me, how is my dear cousin Phyllis?"

"Phyllis is fine. She's in the best of health. She has a lovely family and a lovely home. We see each other often, whenever she's not helping her husband in his photo business. She's a real angel. My very best friend."

"Her father, Cousin Bob, used to live in Palmyra where our family comes from. Then in his travels he became infatuated with a southern belle. Is that a fair word? A complimentary word?"

Marg smiled. "I knew Phyllis's mother; her father had passed on.

Such a lovely woman. Capable, smart and dignified. I named my little girl after her. Nowadays, a belle means somebody spoiled: a pretty, wistful somebody usually on a plantation."

"I won't use it again. Thank you. Isn't it terrible that we're getting to be two nations? Tell me, are times getting hard for your people? No. I don't mean that. For *our* people. Margery, I've taught myself to think upwards. And I knew, dear, the moment I saw you that we're the same."

Flushing, Marg studied Angela again. Now she remembered that she was anti-black. "I know what you mean, Angela. If war comes we must stand and be counted. Now we're hems in pretty dresses. We must consider if we're whole and if we'll have a place to go. Today in the South we often are attacked, if we're visibly mixed."

Angela quickly put her finger to her lips, warningly. Cook was coming with tea. The big woman entered the room, made an artificial quick smile, then set the tea service down in front of Angela for her to serve herself and her friend. Cook was gone with a little bang of the door. "She really doesn't know," Angela whispered. "And it's such a joke because Mrs. Jerome, her employer, is herself a—"

Just then a huge dark-skinned white woman stepped into the room. Elegantly dressed, she walked like a princess. Her wonderful perfume took over the air. Her smile was stern but not as mean as Cook's. Marg could tell from Angela's sudden erectness that this had to be the lady of the house, Mrs. Catherine Jerome. As the yellowish diamonded hand was offered, Margery stood up.

"My dear, Mrs. Spence," cried Catherine, warmly and stilted. "Welcome to my home! Is this your first time out of Georgia?"

"Yes, it is, Ma'am." Margery then was given a short lecture on the difficulties of running a large house in the North with inexperienced help, people who need watching and scolding. "I presume in the South with all your slaves you have no problems like this," laughed the rather tense Mrs. Jerome.

"We have only two servants," said Marg, thinking suddenly of her nemeses Jane and the four slaves she had taken.

"It takes a minimum of nine to run this house," Catherine continued. "Of course, I'm not a social bug like my sister, Clara, who is building a gorgeous new mansion in Madison Square. They've just come back from a stay in Paris where they were entertained by royalty. Mr. Leonard Jerome, my brother-in-law, is no slouch. He must have the best, and the best they're always going to have. Hah! Now, Angela here is my precious. She helps me so much, but I don't count her with the servants. She is my housekeeper, my confidante. When we moved here from Rochester she was superb in getting everything packed and labeled. I don't know what I would have done without her. My two boys now are away at school. However, I've got my sister's three girls while their great house is being finished. They're very European and no bother—"

Just then, two athletic young ladies sallied into the room and grabbed Mrs. Jerome by the hand. She introduced them as Clarita and Jennie, and coached them on speaking to the visiting lady. One was blond and white-looking, and the other was dark and mulatto-looking. Mrs. Catherine Jerome explained that President Millard Fillmore had first sent Mr. Leonard Jerome to Trieste in 1851 as U.S. Consul. They returned home when the Democrats took over in 1853, to this beautiful Brooklyn neighborhood. Jennie was born then and named after the celebrated Swedish singer, Jenny Lind. The family had another child, Camille, who was born in 1855, and it was then that the family's fortune soared. Soon, explained Catherine, the Leonard Jeromes were millionaires, and they rented a summer home in Newport, and bought a yacht so Catherine and her family could come up on visits. When Leonard took his family to Paris in 1858 their elegant apartment was on the Champs Elysees. Catherine was bubbling all over as she told this story of her brother-in-law's success. Angela too looked pleased. The two girls just stood by, the little dark one milking Margery's fingers.

When Catherine paused Marg quickly and politely said: "They've truly been blessed by Jesus to have had so young such an exciting and full life, and a wonderful father, and mother and aunt—"

Catherine was satisfied. She stood, rared back, then looked down her nose at the plain seated guest from Georgia. "I must get back to my invitations. Some very important people are coming here Tuesday night, to discuss Abraham Lincoln. Angela, don't be too long!"

The two young ladies scurried behind their proud aunt. They waved at Marg as they left. Then the little dark one broke away and came back to feel Margery's hand. Grinning a bit, she then raced away making a scream of glee. Angela felt she had to explain something to Marg.

"A few people are quick to notice Jennie's darkness. Her mother always explains it away as a little Indian blood . . . in our family." She laughed and led Marg to the armoire where her shawl had been placed. Marg got ready to leave. At the door Angela hugged her. Their secret of African kinship was warm and comforting. "Next time, I hope you can meet my wonderful employer, Mr. Lawrence Jerome. He's just as fascinating as his brother Leonard. He too will soon be a millionaire. That was on Catherine's mind today. Usually she's not so talkative. Well, my dear, you see why I'm proud to be here? Someday the Jeromes will do very important things for the country."

As her carriage pulled off Marg had mixed feelings. Her Bible said: not to be too proud of luxuries. Or living high over humble people. Poor Angela was living the fancy life serving these charlatans and not discovering her true self. Marg liked Angela. She would ask Phyllis's permission to write to her.

Sure enough, Margery was to hear more about the Jerome brothers when next she saw her broker, Mr. Haney. He claimed that the Jerome brothers were very successful in the finance business and now owned a racetrack. He was impressed that Marg knew such important people. Now reaching into his top drawer, he produced a thick yellow packet. This was top secret stuff. A copper mine in Wyoming, belonging to his family. If Marg wanted to buy into it, chances are she could have a voice in the company's operation. She laughed, saying she knew nothing about mining. Haney then drew out some pamphlets, urging her to read them on her trip back home.

"Then you're not askin' immediately for my decision?"

"Oh no, Mrs. Spence. Think at leisure. If you feel comfortable about it, send me a draft for one thousand dollars. Now don't take too long! The limited shares available will be gobbled up whenever this is offered on the market. Say, in three weeks' time."

She laughed again. This man was a real operator. But she still trusted him. As she was leaving he mentioned that the Jeromes were paupers five years ago. Then quickly he said something about their mutual Irish blood, and luck, and neither she nor Anthony denied it.

When she told her brother about her experiences with Angela and the Jeromes, he scolded her for calling them charlatans. They were indeed respectable people, and she'd never know better Americans. Marg's problem was always giving value on religious terms. She insisted it was God doing the judging, not herself. Anthony said to be persuasive among people one had to admire earthly nuggets, and that meant money and jewels as well as education, poise and beauty. It was the society, and not the Jeromes, who made the rules. She considered her brother's remarks. Material worth could be responsible. And with it she could draw in people, and still serve God. Yes, Anthony was right; she had to live in this world.

Their trip had been daring. Now she would go home to her southland and all its peculiar charlatans, and to the confinements of her aristocratic half-black world. Her society was truly weak at the seams. Yet, that controlling white world would be curious, not suspecting that they had clinched hands with northern people of substance, with the freedom to make themselves a better future. Perhaps they were all like greasy-handed gamblers, that was Anthony's light turn of the conversation. She liked his humor.

On the way home they decided to spend four days in Washington, D.C. They had not wired ahead. It took an embarrassed Louise to talk for them, to get them two rooms at the fancy Willard Hotel. It made Louise nervous because here in her work she was known as a colored woman in charge of the chambermaids. None of the guests were colored. Marg understood and appreciated the acting Louise had to do. She and Anthony would be white guests, upper-class white people. Such a farce, thought Marg, since the town was full of well-mannered, beautiful Free-colored. But class was class and everybody in Washington knew his place. And she would ignore distant kin and friend, Louise, while she was on duty. Then in evenings that same Louise would knock cautiously at their well-polished oak door. They'd invite her in stealthily. Inside they'd laugh over a glass of wine, relaxing and talking normally about many things. Who was the public that made these rules? Nobody knew. After a few days, in daylight outside the hotel, Louise was bold enough to take them sightseeing. Finally, they went to a fancy restaurant with Louise herself, over-powdered, stiff with mannerisms, posing as white, and beautiful in her best garments. She had picked a pleasant nice place but one where none of the senators she knew would go. Marg understood her being careful about her job. But in her mind the false world of the Jeromes in New York kept coming back. Pretentious people who had been poor a few years earlier, yet so full of power and respect. America's ruling class!

Marg enjoyed Washington. Her only disappointment was that unfortunately they didn't see Lydia Farley Smith. She was back in Lancaster. Louise told them that Lydia was getting to be very well known by the politicians who ran things. They knew her as a colored woman, Mr. Thaddeus Stevens' friend. And in that connection was all the power and respect a woman could expect. A woman of any color.

"Isn't it sad how we have to be devious to be accepted by those in power," Louise exclaimed to her guests while seeing them off at the railroad station. "And we must act as if we're other persons even in a strange town."

"I felt ten years younger in New York," laughed Marg.

"Listen, I have a secret to tell you-all," said Louise, looking around. "One of our distant old cousins from Carolina is now a man gaining power in Washington. As a poor young man he took his family to Tennessee where he became good at politics. Now he's come to Washington as a congressman. A *white* congressman."

"Oh, Louise, that's splendid! Who is it? Someone from your side?"

"He's a McDonough. But I'm not goin' to tell you precisely. His whole career would be threatened if they knew. He knows who I am. We have an understandin'. We bow without speaking. It's a wonderful trust, Marg, and I wish him well."

"I think it's terrible," she replied with a frown. "What kind of country are we becoming that people have to hide and whisper because they have a little African in their blood?"

"The pure whites insist," said Louise stoutly, "without bein' ashamed of their behavior."

"Well, I don't want their guilt on my back," said Anthony. "I'm beginnin' to understand what makes a southerner love his guns. He has to force society to behave his way!"

"Don't say that," laughed Louise, kissing his cheek. "We don't want war. You know that."

The beautiful steaming Coastline Limited came in with a gush. The three hugged and kissed again, not realizing a real war would come and keep them apart for many hard years.

Once comfortable on board, sitting in her purple velvet seat, Marg raised her window for one last word to Louise. "Honey, write an' tell me who it is, this congressman kin."

"Oh no," exclaimed Louise. "It just wouldn't be fair. An' I don't ask you for all those secrets you're findin' at Maple courthouse, do I, Marg?"

Marg laughed. "When I get something good, I'll write you!"

"No, no. Letters aren't safe. Margery dear, be careful!"

"Louise is right," said Anthony as the train pulled off. "I'll bet you, Marg, if politicians back home knew ours was a money trip, they'd be clamoring all over us. Jealous whites ready to steal! Hah! That's their birthright exclusively."

"I did learn one thing from Louise, about this mystery congressman," said Marg, reflectively. "She said he loves America. She called him an honest man among thieves. I think we can be proud of that kind of blood."

"I've always been proud of my blood, Marg."

"Even that little touch of blackness?"

"That too," he laughed, then ordered his wine from a black unsuspecting waiter, a slave.

The trip home was uneventful up till Charleston, but there the deluxe coach had to be vacated. It had a bad wheel. They decided on a day or two layover to see the quaint town. Their fair cousins made it a pleasant stay. Coming back to the railroad station, they were saddened to learn they'd have to continue on to Georgia in a normal night train. Immediately the southern type of white man came into view. He was loud, messy, boisterous and evil. There was so much drinking and comradery that Marg didn't get a wink of sleep. She sat back, with closed eyes, listening to all the conversations, the accents. All these different types of Americans. It was an education. And the poor black man, whom they despised, was the brunt of all their jokes. They talked about him constantly, always sharp derisive words making him the bottom of the society. A tear came, as Marg thought about all those dark-brown faces in their damp dark cabins, working so hard for nothing. In New York she had bought two copies of Harriet Beecher Stowe's novel *Uncle Tom's Cabin*. Now she realized she could really cause a commotion on this train, or in Georgia, just by exposing her purchase. To live with them, these rulers of the land, one had to be discreet. She could not reveal her simple, handsome books, her gifts. They were weapons in this freedom struggle!

Finally the train reached Maple, in daylight, almost noon. Upon seeing the red-brick stationhouse and the two huge palm trees out front, with relaxed green fronds waving, Marg had very warm feelings. This was home. And there on the platform were her three fair children, looking neat and handsome, and her lovely friends, the Korners, the Simpsons. Matilda had flowers. Little purple violets. As she ran forward to hug, Marg noticed some anxiety in her eyes. Then she saw Charles getting out of their shiny carriage. He too had flowers. She watched him cross the lawn, youthful, handsome and a little brown. People were staring, mostly because of black Matilda being among these white faces and near-white faces. Marg really felt they were staring because of the handsomeness of the group. Seldom could you find a pure white group so full of good looks. Her father had said that a Scotch-Irish, German, Indian, African mix made the most beautiful people in the world. Marg now tried to forget the public's scrutiny as she stepped into her family's best brougham carriage. On the way home she suddenly realized they were already rich people. She had seen so much poverty up North. Yes, it had all been an education.

"Would you like to live there," asked Charles as the carriage pulled into shady Plum Avenue.

"Oh no," she said, lightly. "This is home." In the silence her voice sounded strange. Then a horse stumbled on a cobblestone and at the same moment Malcolm House came into view. Grand and beautiful. Thinking of damp courthouses and jails, Marg allowed her tears to gather. She needed support to get inside. The train ride had been tiring. Or was there another reason for her weakness? Once seated in the parlor she saw immediately a magnificent rosewood piano by the great fern. Charles said it was a belated birthday gift. Her birthday was in April. She was thrilled. A kiss, then more tears came. Then Cousin Sue arrived with posies, and began playing all sorts of fancy pieces. The new piano had a more brilliant tone than the old one. She'd grow to like it, like one of her children. Now she felt very much at home. Soon the house became filled with people, music, and the smell of good food. Matilda had a hot bath ready. As Marg excused herself she realized her children were tugging at her skirts, wanting their proper attention.

"Did you see any Indians?" asked John, towheaded and serious. "Any Egyptians?"

"None whatever," she replied, sitting at her mirror and removing hatpins. "I did see a lot of new Americans. New York has many different kinds of people."

"What were they like, these new Americans?"

"Oh, nice people." She didn't want to talk about greed, color, or bad manners. What stuck in her mind, the Egyptians at the museum were colored yet revered by whites. New York Jews and Sardinians, the new people, were much darker than the colored she knew. Yet, the Jew and Sardinian would be thrown in with the ruling caste, to be regarded as white persons! "John, they also were very poor. We should be thankful that the Good Lord has blessed us. We live a very comfortable life. In big cities people often go hungry."

Next, roundfaced, first-grader Beth had her question. "Mama, tell me about school. Do they have to wear ribbons like we do?"

"I don't know, precious. I didn't go into any schoolrooms. Now did you behave at Aunt Phyllis's house?"

"Beth was very naughty," offered John. "She put lampblack on their cat."

"Oh, how terrible!" screamed Marg, taking up Meg, her little one, into her lap. "Why did you do it, Beth?"

"Oh, I wanted to see if he'd turn black, like you do, Mama, when you go to the courthouse."

"Hush up," scolded Marg, turning red. She had not realized that the children knew. "Now run along and help Matilda get the table ready. An' be careful you don't break my good dishes."

It was a party for good dishes. Gregory and Valerie came with their children and that made eighteen for dinner. It was too much work for Elias and Matilda alone; as usual, the free mulatto women all helped out in the kitchen, while the men sat around smoking and drinking good wine. Soon Marg came down, looking refreshed and simply gorgeous in one of her new frocks from New York. It was a magnificent Charles Worth gown from Paris; a flowing skirt of rich green velvet and Madras cotton matched a cool white linen top with dainty embroidered sleeves. While everyone raved at how wonderful she looked in the exquisite gown, she allowed shy Frank Korner to take a portrait photo at her piano, and one at her handsome staircase. Charles even gave her a special smile, but the house grew very calm when his Negro friend, Mel Young, came in. This big, bumbling man behaving his best, still talked in a loud drawl, while all others had their quiet, stilted big-house English. They were courteous to him but somehow the chill remained. Charles knew better than to invite him to sit down and eat with them, but there was nothing wrong with having a drink; so the two of them went off to some back room with a bottle. This upset Marg, but she would not let it delay the homecoming meal. She was still sore when Charles finally came back to the table, alone. Like a lady, she served him his dessert and coffee. He'd have to go to the kitchen if he wanted dinner.

"Brother Charles," said cute little Valerie, "you've missed a fascinatin' tale of yo' wife's exploits in the big city. She was hobnobbin' with millionaires."

"Really?" said Charles, in his elegant manner. "Shall there be no repeat for me?"

"She was tellin' about my cousin," offered Phyllis. "Angela Baker lives with the famous Jerome family. The Hall sisters, my cousins, married the Jerome brothers in Palmyra, New York, They moved to Rochester, then success took them to Brooklyn Heights, and society. I hear they're building a new mansion in New York itself. The house will require more than a dozen servants."

Matilda came with food for Charles. He carved himself a piece of dark meat. "Well, that's as good a judge as any of a man's worth, I guess. Just think of all the good people who have no help at all!"

"I love havin' help around," said Valerie. "It makes me feel like a teacher. I have to know things, an' see that everything's in order. When things go wrong, God will blame me because I watch over people for Him."

"That's an argument of the whites," said Lilian Simpson, coldly.

"It's all airs! Let simple folk watch over themselves. That's true freedom!"

Very soon Charles, still smiling, excused himself from the table. Now Marg frowned profusely. Where on earth could he be going? He whispered nicely that one of his horses was in trouble, but she saw him cross the front lawn with that black man, Mel Young. She didn't like this friendship, yet if she mentioned it, people would say she was prejudiced. No, she had to lighten the party by telling more New York stories. After mentioning the excitement in the faces of the well-dressed young ladies coming to their hotel, she decided to talk about the individuality of colored people up North. Valerie wanted more to hear about gambling dens and showgirls. In the end Marg talked about Mr. Haney, his nice Irish manners, but she would not mention money or investments. She did not want these people to know her secrets, to be blabbing them all over town.

Chapter 5

Marg woke up to the cheeping of birds, and a glorious warm sunlight flashed across the pink chintz stretches of her four-postered bed. Her waking thoughts were about tariff protection for northern manufacturers. This was Tom Haney's talk. Why was she thinking about him? He had promised to take her to a New York dress factory, but time ran out. While being the first northern man she had gotten to know, his easy manner made him like an old friend. No fierce brashness like most white men. They could talk. And he agreed with her that northern poverty was just as bad as black slavery. She had tried to explain to him that there were good homes, as well as bad, where slaves lived. Setting Christian example, her family had always treated the slaves with respect. No, not respect, perhaps with loving kindness. No, not that either, because she had seen Fred Thurston, the overseer at Edgewater, beat the black ones with a cane. No, the family treated them as business partners. The plantation could not produce cotton and tobacco, peas, potatoes, cabbage and corn, without the black field-workers. It could not work without their cooperation. That was why Neelys had failed, and Proxmire's too.

Where southerners had been cruel and nasty to slaves they were having trouble with production and harvest. So the slavery question was social and commercial, as Mr. Haney had maintained. And politics too. The South in 1860 felt it needed having slavery extended as an institution in the West. Washington had long leaned towards pro-slavery factions. The new Republican party, wanting to restrict slavery, seemed popular in New York, yet Haney claimed their numbers were small compared to the Democrats North and South. Marg knew that the delegates from her town would go that summer to Charleston demanding that slavery be recognized as a national institution, or they had a right to secede. Mr. Muggeridge, their next-door neighbor, was one of

65

the delegates. He had angrily discussed his views on her front porch many a day. In fact, she now had the kind of headache she got from his shouting. One of her girls was thumping the piano downstairs. Marg had them studying under Cousin Sue whose diligence only showed with John.

Marg got up and went to the blue-flowered basin and bathed her face in cool water. She didn't want to take any drugs. Grandma Margery had taught her to avoid drugs as long as possible. To live longer. She smiled, wondering why she would want to live longer. She didn't feet particularly happy this morning. And she didn't want to blame her feelings on Charles.

He had been up and gone since daybreak. And now without the vegetable business there was no need for this early-rising. He'd probably say it was the horses again. That was his standard excuse. She knew that sooner or later she'd have to face him with this and they'd argue. Poor Charles. Anger always upset him. Life never left her free of such dark decisions. She felt as tied down as the average nigger in bondage. She thought of Mel Young when that word came into her mind. Then she quickly got to her knees to ask God's forgiveness. The soft words of her morning prayers mingled with the soft fluffiness of expensive sheets and chintz quilt. She asked Jesus to grant humility, strength and direction to her misguided soul.

As soon as she rose Matilda came in with tea and toast and a bouquet of pink roses. "Mornin', Miss Margery, honey."

"Mornin', Matilda. Oh, these are beautiful!" Marg got into her robe sniffing at the fragrant flowers nearby. She thanked Matilda again, remembering her father's lecture on the inferiority of the Negro race. Of course he was wrong in this; her dear mother and other Christians had told him so. And he was ambiguous, so vulnerable with half-caste women. As his daughter, she felt she had some of that same evil and ambiguity. Perhaps all near-whites had it. She always had had to put effort into being nice to Matilda. And the black woman was wise, knowing all educated southerners felt themselves superior to any Negro in subjugation. Marg kept trying to conquer Matilda's suspicions.

"Oh, Matilda, you make me feel so wonderful to be home!" she exclaimed exuberantly while getting back in bed.

"I 'spects I know jis how you feel," smiled congenial Matilda. "Once at de plantation overnight I had to sleep on straw, an' it was itchin' and dirty an' rain was fallin'. Hah! Lawdamercy, I was so happy to git back to my own bed. But yo' brother, Miss Margery, tells me yawl had real luxury quarters in New York."

"Yes, it was real nice, Matilda. Did you try on that new dress I brought you?"

"Lawd, Miss Margery, I had it on six times already. I was struttin' around dis mornin' at five a.m. when Mr. Charles went out—"

"Five a.m.?" Marg frowned. "Matilda, where is he goin' at that time in the mornin'?"

That look came into Matilda's deep brown face again. Marg noticed it. "Well, ma'am, he didn't say nothin' to me. I was at my mirror an' 'course he couldn't see me. Lawd, I was havin' myself a time! Ha-a-a!"

Marg let the question go unanswered. She got up and took off her braided hair-cap, admiring the way they had curled her straight blond tresses in New York. She'd keep it this way for a while. Slipping into her new soft-leather slippers she reached for her gardenbook. "I want you to help me water my garden this mornin', Matilda. That is, of course, if you haven't got somethin' better to do."

"Me?" Matilda rolled her big dark-brown eyes. "You know, Miss Margery, I do whatever you say. Nawsuh, ain't got a thing pendin'. Happy to—"

"Matilda, do you ever think about bein' free?"

"Lawdamercy, Miss Margery, why you question me so? Ha-ha!"

Marg put on another item from New York. A waistcoat of leather and velvet which she had especially bought for work outdoors. But it was too hot for this. She got into her old gingham. "This Mr. Haney up North kept askin' me how I treated you and Elias. I told him the truth, Matilda."

"What's de truth, Miss Margery?"

"That there are good homes and bad homes. That people are treated with love and respect in many good southern homes. Isn't that right, Matilda?"

She was quiet for a second. "Dat ain't the same as freedom, Miss Margery."

Downstairs two new young girls were busy in the pantry. Another one of Charles' surprises. These additional slaves meant he and Ned were doing all right. Since Charles could spend money recklessly, she had decided not to tell him anything about her New York investments. And she told Anthony as well not to talk about it. With the children now knowing about her courthouse visits, everything in her life was getting too public.

"I think I'd be restless livin' here again," sighed Anthony over his breakfast. "September can't come too fast for me. The heat here is outrageous. It's morning and already ninety degrees outside."

"No one's begging you to go outside," said his sister. "Matilda will help me. I know you're not a man for hard work. Ha-ha-a! What were all those meetings you had in New York, Anthony?"

"Well, first of all, I was trying to see Rev. Henry Garnett. I wanted him to accept my application to teach at Wilberforce University."

"Is that the Negro college in Ohio? Mercy, Anthony, you're not a teacher! Dad wants you to continue until you finish medicine."

"I probably will, but I'll also teach. With more than a quarter of a million Free-colored in the North the schooling for them is terrible. Only Massachusetts allows them in the public school system as equals. In Illinois, a black man has to pay a fine to enter the state. In the West when he wants to buy a home he's put on the block just like a slave. I went to the New York Manumission Society and registered as a teacher. They had a job for me at Avery College in Pittsburgh, but I want my degree first. Charles Sumner and Wendell Phillips who have pleaded so hard for our cause both stress that to be qualified we too must have the degrees."

Marg sipping her second cup of tea, set it down hard. "They don't have them! Believe me. But I'm glad to see you identifying with black people, Anthony."

"Not with black people, sis. We could never be black."

"I'm not so sure about that. Now that Dad is dead, they don't see us as white."

"That's because we allow busybodies to manufacture an inferior slot for us. Marg, we're weak politically! Near-whites should fight for their culture an' position."

"Anthony, the American prejudice is against the whole dark race."

"An' where do you divide the races? Tell me."

"No. Let's not discuss it. Wasn't it nice in New York? Your Mr. Haney says it's only money that talks."

"We have money down here, and suffer all that scorn. A double standard of treatment based on family facts people know. Otherwise invisible! Our blood for generations has been more of Europe. We have more European ancestors, yet, why should we let these bullies point us only towards Africa? I hope you'll teach yo' children to respect their European roots. In a society thinkin' black what will happen to them?"

Marg laughed. "You remind me of Lydia Farley Smith. She took Dad to task, accusing him as if he were a redneck philandering among colored women. I was shocked by the thought and words. It made us nothing but—"

"You have to grow up too, Marg. We are not angels. None of us. It would be nice if men respected me for my roots, bearing and culture. How easily they could treat me with the same respect accorded other gentlemen. No. They want me a worthless black. An' I'm ready to fight a duel if a man tries to belittle me so, while he falsely builds himself up. Yet, my longing for respect is with every colored man. We get not an ounce, dealin' with this brazen a-little-more-white devil."

"Mercy! Let's not continue this. That's all I've heard for days is this racial talk. I hope this man Lincoln will win and change it all. The states won't divide if he can put people's minds on something other than—"

A big black carriage pulled up in front of the house. Marg immediately knew it was from the Malcolm family. Anthony quickly disappeared. She thought of Jane coming to take more slaves. Or, now she feared maybe they'd come to scold her and Anthony for their trip North. As she reached for protection, she saw through the curtain a big woman in flowing skirt crossing the lawn, followed by a slim, slightly-bent old man. Who were these people? In just a few moments two of the loveliest faces she had ever known came through the back door. It was Celeste and Winston, two favorite servants from her childhood.

People had always admired fair, ivory-colored Celeste and Winston because they looked so wonderful together. God had blessed them both with fine features and beautiful skin tones. Even the whites who called them slaves had to admire their beauty as well as their dignified carriage. They had been husband-and-wife houseservants at the Malcolm main house for years and years. Such couples with just a hint of Negro blood had been in demand among the richest families. Such people would marvel over the whiteness of their skin, the straightness of their hair. Celeste and Winston had always tried to be expert in their work. And their gracious manners had also made them famous in Maple. Judge Edward had been very proud of them as his most handsome slave couple. He also was proud of their wisdom and skills.

Celeste had been pastry cook as a young girl, and later the head cook at Edgewater. None of her three cute children had been born of her union with Winston. Her blond son, John, was fathered by Judge Edward; another quadroon boy, Joey, came mysteriously; and she never told who the father was of her most beautiful little girl, Effie. Celeste had been trained by her own dignified Christian mother to accept the bonds of slavery without scarring your character. Her tears cleansed, and Winston alone knew that she was a very chaste woman, as much as any pure white woman sitting back with fancy airs and finery.

Marg ushered them in to seats around the breakfast table. Celeste waited for her husband to sit down first, then he came rushing over as she sat down, to push in her chair. Marg now remembered Celeste's lovely green-eyed daughter Effie who was a proper beauty. Celeste was heartbroken when they took her off to New Orleans, to be a dancehall hostess. But Effie did very well at it. It is said a white banker married her and now she moves in the best circles in Crescent City. It made her mother so proud. Winston too was proud, because he had accepted Celeste's children as his own, and he was a good father to them. Now his health was not good. Marg realized he had to be past sixty. Having been sold to the Malcolms in his twenties, he first served as a groom, then a footman, then became Judge Edward's most faithful personal valet. Now these two marvelous people had been allowed to live in retirement in their neat attic rooms out on Peachtree Drive, just as Margery and her mother had lived in the attic rooms in this the original Malcolm House.

"You keep it so lovely here," said Celeste with relaxed folded hands. "Whenever we drive by here I takes it all in. Hah! In admiration. Yo' dear mother would be very proud of you, Margery-baby."

"I suppose she would," laughed Marg, bringing eggs, bacon and toast. The two servants moved eagerly for the food, which made Marg remember that contained servants even in the best homes were not getting the best of food. She went back to the warmer and brought hominy grits, buttered hot biscuits, and sage sausages. Their eyes lit up as if a feast were being served. Right away they asked her about New York and Marg quickly had to think of a gift she might give. The Longfellow book of poems had gone to Cousin Sue. She couldn't dare give them a copy of the Harriett Beecher Stowe book. And Anthony wouldn't part with the Niagara Falls painting he had by van Starkenborgh. Well, there was the crystal hand-warmer she had bought for Lilian. That would do. She rushed upstairs to get it while Anthony came again to say a few words. He was off for a swim at his favorite boyhood spot, in Cobb's Creek.

"That's such a long way off," cried Celeste in her customary melodious drawl. Knowing good English, she allowed her voice to make musical ups and downs the way southern ladies did it. Celeste had always been as proper as the most gracious southern ladies (white). "We can take you, if you can wait a while, Anthony-baby."

Winston sat forward. He didn't seem to agree with his wife.

She grabbed Anthony's hand. "There's something very personal we have to discuss with yo' sister. It won't take long. Say, a half hour?"

"Oh, I'll go on and walk," said Anthony. "Remember, for me, it's like a vacation being here. I want to take in all the sights."

"We might catch up with you on de road," said Winston, his English not being quite so fine as Celeste's. "You young rascals have all de energy, like you has all de girls an' de money! Ha-ha-a!"

Marg came back with her gift beautifully wrapped just as Anthony went out the door. While Celeste made her musical ohs and ahs Marg sat down to her third cup of tea. "Angel, this is so beautiful! I thanks you from the bottom of my heart. You know, when I was a fetchin' young thing I wanted one of these gadgets, 'cause all the fine ladies in society carried them when they went to dances. See, Winston, you just squeeze it! It's to take the sweat out yo' hands. Isn't that somethin'?"

After a while, they got down to serious conversation. "Miss Margery," said Celeste, now in formal respect to the free woman, "we in deep trouble. Ever since yo' father died. You see, how it is, Miss Jane's so fussy. Now she's botherin' us to get us out our rooms, and yo' father said we could have them rooms as long as we live . . ."

"By all means," agreed Margery as her headache came back. "Is there any help I can give?"

"Well," Celeste took her time getting around to the rest of her story. She pinched the corner of a biscuit and ate it slowly. "Doctor says I'm not to eat too many of these things, the way I'm bustin' out of my clothes. Ha-ha-a!"

"Celeste, if you want me to speak to Miss Jane, I will."

She and Winston exchanged glances, then her face became serious again. "She scandalizes us. An' this has been goin' on a long time, Miss Margery. Even before yo' daddy's stroke. An' I came to the decision we should leave. We're old now an' they can't do nothin' but kill us. I told Winston I'd first try to do best by him. He's ailin' too much to be a runaway. An' we talked it over, my idea, an' he thought Jesus had given it to me, to tell to you—"

"How can I help?" Marg urged her on. "Cousin Don has connections with northern people. Do you really want to try to leave, Celeste, at yo' age? I'm sure there must be some easier solution."

"We want you to buy us," said Celeste straightout. "If we could come here to live, I'd work an' work, like a sixteen-year-old, Miss Margery."

"Bless yo' heart," Marg couldn't stand tears, and Celeste was crying now. She couldn't take more tea, so she just had to sit through it. With clasped hands she breathed deeply, while Winston stood up, went to his wife, and kept hugging her, kissing her, and patting her hands. Celeste then made a loud moan. A lump came into Marg's throat. Pretty soon she herself would be crying. "Instead of buying you, I could take you in as fugitives. It would be our secret. You could live up in my attic. Nobody would find you here. To buy you would mean negotiating with Jane, and as you know, she's terrible. Miss Jane would give me all kinds of trouble. Just as soon as Daddy died she came here an' took my four girls—"

"An' sold them!" screamed Celeste, not tearing any longer. "It was so heartless, Miss Margery. All she wanted was the money."

"You mean, my Coogie has been sold?"

"Yes'm. She's in South Carolina. Wanda's down in Dothan. Johnnie Mae and Fanny, nobody knows where they is. They put 'em on a boat goin' down the Chattahoochee. Lawdamercy!"

Marg now touched the wrinkled ivory-colored hand. "Angel, why don't you come here as a fugitive? If a war comes I'm certain I could keep you without suspicion. Safely hidden, an' we'd have lovely times together! You'd have your freedom!"

"No, no. War ain't that easy. We wants you to buy us, Miss Margery. All straightforward and legal. I've talked to Lawyer Perkins about this. I've told him this plan an' explained my feelings in detail. He knows I would never ask it if Judge Edward was alive, Lord bless him. He said he'd talk to you."

"When was this, Celeste?"

"Last week Monday."

"I was in New York. Don't you fear Lawyer Perkins will tell Miss Jane?"

"He won't do that. You see, he owes me a favor or two."

Marg had never liked long and lanky Lawyer Perkins, with his strict face, skinny bald head, and chicken skin around a bulging Adam's apple. In fact, she was afraid of him, this wicked man who had come to her with Jane's threat of slavery so soon after her father's death. "No, Celeste, I could never trust him. You'll have nothing but trouble."

Celeste now smiled. "I doubt that, Miss Margery. You see, he's the father of my daughter, Effie."

Marg had never suspected, all these nineteen years she had been admiring beautiful near-white Effie. "Well, I don't know. I have to think about it. Excuse me, I have this terrible headache. I think it's from all that train-ridin'. Maybe yawl could come back in a day or so—"

Celeste and Winston stood up. They knew how grave the subject had been. They would not press for an immediate decision. At the door

Celeste, clutching her gift, turned with mournful grey eyes. "During yo' trip I happen to mention it all to Mr. Charles."

"You told him? What did he say?"

"He said you would decide, that it was yo' house—"

"But we'd have to do it as a family. Celeste and Winston, I love you very much. I want you here with me. I think Jesus is tryin' to tell me something. Even so, I have to speak with my husband."

Celeste understood, and Winston too. They went out into the thick morning heat feeling relieved. They knew Miss Margery was a Christian woman, deeply so.

Chapter 6

As soon as they left Margery took a pill, then went out on her shaded backporch to read the morning newspaper in her swing. The first thing she read was an article by slave-trader, W. B. Gaulden, saying he would go to Charleston's Democratic Convention urging support of the South's rights. In his view, boats bringing black slaves from Africa should start up again, and if the rest of the world went along, the price of slaves could be reduced. Next she read an article saying Convention delegates should support the views of William Lowndes Yancey, the orator who had led the 1848 endorsement of the Alabama platform calling for slavery in the Territories. The paper tabbed Lincoln as swarthy and black. True, he was much darker than many colored she knew, but why did the color of a man have to make him bad? Yes, if Charles agreed she'd be willing to take in Celeste and Winston. But she should have bargained for something from them. The family's big house on Peachtree Drive was full of secrets. Celeste could get to those secrets for her. First of all, Marg wanted to know if there was another will, or, a home copy of the deed to the Broad Street property her father had given her as a fourteen-year-old girl. She became excited thinking that answers could be found in her father's oak desk. Yes, Celeste had to look around before she left there.

"Lawyer Perkins may be all right," said Charles that evening at dinner. "Ned uses him for all his business. If you don't trust him we could go to Judge McKnight whom you like. What about that?"

"Charles, why do you leave me so early in the morning? On the first morn I'm back? I'm beginning to think there is somebody else in your life."

"Ho-ho," he laughed. "What brought this on? You know I don't like hot weather. I went out early to Cobb's Creek—"

"Anthony was there. He didn't see you."

"Hey, come on. He was some six hours later. Don't you trust me, sweetie?"

"None of that sweetie talk. You're a hypocrite, Charles. You cleverly go along with my schemes when you don't agree. Matilda says you told her that you don't want Celeste and Winston in this house. Now I hear compromise. What do you really think?"

Charles bit his tongue, and dimples came into his youthful cashew-colored cheeks. "Well, you're only askin' for trouble. My business is goin' pretty good now. We've got a small fourth blacksmithy. A tiff with Jane would wipe it all out. Besides, I've got you Mamie and Carrie now. You don't need any more help."

Marg sighed deeply. "It's not a question of help, Charles. It's a question of humanity. You mean you'd let people suffer without liftin' a finger? Old dear friends? Actually Celeste's son John is my half-brother."

"Go to Judge McKnight. I think that's the best idea. Let him advise you. I see the circus is settin' up again on yo' Broad Street lot. Now would be a good time to ask about it."

"I have a plan. See if you can get Bubber to take a note for me." Bubber was the errand-boy who lived next door with the Muggeridges. He was their teen-age slave. A tall likeable brown boy with skinny legs. In summer he always wore cut-off pants and Marg like the looks of his bare legs. He was clean in his neat briefs, and that was better than the tattered things most slaves wore. When Bubber came she gave him a piece of sugarcane, then explained carefully that the note was to go only to Celeste, nobody else. He was to say: "I'm the boy from the Muggeridges." He wasn't to mention her name.

Sure enough, by sunset the familiar carriage used by Celeste and Winston was before the house again. The two of them got out slowly and crossed the lawn. Marg was thinking of the freedom they had. It was almost as much as Free Negroes.

"Have you had yo' supper?" she asked as they sat down at the table again. This time they refused all food. It was strange, as if somebody had coached them. Marg boldly told of her Broad Street property that was not mentioned in her father's current will. She told Celeste that such papers could be in his locked oak desk. She wanted Celeste to get the key and systematically go through all the papers, say, after midnight, and bring her anything mentioning her name.

Several days passed and there was no word from Celeste. Marg was preparing to resume her Friday night blackface visits to the court-house. Then word came that Humphrey had been killed. Bubber brought the news. It seems he had had a fight with another Negro. Got knifed in the neck. Marg didn't believe it. Humphrey, a calm Christian person, would fight nobody. The hardest thing was telling the news to Matilda, who immediately went screaming and raving. She broke dishes. Marg had never seen her so angry. She even ripped the new dress Marg had brought her from New York. Maybe it was a way of blaming her mistress for the tragedy. Marg decided to do what she could for poor Humphrey.

As he was Judge Barlow's slave, she couldn't claim the body but she could send flowers. The biggest bouquet a slave ever had. And people talked about it. Marg didn't worry. She felt it was appropriate. He was Elias and Matilda's brother. And Matilda was hers, almost another Malcolm.

The best white lawyers in town had their offices in the County National Bank Building on Broad Street. The building was kept elegant by the pure white Malcolms who owned it. Marg went there to see a northerner, Judge Horace McKnight, who had a few private clients but was known in town as the Federal judge over Circuit Court. Finally getting an appointment, now she was seated across the big mahogany desk, talking to bright-eyed and smiling Judge McKnight. Several weeks had passed and the circus now was gone from her lot. The profits had gone into somebody's bank account. She wanted Judge McKnight to find out who. In his polite Indiana manner he said he would, taking her forged copy of the deed. On that other matter, that of taking Celeste and Winston, he said he'd speak to Miss Jane. Marg said no, no social formalities. She wanted him to prepare a court case and have it tried. While the Near-whites did have court privileges, Judge McKnight advised against it. As a Federal judge, the case would not come under his immediate jurisdiction. He felt the power of his office could make Miss Jane behave properly, and settle the matter out of court. Reluctantly Marg went along, agreeing to a meeting, but she made it clear, she herself didn't want to be there. She didn't want to see any more of Jane Malcolm.

Summer passed and the Muggeridges came back from South Carolina. The Democratic Convention of 1860 had been a disaster. There was a split in the party with the South nominating a proslavery Kentucky aristocrat, John C. Breckinridge, while northern Democrats nominated Stephen A. Douglas. Mr. Muggeridge was very happy about Breckinridge who had presided over the senate and had served as Vice President. He felt confident the South would win in the November election. When he and Mrs. Muggeridge began telling all the grand stories of their stay in the delightful town of Charleston, they suddenly realized that Marg and her brother had been there before them. Then they turned sour. More and more they were classifying Margery Malcolm Spence as a colored woman. Their friends had told them to build up a fence between the two properties. Muggeridge himself wanted to move into a new finer house, but his wife said no. This was her family's property and she still thought of the land next door as belonging to the white Malcolms, who'd get it back if a war came.

"I've concluded my discussions with Miss Jane," said fiftyish Judge McKnight that September morning. "She'll give you Winston and Celeste, but she wants four thousand dollars for them."

"Four thousand?" gasped Marg. "That's top price and they're old!"

"That's her figure, Margery. And it's firm. I tried and tried to get it down. She thinks you have the money. If so, I'd advise you to settle now, before some new ideas come into play."

"Trouble is, I don't have that kind of cash. We'd have to surrender some investments and I don't want to do that."

"Well, now." He poured himself a glass of icewater and drank it without offering any to Marg. "Let me offer a little suggestion. Finally after all these months the family has located your father's papers on the Broad Street lot. It is yours, as you have said. With a little matter of reimbursing the family for clearing away debris, and for taxes they have paid, you may claim it legally. And I've been talking around about it, and I have you a buyer. Unfortunately, you wouldn't make four thousand dollars. In fact, the highest figure offered is eighteen hundred. That's very good, Margery. I'd advise you to agree. Can you raise the additional $2,200 for the slaves?"

"I have to talk to my husband," Marg told him. Charles had told her that the Malcolms would be very tough to beat in money matters. Maybe Charles could suggest something now.

At home, as he lounged in his bath, the subject did not impress him. He had been helping Mitchell to clear nine acres of bottom land near Edgewater, for more vegetables and flowers. A piece of that land belonged to his family. A dam had to be put up to keep out the waters from Cobb's Creek. Charles couldn't see paying four thousand dollars for Celeste and Winston. Marg made a few false tears and he finally came up with a suggestion.

"You know, by chance Mitchell and I ran into Mr. Gilbert Myers. Remember him?"

"No, Charles, I don't know those country people."

"He's a rich man, Marg. Owns all the land on the North and West of our property."

"Oh, you mean the railroad man. Cousin Sue said he was after her once. Yes, I do remember him now."

"He's a decent sort, Marg. He told Mitchell and me that he'd help us regain our swamp land. All he wants is another two acres to put up a barn on the main road. Claims horses can't make the grade to his old barn. Mr. Myers says for one thousand dollars he'd get us a solid dam in there. I think that's the better investment."

"Oh, Charles, how could you? That's not even our land. It belongs to Sue's people. Besides, you've given up the vegetable business. You don't need it."

"I don't know about that, honey. If war comes, Ned may ease me out."

Marg looked up with startled eyes. "I thought he liked us."

"No. He's a cracker at heart. You know that. In Mr. Gilbert Myers I feel we have a friend. He's honest, with none of that bigotry of most southern planters."

Marg threw down her book. "Lord, every question of our lives is this racial business. What I feel we ought to do is like Daddy said, completely sell out! I'd like to give every penny we have to Mr. Haney up in New York."

"Say-y, now that is an idea," chimed Charles. "You did take that insurance he suggested. The way I hear it goes, we can borrow money on that insurance. Did you know that, Marg?"

"Charles, do we want to be in debt? My father was always against it."

"These are different times. Sure, let's try. Get some of that northern money down here!"

The next day, a letter arrived from Anthony who was back in his plosh university up North in the state of Michigan. It read:

September 29, 1860

Dear Marg,

By train and carriage, I finally arrived back in this Gothic place. Beer, football and studies. Already the steam is hissing in my radiators. We feel so fortunate to have central heat. My room is over the furnace and the guys dry their clothes here. It means I have lots of company. But I'm not all that popular. Last week I had to give an oral book report on Charles Darwin. I argued against the racial theories that have been proposed. Our professor was teaching that black is always dominant, and I maintained that it was not. I said my children would be blond and white even if I married a brownskinned girl. Then they wanted to know about my roots. Some guys stopped talking to me upon learning that we're near-whites. Yet, I've made a few better friends. Only thing, my professor doesn't give me any credit any more. One would think I had done him wrong personally. If he gives me a low grade I can't make Phi Beta Kappa. But in this so-called scientific matter I wanted to be truthful, especially in these times when doctors color their teachings, and the next scholar has his own idea of who is the typical American. I feel we are that.

Love,

Anthony.

Marg put down her knitting and answered her brother right away. She wrote:

October 10, 1860

My dear Anthony,

I was delighted to receive your fast letter telling me that you're comfortably back in your Michigan rooms. It made me shiver when you spoke of the central heat. I suppose it's already snowy and cold up there. We're still having nice balmy days and the nights aren't so bad yet. The children still play outside and Charles and Mitchell stay busy with the land. I think you did right telling those boys off in your classroom. And don't worry if it cost you the friendship of your professor. I am sure there are other professors who'll agree with you. If not, you must quickly try to find a friendly professor. You must always balance life that way. That Darwin talk is down here too, but most of us know that it is the greedy ones who speak of inferior and superior men. Let them try to do without the labor of the dark race! Amen. Honey, we've always been American, and Christian. You keep on fighting, and write me again soon.

Love,

Margery.

As the cool nights began to reach the Georgia middle country, Margery and Charles, with careful planning, managed to be successful in several business matters. In the first place, Mr. Gilbert Myers paid them well for the two acres of Spence land he wanted for his barn. They were able to take possession of the Broad Street property just by paying the lawyers. Elias took her up in the carriage and she got Korner to photograph her walking on that land one time, then they went back into court, selling it this time. Judge McKnight's buyer turned out to be the Innis family (white), but Marg didn't have to deal with them. The lawyers handled everything. She and Charles were glad to find funds to give Mitchell for the new concrete dam. As the swamp land became useable they planted seeds, and soon green shoots were everywhere.

Marg had secretly bought into the Haney family's copper mines without telling Charles. Now she put up her stocks temporarily to get the money needed to buy Winston and Celeste. It all worked out, with Judge McKnight's constant help. The two grateful old people were to move into the central attic rooms at Malcolm House on the 6th of November. No one had remembered that that was election day. Soon after dawn, whites around town were standing in groups at polling places. A misty rain fell, but that business kept them outside. Later, the railroad station was jammed with the curious wanting to get the latest information from the telegraph.

That evening Marg, bone tired, sat down with a beaming Celeste, to have a soothing cup of hot chocolate after a day of moving furniture and boxes around. At ten o'clock Marg put the lamps out in the front of the house. Just before her own bedtime, Celeste came down again wanting to read her a passage from the Bible. Just then, Charles walked in, looking very depressed.

"Well, it's happened," he sighed. "The northerners won the election. That fellow Lincoln has gotten in."

"Are you sure?" asked Marg, screwing up her face.

"Well, they're still counting but it looks like he'll win. He's way ahead of Breckinridge, Douglas and Bell."

"Tomorrow morning you go down and find out for sure. I think, Charles, we have to prepare for our future." Then she smiled. "Isn't it wonderful to have Celeste here with us? It makes me have a happy feeling, as if my dear mother has come alive again."

Matilda, in no uncertain terms, disliked the idea of having two more servants in the house. The part of the house where she and Elias lived was the East wing attic over the conservatory. A little back stairway led up to these rooms. She had no heat but it didn't matter. What Miss Margery had done for the new two was to open up the main attic rooms in the center of the house, which meant access straight up from the main staircase. And they had heat too. A brick fireplace in two of the three rooms.

Marg waxed sentimental in opening up this area of the house, for it brought back all the good memories of her childhood. The flowered wallpaper had an old smell but that was a part of the charm. And the big brass bed her mother had died in. Those huge expensive china pots were still under the bed. The Swiss musicbox. And the black mantel clock chiming the quarterhour. All the gifts her father had brought which she had put away to deaden memories. Now it was all right for memories to come alive again. She had achieved victory, freeing two human beings from slavery. And with all the fine bedding, copper pots, crystal vases, it certainly didn't look like quarter for slaves, even with the sloping attic roof. No wonder Matilda was mad and jealous. Neverthless, Marg promised her some good things from this new adventure. For one, she would no longer do the ironing. Celeste had volunteered in this category. And Winston would take out the ashes from every grate. Matilda felt they should chop the wood as well, but Margery didn't give in on this. After all, the old couple was in retirement.

"You don't pay no four thousand dollahs for no retired people," sassed Matilda with knitted brow.

"Now, hush up," said Marg. "The money part of it is not your concern. God Almighty, I simply don't know how all my business gets out into the streets. Don't you mention that sum again, young lady."

Matilda didn't say anything. She just smiled and went on with her dusting. She knew more than Miss Margery suspected. Ned Malcolm was friendly with a vicious bunch of white thieves, the Innis boys. Nothing but white trash, but they were getting their hands into many things that had belonged to the mulatto aristocrats. They had shrewdly taken jobs in the blacksmith shops which Mr. Ned and Mr. Charles were supposed to own. Rumors among the slaves had it that all seven Innis boys from the swamps near Cobb's Creek were buying houses in town. One of them was now in the fire department and another was in the courthouse. The toughest one, Brady Innis, who owned the grocery store, was interested in politics. He had gotten Jack Malcolm to lease him Margery's Broad Street lot for five years; he had made a fortune with the circus there. Now he had bought Marg's same Broad Street property, and was selling it to the city for a new Town Hall!

In the old days Matilda would delight in telling all this gossip to Miss Margery, but no more. Every black person knew that poor Humphrey was killed because of her. The Innis boys had a hand in that too. Matilda knew it was dangerous to talk. She never wanted any poor white trash hanging around threatening her. Best thing was to forget it. And she had her own new wealth as comfort.

Matilda through smiles and coaxing had gotten Celeste to bring her a piece of good jewelry from the main house. It was a beautiful diamond brooch that Miss Wanda had owned. Miss Wanda had loaned it to Celeste as a token when her beauteous daughter Effie was abducted to New Orleans. No, actually Miss Wanda had given it as an appeasement since she grieved too at seeing them take a princess like Effie away. It had all been Mr. Tom's idea. He needed the money. Then as months passed, the jewelry was forgotten, as poor Effie was forgotten. Nobody knew that pretty-faced Effie, so faithful and honest with her mother, tried to send letters home. Then when finally she and the rich white banker were married, one of the first things she did was to return the brooch by post to her mother. Poor Celeste thought of giving it back to Miss Wanda, but this sparkling spray was truly the only grand reminder she had of her daughter. So, over the years, she kept it, until Matilda was bold enough to ask for it. And just like that, Celeste in her old age was willing to part with it. She thought it would buy her peace in the new house.

Charles was right in his election news. Lincoln got 180 electoral votes, Breckinridge 72, Bell, 39 and Douglas, 12. He had won in every northern state except New Jersey. But in the popular vote he had only 1,866,452 votes as against 2,815,617 tallied by all his opponents. Unfortunately, Breckinridge failed to carry a majority of popular votes even in the South. But no one could say he was a strict secessionist. So the country got Lincoln, a minority president, who was lacking majority votes. He had won mostly because of the voting in populous states. As expected, almost immediately the legislature of South Carolina was assembled at Columbia and they voted to have a convention of Southern states. The excitement was great. There were parades and fireworks, and lots of cheering.

Now Margery read the newspapers every day. She told Charles to renew his vegetable connections. No, she didn't want him back in that business, but she did see the need to store food. She put all four of her girls, even Celeste, to work canning fruits and vegetables. When they ran out of bottles, she got more. When they ran out of space, she created more space. Even the brand new piano was used to store things. Not food, but documents. Under the lid, in velvet wrappers. In a way she was getting ready for war.

Chapter 7

On December 20th, 1860 the South Carolina Convention, by unanimous vote of its 169 members, passed an ordinance declaring that "the union now subsisting between South Carolina and other States, under the name of the 'United States of America', is hereby dissolved". She maintained that the colonies had decided in 1776 that they were free and independent states. Declaring that she had been deprived of her property rights stated that on 4th of March a sectional party would take over. She blamed the problem on politics and erroneous religious beliefs. The people of South Carolina, now an independent nation, were appealing to a Supreme Judge. Margery read all this thinking of her father. He could have been their supreme judge. Men can make such big problems from little disagreements. Now she was having to cook her own breakfast. Matilda wouldn't come down. Claimed she was suffering from some malady that made her oversleep. Marg knew that it was nothing but spite and jealousy, but she wouldn't beat Matilda as pure whites would. She just went on letting her tie ropes on their friendship. She thought she had raised Matilda as a true Christian. If so, some day soon she'd see the light and beg forgiveness.

On 21st December Margery received a curiously heavy invitation in the mail. She marveled over the thick envelope and the beautifully-embossed handwriting. She had seen such lavish invitations before but she and Charles had never received one. This was from Judge McKnight. He and his wife Edna were having a few friends in for a pre-Christmas party, on the evening of the 24th. The "RSVP" meant a reply message had to be sent immediately. Marg waited until 6 p.m. for Charles, then she called Bubber over for him to take her written reply to the McKnights. Of course, she and Charles would accept.

Poor Bubber came in a moth-eaten sweater. He had no overcoat and the temperature was down in the thirties. Instead of sugarcane this time, Marg, feeling sorry, gave him one of Charles' old sweaters. That was for the message. And the something extra for Christmas was a big piece of fudge candy. Matilda made it every year and Marg actually didn't expect it this year because of her onery behavior, but Matilda broke down and smilingly produced the candy as usual. Marg really didn't want to eat it. She feared it might contain poison. The cat got some of it, for Christmas, and now Bubber would get the rest.

On the evening of the 24th the children were put to bed early. They would get their gifts in the morning. Celeste stayed in their warm rooms wrapping all their little surprises. Matilda, in drafty barewood room, felt somewhat left out but happy too, for the mistress had gotten her a kerosene heater and it made everything nice with warming breezes.

In the main bedroom on the second floor Marg got dressed near a crackling hot fire. She would wear an expensive brown velvet Parisian frock she had purchased in New York. Now the Korners were carrying jewelry in their photo shoppe and Charles had purchased some nice little rubies for her ears. Next, her mother's lace blouse and gloves. Now Marg felt like a million dollars. And she looked gorgeous too. As usual, Charles came late. Too late for dinner. They had to be at the party at eight o'clock and she had no intention of arriving late. In their inexperience they had no idea that dinner would be served. Mainly she made sure he wore his best cutaway suit, with silver watch and chain. Charles looked like a handsome young bridegroom, in spite of little grey curls that now appeared at his temples. Elias would drive them over to Walnut Street, to the former Bowne mansion where the McKnights lived. And he'd bring them promptly back at eleven p.m. Marg wondered what she would do for three hours in a house full of pretending white know-it-alls. She would be out in society, Celeste told her, and this was something to soak in. Yes, in truth, she'd be with some of the most prominent people in middle Georgia.

Elias had the carriage all polished and shined and it looked as grand as the couple inside. He was proud to be taking them out. Matilda didn't want to see them in their finery, but Elias insisted. He would not drive off until Matilda came down. She mumbled a few nice words. It was Christmas time. Happy for a quiet house, she rushed back to her books. She was trying alone to learn to read. It was a gift she wanted to give herself.

As the Spences arrived, the McKnight mansion was all aglow. Crystal chandeliers twinkling in high ivoried walls. Marg was fascinated by the architectural beauty; she stared upward at the detail in the vaulted ceiling as the foyer greeted them with cultured music and happy voices. Marg felt right at home although she saw no one she knew. Their fair faces were not out of place. Charles' ivory-colored cheeks had a pink glow and Marg herself was white with powder. And they were just as well-dressed as the pure whites. Sparkling eyes met her sparkling eyes. Then, almost too soon, some sneering lady in grey gown with red bows came up and deliberately splashed wine in both their faces. Charles and Marg took it in stride. They knew that people knew them, and some striving whites would be jealous. In a darker hallway, they tidied up. Just as they finished, Marg's half-brother Jack came up smiling broadly and offering his hand.

"Well, well, it's wonderful to see you," called the blond man. "I had no idea you're friendly with Judge McKnight."

"Oh, Jack," smiled Marg, "I'm sure Jane has told you. He arranged for us to get Celeste and Winston. Also my lot on Broad Street."

"Oh-h, that's right. Well, how're things goin'? Are those two retirees happy at yo' place?"

"Yes they are. They don't miss your house at all—"

"I'm no longer home," Jack told her. "I'm married now, an' I'd like for you to meet my wife. Sarah, this is Margery. I've told you about her. An' her Charles."

The pure white social woman's face wore a visible sneer. She would not shake hands. She just nodded a half-smile, then turned to walk away. Jack grabbed her hand, and Marg's too. "I think it's good for you to get out like this once in a while."

"Yes it is," chirped Marg, not saying that nobody else had invited them.

"With all the war jitters, we need a party like this. Did you know it's a farewell party? Judge McKnight's been recalled back to Washington City."

"Oh, I didn't know," gasped Marg. "How sad. I must speak to him." Jack was going to say something, but his wife led him away without another word.

Marg and Charles followed the crowd and soon reached the punch table. A deep red liquid glowed in a huge crystal bowl. They were offered cups of the hot drink and found it full of spices. "Bishop's wine," called an elderly lady pleasantly as she sipped her own. "Some concoction they've brought down from Indiana. I like it, do you?"

"Yes, ma'am," stammered Marg. "I-I think it's fine."

Wrinkles came under the lady's glasses. "Yo' face is familiar. Do I know you? I'm Jessica Bowne."

"How d-do you do, Mrs. Bowne." Marg certainly knew this distinguished lady's name! She was reputed to be one of the richest dowagers in the county. "I'm Margery Malcolm Spence. And t-this is my Charles."

"I knew yo' dear father, Judge Edward," said the sharp-eyed Mrs. Bowne. She of course knew this half-caste Margery Spence. "It's brave of you to be here. It's a buffet supper. Some are eating, but others are drinking too much. I would never let all this riff-raff in my home!"

Marg didn't know what to say, whether she was being included in the "riff-raff" category. Charles decided to be sociable and spoke up. "Yo' brother, Mrs. Bowne, used to bring his horses to our place for shoeing. Haven't seen him lately."

The old lady laughed. "That's because we've got our own blacksmith shop now. You see, you didn't know you were gettin' competition, did you? My goodness, we have so many horses it pays to have our own. Over a hundred now."

"A hundred?" asked Charles in amazement.

"Well, you know part of our business is representin' the McCormick reapers. So, we have to have a decent show. Have you ever been to Claremont, Spence?"

Charles' cheeks grew warm. "No, ma'am, I haven't."

"Well, I'd like you and Margery to come out and visit me sometime. I like brave people. Hah!"

Just that quickly she was gone. The crowd had swept her away. Marg and Charles stood staring at each other. They didn't know which way to turn. They decided to follow their noses. The food smelled good. They came into a festooned dining room. It was ivory and gold, candlelit and crowded like all the other rooms. A long table was laid out with hot dishes of every kind. The little gardens on fine china plates were shining among heavier green garlands and red balls. Marg picked up a large silver spoon and served herself some fish, and Charles took ham and oysters. All the while, the pressure of people behind kept them moving towards some unknown destination. They began eating on the way. Marg found the salmon and turkey delicious, as was the baked yams, creamed limas and asparagus. They became pushed out into a cooler quiet hallway. As they stood there eating, little beady eyes were watching them—three red-faced drinking men at the end of the corridor, under a shining but smoky mirror. One of the men started shouting: "Hey, Gus, look here! Whatchu got, man, a nigger in the woodpile?"

"I ain't got no nigger," was the singsong reply from Gus. "Luke, whatchu talkin' 'bout?"

"Look, man, a nigger! Don't you see him, man? You blind?"

Marg and Charles, with burning cheeks, stood alone, in the stares of the three, hallbound wild foxes, or ignorant crackers. No other guests were around.

"Hey, nigger," the third one shouted to them. "Whatchu doin' here? We don't eat with no niggers!"

"You must be drunk," whined Gus. "I still don't see no nigger. Where?"

"Right there, man," shouted the first one. "them two! That gal an' that dressed-up dude. They sho ain't white. Them's niggers! Niggers!!"

Just then, Ned Malcolm sallied into the corridor with a plate loaded down with drumsticks. "Oh, hi," he said to Charles, offhandedly. "Didn't know you was comin' here. You seen my Molly around?"

"No, I haven't," was Charles' husky reply. "It's really a big crowd, isn't it?"

A yell from the corridor's end: "Did I heah crowd or cloud? Nigger in the crowd!"

Ned now noticed the three at far end. He stood there in the hall's middle, chewing his drumsticks, and surveyed the drunkards too. "Ned Malcolm," called one of them, "whatchu doin' with them niggers?"

"You m-mean Charlie here," Ned called back, weakly. "My business partner?"

"Some partner, a nigger," laughed Luke. "Hey, nigger, you wanna bootblack my shoe? You wanna kiss my arse? You wanna make somethin' of it?"

The three were moving slowly towards Ned, Marg and Charles. In the atmosphere's silence Ned's greasy fingers stayed busy, and his cheeks ballooned with drumsticks. "This is a nice party," he spoke through his food. "Now, yawl don't want no trouble!"

Just then, the tall rangy one, Luke, with black hair, bluish beard and darkish Adam's apple, reached up a threw a plate full of food at Charles. It crashed in a corner. Nothing landed on Charles, except some lettuce on his shoulder. Marg saw ugly food splotches on the beautiful walls.

Ned took them both by the arm. "Come on, let's get out of here."

He steered them back into the crowded dining room. "I think yawl should split up. Then you don't look so conspicuous. Charles, introduce yo' wife to my Molly. There she is by the door." He pushed them forward while looking back for the rednecks. Entering the dining room, Charles obediently took his Marg to meet Molly. The youngish white woman, with long neck, looked cheap, was the first thing that came into Marg's mind.

"Well, well," whined Molly, with little shiny lips also working on a drumstick. "Ned's talked about you a lot." She eyed the pretty, more dignified woman. "I didn't think you'd be so nice-lookin'! Hah! Did Miss Wanda give you that dress?"

Marg, shocked, didn't know what to say. "Charles, maybe we'd better leave."

"Naw," drawled Molly, touching her arm. "Don't go. Party's jis gettin' good. Don't know about you, but I got a house full o' young'uns always buggin' me to death. Thank God, tonight's Christmas Eve, so they's all asleep early! You know, you've got the same hair as us. Never would have thought it possible. Ha-ha-a!"

Marg tried to think of something to say. "The food is good, isn't it?"

"Oughta be," laughed Molly. "It's government food. May be the last Yankee stuff we'll evah get if these folks go to war. Ha-ha!"

Their distinguished host, Judge McKnight, suddenly came before them. "Oh, Judge McKnight," cried Marg, reaching to shake his hand. "It's a wonderful party. I don't believe you've met my husband, Charles."

The smiling judge nodded, shaking Charles' hand. At that moment Marg spied the hateful woman in grey gown who had splashed wine in their faces. Quickly she asked Judge McKnight who she was. In his usual calm manner he said it was Mrs. Callie Jones, wife of the Presbyterian minister. Marg noted it in her mind, then turned back sweetly to her host. "We're so sorry to hear that you're leavin' us. It's really sad. An' we'll miss you very much."

"Thank you, Margery," he replied. "It's likely we'll meet again some day." He wanted to say "after the war" but protocol wouldn't allow it. "I had to show my gratitude to all these nice people of your town and county. My wife and I shall miss Maple, an' all these spirited citizens."

"We made you so many difficulties," Marg continued as Molly moved away with Charles. "I personally don't know what I would have done without you. So few will accept us as you have."

Edna McKnight came up and grabbed her husband's arm. She was smiling at Marg. "Horace, this is a brave woman. I hear some of our drinking guests were rude to her."

"Really?" he exclaimed with raised eyebrows. "I didn't think to have any militia boys here, but any time you get a mob of citizenry there can be trouble. Edna, take up the spirits. Maybe that we should do."

"They have their own," chirped Edna in a holiday fashion. "Maybe we should sing some carols, to keep it moving in the right direction."

Charles came back with his watch in his hand. It was twenty past eleven. Elias would be waiting for them. Marg then began saying good-night to her host and hostess. "We leave next Thursday," the Judge told her. "I hope you'll drop by. We must keep in touch. After I finish a legal study in Washington President Buchanan has me slated for service in Pensacola. Then after a few months I'll be serving Mr. Lincoln in one capacity or another."

Suddenly Marg realized how small the world was. This man would be shaking the President's hand. Her hand found its way again into the Judge's soft hand. The warmth was reassuring.

Outside in the nippy air seven or eight black carriages hugged together around the entrance. Farther out at the curb, there were more silhouetted carriages. Charles spotted theirs about eighty feet to the right. As they came near, they didn't see Elias. The carriage was leaning forward as if a wheel were broken. A wheel was broken! Half its spokes were missing. Actually lying scattered on the ground. This was strange. Charles rushed to check his horses but they were okay. Marg looked inside and immediately let out a scream.

Elias was stretched out, panting, on his seat, with blood staining his white shirt. He began moving and whimpering as they got to him. Charles propped him up and loosened his collar. "Dey attacked me!" he shot out, in gravelly voice. "Dey come right up, callin' me names. I ain't no Malcolm. Dey said I was!"

Charles helped Elias to the ground. He was going to take him inside the house for water and attention, but Marg said no, she wanted to go immediately home. Charles got out his tools and worked a bit on the wheel. Then he put Elias back up into the cab. Marg and Charles sat on each side of him. As Charles took up the reins a terrible odor came from the backseat. Some human excrement was there. Marg shook her head looking up at the bright moon. It was the Lord's day. His first day on earth, and human fools were desecrating and polluting.

Cleaning up the mess, she thought of Mary and Joseph. As they rode off the cold air nipped at her shoulders. Then the stable smells came back again. Charles was quiet all the way.

"Well, was it worth it?" she finally asked him.

"Oh, I don't know. Maybe. I saw that Mrs. Jessica Bowne again. She insisted that you come and see her."

"Maybe I will," said Marg, hugging Elias to her bosom. "With Judge McKnight gone, we do need one friend in this town."

Charles thought she meant "one white friend" but he did not press the issue. Their own people were so weak. And feelings rather weak too. He too preferred to think about the moon. He nudged Marg, pointing to it with a smile. "That newborn babe, the Saviour, is our friend, Marg. He's watchin' over us."

Chapter 8

Margery tried to concentrate on her children that calm balmy Christmas Day. Handsome John, 11, came knocking at her door at eight o'clock. He wore a special smile and was all neatly dressed, anxious to give out the gifts he had made for his family. Marg received a beautiful carved-wood jewel box. It looked professional and it made her very proud of her blond boy. Beth, at seven, was not as artistic. She had made a bird's nest of paper, full of colored eggs. The white people in Maple had a custom of painting hen's eggs for Christmas and Easter. Someone would make a pinhole and suck out all the insides. Beth's eggs had gotten smashed a bit, but when Marg studied them again, the designs were not bad. Maybe her little angel had talent after all. Meg, at 4, with stringy blond hair like her mother, was only able to hand over a gift somebody had put in her stubby white hands. Charles had it a blue silk scarf, and Marg thanked him for this, just as she had kissed him warmly for the fur muff which had come in his name. They went out to Uncle Gregory's for dinner. This year, all their friends and relatives were a bit preoccupied. There were rumors that the state of Georgia, too, would secede from the Union.

By late January 1861 South Carolina was happy that the six other cotton states—Georgia, Florida, Alabama, Mississippi, Louisiana and Texas—had seceded. They met at Montgomery, Alabama on February 4th and organized the "Confederate States of America". Montgomery was just fifty miles across the border from Maple. Townspeople were most excited about all this important political activity in their backyard. Some delegates even got down to Maple to shop. They told that the group had elected Jefferson Davis of Mississippi as President, and Alexander Stephens, of Georgia, Vice-President. A warm spell hit Maple and people were all in the streets. Marg donned a warm sweater and sat out on her backporch reading all the newspapers.

She had been receiving regularly several northern papers, mainly *Freedom's Journal* and *The Colored American*, which her postman hated to bring. She had merely continued subscriptions started by her mother. Through them she had gotten to know Frederick Douglass and a number of other prominent Free colored leaders, as well as the views of the country's leading abolitionists. Anthony had said that this was one of the reasons the townspeople were angry with them as a family. He had gotten Marg to take the New York *Evening Post*, which William Cullen Bryant had run for three decades. Gregory said that southerners didn't like it any better, because of its liberal views. She also took the New York *Tribune* because its editor, Charles Dana, had been her father's friend. Right now, they were all stressing that America was a Union, not able to tolerate a dissenting group. She read the reprint of Webster's view, that the Constitution was not a compact between sovereign states, that they were one and inseparable. The New Orleans *Picayune* had a piece by Calhoun who had taught the South so much of its separatism. Marg learned that the North thought its population its advantage: 23 million against the nine million in the South. The North too boasted about its factories, businessmen and great wealth. And when they mentioned the navy, she realized this was war talk.

From local papers Marg learned that an Alabama man named Leroy P. Walker had been made secretary of war for the Confederacy. She knew that name. She felt certain he was a person in her mother's family. She'd write to Cousin Lucy Walker in Selma to find out for sure. Maple's afternoon paper, *Star-Journal*, stressed that they had nothing to worry about. The South was strong. She had the most experienced generals in the country. Within days they began seizing Federal properties, forts, arsenals, the custom-houses. It did look like war.

Marg read that early in January the Union's President Buchanan had sent a merchant steamer named *Star of the West* to its Major Anderson at Fort Sumter, with men and supplies. Confederate troops at Charleston had fired on the vessel preventing her from reaching the fort. The South had also secured the Mississippi River. For the most part, things were quiet in the country. A sort of waiting period. Marg wanted to talk about this to Charles, but he was absorbed in his own problems.

"Marg, you know Ned gambles. I think in time he will cause us to lose our business. I want to separate from him. Each of us would take two of the blacksmith shops to run on our own. Naturally, he wants the best two, the ones Uptown. I'd have to take the one out at Post Road and the other by the ballpark. Besides, he wants eighteen hundred dollars from us."

"Oh, bosh!" screamed Marg. "He's just another Malcolm bleedin' people for money. Why should you pay him anything?"

"It's to settle the debts of the partnership. I don't have eighteen hundred just now. Do you?"

"Frankly, Charles, I don't have it either. I had to send Anthony money for his schooling."

"Well, maybe we can sell something," said Charles quietly.

"You were too generous in improving Mitchell's land," she replied, squeezing his hand. "I suppose a good bookkeeper would say we don't need six servants. If war comes, how can we feed them all?"

Charles smiled. "I think we're goin' to have to live day by day, like everybody else. Unless you want to fight for yo' father's true will."

Marg had had another important Christmas present. Winston and Celeste had come down early, looking rested and smiling divinely. Before breakfast Celeste handed over her little gift. It was a white scroll of papers donned in pink ribbon. It was something from Marg's father's oak desk. A copy of the will that never got to court! His Last Will and Testament dated May 14, 1859. It had all the right things in it. Marg, Anthony, Paul and Gregory were to get 300 acres of Edgewater, the south end nearest Cobb's Creek. This never came to them in the will that was publicized. Now Marg had forgotten the date of the probated will, and poor Humphrey was not alive for her to go looking again at it in the courthouse. She'd simply have to go to court, and fight for her father's true wishes, like she told Judge McKnight she'd do. Now with war in the clouds she wondered about the timing.

"No, Charles," she told him. "I think we'll simply have to take a long rest, an' be happy with what we've got, the eighteen gunshot houses he left me, also that piece of land near Mitchell, this house and yo' business. We'll make it all work somehow." She didn't want to mention her northern investments which were by far the greatest assets they had.

"I think you should talk to Mrs. Bowne."

"Mrs. who?"

"Mrs. Jessica Bowne, the lady we met at the Christmas party. She's very rich, Margery, and could help us a lot."

"Charles, people are not going out of their way to help us. They think we have too much already."

"I want you to know Mrs. Bowne as a friend. We need that friendship, Marg. Why can't you visit her like she asked you to?"

"I could *never* go out to Claremont like that! It would be impertinent. Anyway, she's probably forgotten us."

"I don't believe that. I think that's why God had us go to that party, to meet Mrs. Bowne."

Marg laughed. "Charles, I nevah knew you to be prophetic, or so much a religious man. You don't even come to church."

"I'm gonna start goin'," he said, shaking her shoulders. "Right next Sunday. There's something I want to talk over with yo' Cousin Don."

Sure enough, Charles started going to church that very next week. St. James Methodist, the mulattoes' church, had about sixty families and lots more children. Rev. Don Malcolm was known in the community for running the only school in Cobb's Creek for the near-whites. People like Mrs. Jessica Bowne had given money to it, and Charles knew that. What he had in mind, to talk over with Don, was the moving of the church. The handsome white wooden building with square cupola and steeple, was nestled in a grove of maple trees, and the carpenter ants were doing it great damage. Cousin Don had talked of moving it down the hill a bit. There was a large clear meadow that belonged to the church only about two hundred feet away. Charles now wanted to supervise the moving. All he needed was some oak logs and about twelve strong horses. He wanted to borrow the horses from Mrs. Jessica Bowne. She'd remember him from the party, and maybe she'd ask to see his wife again. It was all a hunch, but Charles wanted to try it. Naturally he couldn't detail his plan to Marg. She had too much Malcolm pride, in spite of her little color.

The scheme worked out. Mrs. Bowne was willing to loan the horses and she certainly did ask to see Marg again. After an exchange of notes, Marg decided to make the visit on the first day of spring. A balminess prevailed in spite of rugged tracks in the road which had suffered incessant March rains. Marg came alone in her surrey.

"Mrs. Bowne, my shoes are not clean," she cried upon entering the huge plantation house. "I'm afraid I'll spoil your beautiful red carpet."

"My dear, you're not to worry yo' pretty head about such things. I have loads of servants here to take care of any problem. My dear, let me look at you. Marvelous! You have all the good looks the Malcolms ever had. And I suspect the sense as well. You know, yo' father was not all that pleased with his boys. Jack was to be the brains but turned out likin' womenfolk too much. Then Edward, to be the money genius, lacked the understandin' of people to get 'em to work and not steal.

Hah! I shouldn't be talkin' this way but I think you should know, I was yo' father's confidante."

"Really?" was all Marg could think to say. She sat down in a deep cool velvet couch. Already slaves filled a low table in front of her with tea things and goodies.

"As a young girl he tried to court me, but my father wouldn't hear of it. He knew the Malcolm boys liked colored women and he didn't want me in a family with colored people."

There was a silence. Marg didn't know what to say. She had trouble looking at sixty-year-old Mrs. Bowne in daylight. Her face was too wrinkled. It bothered Marg. But the sincerity and warmth of her brown eyes came through the glasses and captured Marg. She couldn't escape that glance, that waiting for an answer. "Well, I suppose your father was right. People should stay with their own kind."

Pleased, Mrs. Bowne sat forward to pour tea. "Precisely. That's exactly why I've invited you here. My dear, I'm bored with stupid people! I knew you and I should be friends from that first moment."

Marg sipped her tea. Three long months had passed since the Christmas party. Mrs. Bowne had not made a move to invite her until Charles borrowed horses to move the church. "Please don't say that unless you mean it, Mrs. Bowne."

"My, you're an impertinent one! My dear, I was ready to fight for you at the party when Rev. David Jones' wicked wife Callie deliberately splashed red wine on you and yo' husband."

"Do you really mean fight, Mrs. Bowne?"

"I certainly do. That Presbyterian witch could have had me turnin' that party out! Hah! Of course, I don't mean physical fighting. Leave that for the lower classes. But there are ways to get back at people. If I lash out at Callie in public, she'd never again do a disgusting thing like that. Mind you, the Presbyterians are supposed to be liberals like the Quakers and Congregationalists. What are you, child?"

"Originally the family was Baptist, but I'm Methodist right now."

"About the same. And yo' husband?"

"His family were Episcopalian—"

"Terrible! They, the Catholics an' the Unitarians . . . couldn't care less about the rights of colored people. I originally went to Elizabeth Female Academy, a Methodist school in Mississippi, but I got my degree at the Georgia Female College."

"Your degree, Mrs. Bowne?"

"Ha-ha-a-a! I guess I don't look like an educated woman. My dear, I'm the one who brought Dorothea Dix here on lecture. All the feminists up North know me, Lucretia Mott, Elizabeth Cady Stanton."

Now she leaned forward and whispered: "And even a few abolitionists know me. No-o, I'm not just a plantation wife."

"You mean you'd let yo' slaves go free?"

"No, I didn't say that. Mankind wins his rights through duty an' through slow intellectual churning. It's high time, I think for us women to be votin', and some of the Nigras should be free. But I'm a wise woman and I know none of it will happen just like that. There must be stages of preparation an' acceptance."

"Then you believe, Mrs. Bowne, that some day the slaves might be freed?"

"The qualified ones. I'm not for releasing' the ignorant ones. And to get them ready might take a hundred years! Have more tea, angel."

Marg frowned. "You confuse me, Mrs. Bowne. First you told me you believe in racial purity and now you speak for freeing qualified black men."

"Oh, it's a complicated subject, my dear. I had no intention of speaking it with you. First of all let me say, the black man doesn't belong here. He belongs in Africa. Yes, free him, and send him home."

"And what about people like me?"

"Well, you're a puzzle, the real obligation Americans have. We made you! You're neither one nor the other, so you have to keep on bein' American!"

Marg smiled. "That feels okay. I can accept that. But it's a real fight. Things such as what happened to us at the party don't make people feel right. I told my husband we should have stayed home, yet he said God sent us to the party, just to meet you—"

"Oh-h, I like that!" She got up and hugged Marg, "Now, come. I want to show you my house. The plantation is run by my brother, Mr. Lance Folsom. He's away on a trip. The house is my pride and joy."

Marg followed her hostess through Claremont's deep caverns. Colorful furnishings at every turn looked attractive and comfortable. The rooms led out into a high-arched light-blue corridor, which seemed as mammoth as a church. "My late husband, Mr. Carl Philip Bowne, and I picked this Carrara marble on our first visit to Italy, and had it shipped here."

"You've been abroad?" exclaimed Marg, gaining excitement.

"Several times, my dear. Come, I want you to see my Mexican room. It's where I do my sewing."

"Then you do do things? I thought at first you let the servants do everything."

"No, no, don't ever oversimplify life, Margery. It's all very complicated."

Marg agreed. "I think you stand out as a religious woman of conscience, Mrs. Bowne, an' also you have an aristocrat's good taste, an' other sterling qualities by being an abolitionist—"

"Heavens, I'm no abolitionist! Don't put tags on things. I would never call you a negress or a quadroon. To me, you're just another person. A marvelous person!"

"Thank you, Mrs. Bowne." Marg was beaming. She now remembered she had brought a little gift for Mrs. Bowne. Without words, she handed over a little jar of pear preserves. Delighted, Mrs. Bowne kissed her cheek. "Grown in Georgia?"

"Yes, ma'am. China sand pear. My father's sister, Aunt Bess, brought the original tree from China. They're nice and sweet."

"Thank you! for this rare gift, and yo' rare visit!"

Marg went away feeling this rich white lady would be a true friend.

Chapter 9

Jefferson Davis and his Congress had hoped South Carolina would not push on the northerners at Fort Sumter until after his inauguration. Fort Sumter had a Federal force of merely eighty men, while Confederates had six thousand nearby. President Lincoln decided that the garrison needed it supplies. When General Beauregard, in command of Confederate troops at Charleston, demanded surrender of the fort, Major Anderson refused, and Gen. Beauregard opened fire on the morn of April 12, 1861. The garrison held out for thirty-four hours. Then on Sunday afternoon, the 14th, Union soldiers saluted the flag, and marched out with drums beating "Yankee Doodle". Somewhat in shock, they embarked for New York. While in the bombardment of the fort, no one was killed, the secessionists now realized they had begun the war.

When North Carolina, Virginia, Tennessee and Arkansas were asked to supply troops for the national army, they refused. Then they seceded. On 21st May the decision was made to transfer the South's capital from Montgomery to Richmond, Virginia. Hostilities in the East began when the Union tried to preserve the new state of West Virginia from ancient and powerful Virginia. General George B. McClellan was in command; he had a small success at Philippi, saving the Baltimore and Ohio railroad for the Federals. Next, General Patterson commanding the Pennsylvania forces was to recapture Harpers Ferry, from Gen. Joe E. Johnston. In early June, there were logistic successes at Annapolis and Baltimore. Gen. Butler had a *fiasco* at Big Bethel. No one had dreamed that the South was so well-prepared for war. The Union worked fast to get two hundred thousand men under arms. The Confederates at the time had a force of just half that many.

Marg went again to Claremont in late June. This time she had been summoned by a sweet but peppery Mrs. Bowne, who wanted more pear preserves. She claimed the jam was tart and perfect, and she wanted an orchard of those same pear trees. Charles got the rare saplings ready, after Marg explained to Mrs. Bowne they needed a cool spot. She said she had just the knoll for them. This time, with gunny sacks and dirt, Marg came with Charles, in his work wagon. He hadn't yet broken away from Ned, but he had paid him some money. With Innis boys getting into the operation, Charles knew that if he did not legally separate, soon they might steal everything from him. Feeling desperate, and he didn't tell Marg, he would be bold enough this day to ask Mrs. Bowne for a loan.

Mrs. Bowne, powdered and perfumed, was ready to receive the two of them out on her cool East veranda. The caste system of the South was a peculiar animal with twists and curls of every description. In the Maple area it was all right to entertain a fair and free mulatto woman, but you did not have her and her husband together in your house for any social affair. What Judge McKnight did was all right for a northerner, but Jessica Bowne stood by her community. She'd merely give them a quick bit of tea out on the veranda.

"It was good of you to bring yo' man," the white lady told Marg as the quick sitting session ended. "He can go right to the knoll an' set these out. Charles, I've got good black dirt for the transplantin'. I know you ain't supposed to move saplings this late. How 'bout these Chinese things?"

"They'll do all right, ma'am," said Charles politely. "With manure. An' provided you water good, every day for about a week."

"Do you want to stay here a week an' do it?" asked Mrs. Bowne, jokingly.

Charles looked at Marg. "Well, I could come every mornin' . . . an' every night, I guess."

"All right, then, we've got a deal. An' how much you want to borrow from me?"

Flabbergasted, Charles wondered how she could read his mind. Old wrinkled Mrs. Bowne smiled at him. "You shouldn't talk yo' business so much. My black boys tell me everything. Seems when you were movin' the church you let it out. I been wonderin' when you'd get around to askin' me. Hah!"

"I'm deeply ashamed," said Charles, turning a little red.

"You needn't be ashamed," she clipped. "Money matters can always happen between respectable people. How much is it, Charles, that you want?"

He again looked at Marg. "Well, maybe two thousand, Mrs. Bowne," he said very quietly.

"What! You want me to give a nigger two thousand dollars?"

"I'm not a nigger, Mrs. Bowne."

She looked at him for a while. "I guess you aren't," she said with a strange serious look on her face. "I thought you meant somethin' like three hundred. How in the world can you pay me back two thousand dollars, boy?"

"You could be my partner in the two blacksmith shops I will own. Or, I could help you with your shoeing. I've seen yo' shop, Mrs. Bowne. The ventilation isn't right. The place could catch on fire. Also the anvils are out of place. The sparks hit the animals."

"You want to run my shop?" she screamed at him.

"I still, ma'am, would rather run my own shops," he continued quietly.

There was a silent moment. Mrs. Bowne looked to Marg to settle the matter. "Well, tell me, is he worth it?"

"I-I didn't know, Mrs. Bowne, h-he would ask you."

"Never mind. Is he worth it?"

"Oh, yes. Charles is a good man. A very good worker, Mrs. Bowne. We would pay you back—"

"Of course you will . . . an' I want these peartrees to catch on. An' if they don't, I want *you* to keep on until I have an orchard of these same pears! You understand?" She was shaking a dipper at him for emphasis.

While Charles did not like Mrs. Bowne's superior attitude, he said "Yes, ma'am" to her, as if he were a small inferior black boy.

The deal was clinched. The papers were signed, and the partnership with Ned Malcolm was dissolved. That was the same day that General Hood's troops marched into town. The Confederate Army had decided to make Maple a supply depot. Goods were being shipped down the Chattahoochee River, on to Mobile where they'd be taken overland to New Orleans, to beat the blockade the Yankees had at sea. As the South tried to hold the Mississippi, this was all important in the conduct of war.

Momentarily Gregory and Valerie grew rich making uniforms for the soldiers. Then the white tailors in town got together and decided not to send him any more business. They'd rather use inexperienced white women sewing at home. It was a loyalty issue.

Many young white boys of Maple had gone off and joined the Confederate army, and the first sons of the great families were serving as officers. The black slaves did their share too; on most plantations working hours were moved upward of ten hours a day. There was a cause, and the people rallied to the cause.

People in the North wanted the Union Army to advance on Richmond. General Irwin McDowell at Washington City had about 30,000 untried troops. The Confederate army under Beauregard, with about 22,000, was stationed at Manassas Junction, about 35 miles from Washington, on the little stream of Bull Run. McDowell attacked the Confederates on July 21st. At first he seemed to be victorious, then the Confederates were reinforced. The Union army's raw troops fled in panic. The equally green and crippled Confederates did not pursue them. The North now called on Gen. George McClellan who had been successful in West Virginia. While he concentrated on fortifying the North's capital, Washington, the Confederates, thinking themselves victorious, began fortifying beyond their capital, Richmond.

In the Battle of Bull Run officers on both sides had fallen in great numbers. In the Confederates' call-up Marg's white brother Jack joined with a group of well-to-do neighbors making their own company of Maple boys. Next, to everyone's great surprise, Frank Korner volunteered. He too went in as an officer. Phyllis came over excitedly one morn, to tell the news to her good friend. Marg was less than pleased. "I think the best place for us is at home," she said stoutly. "Since now they think of us as free blacks, we've taken our children out of the mixed school. Next fall they'll go to Cousin Don's school out at Cobb's Creek."

Phyllis smiled. "My Mark will continue public school. It's right by our house an' Frank wants him there. Marg, do you think the war will last long?"

Marg smiled. "As long as young men and bullets keep in supply. Mrs. Bowne's brother, Mr. Lance Folsom, went on a mysterious trip to get the Government of France on the South's side. Somebody shot at him in New Orleans. She's all upset."

"I heard guns while I was sleeping, the other morn," said Phyllis mournfully. "I think it's the garrison boys out in the woods near Cusetta Park. When I get frightened, I take Frank's little pistol with me. But it frightens me too!"

Marg decided to read to her friend a letter she had received from Louise in Washington. With the interruption of mail, she had received it only through the courtesy of some travelers. It was four months old. It read:

April 2, 1861

My dear Cousin Margery,

As you might expect, there is gloom all over Washington. The break in the nation came and Mr. Lincoln came like a troubling dream. The President arrived secretly in the capital by night train, and he set up his first office here at the Willard Hotel. I had to serve him in many ways but unfortunately I never got to speak to him personally. Lydia Farley Smith has been more fortunate. She's met President Lincoln at Mr. Thaddeus Stevens' house, where she is in charge. She claims he is genuinely interested in freeing the black people. While Mr. Lincoln does not openly talk of freeing the slaves, there are radicals in his party who are working on him, and Mr. Stevens is one of them. The two strong men in his cabinet are Mr. Salmon P. Chase of Ohio and Mr. William Seward of New York. While many men talk of slavery, the rights of men under the Constitution, these men talk of a higher law, God.

There was a large military display on Inauguration Day. Mr. Lincoln said there'd be no bloodshed or violence in getting back government property from the secessionists. Lydia says Mr. Stevens says Mr. Lincoln was a reluctant Republican to begin with, and that his wife's people are aristocratic slaveholders, so he needs prodding to keep the Republican vow. But we know firmly he believes in the Union and in peace. Right now, his Party still wants to keep states in the Union, with no more compromises. Yet, Mr. Seward himself believes Sumter should be evacuated. Lord, help us.

Love,

Louise.

"I would save that letter," said Phyllis, quietly. "Some day it may have historical value."

Marg smiled, with muscle tension lines going down to her chin. "Child, I have an attic full of history, all of my mother's things. If we're of no value as people, nothing we have is of value. Just the same, I do treasure everything, for my children. An' I try to prepare them, just in case this war is won—"

"You don't sound hopeful."

"I'm not. Phyllis, I'm having so much trouble with Matilda. Since Elias was hurt on Christmas Eve I can't get her to do her old chores, like the windows an' wood. We have to hire the boy next door. Last week I had a serious talk with her. I said if she didn't improve I would sell her on the block. Oh, she turned sassy with me then. I hit her with a batch of newspapers. Now she sulks in her room."

"You're the lady of the house," cried Phyllis sweetly. "You have to keep a firm hand. I have to do it now with Frank gone."

"I don't understand how he could leave you alone like this and volunteer."

"Oh, Marg, this war is very important to Frank. He's very patriotic."

Marg wanted to say something positive about race, but she put it in the back of her mind. The teapot was ready. Without a word, she poured out tea while her two girls raced around noisily in the yard.

"I have a letter too," said Phyllis, after they had sipped their tea. "It's from Angela, and she asks about you."

Phyllis read aloud:

June 12, 1861

My dear Phyllis,

Now that we are a severed nation I pray to God this letter reaches you, and that you and your family are safe and sound, and eating well and in good health. We're all right but greatly saddened by the events. Mr. Leonard Jerome was kind enough to offer to post this for me, so that it reaches you. He has influential friends in Washington, and maintains that in matters of finance there are still continuing valid connections between the two parts of the country.

My work goes on as usual. Catherine Jerome is kind to me. Together we enjoy the many successes of her family. The racetrack has gone well. They now are trying to buy another bigger place, the old Bathgate estate in Westchester county. It's like a farm, so many acres. The Leonard Jeromes now live in their magnificent new mansion in Manhattan. My employer, Mr. Lawrence Jerome, is even considering getting us one. I still have the Jerome girls to care for, but not for long. They've hired a huge Negro woman, Dobbie, and she takes over next week. Their family is growing: there is Clarita, 11, Jennie, 7, Camille, 4, and Leonie, 3. I love these girls!

I'm still remembering their Grand Ball for the Prince of Wales last year. I was dressed like a princess and a few eligibles even looked at me. Jennie's always asking me to put on that dress. I'm afraid she's very clothes-conscious. She still asks me about your dear friend, Margery; she calls her "the lady in the pink satin gown". Once she asked if she could write to "Mrs. Spence in the South". It seems they're teaching them about the war in school. If this letter does reach you, please give my regards to dear Margery, from all of us. When you write please send me her birth date. That's one way of keeping in touch, if we all don't get blown to the moon! God bless and take care of you, always.

Your devoted cousin,

Angela.

"I'm goin' to answer, but haven't got the slightest idea of how to post my letter so that it reaches New York."

"Give it to me," said Marg anxiously. "Mrs. Bowne's brother, Mr. Folsom, is now passing through, on his agent duties for the Confederacy, an' he'll soon go to Washington. Secretly."

"How do you know, if it is a secret?"

They both laughed. "Because," sighed Marg, giggling over toast, "people like to share secrets. I'm gettin' him to take some money to my brother Anthony, and a message to my New York broker, Mr. Haney. It seems I made a good choice in stocks. Both copper mine and textile company I bought into are doin' record business. The latter, in soldier uniforms."

"Oh, Margery, I'm happy for you!"

Marg looked down. She had seen something in Phyllis's eyes. It wasn't exactly jealousy, but something strange and different. It startled her in a way. "I suppose you think I'm disloyal to the South."

"I didn't say that!" screamed Phyllis, in her little girl manner. "You couldn't know a war was coming. Both yo' father and mother would be happy to see you movin' forward in finance, and with other adult successes, Margery dear."

"These adult successes," Marg replied. "They please me, and sadden me." Then tears came into her eyes. She didn't want to tell Phyllis what was really troubling her. She wanted her, and everybody, to believe that Charles still loved her.

"Will you miss Frank?" she quickly asked, drying her eyes with her thumb.

"Of course I will, an' I'm not brave enough to talk about it yet. Now you don't want us both cryin'! Do you?" Phyllis rose to leave. Marg didn't see her girlfriend for another ten days. It seemed the daily visits were no longer necessary. They each had matured. Their time would be occupied, perhaps in some things for the war.

END OF PART ONE

PART TWO

1861-1865

Chapter 10

As the year 1861 dragged on gloomily, hopeful people read newspapers and magazines, looking for Glory. Others who were distressed and worried often carried Bibles on the street. Marg knew the important part of their lives was "family". Usually it didn't include colored people, but she couldn't hate them for that. She thought of border state families who often had boys fighting on both sides. In her own decision to be ready to meet the Lord, she knew she had to find a way to settle Charles' debt with Mrs. Bowne. By selling her father's treasured diamond stickpin, she was able to give over all the money. That evening she felt refreshed, as if she had new religion, or just finished giving birth. The strain of life she could always deal with by giving up something. Poor Charles never worried enough about his obligations in life.

The mid-year terrible battle of Bull Run, while viewed exultantly in the South, actually worked in the North's favor by cementing its people together. McClellan was put in charge of the Army of the Potomac, and there remained the heavy task of creating a unified and strong fighting force. Wintering on the Potomac, he organized his men, with constant drilling which helped them to learn discipline. The South, as a family, was happy over the small victories of General Robert E. Lee who tried desperately in West Virginia, but the Union's Gen. Rosencrans also did well in those mountains.

Farther West, the Confederates scored in Missouri but General Pope held on vigorously; Gen. Halleck's strategic abilities were recognized; General Grant broke up Belmont's strongholds at Cairo. With few decided victories the North's abolitionists criticized the Government, the Republicans in particular, for making a mess of the war. The crucial division in the North was caused by two-party politics. When November's elections came, more seats in Congress went to Democrats. However, soon after the new year began, northern people could relax, in that the Union Army had soared to over a half million men, with a fleet of 212 vessels behind it.

General Halleck as commander of the western armies held out in Illinois with Grant and Pope below him. They had to penetrate the Confederate line of defense. There was a vigorous January 1862 campaign. Early in February Grant's 17,000 men were sent up the Tennessee river to attack Forts Henry and Donelson. The weather was severe, and the men, inexperienced. The fleet aided Grant; he was able to break through the center of the Confederate line and capture fifteen thousand men. Now there was plenty of activity on the upper Mississippi; in March 1862, it was the battles of Pea Ridge and New Madrid.

In Maple, soldiers were now seen all over town. And the community enjoyed some prosperity. After finding a rich general to buy Marg's diamond stickpin, Phyllis expanded the jewelry and gift business of her shop. She had a black slave doing the photography work Frank used to do. She asked Marg to come and watch the counter with her, but Marg refused. While she was grateful for her friend's resale help, her mind was on shifting values. She was deeply disturbed by the fact that Phyllis had kept her son Mark in the white school. The local people now were very nasty to the mixed-bloods. Gradually the mulattoes had given up the white schools and churches, since they were not welcome in either. Cousin Don's Cobb's Creek school was flourishing, but the folks in town had problems. There was a small well-kept Free-colored school, but it had been for years primarily an institution for brownskinned people. While the near-white mulattoes had never had to mix with brown people, now some of them relented, because of the war. Most felt themselves far superior to ordinary Free Negroes who had brown coloring, simple homes, and less distinguished family names and backgrounds.

Since Marg couldn't convince Phyllis to support the idea of a new school for their class, she went to Mrs. Bowne. The white lady quickly saw the need, to keep caste lines in tact. Mrs. Bowne, thinking herself both Christian and patriotic, bought an old flour mill and turned it into a school in town for the mulatto children. It naturally made her some enemies on both sides. Callie Jones, from the Presbyterian church, was furious; she openly led the fight among white people. The Free Negroes, who felt disturbed by the Maple Mulatto School, blamed Margery Malcolm Spence. Everybody knew she was inclined to pull away from the colored race, and she was friendly with that hateful Mrs. Bowne.

On the first Sunday in March, a rock went sailing through Marg's front window. What disturbed her about the attack, she saw Mel Young standing in the crowd, laughing. She told Charles he should have nothing further to do with that man.

Charles frowned at her points, saying Mel was his best worker, his friend. Marg cried a little, knowing that on those many evenings Charles came home late saying he was out taking care of Mrs. Bowne's peartrees, he was actually with Mel Young. Matilda had let it slip out of her evil lips that Charles had a brownskinned girlfriend out at Cobb's Creek.

Marg had been a half-sick woman ever since hearing those malicious words. She had brandy the night she confronted him. He didn't deny it. He claimed a man was a different kind of human than a woman. He needed to stay young his own kind of way.

Marg never forgave Matilda, who was past forty and mature, for this gossip about her husband. She even went to Lawyer Perkins to ask details of selling slaves. Of course, she never told a soul that it was Matilda and Elias she had in mind. And from that day, she acquired a malady of poor sleep and nightmares. Her deep mind had Matilda and Elias firmly connected to her family.

The northern money from Mr. Haney had stopped coming in. No letters from him, or from her brothers Anthony and Paul. She assumed Anthony was still in Michigan, and Paul in California. The only person she could talk to was Mrs. Bowne, and she really didn't want to discuss details of her personal life with Mrs. Bowne.

Lean, uncertain war days also meant some bargains, said Mrs Bowne. Wood was cheap and Marg decided to take her rich friend's advice about modernizing her house. She had wanted everything to stay exactly as it had been when her mother was alive, and as her father had built it. But Mrs. Bowne made her realize that life had to change. There would be nothing wrong in eliminating the cookhouse out in the yard, and bringing the full kitchen inside. Also she encouraged Marg to have an ultra-modern indoor toilet and bath upstairs, leaving the outhouses to the slaves. When Marg finally found funds to do this renovation, it was spring again, and she enjoyed cooking for the Claremont workers (slaves) who did the job. It was on April 25th when Jessica Bowne drove up to Malcolm House in her resplendent carriage to inspect the new rooms. Marg, all excited, had gone through the house three times, with Celeste, Carrie and Mamie, dusting and polishing so that everything looked magnificent. Mrs. Bowne had visited before but this time Marg had to show her gratitude by having the house perfect.

"Here she comes!" shouted Celeste peeking through the curtains. "Shall I give her these flowers?"

"No, I'll do it," said Marg, coming forward and taking the big bouquet of peonies. "Welcome, Mrs. Bowne! Welcome to Malcolm House!"

"I'm happy to be here," cried Mrs. Bowne, hugging Margery. The five active servants were lined up and bowed deeply with courtesy. Only Matilda was missing, and Mrs. Bowne noticed this. "Don't tell me that Matilda is still ailing. All she needs is blackstrap molasses, and I brought some!"

Marg thanked her profusely for the gift. With the war many things now were in short supply; Mrs. Bowne also brought bacon, grits, cornmeal, woolen socks, sandals, soap, cotton and witch hazel. "Oh-h, thank you," screamed Marg. "This is wonderful!"

"Tell Charles I also got some horseshoes. He'd been complainin' because they all were worn down so. Aren't you gonna ask me how I got so lucky?"

"Yes, please tell me."

Jessica sat down in the tan velvet couch by the window, running her hand over the nice fabric. "Well, President Davis wants Maple a factory town, to make a number of things for the war effort. With my brother's help, we now have out at Claremont something of a textile mill. An' I'm supervisin' in town a new shoe factory. Do your slaves need shoes?"

"They certainly do! We're usin' cardboard now to patch'em up. Oh, Mrs. Bowne you don't know how much I appreciate your generosity."

"It comes with a pricetag. I want Charles to plant me some more peartrees. Where is that rascal . . . out with his girlfriends?"

Marg turned red. "Mrs. Bowne, I didn't know you knew."

"Of course, I knew! That Laurie he runs with is one of my girls. You want me to stop it?"

Marg didn't know what to say. She came and sat down close to her friend. Celeste now came in with war-flavored coffee and sandwiches. Mrs. Bowne inspected her napkin, then asked for a cleaner one. As soon as the door closed Marg said: "I don't want to change him. He's goin' to church now. Maybe in time—"

"Of course, my dear. But I should tell you, Laurie is pregnant."

"Pregnant? With Charles—"

110

"Exactly. Now you know the child will belong to me. Laurie is not a free girl."

That evening when Charles came in there was a terrible scene up in their bedroom, Marg crying and accusing him of everything. Celeste came knocking twice, but Marg wouldn't let her in. "How could you, Charles?" she went on as he sat on the bed looking dejected. "And with a slave girl at that! A field hand!"

"I love Laurie," he confessed quietly.

"Well, you go to yo' Laurie, and leave me alone!" Marg didn't mean it. As he got up and started for the door, he reached for her hand. She relented. "Charles, you could be in great trouble about this. If Mrs. Bowne insisted, they could arrest you."

"I know that, Marg. I've confessed to my Lord. I'm ready to take any punishment."

"Think of yo' children, Charles. You can't slur them like this. Why don't you give her up? You can't play halfway with sinning. Give her up, Charles."

"Maybe I will," he said, starting for the door. "If I can."

"And Charles, promise me, you'll stop this friendship with Mel Young. He's uncouth and not good for you. If you have any integrity an' feelin' for me, you'll stop socializing' with trash like Mel Young."

"Okay, Marg. I'll do as you say."

That same evening Gregory came by to tell Marg that there was great excitement down at the railroad station. News had reached town that Union forces had taken New Orleans. The South, in vigorous resistance, had defended its river forts against Admiral David Farragut's onslaught. The Mississippi could not be lost. Celeste screamed at the news, thinking of her Effie and her two boys who had gone there. Later that evening Lou Simpson came by bringing his father Vincent who had just returned from another year at sea.

"This time I cooked for the merchant marines," the white-haired tannish man explained. "I've been all over the world. And you should hear how the world feels about this war."

Marg grabbed his knotty hands. "Oh, it's so good to see you again, Uncle Vincent. My children will love these toys. How did you get through the blockade?"

"A friendly ship in friendly waters." he told her. "Only thing, I had to slip through the lines to get home."

"Wasn't that dangerous?" asked Winston standing in Marg's new kitchen as if he were one of the family.

"Yes, indeed. But if a man walks and asks questions, he can find out soon enough if he's in enemy territory or otherwise. You see, the minute I was on land, I was a southerner again. Ha-ha-a!"

"You're brave," said Marg giving him more of the real South American coffee he had brought her. It was excellent. Her tea supply had disappeared. "While in New Orleans did you take any time to ask about Effie?"

"Yes, how is my daughter?" drawled Winston, coming closer.

Simpson scratched his curly white locks. "Well, I knew she was there. Her name's Lacroix now. But she's way up in respectable society. Way up!"

Dr. Lou had been sitting opposite his father with his right hand propped under his chin, holding up a tired face. "Pop means she's in white society, no longer colored."

"Oh, there's a lot of that in New Orleans," said the old man. "An' in Charleston, an' Washington. People around the world ask me why do I insist on bein' a colored man, an' I say 'dat's my blood; you can't change nothin' forgittin' part of yo'self'. Hah! Dat's right! But I wouldn't stop Effie, or her two brothers over there now. I saw Joey—"

"Where?" asked Winston, really concerned about this sensitive son.

"In a barbershop. He's real happy in New Orleans. A free man."

Lou sighed loudly and looked up. "Pop was there before the Yankees came. Things could be different now. I sho hopes the Union or somebody comes here soon. Marg, they're tryin' to kill me with soldier patients."

"Poor Lou," cooed Marg, pouring him more coffee. "You're gettin' rich."

"No, I ain't. I have to take all these guys, maybe forty a day, without receivin' one copper coin."

"Who sez so?" asked Marg, contrarily.

"Maple's new Commissioner of Health. His men came to my office layin' down the law."

"Who is this new Health Commissioner?"

"None other than an ole beet farmer, Rayford Innis. He got elected last year."

"What would happen if you refuse?" asked Marg.

"You don't refuse Innis boys," laughed Lou. "An' in war times? Listen, I probably could be shot for treason. Ha-ha!"

His father's brow wrinkled, and he signaled for quiet. "Listen, you-all, time is gettin' short. We all have to think seriously about this matter. An' each man has to decide in his heart which side he's on. If you're with Union, then act like a spy an' get somethin' good done. At sea, I only helps good officers. An' Lou, my boy, you don't have to pull teeth so good, if'n they's enemy teeth. Ha-ha!"

Later, when Winston told Celeste about their Effie, she was delighted. She had had a vision that Union soldiers had come to Louisiana and raped her precious princess.

While some worried about New Orleans, fighting in the East went not so badly for the South. Lincoln wanted Generals Frémont and Banks to trap Stonewall Jackson. When Jackson got away Lincoln wanted the East under a single command. As June ended the Army of Virginia was created, under Pope. Halleck was ordered to Washington as General-in-Chief. The Peninsular Campaign had brought McClellan down the Chesapeake capturing Yorktown and Williamsburg, and getting ready to attack Richmond. With the South still strong in the Shenandoah Valley, McClellan was pushed back to the James River. That August, competition rose between Pope and McClellan; a boastful Pope was ready to meet Lee, but a river rose. Jackson started after Pope's supplies. With Confederates all around, Union forces suffered defeat at the Second Battle of Bull Run.

Forgetting the war, Marg rode out to Claremont on a pretense, to get a good look at Laurie. She told Elias the purpose of her visit, wanting him to lead her to the beauteous young wench, without Mrs. Bowne in the house knowing about it. Their difficulty, the overseer, Mr. Easley, had told Elias before to keep his carriage outside the gates. He made no bones of the fact he hated Margery Malcolm Spence, and all the fair ones like her. Marg had complained to Mrs. Bowne about his treatment, and like her father on Thurston, Mrs. Bowne just shrugged her shoulders. With her brother Lance away on war business she needed Mr. Easley and would tolerate his views. As a consideration, Marg was allowed to take a donkey cart from the carriage shed up to the house. This day at the carriage house Marg picked a sleek surrey and had Elias chauffeur it to her destination. The cook had told her that Laurie, tall and lanky, always wore a red and black dress, and had a man's stride. Her brown face and figure were quite gorgeous.

First, Marg went looking in the cotton fields. She didn't ask any questions. She didn't want these fools knowing her business. Next, she looked in the smokehouse, then in the laundry shed. There were stares as she sashayed around in lovely white gown with pink petals and ruffles, and matching parasol. The idea was to look "pure white". And many of the slaves knew who she was. They knew Elias. Their excitement grew as she approached the new textile mill. The black boy at the door said Mr. Easley had just gone to town with a load of soldier shirts. Good! Marg entered assiduously and confident. Sewing machines were humming among bolts of greyish material. Plenty of darkies, but no Laurie. Coming out, she tripped over a splintered door saddle in the hot steamy vestibule. The black boy guard came forward as she inspected the damage to her white satin slippers. Then somebody touched her on the shoulder.

"You lookin' for me?" asked a tall lanky brown girl in red and black dress.

"Are you Laurie?" asked a squinting Marg, noticing the girl's impertinence.

"They tells me I is," laughed Laurie, sternly.

"I don't want you for anything," clipped Marg, imagining an odor in her nostrils. "I just wanted to see you. Go back to yo' work!"

Laurie stood there smiling. "Charles loves me," she said.

"How dare you?" screamed Marg, looking around and picking a whip from the wall. "How dare you! Go back to yo' work!" She struck Laurie several times, and now a commotion rose up inside. Elias came quickly and grabbed her arm, putting the whip back in its position. Mr. Easley's bottle of whiskey was right there on the ledge next to the whips. Marg flipped open her parasol, allowing Elias to lead her back to the surrey. "I lost my temper, " she told him, shading her face from view. "I'm glad you stopped me. Drive on, Elias!"

"You goin' up to de house, ma'am?" he asked.

"No, Elias. Back to the carriage shed, then straight home. I'm embarrassed." Actually what embarrassed her, she had taken Mr. Easley's whiskey, and had hidden it in her skirts. Some one of the slaves would get a beating for this. She hoped it would be Laurie!

Charles heard about what his wife had done, and he stayed away from home for three days. Matilda came down with glee on her face. Somehow the news had gotten to her, cooped up as she was on the third floor of Malcolm House. "I wants to do better," she told her mistress. "Even though I'm ailin'. I guess I could iron a few things."

"Well, you see Celeste," was Marg's businesslike reply. "She's in charge down here now. You're to do whatever Celeste tells you."

"Yes'm," said Matilda, still wearing a smirk. "Did you hear the news, Miss Margery?"

"What news?" snapped Marg, wishing she had a whip nearby.

"Mr. Lincoln done said the slaves is to go free. It came ovah de clickety-clack yesterday afternoon. Says dem slave states gotta release us come January, or he himself will do de job. Ha-ha-a!"

"Has the paper come yet, Matilda?"

"If I's free I don' fetch no newspaper, Miss Margery."

"Now, don't get beside yo'self again, Matilda. You oughta have some sense. Nobody can move around in this world alone, slave or no slave."

Matilda went off quietly, and brought back the newspapers and other mail. The first thing Marg saw was a note in Mrs. Bowne's handwriting. It read:

September 24, 1862

Margery,

Was that a sensible thing to do? I'm having enough trouble with these darkies looking for reasons not to work. Next time you consult me, and I'll take care of the problem. Tell Charles to keep himself free next week. I want him to clean my stable. We're to give half the horses over to the army. He'll accompany my boys down to Camp Edwards, and see a taste of soldier life. It should do Charles some good. You spoil him.

Love,

Jessica.

Strangely, the note made Margery feel very happy. It was the first time Mrs. Bowne had used "love", and the first time she had addressed herself by her first name. It was good to have this now that Phyllis was acting strange. Marg had gone into the shop while others were there (whites) and Phyllis almost ignored her. Her business was so good she was getting rich. But people should not behave badly because of worldly riches. Marg took a sniff of Easley's whiskey, and threw it in the trash. Then she got herself a taste of her own French brandy. She was now down to the last bottle. She wanted it to last until Christmas, so she and Charles could take their usual toast. What would it be this time? Victory or a slave baby?

After the bloody battle of Antietam (Sharpsburg), people were getting panicky all over the South. McLaws and Hood had done the best they could. At least McClellan's claim of victory lessened the threat of European intervention in the war. In Maple, they worried about the fighting in Alabama next door. Michel had captured Huntsville and the Memphis and Charleston Railroad. Religious leaders were telling people that it was just a question of time before the horrors of war could be right in their town. Some people had closed up their houses and moved away. Food and other provisions were getting harder to come by. Everyone was angry at the blacks, and at the mulattoes. The reason they hated the near-whites, President Jefferson Davis had

115

had Congress pass a law on Aril 16, 1862 giving the South its first conscription, which called for all white men between the ages of 18 and 35 to join the army. In September, the act was amended extending the age limit to 45. The whites were really angry that the well-to-do mulattoes were not included. They assumed they'd go scot free through the war, to get richer and to have a free run with women (white).

In truth, colored people were suffering. Mitchell's vegetable and flower business dropped to a trickle. Charles' blacksmithing was floundering while Ned was getting both civilian and army work. Gregory's tailoring business was terrible. What little activity he had was his doings for low-rank soldiers, and it wasn't paying. He and Valerie had to give up their horses, so the children now could no longer get out to Cobb's Creek to school. One morning he came by to borrow money from Margery. She gave him what she could of the money from their rental houses. As it wasn't much, she also gave him canned preserves and some of the things she had gotten from Mrs. Bowne.

"We're now seeing refugees on the road," he said, packing his gunnysack.

"And beggars too," said Marg, trying to be cheerful. "It's all predicted in the Bible. This is the Age of Fire. Those guns will destroy us if we don't pray and pray."

"You should close this house and come stay with us," offered Gregory, wearily. "I doubt this winter if there'll be enough coal and wood to keep this place warm."

"We have blankets an' sweaters and kerosene and candles, Gregory. Besides, under the house I've saved all the wood from the old kitchen. There's really no need to worry. The Lord will take care of us."

"I hope you're right," he sighed. "Anyway, I'd advise you to keep some things packed in a valise. For the children too. In case the soldiers and bombardment come close."

Marg did worry about her children. They weren't going to school anymore. Mrs. Bowne had had to close her mulatto school. There simply was too much objection from the townspeople, thanks to Callie Jones, the Presbyterian minister's wife. Marg could not understand why people hated them so. Like she told her father, she still thought it was jealousy. Every pure white felt he had to be better than every near-white, and every brown person. In spite of the war her house was sparkling inside and out, just like the homes of rich people. Few whites had such a home. And many who had decent homes were letting them go down. The Muggeridge house next door was badly in need of paint.

He was off in Richmond, doing the same kind of work Lance Folsom was doing. Plum Avenue was now like a main parade street. The children sat outside and watched it all day. So many strange people coming and going.

"A man gave me a northern flag," John told his mother. He was now getting tall, looking Anglo-Saxon with whitish-yellow sun-bleached hair. "Maybe we can put it up if the Union wins."

"Don't talk that way," said his mother. "We have to be neutral. We have to live in this town. If you want to keep it, go hide it in yo' room."

"I got a souvenir too," cried Meg, showing her mother. "A little golden bullet."

"Throw that away," said Marg taking it from the child. Then she realized it was likely to fit Charles' pistol. She put it in her pocket, and she reminded herself to check his two shotguns and his flintlock.

"The man gave me a flute," said Beth now acting ladylike. "If I wash it, Mom, can I keep it?"

Any other time Marg would have said a definite no. Now she nodded her consent, deciding too to take Mr. Easley's whiskey out of the garbage. It might come in handy.

"Look, Mom, another parade," called John pointing to a new large group coming down the street.

Gathering her three, Marg stooped by the curb to watch the company of soldiers coming their way. They were southerners and she breathed a sigh of relief. There was a drummer beating rhythms. The boys looked very tired and unkemp. They probably were going to Camp Edwards for a rest. Barefooted white children raced beside them, begging for handouts. At the end of the column there was a thin white woman with two small children. She too was barefoot and it seemed that her feet had been bleeding. Marg wanted to offer her some sandals she had gotten from Mrs. Bowne. She looked hard, studying the expression on the woman's face. To her surprise, it was somebody she knew.

"Lucy! Is that you, Lucy? Oh, my God, Lucy Walker! My dear, what are you doin' in Georgia?"

It was her own dear cousin, Lucy Walker, from Selma, Alabama.

"Hi, Margery. Bless you, honey. I knew you lived somewhere on this street. We walked all the way from Montgomery."

"Oh, you must be exhausted. Come in, darling! Are these your two children? These are my three. John, Beth, Meg . . . speak to yo' cousins!"

Chapter 11

Marg gave her straight-haired brunette cousins the pink guest bedroom on the second floor. Lucy looked much better after taking a hot bath in Marg's new indoor bathroom. Next, they all went downstairs to a nice hot meal. Celeste and Matilda had put out the best linen and china plates. The children's old baby chair had been polished and placed, for Lucy's boy Jimmy. The big-eyed girl, Ruth, was seven and hungry. She had good manners, good enough for Marg's formal table. The meal was whole-kernel corn fried in bacon grease, and a stew of limas and tomatoes from Marg's own garden. Nothing to drink but water. Boiled figs from the yard made an excellent dessert. Lucy, satisfied, asked about Charles who was absent.

"Oh, he comes and goes," said Marg, lightly. "I stay too busy to be worried about him. How about yo' own husband, Lucy?"

Lucy shook her dark flowing hair, then bit her pink lips. "Kenneth went to Chicago before the war. I was to follow but couldn't get out in time. It's been a year now since I've heard from him."

"How have you been living?"

"First, we stayed with kin in Selma. Then I got a job teachin' in the mulattoes' school in Montgomery."

"We had one here but the pressure was so great they had to close. Did you get my letter?"

"Yes," said Lucy, putting a napkin to her lips. "I meant to answer but life in Montgomery is hectic. They closed our school too. That's why I'm here. For months I've been desperate, Marg. Yo' letter made me start plannin' anew. I said maybe I can get to Maple. I thought too of Mr. Leroy Walker. He's ailin' now. He'd probably help me, but his family are very evil people."

"Is he the same one? Did Jefferson Davis make him Secretary of War?"

118

"Yes, the same indeed. And he served well. But in high office there are always people lookin' to blame you. They said he gave the order to General Beauregard to fire on Fort Sumter, thus it was his fault the war started. Actually it was this racial bit whispered about that made him resign. Mr. Judah Benjamin of Louisiana took over in his post. Mr. Benjamin had been Attorney General and Secretary of State. He was havin' troubles too. You see when Mr. Jefferson Davis's popularity sags, his cabinet takes the brunt of public criticism against him. When Mr. Leroy gave a donation to our school, his white family hated it and the fact that I was in Montgomery because people could whisper about me bein' his Free-colored kin. But pressure on me changed when a big congressman came down from the North, an' when they found out he too was my kin. Hah! They couldn't scorn me any more as bein' so inferior and beneath them."

"Who was this congressman," asked Marg, serving a little punch made with Mr. Easley's whiskey.

"You know, he's your kin too. Originally from Carolina, Cousin Frances's side. The McDonoughs. Very nice. I liked him. He brought me a gift from Louise."

"Louise Johnson, in Washington?"

"That's right. His name is Johnson too. He was Congressman Andrew Johnson then. We had a nice chat. The President, Mr. Lincoln, had sent him that very first week the South's leaders met at Montgomery. He had talks with Mr. Davis and with Mr. Leroy Walker. Then had time for li'l ole me. I was very flattered. Now President Lincoln's just made him Military Governor of Tennessee."

"Wonderful," smiled Marg. "As a whole, our family people are not bad, but now that everybody's bein' white, we have no family!"

"Marg, you're absolutely right. Mr. Andrew Johnson kept cautioning me. I wasn't to tell a soul that he'd come by to see me, or that we're related. Why across-race-lines kinship is a dangerous subject to these people."

The children were screaming at one end of the table. Marg called Celeste to take them out to play some games in the yard, to digest their food a little. Poor things were probably still hungry.

"The country's gotten into a terrible mess," Marg now exclaimed, closing the dining room door. "Everybody has a great thirst to be important. White means important. An' they're killin' innocent young boys by the thousands. Nobody will evah say it's wrong! In the end, they could be puttin' us up before a firing squad. When I saw you today, that's what I was thinkin'. I was goin' to find my husband's guns. Lucy, how was it in Alabama?"

"Union soldiers already in Huntsville! It's just a matter of time, Marg. Some say we shouldn't stay in cities. We should get out in the country an' maybe the bullets'll miss us."

"How much time do we have?"

Lucy turned pale. "Oh, maybe they'll be here by Christmas. Now the hard war is all over the South; and, it's racial. Is there anywhere in the countryside we can go?"

"My cousin, Sue Barrows, has—"

"Oh, Sue! I remember her. How is she?"

"Okay. She had a stint up in Oberlin. That turned her head. She wanted to marry an Irish fellow. Then the war came. Now she finally wants to marry Jeeter Brown, her childhood beau. But white people in the courthouse won't give them a license now. Cousin Don's goin' to another town to try to get one for them. Well, Sue's invited me several times to come out to Cobb's Creek, but I want to stay here with my house as long as I can. Gregory told me today to get packed. I'm ready, but, Lucy, I don't think I want any longer the burden of six servants."

Lucy bucked her eyes. "You see how war changes our priorities?"

"Yet, we can't let them go. One told me today President Lincoln has freed them, as of January 1, 1863. Do you believe that?"

"It's true," sighed Lucy, standing up. "Marg, I wanted to walk to Chicago, but this was as far as I could get. Oh, yo' food was so delicious! Now, I'm so sleepy I could fall over. I'm sorry, honey. I thank Jesus we're here."

"Oh, you poor thing! Why didn't you tell me sooner? Come, let's go up to bed, an' you sleep as long as you want to. Shall I call yo' children?"

"Let them play," called Lucy, following Marg to the staircase that reminded her of white people. Rich white people.

Chapter 12

Lucy Walker Shaw and her children relaxed at her cousin's fine house, and it was much like being in Heaven. She woke up looking at beautiful figurines, white bone china, cupids with angel wings while clocks chiming prettily put music in the air. She stayed in bed, as she was invited to do, reading *Uncle Tom's Cabin*. Finally she got up and went outside to get some sunshine and air. The children were kicking up leaves finding fat pecans. Lucy joined in the fun. Soon they had three bushels full. Lucy started talking about a pie she'd make. Margery said no; she'd take all three bushels to a white man who would give her money for them.

By November Lucy had recovered from her ordeal with war, and she felt tired of sitting around. She began helping out with the cleaning. She thought too of starting a school in Malcolm House, for the mulatto children. Marg told her no, she didn't want trouble from that new bunch of whites running the town. She didn't mind if Lucy taught her own children. So, Lucy made a classroom down in the conservatory. The five pupils were ecstatic. But it was cold there because of the big windows lacking curtains. John offered his big room so they moved upstairs. Somebody found a globe and slates in the now empty chicken-coop. Marg gave them an old desk from the attic; soon it was looking like a real schoolroom. Beth wanted her friends down the street to be invited in, but Marg said a strict no. She didn't want any trouble with the authorities.

That autumn Generals Rosencrans and Bragg were fighting hard for Nashville and Chattanooga. Everybody in Maple got excited because the Chattanooga campaign was pushing in on northwest Georgia. Union troops were at Dalton; that was less than a hundred miles away! The white people were whispering gossip not wanting the colored to hear it, and the colored knew as much as the rest of them.

Weren't the armies' best scouts the black people? The distrust among civilians was great. The atmosphere of hate was depressing. Cousin Don got back from Macon with Sue's license to marry. She decided she'd have a big wedding. Maple crackers in their offices turned red at the news. She even invited some of them. Anybody who was in any way in her family or Jeeter's family.

Fabled and elegant Miss Wanda came, all powdered and bejeweled. The only one from the white Malcolm family. The shrewd old woman right away saw the stranger among them, Lucy Walker Shaw, who looked very pretty in one of Marg's old party gowns. Lucy did no talking about kin; she told Miss Wanda as much as she knew about politics in Montgomery. Of course now everything was happening up in Richmond. No, she didn't know Jefferson Davis. She had never met him.

"They say," whined Miss Wanda, "that his family is very good to their nigras. When young Jefferson got out of West Point he went up in Wisconsin for a spell, an' got very sick from the cold. His Negro, Pemberton, brought his health back. I knew Mr. Davis' first wife. She was the second daughter of Colonel Zachary Taylor—"

As politely as possible Lucy suggested they go off and get some of the delicious wedding food. She didn't want to tell the old lady she was too much wrapped up in southern white society. Suspiciously Miss Wanda tasted the food. For war times, it was delicious. Everybody marveled over the hamhocks, chicken wings and feet, the potatoes, cucumber salad and bridal cake (made out of cornmeal). Miss Wanda had her chicory-coffee, then left after giving the bride a pretty box containing an old piece of jewelry. A sunflower brooch, with real diamond in its center. Nothing like the spray Matilda had from Celeste. Effie's spray. But Sue was most delighted with her gift. The biggest gift she and Jeeter had was from his father. He had built them a nice one-room cottage on two acres of land. Sue would still have to go to her mother's house to play her piano. Feebled Amy Barrows, wearing rouge, with dignity lines stretching her old ivoried skin, carried a Chinese fan to hide the fact that she was rather toothless now. She claimed she wouldn't part with the piano. It was the tunes that kept her alive— her daughter playing tunes from her childhood.

Charles came nattily dressed to the wedding, and Marg was pleased that he acted civilized, although that darky Mel Young was waiting for him outside the door.

Jessica Bowne decided it wasn't necessary for her to come to the mulattoes' wedding. She had thought of coming until Marg shocked her by telling that Celeste and Winston were coming as guests. Mrs. Bowne had never heard of free people inviting servants to a social function. She called it poor judgment, telling Marg that educated near-whites had to erase African practices from their lives. Marg decided to stay away from Claremont awhile; maybe it would teach her eccentric and racist friend that she wasn't infallible.

Christmas came, with a steady stream of tiny snowflakes falling from the heavens. Alone with the children, Marg dressed her tree in the usual necklaces of popcorn and cranberries. She had saved them from the previous year. Her mind was on the chinks of paper wedged into brown cabin walls. Cold terrible places! Yet, black people could still smile. She thanked Jesus as sprinkles of sunshine began to sparkle on wet grass. The holiday atmosphere came as usual with strong pine odors.

Early that morn Elias drove out to Edgewater Plantation with a weak, bony horse. Happily he came back with chicken gizzards, enough for them all. A grateful Marg had worried that her feast would have no meat. Now she was glad too that Charles had stuck around home for a change. Secretly she had knitted some booties for Laurie's baby, but there was no news of a baby. That evening, Matilda came down in starched cuffs, carrying her fudge. How in the world did she get ahold of sugar, and chocolate? Marg grabbed those fat brown cheeks, and kissed those lips. Matilda was happy that hers was the big uplift. As the house got quiet after carols, Marg dimmed the lights, then made a ceremony of starched linen and crystal glasses. She and Charles, alone, drank their last bit of French brandy. Soon his eyes were shining brightly. She went up, got into bed, but he never came. She heard him going out, and with head in a perfumed pillow, she cried herself to sleep.

Chapter 13

One January 1863 arrived, and everywhere in Maple seemed cold, naked and anemic. Nobody much talked about Lincoln's Emancipation Proclamation. There was disorder at some of the plantations. Others ran in their usual manner. Edgewater had trouble. The overseer, a cranky and aging Thurston, had been too cruel. Some rough black boys fought with him and got away. Runaway slaves! But they didn't have far to run nowadays. Freedom was merely getting to Union troops; slaves could walk barefoot into Alabama, or across icy roads into Northwest Georgia. Now on most roads there were ragged groups of Negroes, happily going to find freedom. They used to follow Union armies until General Butler labeled them "contraband", and detained them. Freedom now meant a walk to food and warm clothing. Matilda came down and greeted the new year staring out of a window. But she didn't go anyplace; and she didn't talk it either. The house was warm, and she was happy about this.

Later that month, Laurie's baby, a boy, was born out at Claremont Plantation. Jessica Bowne took charge. She gave the mother some milk, a clean bed, and two teen girls to look after her brown-faced infant, but she didn't want Charles coming. After all, his act had been a sinful one, nothing to take glory in. And Marg too was not invited out. Celeste was able to give the gossip from Claremont Plantation. Most didn't believe it was Charles Spence's baby boy, because the child came looking so Negro, and none of the Malcolms had ever been brown. Pacing her drafty corridor, Marg was inclined to believe like others that Charles had been duped by that Laurie girl. A kind of blackmail for his fooling around with her. Well, now it could be over if Charles kept his senses. And she, Marg, could forgive her husband. The war was enough to wreck anybody's composure and practices. Yet, she doubted that Charles had repented. Her poor life! She had so much wanted to be looked up to, as the best people.

All of a sudden, the Spences had to give up their transportation luxuries. All the remaining horses, but one, had to be surrendered to the Confederacy. And, as requested, they sold their fine carriages to the new white rednecks running the banks and the new Town Hall offices. Marg saw the good side of it: money for coal and firewood. The winter still boasted two months to go. And they'd stumble into each day expecting war on their doorstep. Hardship now was as much with people of means as it was with the poor, and the straggling troops.

It was true the North had a problem of generals, with the better-trained ones being with the South. Nevertheless, as a new year of fighting began, the war was soon to turn in favor of the Union. When in December 1862 General Lee had defeated the Army of the Potomac at Fredericksburg, the North retired Gen. Burnside to winter quarters while Lincoln, with anxiety, put General Hooker in command. He soon had 113,000 men to attack Lee. However, the Army of the Potomac was again defeated in a heavy battle at Chancellorsville, in May 1863. Washington City's Executive Mansion grieved knowing that Lee would try again to invade the North. It was on the 1st of July that the two armies met at Gettysburg. Fierce fighting went on for three days, and Lee was defeated. At the same time the North was victorious at Vicksburg down in Mississippi, with General Grant in charge there. This nibbling in towards Georgia seemed to be the Union's barometer of its success in the war. Marg worried; she could get no advice from Jesus or her dead father.

The gossip was that Grant had dug channels around Vicksburg, like a river rat. The Yankees were now running boats down the Tallahatchie and Yazoo. They had stopped the boatbuilding at Yazoo City and seized a considerable depot of supplies. Pemberton's men were slashed down, while Sherman created a diversion for Grant. There was controversy in the South's forces when Johnston ordered Pemberton out of Vicksburg to attack Grant's flank at Clinton, while Pemberton decided to hold on to Vicksburg. He did abandon the bluffs north of the city to Sherman. The city was besieged, and the northern press was glad to have a new hero, General Grant.

The southern troops did not disappear so easily. There was mining and countermining. Lack of food was one big problem. Johnston feared mutiny. Pemberton's officers advised capitulation. It seems Grant had laywasted the countryside for some fifty miles and the July heat was killing what vegetation was left. Johnston fled to Jackson and telegraphed Richmond that it was too late to retrieve the campaign. In Maple the talk was that Johnston didn't try to attack, that Lee, if there, would have. Thus, the North was to have its Independence Day celebrations with the victories of both Gettysburg and Vicksburg.

Down South in many communities criticisms were now flowing against the Jefferson Davis government. It had been praised for being nonpartisan. Marg and most of the other mulatto aristocrats from Richmond to New Orleans felt that the Confederacy had made its biggest blunder in limiting conscription to *white* males. This made everything in their society racial. They were now taboo people, to be ignored or set upon. The edict not only put the average whites against the mulattoes in war matters, it cut the near-whites off as well in civilian affairs where they had long been silent partners with the rulers in the South. Now with most of the sons and fathers of blueblood families away at the campaigns, a new conniving group were in power in the towns and cities, weaving plots to steal wealth from where it was most stealable, from the half-niggers.

The South was not alone in its racial troubles. Up North at this time there was much hatred towards Free-colored people and many were killed in a four-day riot in New York City, which began that July 13, 1863. The reason, the Government had found it necessary to resort to conscription, or draft, since volunteer troops were not enough. But whites knew how to make money even in the game of war. A bounty was paid to enlisting new soldiers. Many would immediately desert, then go to another district or state to collect another bounty for their enlisting anew. While Negroes were not drafted, many had volunteered and there were many black regiments in many successful battles. The fact that the Government nastily gave them only half the pay of white soldiers was forgiven by the Negroes, who had a better understanding of Christianity and patriotism.

General Lee, in retreat from Gettysburg, decided to surprise the Army of the Potomac by seizing the Orange and Alexandria railroad in its rear. But the North crossed the Rappahannock and got strongly posted at Centreville. It was now late October and Lee didn't have the strength to push Meade out, so he destroyed what he could of the railroad. Meade's outfit kept repairing and pushing. However, it had been cut aloose from its base with only ten days' rations. While Lee was entrenched at Mine Run the battle there raged for the last four days of November 1863. Each army had a brilliant general, but they had to retire to old locations for the winter.

Out of nowhere Marg received a lovely Christmas letter from Angela Baker. It read:

December 18, 1863

My dear Margery,

I hope this reaches you by Christmas. Mr. Jerome is going to Washington and he assured me you'd get it. How are you, dear? Is the war treating you all right? I hope so. We're buckling down after a tragic year. One of the girls died of fever. Poor Camille. She was only six years old. And Mr. Jerome's brother, Addison, died. Our personal sadness is not helped by war news. We had a dreadful time here in July during the draft riots. It was purely racial. The whites blamed the Negroes for the war, and were killing and wounding them all over New York. One gang broke into a Negro orphanage and threw children out of the windows. Then they went over to the the *New York Times*, threatening to destroy the building and to hang Mr. Horace Greeley. Mr. Jerome was on duty over there (he owns 1/5 interest in the *Times*); the Army had given him this new breech-loading machine gun. Thank God, he didn't have to use it. We even saw in our neighborhood mobs with pikes and torches. My girls were crying as they watched.

The Jerome Brothers are deeply committed to the Union cause. They got up a fund for families with killed and wounded in the draft riots. They gave $35,000 towards the construction of the warship *Meteor*. They've been to Washington working on a plan to resettle 5,000 Negroes in Haiti. The family has agreed to be responsible for 450 of them. I feel the Lord is with us.

All the best to you and family. Let's hope the war ends soon!

Love,

Angela

Here is a note from Jennie to you.

Dear Mrs. Spence,

Hello from New York. I still remember your lovely pink dress. I'm going to dancing school now. Well, Merry Christmas, and a Happy New Year!

Jennie Jerome.

This letter gave Marg a lift; she sent a little reply to Angela and Jennie on very pretty stationery, hoping it would reach New York. Christmas found the house with no special decorations. They gave little things as gifts. And were thankful for food. Lucy kept the kids learning their lessons, and Celeste kept fanciful vegetarian dishes on the table. Matilda took on a chore of finding kindling and coal, feeling proudly like Harriet Tubman. Lilian Simpson had forged her some papers to show that she was a Free Negro (and this was done with Marg's approval), and Matilda happily went about town with an old wheel barrow, picking up wood and anything else she could find. In many ways she became the household's provider. With her bold way, she could even get handouts of food. These forged papers of freedom made Matilda very confident in her skills. And she proclaimed they didn't have to eat rats like the people down in Vicksburg.

1864 started with rain, rain, rain. It made Marg deeply depressed. It reminded her of how she used to go secretly at night to the courthouse, with lampblackened face, and Humphrey helping her to find family documents. Now, this January night, she had that same itching to get out and be a spy or a thief. Feeling suddenly gleeful, she rushed up to the east attic and got Elias out of his bed. She bribed him with one of Charles' felt hats. Yes, she wanted him to get the wagon out. They'd go riding at midnight.

Elias was feeble now, and his vision wasn't so good. But he could see that lampblack on her face. He grinned. "Miss Margery, we's goin' to de courthouse?"

"No, Elias. Some place else. Now hurry an' get yo' mittens. It's cold outside."

When they reached Walnut Street, the fancy district, she led the horse, now telling the black man they were going to Peachtree Drive Malcolm House. "I have a sudden taste for brandy, Elias, and I'm sure there's plenty in that house."

"Miss Margery," gasped Elias. "We can't go in dere stealin'. Dey'll shoot us for sho!"

"No, no, Elias. It's not stealing. This is my father's house. He would share things with me. In fact, he gave me the suggestion in my sleep, my dear departed father—"

"Judge Edward? His ghost?"

"No ghost, Elias. Just a saintly communication. I'll go quietly into the family house. An' in the library's alcove is my father's whiskey. An' he wants us to have some."

Elias grinned. "Maybe, Miss Margery, if we's lucky we can get some ham, some chicken, o-or, maybe jis some fatback an' greens. I's hungry, Miss Margery. Deeply hungry."

"Now, now, Elias, stop whinin' like an old man. We'll stop here. I'll walk the rest of the way. Take the reins an' keep yo' mind on business. If I'm not back when the clock strikes one-thirty, you go on home without me. But mind you, come back smartly at five. I'll especially need you if I finish at daybreak."

"Y-you mean you gwin stay here all night, Miss Margery?"

"I don't know, Elias. I'm only telling you in case of trouble. I may—"

He blinked with tight lips. "I stay with you, Miss Margery. I ain't goin' nowhere without you."

"That's mighty brave of you," she said, patting his arm. Then she got down. "Remember, the Lord sanctions what we are forced to do in wartimes. Amen."

Marg was gone a long while. Elias couldn't see much of anything in the black of night. Soon he got cold. Chilled to the bone, his teeth were chattering. He started singing a little song, but when a dog barked in this ritzy neighborhood, he realized somebody might aim a gun at him. He got down and walked about the wagon. His horse, Lizzie, was cold too. Taking an old floor rug to drape around the animal, he heard footsteps.

Marg came through the evergreen bushes with a little black boy at her side. The boy released a big loaded basket into her hands. She kissed him and gave him a cameo brooch from her jacket. The boy went running happily back into the black bushes.

"Dat's a shame, Miss Margery," scolded Elias. "Teachin' a po' innocent chile to steal."

"Thank God, Elias, there was no such teachin'. Cook was up an' I explained our plight. An' Abigail gave us so many leftovers an' things, I gave her my weddin' diamond!"

"Oh, Miss Margery, you shouldn't have done that!"

Margery, the provider, went putting foodstuffs in back. She didn't want to mention that her husband Charles hadn't brought home any food or money for months. Elias probably knew this. The slaves talked about Mr. Charles spending a lot of time out at Claremont. "Elias, in war times we have to make many sacrifices. We can give up material things. Perhaps you're right; I shouldn't give away my jewelry. But in this case, it made Abigail so happy, I didn't mind."

Elias looked over now and saw that Miss Margery's face was no longer black. He wondered whether she took it off before or after she saw Abigail. Later when he told the story to Matilda they had a big laugh. Miss Margery was too proud to let a slave woman see her in blackface. She would have been real embarrassed.

Next day, Matilda walked three miles to find out what had happened. She was almost there, at the Peachtree Drive house, when she heard bombs. At first she thought it was thunder, but never so in January. When she realized it was war sounds, she became a little girl with

129

fright. She made her short fat body run all the way home. She'd see Abigail another time.

Even the North's armies were suffering lack of victuals that winter. The big Battle of Chattanooga was sapping strength in all directions. The Ohio and Cumberland armies now were under Grant, upgraded to Lieutenant-General, in a huge outfit called the Military Division of the Mississippi. That spring of 1864, Sherman had to rendezvous at Huntsville, to join the great onslaught towards Atlanta. He moved into Georgia with four divisions at the mouth of Chickamauga Creek. All Maple hoped that Breckinridge's boys could hold them back.

The Army of the Cumberland, under Thomas, and the Army of the Ohio, under Schofield, and the Army of Tennessee, under McPherson, had a total of one hundred thousand men, with two hundred and sixty big guns. The South had Joe Johnston with his 65,000 men. He was good in a defensive situation. Restless and sanguine, Sherman kept at his heels, and that spring was a rainy one. Rations were short and the men took privations cheerfully. Johnston knew that Sherman was apt to follow along the railroad lines. The South blew up rails and bridges, only to have the North repair them quickly and keep following. What Sherman really wanted was a contest out in the open. Inch by inch, they were nibbling down, nearer to Maple.

White people in town felt the enemy was trying too much; they were in western Louisiana, on the Red River, and in May General Steele started marching down from Little Rock. More Yankees were crowding in on the city of Mobile, Forts Gaines, Powell and Morgan. The fighting lasted all summer. And Old Farragut was there, not worried about the heat or humidity.

Desperate, the Maple authorities now prohibited stores and shops from selling to Free Negroes and the mulattoes. Marg and her family took chances by going to stores that did not know them. That way, they could pass as pure whites and buy the things they needed. Marg's delivery of newspapers was stopped. Luckily Mrs. Muggeridge next door let her have some of hers, after they were a few days old.

"Lucy," screamed Marg, as she sat in her swing early one June morning. "Come quick!"

"What's the matter?" asked a frowning Lucy, bolting through the screendoor.

"Look. Read this. It's about the North's convention in Baltimore. The Republicans have nominated Mr. Lincoln again. But do you see who will be his vice-president?"

Lucy sat down next to her cousin. She read intently, not saying a word. Turning pale, she set her feet in a swinging motion.

"Well, is it him?" asked Marg, with confused look in her longish jaws.

"Yes, I think so. Unless there is another Andrew Johnson from Congress. So, he'll be Mr. Lincoln's vice-president. We'd better not say a word of this to anyone. He's only distant kin, but knowing your local people, they would just hate us all the more. Yes, Marg, you must make sure this stays our secret."

"I will," said Marg, tearing out the article. "I may save this for my children. After the war, of course."

"Yes," sighed Lucy mournfully. "After the war." She got up sighing and went back into the house where she was cutting down a dress, and with no thread, she was actually tying together pieces of old thread. This took steady hands. Recent local edicts had brought some nervousness to her hands.

Now Maple authorities declared that any slaves who had walked away from southern homes who were now on the streets were to be shot or arrested. Out at Camp Edwards they had gotten the Confederate Army to establish a big block of prison barracks. These were set aside to hold runaway blacks who thought they were free. Next came the problem of feeding them. Farmers were asked to donate their leftover slop the pigs didn't eat.

Just ten miles north there was a lynching. So, some citizens felt the harsh local edicts would drive northern armies direct to their door. Newspapers were asked not to discuss these matters of treatment of blacks. Jessica Bowne made ample donations from her locked barns, telling the authorities to remember they were Christians. She personally saw no harm if they were the center of northern gossip, for if those armies did come, perhaps they'd get it over quick and help the people stay alive; she preferred being gobbled up rather than dying of starvation in a long drawnout campaign. Now she felt a little guilty for having let her friendship with Margery fall apart. She decided she had to do something about it. So, one lovely June day, she got into her carriage and started for Malcolm House. She had heard that the whites were now leaving *en masse* from Marg's eighteen rental houses up near Rose Hill. It would be a pity if she and Charles thought of renting to blacks. Entering Plum Avenue, Jessica decided to stress class. She moved to exit cocking her flowery hat, leaning on a black slave, and clutching a basket of rutabaga, and preserves from the first pears from the trees Charles had planted.

"Oh, I'm delighted to have these," screamed Marg, since her own cannings were all gone. "Do sit down, Mrs. Bowne. Would you have a lemonade?"

"With sugar in it?"

"Oh, I'm sorry. We have no sugar. Just lemons squeezed in water. I find it refreshing in the heat. We've gotten used to the bitterness."

"Haven't we all!" sighed Jessica, sitting down. "My dear, I've come to aid you somewhat in your misery. I have a plan. I see yo' houses up on Twelfth Street look horrible. Half of them are empty an' the other half are fallin' down. I can get my boys to nail up a few boards, and fix the windows, then decent people might come again to rent them."

"Oh, Mrs. Bowne, we were goin' to take care of it, but I have so much to do tryin' to feed and clothe my household."

"Is Charles helping you?"

"Oh, he tries. He's a good man, Mrs Bowne, but he has enough to do keeping his shop open." Mrs. Bowne was staring at her hands, and Marg quickly hid them under her blouse.

"Well, now listen. My plan will get good people back in yo' rental houses. I know the Innis boys and the Wheatlands now runnin' this town have encouraged white people to stay away from yo' kind. But it doesn't mean you have to rent to blacks. They simply don't have the class or money, Margery. I can get you some good people."

"How, Mrs. Bowne?" asked Marg anxiously.

"Well." Jessica reached in her purse and took out a little ball of white tissue. "Take it," she ordered Marg. "It's yours."

Marg was dumbfounded to find inside her diamond ring. "How on earth did you get this?"

"Miss Wanda found her Abigail wearing it. How can you be so stupid, Marg? If you need staples, don't go to them. Come to me!"

"Poor Abigail," sighed Marg. "Did she get in trouble?"

"No. The Malcolms aren't really hard on their house staff. Perhaps the ones in the field suffer under that Lucifer, Thurston, but not the house slaves. Abigail told them the truth, and they were glad to have it."

"Jane must be furious."

"No. She understands your need, my child. The war has calmed Jane a bit. I think the poor dear is ill. She looks very pale. Now, out at Camp Edwards there is a Captain Pitts, a friend of mine. He's got some nice noncommissioned officers who need housing in town. Would you like for me to send them around?"

Marg was grateful, and Charles too. When the slave boys from Claremont came to do the repair work on his houses, he pitched right in, and as Mrs. Bowne put it: "Charles worked as hard as any nigger."

The Free-colored community did not easily forgive the Spences for their breach of propriety. They needed housing too. They simply could not understand how she could side with whites. They sent a wise Mr. Wilkins to talk to Marg. She met him out on her porch.

Marg, right away, resented the brown man's audacity. "If it's rumors that brought you here," she said, "I can't answer rumors."

"Well, Mrs. Spence," he grinned through a bushy moustache, "I appreciates yo' perdicament. Next time, if we gets dere first, maybe you'll help us?"

"I don't know about next time, Mr. Wilkins. If I can help you in any way, you just speak up now."

He was quiet for a long moment. "Maybe you could hide somebody in yo' attic?"

"Heavens, no!" screamed Marg. "Everything in this town is known by everybody, people gossipin' so. Now you want me in real trouble." Then she realized perhaps the favor he asked was crucial.

"There won't be no gossip, Mrs. Spence. Trust me. It's Big Jim, from Edgewater Plantation."

Right away Marg knew that name. He was the big tough black who had caused the slaves to riot several times when her father was alive. Now she remembered that he was in that runaway group who had fought with Mr. Thurston back on Emancipation Day last year. "I-Is he still alive?"

"Oh, yes'm. We've kept him hidden real good. Only thing, Big Jim is ailin' now. Got consumption. Ah don' think he could spend another winter without heat, Mrs. Spence. Ah heah yo' attic's nice and warm. Now you think about it; dere ain't no hurry."

Marg looked at the brown man's fat cheeks. He had liver spots, a straight nose. At first she saw Mel Young in his face, then she saw something warmer. He was a bit like Lou Simpson's father. "When winter comes, you can come to me again. I'll give you my answer. But if I hear a word of this any time, anywhere, don't you come back."

He tipped his hat politely, then backed away from the porch. Marg watched him go down the street, wondering how a fifty-year-old black man could stay so strong and healthy-looking in these wartimes.

Little did Marg know that Henry Wilkins really didn't want to come and see her. The group had picked him since his English was best, and his clothing was best. Meeting the near-white Spences was like meeting white folks. And it was rumored that the Spences were trying to be pure whites, like the Korners and a few other fortunate families. Marg had as a young girl done hospital work with Maple's brownskinned ladies. Now they didn't want her kind in their groups. Their churches no longer had contact. It was the war, and also a matter of color, spite and fear.

With Lucy coming, it helped the Spences' position a bit. While Lucy wasn't white, she wasn't brown either. This yellow woman was mostly Creek Indian, and both sides were happy to be with the Indians. Mr. Wilkins himself was part-Indian.

Birch Redberry, a tall athletic Seminole, was Creek on his mother's side. He put on his leather clothing, beaded fanfare and his moccasins and walked the long way from Anniston, Alabama to Maple, Georgia. He was coming for a friendly visit with the Malcolms. The near-white Malcolms. Their contact went back years, when they were all bright-eyed adolescents. He had been fond of Margery before she married. Now he lived just across the Chattahoochee in a little town called Girard. Most of his people had been moved off to Oklahoma and Texas. He was allowed to stay because he was an expert at repairing guns and rifles. All the rednecks went down to Birch's cabin whenever their weapons acted up. Now the army was using him to do range firing and to make suggestions about the design of military sidearms. They had him working at the munitions depots in Selma and Anniston. But being a freesoul, Birch would always wander back home to Girard. This time he had been active up at Chickamauga; coming to Maple was like a real vacation. So he crossed that muddy river, smiling before danger, coming to see Marg and Charles.

"They have a checkpoint there now," he told them that first evening of his visit. "Seein' Indian in my face, they didn't want to let me cross. Then I produced my papers from General Braxton Bragg. Oh, that made all the difference in the world! The white man loves humble people his little kings talk about."

"You became a little king by havin' that paper," teased Charles, enjoying the corn whiskey Birch had brought.

"No, not me. Their own people, always the kings. Some white guys I know who were eatin' dirt two years ago are now very rich braves. The war made 'em rich. Cotton they've grown on *our* land, now it leaves for England. Those guys knew what road the planter's usin'. Boom, they got it! Stole every bale. Then they sold it to the British as their own. Hah!"

"Cotton should be payin' good now," drawled Charles. "Ain't so many places producin' any more. I'll stick to my vegetables. But Mitch and I, we don't raise our prices. I was never a rascal in that way."

"You better raise yo' prices, man! That's American!"

Lucy Walker Shaw came into the room wearing a nice cotton dress Marg had given her, and looking especially pretty about the face. "You gentlemen are the ones who'll have to rebuild this society. You shouldn't fashion it on all the old mistakes."

"The lady's right," said Birch, giving her the eye. "White man's culture is built on robbin' the innocent. Charles, when you and Marg gonna let yo' slaves go?"

Charles raised his eyebrows. "We aren't holdin' them. They can go now if they want to."

"Where will they go?" asked Lucy, sipping a bit of Charles' drink.

"It's the gesture," said Birch, serious now. "You should tell them they're free."

"I leave that to my wife," replied Charles, sheepishly. He knew Matilda's forged papers were feeding his house. That brave black woman was doing what he couldn't. "Marg runs the house. And my Marg reads everythin' goin' on! She says the South's armies are only solvent now in Georgia, Carolina, and Virginia. but General Lee is a smart man. He retreats rather than lose so many men, then backs up after 'em again. Hah!"

"Sounds like you're for the South," said Lucy sitting with the men.

"I'm for Lee," Charles told her. "He's really one of us."

"Really?" screeched Lucy. "This whole South is full of mixed people, but most of 'em are smart enough to forget it. I told my Mama one day that I was gonna be all-Indian like her people. Oh-h, she didn't like that. She said my tan father was an honorable man, an' I should never forget him. My children too should remember their colored blood."

Birch bit a toothpick. "Sometimes I says I'm full Seminole. Other times, full Creek. But knowing the history of these lands, nobody can be sure he's full anything! Best thing, American people should forget race, and color."

"Amen," said Lucy, touching the big man's wrist. She liked the way it felt. Warm and strong.

"But not the Indians," laughed Birch, grabbing her hand. "We ain't American yet. Ha-ha-a!"

In spite of the rains, the Yankees grabbed Marietta in June. All Maple was in sympathy for ole Joe Johnston. At the same time they all knew that Sherman still faced a great physical obstacle; he had to cross the Chattahoochee. Strangely Johnston withdrew from the west side of the river. Some say he did this to protect Atlanta, and that he held

Atlanta better than Lee held Richmond. Up North, Lee was having to deal with Grant. Too much blood was shed at Petersburg. Johnston in Georgia was accused by Richmond of not being aggressive enough. Bragg now had been called to Davis's side, as his chief of staff. They knew Hood was the braver man. How about his discretion? Fighting continued around Atlanta all of July; McPherson is killed. Sherman still concentrated on railroads. They got the railroad between Jonesborough and Atlanta, then, the Macon Railroad. The latter made the City of Maple worry, for this ran eighty miles straight down to their front door.

That October the white Malcolms made a gesture that everybody appreciated. They gave up their big house on Peachtree Drive, so that it could be a hospital for wounded troops. The family moved back to Edgewater Plantation. The army came in with beds and linen and nurses. Now that wagon-choked house was a centerpoint of activity in the town. It gave Jessica Bowne an idea. She asked Marg why she didn't give up Malcolm House and move out to Claremont to keep her company. Marg knew that Mrs. Bowne was selfish, but Charles told her it wasn't a bad idea, because the army would pay her big rent for the house. She thought about it, then turned the idea down. She didn't want Charles near that Laurie girl and her baby. Marg felt she had a family obligation to stay in town. Birch Cliff Redberry, visiting again, agreed.

Her father and mother had loved Malcolm House, more than anything else in life. She didn't want to see it soiled or ruined by anybody. Then Mrs. Bowne brought up an ugly subject. She said sooner or later the war would reach their town, and there'd be bombing, shooting and lots of fires. If soldiers were in the house it could be saved both from plunder and destruction. Marg thought about this for a while, then again turned the idea down. If Lord Jesus wanted her to die in this conflagration, she'd rather die at home, in her own comfortable bed.

That night, Marg had a terrible nightmare. She dreamed that the guns were booming all around. And a fire was raging right in her own sweet home. The drapes were all ablaze and the piano too. She went running down the stairs and soldiers kept chasing her back up, to endure the intense heat, and God was waiting there, watching her suffer. When she woke up, her gown was all wet from perspiration. And she was wobbly on her feet. That distant booming was still in her ears. After a glass of water she got back in bed and stayed until noon. It was one of those hot, muggy Indian summer days. Cool sheets tied her down. Finally she forced herself to get up and see about her family.

Nowadays, she spent two hours every day in the classroom, helping Lucy teach the children. Finally she had given in to Beth's request and allowed two neighboring children (near-whites) to come to their school. Preparing herself, Marg salvaged her brothers' books, a few from Mrs. Bowne's defunct school, and from Cousin Don. Poor Anthony. She hadn't heard a word from him in over two years. He could be in the North's army, or he could be dead. A tear came into her eyes. She was weary and crying a lot nowadays. It was her nerves. She made herself sit down and prepare the children's lessons; what she really wanted was a drink: a mint julep, or maybe some whiskey, or just a good lemonade. This took her outside to water her thirsty flowers.

"Good afternoon, ma'am. Is this Malcolm House?"

She looked up and hazily saw a uniformed man standing before her. He was tall and handsome, with deep brown hair. "Yes, this is Malcolm House."

"I'm Lieutenant Waverly. I heard your lovely house might be available for bivouacing troops."

"Whoever told you that?" said Marg, sliding a bit on the front-porch step, in case he wanted to sit down. "I'm afraid to have the army in my house. I'm sure they'd make a mess of it."

"These would be officers, ma'am. Union army officers."

Marg looked up again. *Oh, Lord Jesus*! Now she recognized the uniform. This was a Yankee man standing before her! She stumbled up and caught her breath. It had to be the dream, still. As she turned to run, he grabbed her arm.

"There's nothing to fear," he said in a very clear voice. His accent was strange. She turned around and looked at him again.

"Did you s-say you're a U-Union man?"

"Yes, ma'am. Our outfit came down the Chattahoochee at dawn, and took this town early this morning. There was no fight. It was all done peacefully. Maple has surrendered. And Camp Edwards. We're in charge of everything here."

"I-I don't understand. You m-mean the North now is in charge here?"

"That's right" he smiled. "We're not so bad, Mrs. Malcolm."

"Charles!" she screamed. "Charles, where are you!" Then she went running down the walk. There was nobody on the street. Nobody to help her. The officer just stood there at the porch, looking strangely at her. She was shivering, with cold hands and feet, in spite of the heat.

Suddenly she felt faint. Her body went down to the ground. He came to her.

"It's all right, Mrs. Malcolm," he kept saying. "You'll be all right."

Gradually she recovered. "M-my name is Mrs. Spence. Margery Malcolm Spence. T-this was my father's home. H-he's dead now. Is the war over?"

"No, ma'am, it's not. This is just a lull. And we need the property for our officers. They're now down at Town Hall and that's too busy a place for sleeping too. How many bedrooms do you have?"

"Oh-h, I don't know . . . six or eight. I don't know. I don't know."

"Do you mind if I look around?"

"No, I don't mind." When Marg finally got herself together, the tall white officer had entered her home. Matilda was screaming at him, asking him if she were free.

"Matilda, hush up!" yelled Marg, coming into the room. "Now you go an' tend to yo' matters. Officer Waverly, I'll show you—Is that right? Did I say the right name?"

"Yes. Lt. Charles Waverly."

"Oh-h, your name is Charles—"

"Yes, ma'am. That's it. A typical Yankee name."

"My husband's name is Charles. He's no—Charles, oh, Charles! I wonder where he is. I'm afraid. I can't be alone with you! Oh, Jesus, tell me what to do! Tell me the war is over! Please, Jesus!" Marg was crying again. This time she doubled herself up in a soft chair. The officer waited patiently until it was all out of her system. Presently she dried her eyes, uncurled herself and looked up at him. "I should be ashamed of myself. I'm sorry. Come, I'll show you the house."

Chapter 14

Lt. Waverly only stayed a half hour, but it was catastrophic; the worst half hour Marg had ever known. He stood close behind her as they went from room to room. He looked so healthy, she got hungry thinking about it, and a terrible headache. Finally they shook hands, and he left. It was a warm soft hand. Not a fighting soldier's hand. She just stood there in the foyer. After the front screendoor banged, Matilda came running out from nowhere, screaming that the war was over. Marg pushed her aside and went out to her screened backporch. It was quiet as usual but she had no peace there. Frantically, she began calling Charles again. Lucy came to her. She confirmed that Charles wasn't there; and Birch Redberry had suddenly disappeared. All of his things gone. Marg called Elias to hitch up the wagon. She'd ride down to the railroad station to learn what was happening. She didn't have to go that far. Dr. Lou Simpson met her at the corner of Plum and Spruce. Not leaving his buggy he told her for sure that the Yanks had come. He warned her to go straight home. There were snipers everywhere, shooting at anybody on the streets.

At home, Marg called her four girls together and told them what had happened. She told them that they could go, that they were free, if they wanted to leave. Nobody moved. Not even Matilda.

"Lawd have mercy," said Celeste. "It'll be harder than ever gettin' food now."

"Whatchu mean," sassed Matilda. "I been feedin' everybody! You ain't done nothin'—"

"Now, now, no animosity," ordered Marg, calmly. "We need each other. What I really want to say, that Yankee lieutenant came to rent rooms in this house. And I have agreed. It was a hard decision because it means most of our neighbors will be our enemies now. And it doesn't mean we have to get out. Just double up, that's all. Matilda, Celeste and Winston have to come over to yo' part. Carrie, you and Mamie will stay back by the kitchen where you are, but you've gotta get busy an' put a lock on yo' door. My family, Lucy an' her children, we'll live in the central attic where my dear mother used to—" Marg broke down; she couldn't finish. Lucy took over, giving specific chores to each one. Then she spent twenty minutes trying to calm Marg. "I-I think I'm goin' insane. I feel strange, Lucy. My children need me. Did you find Charles?"

"I think he's out at Cobb's Creek. The boy next door, Bubber, says they fightin' all around town, that Cobb's Creek is cut off from town—"

Marg sobbed loudly again. Lucy got a cool towel and put it to her head. Soon they heard the distant guns booming. It was a prophetic noise, shaking the trees, moving right into one's stomach. Smelling gunpowder, Marg opened her eyes. This was no way to behave. There were things to be done. She had to lead. And they could survive. Now she wondered if she hadn't made a mistake deciding so quickly that Union officers could have her house. Just then, the doorbell rang.

It was her brother, Gregory. Marg confessed to him what she had done. Gregory didn't disagree with the plan, but he strongly advised that all the children be gotten out of the house. He and Valerie could take them in. Their house was off the beaten tracks, near a cemetery. The children would be safe there, and they could continue their studies. Lucy agreed; she got her two ready while Marg called her three and got them all packed. John now at 15 was a young man. Marg kissed him saying he should be a father to his two sisters. She promised to come visit them often. Then as they all left hurriedly, in Gregory's wagon, her tears came again, but only for a moment. The doorbell rang again. It was Lt. Waverly, back now with luggage and two other smiling white officers. They came in, setting their belongings in Marg's hallway.

"Which way?" asked Waverly, handsomely.

"Lucy!" called Marg, straightening her hair. She hadn't done a thing to get ready for them. "Lucy! Matilda! Celeste!"

It was four p.m. when they all stopped moving things around. The heat of the day had dissipated. Now four more well-dressed white officers were standing in the foyer. Marg sent them upstairs where her girls had five of the eight bedrooms ready. "Shall I pay you now?" asked Waverly, politely.

Marg tried to be nonchalant. "What are you payin' me . . . Confederate notes?"

"Whatever you wish, ma'am. I think our greenbacks are better. I'm giving you one hundred a month for all of us. Is that okay? We won't be needing any food. We've brought our own. Maybe we can spare some of it for your family—" He held out a can of tea.

Marg grabbed it, then smiled. She hadn't had a cup of tea in months. "Oh, Officer Waverly, I'm so grateful! You don't know how it's been. Now my husband is trapped outside the city. Do you think you can get him through the lines?"

"It's not safe out there, Mrs. Spence. The Confederates are fighting back. We took them by surprise. Now they're on the South and East. We still have a fight on our hands."

"And all that bombing I hear, where are you aiming those big guns?"

He smiled, putting a finger to his lips. "Can't tell you military secrets. I'll just help you to be safe. Okay?"

She didn't like him now. He was cunning and smooth. "If General Hood knew you were here in my house, I'm sure he'd set it afire. I feel like a traitor."

"Most Southerners feel that way . . . until they know us. You know, actually I'm supposed to free your blacks. They're not to wait on us, or you."

"Oh, come on, Officer Waverly! I know the rules; I can read. If they're free they can still work for me, if I pay them an' if they agree to stay."

"You're right. Maybe you're a rare southerner not having bitterness towards black people."

"Lt. Waverly, I'm half-black myself."

"Really?" His brown eyes looked up strangely. In fact, she was certain she saw rosiness come into his youthful cheeks. "By golly, there are so many fair ones like you! Gee, I feel better bein' in your house. Are you really one of them?"

"Actually, I'm not half-black. Only about one-eighth. But it's not a subject for preciseness. People will treat you like dirt just havin' an ounce. My mother was a Free-colored person, but she had been a slave in her youth . . . right here in this house."

"And now you own it?"

"Yes, my father left it to me."

"And he was white? A rich white man?"

She went to the stove to pour his tea. "It's not right for you to question me like this. I refuse to answer any more."

He met her at the stove. They were close enough for her to feel his

141

breath on her shoulder. "My commander will come soon, and you'll have to answer his questions."

She frowned. "You said you'd help us. I want you to spare me all this questioning, by yo' generals. Will a general stay in my house?"

"No," said Waverly, still bright-eyed. "He's only a colonel. This will be battalion headquarters. We're Infantry engineers, so it doesn't have to be so fancy. You can get your darkies to take those Oriental rugs out of the halls and parlor. His office will be . . . oh, I'm sorry."

"What's the matter?" She saw embarrassment in his strange face.

"I didn't mean to use that word 'darky'. You'll forgive me?"

Marg sipped her tea. It was heavenly. "It has nothing to do with me," she told him, lightly.

"You said they're your people?"

"I didn't say that. You northerners are clever with words. And you cannot simplify life, Lt. Waverly, into clichés and slogans. You would offend me more by using a sly trick of nice words you don't believe. Now, can you get me a pass, to go through the lines? I must get out to Cobb's Creek to get my husband."

"Maybe later. Not now. I tell you, the fighting's heavy out there just now. I'm sorry."

Marg's grey eyes began tearing, and before she realized it his hand was on her shoulder. He kissed her lips. It was a soft kiss. She jerked away, seeing a certain sincerity in his eyes. This was the first time she had been kissed by a pure white, other than some relative. It upset her a bit. In fact, the room was whirling. She had to excuse herself.

Slowly she got up the stairs to her old room. There were two young soldiers in there, picking up photographs and calling Cousin Sue a beautiful face. Marg stumbled out, remembering she was on the third floor now. She continued on up, slowly, letting the teardrops bounce off her cheeks. When she got to the huge attic bedroom with its familiar brass bed, she saw that they had brought up many of her things. She was grateful. She turned on the black lacquered Chinese musicbox, taking in its cedar smell and its music. Stretched out on the bed, she had a strange feeling that this was a new day, a new life.

Marg stayed on top of the cool quilts for one full hour. She had not rested. Her mind was too active. Lt. Waverly's action had embarrassed her. How could she face him again? She knew she had to be adult, firm and resolute. Now she could hear people in the house moving her furniture around. She thought it best to go down and supervise.

She got down to the first floor, and there he was again. Lt. Waverly was in the middle of a work detail. "Hi, there," he called to her. "I thought you were going to sleep" He shooed the other boys away.

"Oh, I wasn't ready for it, I guess. I was thinkin' about your colonel questioning me. I'm terrified of officialdom. You must save me from this interrogation."

He bloused his darkish hair. "I will, if you're nice to me."

"Let's get one thing straight," she said, seriously. "I'm a married woman, and I'm not looking for any adventure. Soldiers too often are mistaken in their judgment of people—"

He grinned, then invited her to sit down to another cup of tea. She accepted. "We have rough times too, Mrs. Spence," he explained. "I was in bad shape in the Vicksburg campaign. We were tired, starving and a little dismayed. I think I was homesick too. Well, I concentrated on the word duty, and made it through okay. That was awful. This is the first peaceful situation we've been in—"

"Where are you from, Lt. Waverly?"

"Elyria, Ohio. A little town outside Cleveland."

Marg smiled. She didn't want to tell him about Cousin Sue and her experience up in Ohio. "It must be nice. They say it's cool like fall even in summer."

"Oh, we can get hot. Our li'l place is eight acres. It has a nice breeze even in the worst part of August."

"What do you grow, Lieutenant?"

"Oh, we're not farmers. My father's a doctor. I'm an engineer."

"You live with your father?"

"Yep. Mom and Pop. I'm not married. I work in Cleveland, which is about ten miles away. I have a brother Bob, my senior, and a younger sister, Ann, who looks a little bit like you. You know, I can't believe you're colored people."

"Well, if you lived here you'd know it. They've prohibited us from shopping in the stores, now that things are scarce."

"Don't worry. I'll give you whatever you need, just say the word. Now, for supper I've got rice, black-eyed peas and hickory bacon. How's that?"

"Oh, it sounds marvelous! Lieutenant, I think it best if you officers eat by yourselves. I'll keep my family and servants strictly upstairs. Of course, we appreciate you sharing yo' food with us. Wouldn't you like for us to cook it? And serve it?"

He wagged a finger. "No, no. We'll play this by ear and see how it works out. Some of our boys may get too friendly, so I'll lecture them on good manners, in case we have a long stay—"

"I'd appreciate it."

"And I appreciate your frankness. For these first days, let's be very diplomatic, and separated—"

She laughed. It was the comic way he was using his hands. Beautiful hands. "I do believe you have the same ideas as these southern whites."

"Oh no. I'll admit our race treatment in Ohio is not perfect. I've learned a lot in these three years—"

She frowned. "You've been three years away from home? Three years in the army?"

"That's right. I was home twice on furlough. But for the last year straight we've been at it. Tell me, Mrs. Spence. What do we do about baths? I could use a good hot bath. Is there hot water?"

She stood up. "Oh, yes indeed. And I have towels enough for all of you. Of course, it will take some time to get hot water for seven. Are you ready now?"

"Any time." He stood up as well. A six-footer. "We don't want to cause you any trouble. Just show us where the pots are—"

"No pots. There's a furnace. It simply needs wood."

"I must say, the modern toilet upstairs is beautiful. We have nothing like it up North."

"Thank you," she said, leading him out towards the linen closet. "I want you to be comfortable in my home. The blankets are here, Mr. Waverly."

He turned and smiled into her face. "Are you glad we came?"

"I don't know. I really don't. I told my girls we'd make enemies among our neighbors. Remember, we have to live in this town after you're gone, Mister . . . I keep forgettin' you're a soldier. Excuse me, lieutenant. I'm sorry."

"Why don't you call me Charles?"

"Oh, I couldn't do that!"

"We're about the same age, aren't we? I'm thirty-two."

"I'm older than you are, Lt. Waverly. I'm thirty-six."

"More reason why you should call me Charles."

"We couldn't do that. All the others would—"

"I mean, when we're together like this. It will make me feel at home. Okay?"

"I'll think about it," she smiled, leading him to the bathhouse.

When Colonel Everett Riggs, the Battalion commander, came in at 6 p.m., Lt. Waverly rushed to introduce him to Mrs. Spence. Reddish-blond Col. Riggs was very polite; he thanked her for taking his group into her home. She then stepped aside while Lt. Waverly and one other gave the commander a tour of the house. Then his junior officers had everything ready for him: his room, his bath and his dinner. They even

144

put flowers on the table, and lit the ceiling candles. Marg was impressed. They were all engineers and Lt. Waverly was the adjutant in charge of the office. It was while they were smoking their after-dinner cigars that she had a sudden shock. She had forgotten all about her eighteen rental houses which had been in the hands of Confederate non-commissioned officers. Surely now with the Union's siege, they had left. And what had happened to her houses? Quickly, as it was getting dark, she got Elias from his attic bed and asked him to hitch up the wagon. She had to go to Rose Hill to see if anything was left of her houses.

It was her first time outside in front since the soldiers had come. She was surprised to see two boys with guns parading up and down. Lt. Waverly came out and explained to her that nobody now could come into the house unless they knew the password. She and Elias were introduced to the guards, and they spoke to her like polite young men. Tired, but polite. Going out to her wagon she had a motherly feeling. No, she did not feel imprisoned.

It was dark when they arrived on Rose Hill. The houses were only slightly visible. No lights anywhere. The row of pointed gables made black silhouettes in the indigo sky. Elias got down and accompanied her on her walk up the gravel path. Then she heard laughter. Strange gutteral laughter. Peering inside one house she saw black faces. They were sitting around a table in dim yellow candlelight. The next house had black faces too! Some were cooking in the firebox and the air was smoky. She now walked the length of the block, looking and listening. She was hesitant to go into any house. Finally there was a loud commotion on one porch in the middle of the block. Somebody was leaving and others were saying goodbye. To her surprise, the man leaving was Mr. Henry Wilkins, the brownskinned man who had come to her house back in June.

"Mr. Wilkins?"

"Oh, Mrs. Spence! How do you do? I was comin' over to yo' place. Jis hadn't gotten around to it. Ha-ha. Now you like what we've done here?"

"What have you done, Mr. Wilkins?"

"We've moved in! As soon as we heard the whites had vacated, I got my people together. There was no time to see you, Mrs. Spence, an' I was sure you wouldn't disapprove. Any other way, the vandals could have taken over an' burned everything. Right?"

"Well, Mr. Wilkins, you should have come to me. There is a question of rent, you know."

"Oh, we'll pay, Mrs. Spence! Provided you don't make it too high. We's poor people. Ha-ha!" Now he came up close to her ear. "I've got Big Jim in the middle house."

"You mean the fugitive from Edgewater?"

"Yes, ma'am. Now that you can't take him in yo' attic. I hear Union soldiers all over Malcolm House. Ha-ha! Can you get us some wood, Mrs. Spence?"

"Wood?"

"Kindling. An' food, an' blankets."

She bit her lip and frowned. "Come by in the mornin', Mr. Wilkins. I'll see what I can do."

Back home, Marg relaxed in her well-lit attic rooms. It was warm up there and the house was full of good odors. Soon Matilda called her down to supper. The soldiers had left them plenty of food, and everything was delicious. They even had canned peaches for dessert. Suddenly Marg felt lonely for Charles and her children. Tomorrow she'd certainly be busy. In the morning she'd take food to Gregory and the children, then in the afternoon, she'd go investigating the checkpoint, to see Charles. Lt. Waverly had told her the fighting was still heavy by the railroad station, that everything beyond it was still in southern hands. Poor Charles. She wondered if he missed her, or, whether he was with that Laurie gal and her baby.

Chapter 15

A tall, silvery flagpole was put on Margery's front lawn, and the Union flag flew proudly in bright sunlight. Some neighbors stopped and stared, others shook their heads in disgust, and still others passed by stoically. October passed, then November came with its chill. The booming of guns in the night relaxed a bit. Also the sniping at civilians soon stopped in town. Once again, people came out into the streets.

Union authorities were polite, and strict in some matters. They made it possible for the mulattoes and the Free-colored to shop again in the stores. The first month Marg saved her hundred dollars. The second month she took this rent money and went shopping for many things: like candles, charcoal, kerosene and hay for the animal. No need to buy any food. Lt. Waverly and his men were wonderful in sharing food with them. Marg did worry that Carrie and Mamie down on the first floor were getting too friendly with the white boys, but all the young ones seemed starved for friendship, as if they were the same class, the same race. Nevertheless, her house retained its Christian atmosphere. Colonel Riggs even turned her drawing room into a chapel where they had regular Sunday services using Grandma Margery's rickety old tread organ. Marg locked her piano but when they asked for the key, she gave it. Loud piano playing, however, she felt was disturbing the neighborhood. Lt. Waverly locked it up again. Now it could only be used on rainy nights, and Sunday afternoons.

Now about fifteen soldier boys lived in tents out in the backyard. They did office work in various rooms of the house, working mostly on documents and maps. They were also allowed in the house for relaxation and food. Lt. Waverly did not offer more rent for them, but Marg didn't care. They really weren't doing any damage, all these mannerly young soldiers. They made the house full of joy. Her canary was singing again. And Tabby, her white cat, came back home. And Matilda was smiling again!

Marg was happy to see newspapers once more. They had really been lucky in Maple. The war was West, North and South of them. Actually pressing in from the North. She called Lucy to show her that Abraham Lincoln had been re-elected. And Andrew Johnson, kin from Carolina, would serve as his vice-president. A new group called Radicals were alive, headed by Mr. Thaddeus Stevens, and they were saying the Republican leaders really were tired of Mr. Lincoln.

"What is it," asked Lucy. "Is America so small, or are we important because we know so many important people?"

"Neither," laughed Marg. "Just a coincidence, my dear. I'm scared stiff we'll have trouble about these soldiers in my house. Lucy, I've made a hiding place under the house."

"Good," said Lucy, chewing a licorice given by a soldier. "Why do you think I was so eager to have my children go to Gregory's? We have to be shrewd, Marg, but ready for anything. Hah! An' take down yo' silver. There's too much in this house. All these boys are not honest."

"Really?" laughed Marg. That night when she told Waverly, he agreed that there was too much opulence showing in the house. For a week he helped her bury many good things under the house. He kept calling it "our hope chest".

The rains came in the middle of November and the girls complained because the soldier boys were tracking up the floors with mud. Marg decided to put down cardboard instead of rugs. Finally Lt. Waverly got her some large canvas pieces and together they nailed them all over the main floor.

"I enjoy doing things with you," he told her as he lifted a stray blond hair out of her face. "I do think your Charles is a lucky man."

"Poor Charles might be dead," she complained. "Thought you were going to arrange for me to go out to Cobb's Creek?"

He raised his beautiful hands. "I can't do it, Marg. I can only get you to the checkpoint Beyond that, you're on your own, and I do think it's risky at this time."

"You said that two months ago when our General Hood evacuated Atlanta and moved down to Macon. The real menace was your man Sherman. He took fourteen thousand prisoners then began burning everything."

"Union's losses were greater than the Confederates'. In the whole summer period around Atlanta we lost thirty-two thousand to your twenty-two thousand. And, as for the burning, it's a way of keeping the war from springing up again. They're even doin' it up around Richmond and Petersburg."

"Such a waste," she cried, busy with her hammer. "Now they got General Hood runnin' back up towards Chattanooga. I did hear that yo' Gen. Sherman let some civilian people ride on the railroad, after burnin' down their homes."

"Don't be bitter, Marg. It should all be over in a month or so. Your General Hood thought he could draw Sherman back to Nashville, but that won't work. He marches on to the sea, on to victory—"

"Destroyin' cotton, crops, factories, an' even the railroad."

"Marg, it's the only way!" He stood up and drew her up as well. "You're tired. Let's rest a bit. When Sherman gets to Savannah, Grant will move down from Virginia and the war will be over. And, then, my dearest, I shall take you in my arms and up to Ohio, to live happily ever after." He kissed her.

"No, no, Charles. I've told you. I do not love you. I'm a married woman. This is my life here, with my children and husband—"

"You've told me too how he's had a child out of wedlock."

"But that's a part of the southern way. You have to understand. The men here and the mores here are not the same as up in Ohio. I'm a Christian and I've taken my vow to live happily with my husband forever."

"Happily or unhappily."

"Charles, let's not argue. You know that I could never leave and go with you."

"All right. By God, I'm goin' to help you see your husband again. Then when you've had the chance to compare us, I'm sure you'll pick me."

She smiled and got her broom, to sweep the newly-laid canvas tracts. "Our life doesn't move that way. I'll always be a happy, satisfied, southern housewife, and a good Baptist."

"You told me you're goin' to a Methodist church."

"Well, it's all the same, like your Congregational church."

"Exactly. Now you're on my side." He looked up squinting his expressive eyes. "You know, my brother Bob's quite religious. In fact, he thought he had to be a priest. My mother's a Catholic while my father's a Congregationalist."

"Then you too are from a mixed family."

He laughed. "It's not like racial mixing—"

"I think it is. You've got two ideas of truth. Two of respect."

"Well, in that way, I guess you're right. You see, Bob, always closer to my mother, wanted to do things to please her. So, in his teens they sent him off to the seminary. He made friends there but somehow the sanctified Catholic life didn't fit him. The school decided to let him go."

"You mean he was expelled?"

"Well, they encouraged him to leave. He made up his own mind. That last night two friends came to his room to say goodbye. Bob says he was really feeling awful. His friends too felt awful. Here was a man who had the best library, the best clothes, and a real gold crucifix hanging on his wall. They had expected him to make it, being best prepared. Also there were Mother's donations. But Bob had had several run-ins with his teachers and the presiding priest. The human side of it was a contest, a war. That night after his friends left he began cursing his crucifix, really saying blasphemous things. He claims he felt better after that. He could face life outside. In a way, he became his own God for a brief moment. It helped him."

Marg touched his hand. "My Jesus has always stood by my side."

"If your husband won't give up Laurie will you come to me?" He reached for her waist but she slid away.

"No, Charles. The women in our family don't behave that way. We're true to one man forever."

"That's what I admire about you," he said, leading her into the front of the house. "You really have principles."

She stopped, smelling a bad odor from her new toilet upstairs. Somebody had misused it again. She quickly excused herself telling Waverly that she had to go fetch the handyman.

The problem was carelessness, and the great number of people using the bathroom. The handyman went under the house where the cesspool was. He said it had not been dug deep enough. More disinfectant had to be used to keep the odor down. And he gave a price for digging a deeper hole, but said he could not do it in this the rainy season. The first nice day, he'd get his men over to do the job.

Marg stood there by the kitchen peering down under the house. They had taken the side boards away and she was thinking about her silver and crystal not too far away. Suddenly it came to her that what she needed was a hole big enough to hold some people. A basement. A real hideaway. Then she went out to look at the chickencoop, to see whether it would be better to dig a room under it. She didn't know why the subject of hiding had come into her mind. This time she didn't tell Waverly her plan. Lucy was right. They had to be shrewd.

Starting back inside she felt triumphant and distressed. When she got up to her room she stretched out on her frilly bed. Then came a very distraught Celeste knocking on her door. Winston had just died.

The soldiers walked quietly through the house respecting the death of Margery's senior slave. They even lowered their flag for one day. The undertaker came and took the waxened fair body, while Marg sat with his ivory twin, Celeste, going through plans, just as if Winston had been blood kin, one of her family. Celeste wanted him buried out at Cobb's Creek. This time Marg went to Colonel Riggs to make her special request, to be given a pass to go through the checkpoint. Colonel Riggs thought about the matter sucking on his briarwood pipe. He explained to her that the enemy lines were just two miles beyond the railroad station. She and her funeral party would be on their own. He could offer no military escort. Boldly Marg decided to take what he could offer. She'd risk it to bury Winston properly.

At noon the next day a small party of seven people in two wagons started out for Cobb's Creek with Winston's coffin. It was beautifully bedecked with bright flowers, and anybody on either side of the war would know that these were peaceful people. They got to the wooden shed at the checkpoint. Marg in her black lace finery presented the papers to the gate captain. Then she remembered something else Colonel Riggs had said—that they probably could get through Union lines but that there would be no guarantee that they would be allowed through southern lines, to come back into Maple. Marg had made up her mind to go because she wanted to see Charles, Cousins Sue and Don, and Mrs. Bowne, all out there in Cobb's Creek. But there was the issue of her children over at Gregory's house. What if the Confederates didn't let her come back? Out at Camp Edwards Confederate troops new in town were quick to learn the Malcolm name and to dislike the near-white Malcolms. Marg now realized she could have trouble. She decided not to go through the gate. She wrote a note to Cousin Don who would preside over the funeral. She folded some Yankee money into a lace hankie for him. Then she sent Winston's cold body on through, to Heaven with fallen heroes, watching now with Celeste, Mamie, Carrie, Matilda, Elias, and dear Lucy who would be the free person going with them. Marg herself would stay behind.

It took her a cold twenty minutes to walk home. There all afternoon, bereft of words, she was too nervous for anything. She had two cups of tea, and some chicory-coffee. At dusk, as she resumed her knitting, Lt. Waverly came in and sat with her. He offered a puff on his cigar, but she declined. She finally decided to take her old buggy, with the Muggeridge's horse, out to the railroad station, and wait there for them. He said he was off duty and would accompany her.

Waverly held the reins, and Marg sat next to him. It was their first time outside the house together! Cold winter weather prevailed. She had her fur muff Charles had given her back in 1860. And the moon was shining brightly just as it had that Christmas night she and Charles were returning from Judge McKnight's party. Marg had told Waverly about the incident. Now taking his arm, she mentioned it again, saying that she felt like that December night had returned.

"An' strangely, I see the face of that vicious redneck who threw food at us at the party," she mused.

"Who was it? Luke? or Gus Wheatland?" asked Charles, sucking on his cigar.

"My, you have a good memory. When I tell you all these stories, I don't expect you to remember any of it. I'm just calmin' my nerves by talkin'."

"I like the way you talk, Margery dear. To me what you're sayin' tonight is that I've become as close to you as your own Charles."

"I didn't say that," she clipped, ignoring a distant petard.

"But that's what you meant, now isn't it?"

"I suppose you're right, Charles. You do confuse me. An' I think Jesus has a hand in it. Why else would He have named you Charles?"

"Hah! I believe you're a sentimental fatalist, aren't you?"

"I do have beliefs of predestination. I feel trouble ahead, Charles."

He was sober now. "Don't think about it." He got down from the wagon and helped her down. Four or five soldiers were on duty at the railroad station. None were senior to Waverly, so he was given their full respect. And Marg was offered a seat inside while they waited for their party to come through the checkpoint again.

Pretty soon the front line sent word across via the telegraph. The party was coming through. The Confederates had let them pass.

Marg and Waverly went outside. Pretty soon there was movement in the dark, and the screeching of wagon wheels. She remarked that she could see them in the distance. Then as they got closer she said she only saw one wagon. Sure enough, only one wagon and one horse reached the checkpoint. Only three people returned: Lucy, Elias and Carrie. The others had decided to stay at Edgewater Plantation. It seemed the hated overseer, Mr. Thurston, had been killed, and Edward Malcolm had told the remaining eighty slaves they were free. The place was running democratically. And Celeste had stayed on to be near Winston. Matilda wanted to stay with Abigail, the cook. Both Miss Gloria and Miss Jane were dead now, and Miss Wanda was in charge.

Marg walked about feeling strange about the news of the death of her mother's rival and of her evil half-sister.

"Jane hated us more than any of the others," she told Waverly on their way back to the wagon. "To her, we were always that separate and inferior race."

"Don't think about it," said Charles, putting his hand on her shoulder. "What happened to your husband?"

"I must ask Lucy," cried Marg, running back to the other wagon. Soon she came back to Waverly. "He's all right. Decided to stay out there." The hurt came through her breaking voice.

Waverly noticed that distressful timbre. He said nothing, merely switched horses, putting a tired one with the buggy as Marg crawled back up into her seat. A knowing Lizzie, the chestnut mare, moved on, leading the other silent wagon into the cold.

On the way back home Marg and the Union officer were silent, both thinking about her Charles. She knew it was racial! He always had hated her edge of whiteness and the power it gave her, over his several weaknesses. Maybe every husband had it in wartimes.

"I'm sorry," spoke Charles Waverly just as they reached Plum Avenue. "You'd think a man would want to be with his family. His wife and children—"

"I don't blame Charles," Marg was quick to say. "He had his reasons. Survival! I'm sure the Confederate checkpoint would have been severe with me or with Charles. We're wanted people in this town! You don't seem to realize that."

"What have you done?"

"For one thing, we've taken you in. That makes us traitors. Don't you understand?"

Charles' beautiful hand reached over in the dark and grabbed Marg's. "Well, the war will be over soon. Don't worry about it. Say, didn't you have another girl on yo' wagons?"

"Yes. Mamie. She didn't come back because a boy she likes is out at Claremont Plantation. We had discussed it. She had my permission."

"Boy, I thought *we* were freein' slaves, yet they'd stay behind southern lines."

"I'm glad Mamie stayed. It may mean she can get married. You know, Charles, I'm just beginnin' to realize the confinements we put on servants. Poor Winston. He survived so much because he was so proud of his Celeste. May he rest in peace."

"I'll miss her," said Charles mournfully, biting a fingernail. "She was very good about bringing me my tea each morning. Yes, I'll certainly miss Celeste."

153

Chapter 16

The handyman eagerly showed up the first warm day early that December, and Marg took him to the chickencoop, and explained about the basement room she wanted there. She had finally told Charles Waverly that she had an important concreting job to do. He got her some sand and fifteen bags of army cement. Some workmen tackled the cesspool digging while others propped up the chickencoop and dug there. Even Marg and Bubber helped out with the digging, while Lucy kept all soldiers out of the yard. It had been a perfect day for all this. That evening Marg was tired enough to cry, but thanked God for everything: no rain, no curious bodies asking question. Not even Waverly knew exactly what she was building. And Tim, her handyman, had been handsomely paid. He was a wise and sensible man, and wouldn't breathe a word to anybody.

On the following morn Elias put hay all around the chickencoop's drying concrete. Soldier tents went back up, and nobody was too nosey about Marg's two projects. Waverly had actually scolded his men about the use of the house's bathrooms. Now those living in the yard had to use the outhouses like the servants. Only officers could use the facilities in the house. Satisfied, Marg got dressed in her Empress Eugenie crinoline. She had missed a day seeing her children out at Gregory's. With Lucy and Elias they started out at noon.

The children were fine. The fact that Union troops had taken over the town didn't matter much with them. They were liking very much their school at Aunt Valerie's. Gregory had turned the double parlor into a proper schoolroom. Aside from Marg's three, and Lucy's two, there were Valerie's three, plus six from the neighborhood. Valerie had one servant and two spinster teachers helping with the fourteen pupils. And now, nobody feared the rednecks at Town Hall. John too helped with the teaching, when he wasn't helping Gregory with some tailoring or household chore. The boy liked his uncle who was more like a father in some things.

Marg and Lucy were both impressed with the learning the children had achieved. At the end of history lesson cookies baked with Union flour were passed out, then Marg made her announcement that she'd take her children home for Christmas.

"You simply can't do that," cried Valerie. "Not with all those soldiers in yo' house."

"We're up on the third floor, Valerie," sighed Marg. "It's a big house and they won't get in anybody's way . . . especially now with Matilda gone, Celeste, Winston, and Mamie gone."

"Oh-h, you're lonesome," said Valerie, ruefully. "Marg, I've already made plans to have everybody here for Christmas."

"How can you feed them?" snapped Marg.

"Oh, we'll manage. Remember it's my turn. Did Lucy tell you, she wants to come here an' live, and help me teach, an' cook—"

Marg knew. The soldiers (maybe one soldier) had gotten to be too much for Lucy. She liked a more feminine house. "Well, more reason the celebration should be at my house, but to show I'm Christian . . . everybody at Malcolm House for New Year's! Okay? An' whenever I visit, I'll bring enough food for children and adults. Wouldn't that be a nice plan, Valerie?"

"Oh, how we do need food! The goat providin' the children's milk is so old, I'm expectin' her to quit on me, any day! Ha-ha!" Then she turned serious. "Thank you, Marg, for understandin' my need."

All that autumn the South had attempted to pursuade Sherman away from Atlanta. As Thomas was sent back to Nashville, Hood moved northward with the big, booming Napoleons, marching on Marietta. The idea was to move the war to the Valley of the Tennessee. Hood attacked Allatoona with heavy losses; Sherman's men concentrated on Rome. Hood moved to Dalton, on to Gaylesville, keeping on the south of the Tennessee until he reached Decatur. Sherman sent Schofield and Stanley to help Thomas at Nashville. When finally Atlanta capitulated, Governor Brown furloughed the Georgia militia. Beauregard was in command but would not interfere with the valiant Hood's field operations. His 54,000 men were trying desperately to draw Sherman back to Nashville. In early November an anxious Hood had to sit three weeks at Florence to accumulate supplies, and this hurt him.

Leaving Milledgeville, Sherman marched to Millen. To keep his men warm, he broke up the railroad between Augusta and Savannah, and made bonfires of the ties. As the Confederates moved up, they took new young men into their ranks. Morale had been low since the heavy losses at Franklin. Hood's flanks were naked without his cavalry and Gen. Forrest was off raiding. The Union had Gen. Wilson with his cavalry working the left flank. They dismounted and attacked the Confederates at Granny White Pike, and Hood's forces, now disorganized, fled towards Franklin. This was the Christmas week. Meanwhile, Schofield was ordered to the Atlantic seaboard to help Sherman who had seized Savannah.

Marg was alone all day Christmas Eve. After breakfast with Charles Waverly she spent time wrapping little gifts. She would give him a velvet watch fob, and a pair of brown woolen socks she had knitted herself. She had another pair for her own Charles, in case he managed to come through Confederate lines. She had heard big guns booming again, not knowing what was happening. For the children there were all kinds of goodies. She even had made them an apple pie, with Union apples from Wisconsin. After dark morning clouds, balminess broke forth, and she felt happy inside. Usually she helped Carrie make beds and they'd finish about noon. This day the officers were out of their rooms by ten, so she and Carrie finished early. She was glad to have extra time up on the third floor where she was still knitting a scarf for Lucy.

The plan was to go to Gregory's early Christmas morn. Waverly said he'd go with her; he wanted to see Valerie's house. He had met her only once since Valerie didn't come by soldiers. Maybe Lucy had told her something. Marg's conscience was clear. Nothing had happened between herself and Waverly, and she was going to keep it that way. He understood.

At Winston's funeral she had sent a little note to her Charles telling him about Lt. Waverly. How he had helped her family. Charles wasn't the jealous type. He knew how strong she was. But she did miss him so. That's why she had made an extra apple pie, if she could in some way get it to him and Cousin Sue, to enhance their Christmas.

She ate lunch alone, thinking maybe the troops would relax their guard at the checkpoint, say, for the holidays. And maybe she could get through as a Malcolm. Maybe there was no need to fear so much what the Confederates thought of her. Even if she were detained, how long could it be? The children would be safe with Valerie. Maybe she should try to go through this time. She needed to do this, for courage and for her marriage.

All that sunny afternoon she tried to steel herself. She even tidied up her room, and took a few important papers out to her secret room below the chickencoop. Now she had a file cabinet out there, a comfortable cot, even water and a makeshift toilet. While she was out there, the house turned from quiet to noisy. The soldierboys had returned. Somebody was pounding a nail upstairs. Somebody else was playing a harmonica in her kitchen. Walking back up the ramp, she felt warmly at ease.

"You're pretty when you're smiling," said Waverly meeting her at the door. "Come, I want you to smell something."

"Hm-m," said Marg as soon as she got inside. "It smells like turkey. Where on earth did you get a turkey?"

"It came down the river," he smiled proudly. "We're having our Christmas dinner tonight. Care to join us?"

"Oh, Charles, I couldn't sit at yo' table."

"You certainly can, landlady, our honored guest!"

"I have nothing to wear," she told him, using her hands for emphasis as he did.

"Now, come on, no excuses! We've seen you decked out, always pretty. Dinner will be at six sharp. Now come, I want you to smell something else."

He took her by hand into the foyer. Marg right away knew what it was. "Oh-h, a pine tree. It smells absolutely heavenly." She fixed the cloth now covering her big Bible, then followed him into the drawing room where three young soldiers worked on Christmas decorations. "I have some shiny balls an' things if you'd like to use them."

"That would be great," called one soldier. Marg was happy to see them happy. She quickly went up to the third floor to get her contribution. On the way, a sharp pain came into her right leg just above the knee. It was from all that bending she had done in the chickencoop. Or, she was the right age for arthritis. Lt. Waverly had teased her about getting old. Now she had to face it. The leg stayed painful so she did not rush down. Soon the soldierboy came knocking on her door, and she gave him the Christmas box saying she wanted to rest for a while.

Soon the smell of turkey was too overpowering. And it was past five o'clock. She had to dress for the party. She picked her designer fancy green velvet, by Worth. She hadn't worn her New York frocks in front of them. Never that rich-white-lady look. Always subdued, as she had been trained to be from childhood. This evening she decided to be another person. She was so long at her face and wardrobe that Charles had to come up knocking a few minutes before six.

"I'm ready!" she called out cheerfully. When slowly she opened the door, she could see consternation in his face. His cheeks turned red; then his eyes became bright as silver.

"Golly, you look great! I've never seen you so beautiful!" He lightly took her hand, and led the way down ten rough steps before they came to the carpeted ones on the second floor. Next, the grand curving staircase to the first floor. Colonel Riggs was right there at the bottom, ready to escort her to the table, as a society gentleman would do. She felt honored, and a little silly, as if she were putting on airs, her mother would say. Well, Christmas was a good time to put on airs.

The meal was absolutely divine. They had appetizers of crayfish and rabbit stew before getting to the turkey and ham. She decided to give them the apple pie she had baked for Charles. She had a feeling some of them would not see another Christmas.

After dinner, the Colonel lit his pipe and directed them into his office in the parlor. There by the tree they sang Christmas carols for fifteen minutes. Marg, oozing perfume, stood in the middle of the group. She was almost tempted to open up her piano and play it as she had done in her youth. But she didn't want to be too showy. Charles made her the center of attention by presenting his gifts: a leather horse-whip and a box of scented handsoap wrapped in pretty paper. Some other boys gave her things, and they kissed her cheek as if she were their real mother. As tears came she decided to open the piano after all. And as they played away, two of them at once, she felt that Jesus had directed this social evening. She thanked him audibly, then told Charles she wanted to retire to her room. Dutifully he accompanied her back up those stairs. He was so wise he knew something was wrong with her leg. She laughed it off, blaming the weather.

At the top of the stairs there was a serious kiss. "Merry Christmas," she said in return. "And thank you so much. I hope this time next year you are back in Ohio with your dear family."

"How do you know they are 'dear'?"

"Because you're such a dear." She pinched his cheeks and ran up the last ten stairs, into her secret haven, her mother's attic rooms.

Marg threw the latch on the first attic door, as usual, then she went up the last steps and threw the second latch, as usual. Now her leg was aching so she decided she had a cold in her muscles. She undid her fancy dress, then stretched out on her bed with a blanket, wondering if Charles was still standing on the stairs. Something impish in her said to go unlock the doors and let him come in. Another voice told her to get her Bible and start reading, that this truly was the Lord's day. Finally she listened to a third voice which reminded her that Lt. Waverly had given her a bottle of whiskey for emergencies such as this. She poured some in a glass while looking at herself in her mirror and continuing the unhooking of skirts and bodice. She suddenly thought of Frank Korner who had taken a picture of her in this gown. In her underthings she went to her truck and found the picture among other mementoes. She thought of giving that photo to Charles Waverly. But what would she write on it? By all means she did not want him carrying a picture of a married woman. No, she had been wrong, encouraging him. She should have kept his mind thinking of duty. And, perhaps, of younger girls back in Ohio.

After two glasses of whiskey Marg felt relaxed. The pain in her leg seemed to dissipate. She could faintly hear the piano below. The house was so well-built the attic seldom heard the normal sounds of living below. It had its own world. Tonight she wanted to mix the two. She went to the first door, opened it, and now the piano sounds came clearer. Somebody was playing Chopin. It had to be that young corporal Sweeney from West Virginia. He played beautifully. Yet, such a shy young man. He was much like her brother Anthony. Then, with quick tears, she knew Jesus had her thinking of family. Her mother again, and that two-faced life she had to live from this same brass bed.

Marg got up hardened, and fixed her final drink. Glancing at Frank Korner's work, she thought of him cruelly. It was he who had put Phyllis out of her life. So many years invested in friendship, to be gone in two minutes, with a war, and with a notion of being pure white. Marg felt that if she were a real Christian she would stop by the Korner home, to kiss Phyllis on the cheek, just as she had done so many times in the past. People had to be ready with forgiveness. This was the whole meaning of Christ. And she forgave herself for loving Charles Waverly.

Pretty soon the piano playing stopped. Then there were furniture-moving sounds. Why on earth would they want to be moving her furniture on Christmas Eve? She fell asleep listening to all the rumbling; maybe some of it was gun noises, the booming over in Alabama. She slept soundly for an hour or two.

Strangely Marg woke up in the middle of night. The moon was shining brightly in her little crescent-shaped window. It was full of vaporous perspiration. She couldn't remember whether this meant it was warmer outside or warmer inside. She felt a bit warm, from the whiskey. Or a fever? For some reason the atmosphere seemed too quiet. The downstairs particularly. She decided to investigate.

Reaching the second floor she lit a wall lamp and started down the hall. The bedroom doors were all open. This was strange. None of the soldiers were around. Once before they had gone on a midnight march. This time it was something else. All their luggage was gone. In Lt. Waverly's room there was nothing there but one dirty shirt on his chair. All his shoes, work clothes, and his beautiful dress uniforms, were gone. Marg now rushed down to the first floor. The grandfather clock chimed three as she looked in the parlor where Colonel Riggs had been. He was gone too. All his papers, gone. Could they have moved out? Maybe that's why they had made such a show of their Christmas party; they were planning to move out. Now she felt a little bit miffed. She went and tried the front door. They hadn't locked it. Alone now, she decided to lock it. She called Carrie, who was sleeping soundly. Together they searched through the house. Carrie spotted a white paper sticking under the door to the central attic. It was a note to Marg. In his handwriting. Marg's heart went thumping. It read:

December 25, 1864

My dearest Marg,

I knocked several times at your door. You certainly are a deep sleeper! We're leaving, my dear. It came up suddenly. Please don't worry. You know the war will be over soon, and I'll be coming back for you.

Love,

Charles Waverly.

PS—Merry, merry Christmas! You made my 1864 perfect. Thanks. I'll be with you (in mind and body) during 1865. Keep the Faith!

He also put in three hundred Yankee dollars, "for the damages". Marg doubled over on her stairs, allowing tears to roll down her cheeks. Carrie, right there, looked equally sad.

"Do it mean the war's over, Miss Margery?"

"No, my dear. I don't think so. I believe they've been forced away, that new people are coming. Maybe Confederates again! Come, you and I have things to do. Are you awake, honey?"

"Yes'm. I'se awake. Do we clean rooms now, Miss Margery?"

"No, we're goin' to hide things. Then we wake up Elias and make an early start for my family's house. We're goin' to Mr. Gregory's, honey."

"Yes'm," said Carrie, rushing behind her mistress who was now in the dining room taking down more silver.

"Merry Christmas, Carrie," smiled Marg, loading the silver upon Carrie's outstretched arms. "This is our future. We've got to protect it. I'm goin' to show you my secret room—"

"Secret room, Miss Margery?"

"That's right, angel. Come. We need every minute we have." Loaded down, Carrie followed her mistress into the black night of early morning. Out in the yard's fresh air they could hear the guns distinctly. They were booming over in Alabama, lighting up the black.

Marg took hay from the horse's stall and carefully spread it over the trapdoor entrance to her secret room. Bethlehem was on her mind. But it didn't look like Jesus's day. Marg thought of Judgment Day, but she didn't want to frighten Carrie. She kept smiling and saying nice things. And Carrie worked like an angel.

Chapter 17

As dawn came up, the house had been stripped of most of Marg's good things. The chickencoop's basement was so cramped with things, a human being could not have gotten inside to the cot and water. Or to the food way down below. Marg explained to Carrie that she was behaving like an ant, since it was Providence making her do things by instinct. She still talked quietly and convincingly so that the slave girl would not become frightened.

"Carrie, when you start out on yo' own life you should remember three things: (a) God made you to accomplish something good during yo' short stay on Earth, (b) work with people but don't let them control yo' life; some of them are real devils. Hah! And, (c) keep faith in Jesus; He will see you through to any goal."

"Yes'm. Miss Margery, what's yo' big goal in life, might'n I ask?"

"Oh, Carrie, I guess I could say my children. Yes, I want them to carry on in the true spirit of my dear mother. She was such a great woman, Carrie. Sweet an' as strong as iron. I really think she made my father the great judge he was. Now you know there are some people who do not want me callin' a white man 'my father'. Well, what else was he? No, they want to invent a truth for you an' me. Angel, don't let 'em do it! Scratch their eyes out, but keep yo' integrity—"

"What's integrity, Miss Margery?"

"Child, it's when the sky is fallin' and you grab on tight to a cloud, to stay up there in the Heavens no matter what. Come, baby, let's have some breakfast."

In the kitchen of the quiet house Marg made her servant sit down while she prepared the meal. It was one egg, two slices of salt pork, two of toast, and each one had a strong cup of tea. Yankee tea. Marg sat in front of her girl, at the same table. "When we finish, I have a Christmas present to give you. Surprised?"

Carrie grinned, knowing all along that Miss Margery would not forget her on Christmas. Just then, a very loud boom went off. It shook the windows. Carrie jumped up screaming. "Dey shootin' at us, Miss Margery! I'se frightened!"

"Now, now." Marg quickly produced the Christmas present. It was a small silver handmirror, with a beautiful embossed pattern of flowers. Carrie looked at it quickly, then pushed it aside. "Carrie, don't you like my nice gift? And sugar, what do you have for me?"

"I ain't got nothin'," she stammered. "Miss Margery, I think we bettah go. We bettah leave dis place."

"Angel, don't you have a gift for me? Remember what the Bible says: it's more blessed to give than to receive. That's what I taught you; now I know you haven't forgotten that, have you?"

Carrie was standing, digging into her pockets, acting confused.

"Maybe it's in yo' room," said Marg, ignoring another big boom that sounded in the distance. "Shall we go an' look? I'm so excited because I knew you wouldn't forget me at Christmas time. Right, Carrie?"

Carrie went to her dresser in the grey room and pulled out a little package of pink paper, and handed it to her mistress. Marg immediately began making ohs and ahs. Carrie's little gift was a pair of black woolen bedsocks. "Oh, how delightful!" cried Marg. "Thank you, Carrie. These are divine."

"I made 'em myself, to keep yo' feet warm in bed . . . since you ain't got no husband now."

"Oh, how thoughtful, Carrie."

"I only had black thread. I knew you didn't like black."

"Carrie, dear, how can you say that?"

"People say it, Miss Margery. Fair people don't like black people—"

"Listen, angel, that's not true. Besides, I've never seen a black person. Look at yo' shoes. They're brown, not black. People are brown, honey. It's evil pure whites who say otherwise. Now, shall we go up and wake Elias an' give him his gifts? He should be up now if we're goin' to get to Mr. Gregory's by eight o'clock."

A fantastic boom sounded just outside. The house shook violently, and the tinkling of glass meant that several of Marg's windows were broken. They heard Elias scrambling and calling upstairs. They rushed through the conservatory wing of the house.

"That noise woke him up good," called Marg as they went up the narrow stairs. "He's old now an' gets excited very easily. We're comin', Elias! Merry Christmas, Elias!"

Marg stopped as she made the turn at the landing. There was Elias, stretched out on the stairs. Apparently he had had a heart attack. He died with his eyes open. Now Carrie really began to moan and whimper. Just as Marg lifted his arms, her bad knee began aching.

"Come, give me a hand, Carrie! We won't carry him back up those stairs."

"I don' touch no dead folks!" screamed Carrie, backing away.

"Don't be foolish, Carrie! He's still warm. Give me a hand!"

"W-where we goin' with his body, Miss Margery?"

They went huffing and puffing through the main foyer. Then several more booms, with floors shaking and several more windows crashed. This time Marg staggered; she could smell gunpowder. "Let's take him upstairs," she called out. "I want to g-get over to Gregory's an' we don't have time to fetch the undertaker. We'll just leave him nice and comfortable in bed, until we get back this evening."

"Who's b-bed, Miss Margery?"

"Go into the first room at the top of the stairs, Carrie. Yes, that's right. Lt. Waverly's room."

Carrie calmed down while Marg stretched Elias out comfortably under blankets. She was going to cover his head with a sheet, then she decided not to. She had closed his eyes and he looked peaceful, as if he were just asleep. She put into his hands her Christmas gift. An old watch that belonged to her father. It didn't run so well but Elias had always admired its gold etchings.

"Silver an' gold," exclaimed Carrie, holding up her own gift.

"Yes, you've got the silver an' he's got the gold. That'll take him to Heaven, all right."

"How long do it take to get dere?" sighed Carrie, as they backed away from the corpse.

Marg grabbed her by the hand. "Don't you worry about that. Come, we have to hitch up the wagon. An' bring all those gifts and baskets I put in the front hall."

"Yes'm, Miss Margery."

Marg turned quickly. "And I'm goin' to get my good blanket. I believe it's cold out there."

In just a matter of minutes the two women loaded down with parcels got outside and into the family's old red wagon. In the cold bright daylight Marg saw that the flagpole now had no flag. They had left it on a foyer table. No, she wouldn't go back to fetch it. But she'd certainly go back to hide it. Her intuition told her to do as much. She rushed into the house one last time as Carrie climbed up, sitting on her usual wooden box in the back of the carriage. Outside again, Marg took the reins, her new leather whip, and got the animal going.

Just as she drew near to the intersection of Plum and Spruce, two big carriages rolled up and blocked her way. A big redneck got out of the first one. He came to her wiggling a toothpick between his teeth. Right away she knew that face. It was Gus Wheatland, now sheriff of the county.

"Margery Malcolm Spence?" he whined as he drew near.

"Yes, I'm Mrs. Spence." She hugged her blanket closer to her thighs.

"Step down," was his singsong annoyed tone. Now two other gentlemen got out of the other carriage and came forward. "Are all the Yankees gone from yo' house?"

"Y-yes, I do believe so," said Margery standing on the ground in front of him. "Why are you detaining me? I'm on my way to my brother's for Christmas Day." As she looked into his brutal fat face for his reaction, she saw that same ugly face four years earlier when he was one of the three drunks at the Christmas party of the McKnights, who had thrown a plate of food at her and Charles.

"There ain't gonna be no Christmas Day for you, young lady. You git in my carriage. You're under arrest for high treason."

Marg bit her tongue, looking at the other two men for support. One was Rayford Innis, the mayor of the town. "What's happened in the war?" she asked him.

"We've taken back our land," said Innis, not quite as nastily as Wheatland. "We've run the Yankees out. Now we have to mop up the traitors, Margery Spence. You should understand that."

All of a sudden, Carrie in the wagon let out a piercing scream. It shook everybody. Now they went back and took her out of the wagon, and pushed her up into their second carriage.

"Why are you botherin' her?" asked Marg, coldly. "She's free. I've given her her freedom. She's a free woman!"

"A nigger ain't never free," whined Wheatland, snapping the reins to get his horse moving, his fat arms touching Marg.

Marg glanced back as the second carriage moved behind them with frightened Carrie biting her sleeve and crying. And the third man had gotten up into Marg's wagon. Already he was sifting through her Christmas gifts seeing what he could pilfer.

Chapter 18

On the ride to Courthouse Square, and the jail in old Town Hall, Marg thought about many things. Actually she felt like a little girl being scolded by her parents. Yet, the ugly man with her was like a steaming dragon, taking her away from all good things. She didn't feel frightened, but she kept looking at the ground speeding away, wondering how far she could get if she jumped down and ran. Outside the courthouse he made her get down, and walk the rest of the way with shackles on her wrists. Being Christmas, practically nobody was around. Seeing one man, and he looked at her, she did feel ashamed.

They went into the old Town Hall. Gus Wheatland took her down a narrow clean hall. Marg knew that the whole second floor of this building was the jailhouse. Driving by she had seen prisoners screaming out the windows. She hoped now that it wasn't a dormitory, that being a woman they'd put her off somewhere by herself. Her mind returned to this beastly devil leading her. "I really don't understand why you're detainin' me," she called out to him. "Other people had soldiers in their homes."

"Now you hush up," he yelled back. "No use'n you tryin' to tell me my job! By local laws, you nigras can't run no hotels without license an' approvals. Atop that, you're a yankee conspirator an' sympathizer, guilty of antiwar crimes—"

"No, no. An' you don't have to arrest people on Christmas day—"

He shook her shoulders; his fat cheeks trembling. "Don't you talk back to me!" They had reached a glass door, a first-floor office. He unlocked the door and went in, then ushered her to a seat. Marg's shoulders were still stinging from his rough finger grip. As he riffled through papers on his desk a younger sandy-haired man came in with two pistols riding his hips. "Jeb, this is that Spence woman; take her across the hall to dat cell. An' give her some bedding. She's liable to

166

be heah a long time!"

Ready to obey his boss, Jeb stood before Marg with a relaxed, resolute face. Avoiding his stare, she felt hatred stir in her system. But he didn't seem mean with his rough blond handsomeness. And her heart was still full of joy. She tried smiling at the man Jeb as he led her away. But fear came.

The cell was huge but horrible. So damp and bare. There wasn't a speck of paint on its cinderblock walls. There was a crooked chair, a lopsided table and a narrow bed with grey dirty mattress. She sat on the sagging bed with her own good blanket still wrapped around her haunches.

"Dere's water ovah there in dat jug," shouted Jeb. "An' a slop pail under the bed. We feed you at eleven an' four. If you kin read, we'll give you a book." It was a recitation he had said many times before.

"Where's the toilet," she asked. "And washing water?"

"I told you, there's a slop pail under the bed. Now, for washin' water, we bring it in morn or night . . . but only once t'day. Understand?"

Marg shook her head. "I'll take the books. And please, tell somebody in my family I'm here."

"They can't help you," he whined, banging the iron bars and putting the key in the lock. "Now you have a nice Christmas."

Alone, Marg tried to relax. The room was disgusting. Just two small dusty windows high up. This made all the light hit the ceiling. She glanced at the book she had been given: a thin volume of poetry by Francis Onnery Ticknor. She had read "Spring" before. Now she read "The Cotton Boll" and "Magnolia Cemetery", an ode to fallen Confederate soldiers. When she finished it, the building was quiet, except an occasional shout from the jailed ones upstairs, the men. Wheatland's office was closed and deserted. He and Jeb had gone. She heard little scratching noises. Mice in the walls. As drafty cold blasts attacked her shoulders, she moved her blanket up around them. Now she could feel the joy leaving her system. This was serious. A vicious man with power had tied her away from civilization. And as her father would say: "Only the laws can free you."

To calm her nerves, she tried remembering her father. He had probably been in this building. This wasn't the new Town Hall. These had been cells and offices a long time. Judge Edward had probably been in this very cell, in his work. Had he been alive, she of course would have been released on bail. She wondered now who would come to her aid. If the Confederates were back in charge of Maple, it meant that Charles could be coming home. And he would bury Elias. Poor wonderful Elias. Maybe Matilda would come back to him now, to take his coffin to the ground in Cobb's Creek. She had evil in her just like Gus Wheatland. Minus power. Marg knew evil ones sharing the world lived parasitically on good people. In the old days the ones with Christianity could make an impression on backsliders. No use now; they simply grab power and don't listen.

As the afternoon sun moved across the ceiling, she found some knitting in her purse. More heavy socks. She worked on them a bit. She had been a fool not to bring her bags of Christmas food and gifts. By now Gregory and Valerie were doing something for her release. And, poor Carrie, what on earth had they done to her? Mrs. Bowne had realized something of these insults colored people had to endure; she had told Marg that she'd always stay active in politics to protect the little people. Now Marg knew that she herself was among the little people, in spite of her white skin, her good background. A bit of joy came back when she realized that Claremont Plantation was now joined again to the town, and that Mrs. Bowne could come and help her. Charles had been right in encouraging their friendship. Now she wondered quickly if Mrs. Bowne hadn't tried to steal Charles' manhood— all that staying-over talk when he was planting the peartrees. The old witch could get away with it by blaming Laurie. No, the pure whites were not to be trusted. None of them were sinless.

Along towards twilight Marg got tired and crawled into the strange cold bed. It was all right with the blanket Jeb brought, and her own. The urine smell was a bit overpowering. She moved the slop pail into the farthest corner and covered it with the poetry book. Now she could rest a bit. She prayed to Jesus to deliver her. It was His day. She was certain He'd answer her prayer.

Sound asleep, she was awakened by loud talk and the banging of iron doors. They were putting somebody in the cell next door. A Negro man. She heard his screams when they cursed him and hit him. Then dragging furniture sounds, then a big thud when they apparently threw him against the wall. It was Gus Wheatland again, and Jeb. Their sick whiny voices. Here again in this jail on Christmas evening. "God, take them back to their families," she pleaded, almost audibly.

There was a grey stove out in the hall. Somebody came and put a few pieces of wood in it. Then that somebody came and looked into her face. Eyes closed, she remained very still, as if she were asleep. Soon they went away. She was hungry now. Nobody had brought food at eleven or four, as Jeb had said they would. She had no food all day. Calling it her Christmas fast, she thanked God again for having given her such a thorough and peaceful life. Maybe now she was paying for her sins, for having befriended Lt. Charles Waverly. That was the big sin. Yes, and the southerners could imagine it too. Who else but a yearning romantic half-caste matron would let a bunch of Yankee soldiers in her house?

The Negro moaned a while, calling Jesus, then he began singing Negro spirituals. This was soothing to Marg's ear. It reminded her of Edgewater and her youth. They had never had a lynching out there. And very few others had been killed, or died mysteriously, even with wicked Thurston in charge. So, in town, in this jail, she hoped that her fate would be as good. She could stand the beatings, perhaps.

The night was long and cold. Each time Marg woke up she listened for sounds of life. Sometimes she heard the rats scratching, and at other times that man next door, coughing or talking out in his sleep. She prayed for his soul, and for the evil ones who had mistreated him. Suddenly Jane came to mind. Miss Jane. She was dead now, not to make another human feel weak and helpless. All her life she had had to approach Jane as one would approach a snake. They'd poke at each other from beyond a striking distance. Her father would only smile at it. He never felt to make them friends. And, Miss Wanda, now in charge, she was his sister. Never a real aunt. And Jack and Edward, never real brothers. Just white people beyond the veil.

Ursula Turner, Miss Gloria's older sister, was the real Christian among them. A spinster like Jane, she had nothing to do in life but baby her hand maimed by polio, and to speak good of His Name. She had given Marg her first Bible, but she handled them, Marg and her mother, as if they were the real sinners. The most the Turners had was their doctor, actually Mr. Tom, really a druggist. He disliked the fact that his sisters Gloria, Ursula and Sybil were not fully-schooled. Not a family man, he was very jealous of Judge Edward and his brother Paul. Mr. Tom spent every day at his slow, dusty store, becoming helpless by the love of alcohol. And Marg thought of this quasi-uncle whenever she was enjoying her little bibbings. Lord, how she would love a drink just now!

The only one who had slapped her hands was Miss Gloria, her mother's rival, Judge Edward's real wife. Miss Gloria, the doyenne, had just died at eighty, to be remembered always as a typical southern white aristocratic wife, who could look the other way and not see people who were there. No concubines! If someone told her Marg was in jail, she's ask: who is Marg? The Turners had one younger sister, Odella, who was a trained nurse, a helpful person. But she would never cross the rest of the family by doing anything openly for the mulatto brood.

Morning came and Marg got up with a hurried toilet while no one stirred. They came at eight. No one looked her way while she waited patiently for them to bring fresh water and soap. It came at eleven o'clock, the same time as some hot soup and crackers. Now there was lots of activity in Wheatland's office. The men who entered kept looking across the hall at Marg. Finally she put her blanket up as a curtain. It was then that Gus Wheatland came in and said Good Morning.

"Did you get some sleep, Margery?"

She didn't want to answer, but she mumbled "Somewhat."

"It takes a li'l time to git used to prison, but you'll do all right. I told yo' folks an' they goin' try to git a lawyerman for you. Judge Barlow's comin' here directly to interrogate you. He's gotta git on to Richmond to see what to do in a case of treason."

Marg knew that Richmond was falling apart, if they didn't know it. Jefferson Davis would have to issue a special order for them to try her for treason, or, his secretary of war. Now she thought of something important. Her own kin down in Alabama, Leroy Walker, had been the Confederates' first secretary of war. Lucy could get in touch with him. He'd come and save her. But then she remembered Lucy saying he was ailin' now, and had a family never knowin' black. Like Miss Gloria! Just the same, it was worth a try, if she could get to Lucy.

"I want to see my family," she told Wheatland. "The colored family."

"Good thing you said that," he laughed. "The Malcolms don' want no part o' you. Town's mighty upset by what you did. Shows you nevah belonged among decent people. Want some mo' soup?"

"No, thank you, Mr. Wheatland." Marg decided to treat him with respect. It might work towards something. "Lucy Walker is my cousin. You'll find her at my brother Gregory's—"

"Hold on!" he shouted. "I don' want none of 'em yellow niggers in here! You jis wait an' let everything take its orderly course. Judge Barlow will see you first."

Judge Barlow came at two that afternoon. Clean and scented, carefully dressed in a business suit. "Well, Margery Spence, you took me by surprise. When I heard you was here, couldn't imagine; 'spects you had run off with the Yankees. Ha-ha!"

"Why would you think such a thing, Judge Barlow?" She had never liked him. He was the evil one working with Jane when she tried to cut them out of her father's will.

"Oh, I know yo' mind, young lady. You think the South is gonna lose this war. Well, it ain't lost yet. General Hood's got his men together across the Tennessee River. That Union Gen. Thomas is no match for our man. He's a Virginian at heart, an' like all the rest of 'em, they're really on our side—"

"Judge Barlow, I want to see my family. I told Sheriff Wheatland about my Cousin Lucy—"

"Wait! You'll git yo' dern turn, as soon as we heah from Richmond. Now this may take a few days 'cause, like in cases of sedition where there's incitin' to riot, bushwhackin' with niggers, or committin' outrages against the government, the review of treasonable acts falls to the central government. The suspension of the habeas corpus privilege may be authorized. The control of such arrests usually is in the jurisdiction of the secretary of state, or, secretary of war. But in yo' case, in the first instance, we'll hear you on code 244, this business of operatin' a hotel without a license."

"Judge Barlow, they came to me askin' for rooms, like any other citizens might come—"

"They weren't citizens of the Confederacy. They were enemy! An' since when do you take *white* roomers in yo' house?"

Marg got angry. "I'm as white as you are, Judge Barlow! My father was your—"

"Just a minute. Yo' mother was a slave. Don' you forget that. Now, to make things easier for you, I'll review the procedures. A special commission is usually called, or grand jury, with appointments recommended by Richmond. The District Attorney may act under the President's orders, or from his Attorney General. The government prosecutors will hear the facts comin' from Sheriff Wheatland and others. Whether the executive authority asks for a summary arrest or not, you are here now for the local offenses, an' you'll be tried first for these. However, under the present dire circumstances of war, in which we find ourselves, I'm sho you can appreciate that the federal an' local activities do become rather meshed together. We're all servin' the same judiciary. Now, you can hire any local lawyer you wish to, an' you can see yo' family. But at the right time, Margery Spence, an' I'm to judge that."

"When will that be, Judge Barlow?"

"It depends on the war! Last night, on Christmas Day, they was fightin' us hard, tryin' to take Cobb's Creek. Oh, they created a conflagration out there. Sherman said burn everything! An' we ain't about to let no treasonable person get away. No-sir! An' if, young lady, you had a hand in this, you'll pay !'' Red-faced, he pushed his belly back from her rickety table and stormed out of the room. Wheatland came quickly to lock the cell again. Marg got up and restored her blanket to its high position over the tall front bars.

By Tuesday of the next week Marg was getting to know Jeb better. He was bringing her water every morning and the first meal. Gus Wheatland always brought the visitors and the evening meal. So far, Marg had not seen anyone in her family, nor a lawyer. She knew it was Georgia justice for nonwhites. Jeb too thought it a bit irregular.

"I heah yo' husband's back in town," he said casually, taking away her dishes. "Looks like they would let you see 'im. But you know one thing, Margery? People tend to punish you for bein' who you are. I know, 'cause they'd do the same dern thing to me. Why you think I'm in a crummy job like this?"

"I really don't know, Jeb."

"Well, I'll tell you. I come from a family of indentured servants. You know what that means? White folks who worked dirt cheap in cotton fields right along with niggers, an' one day bought their freedom. That was my grandpaw. A proud man but they had him marked. Would nevah let him do nothin' decent in this bleedin' town! So we strugglin' today because of it."

"When did he buy his freedom, Jeb?"

"Oh, thirty years ago. When my Pop went to prison, he got me this job. They both dead now, an' it looks like with fo' kids I'm stuck here. People won't give you a friggin' chance at nothin' else. I swear, they treat us jis like niggers. My wife takes in laundry. My sistah too."

Marg felt sympathetic, and miserable in her filthy clothing. She glanced toward the door to see if Wheatland was around. "Jeb, do you think you could get somebody to wash some things for me? Or, to go by my house an' bring me things—"

Jeb took the dishes outside without answering. He emptied her slop pail, brought a fresh candle, then glanced again at the doorway. She knew he was ready to comply. She pulled two dollars out of her purse.

"Is this enough, Jeb?"

He snatched it. "Oh, sure. For one week. What you want from home?"

"Some fresh clothin', Jeb."

"Naw. Sheriff would notice. You gotta keep on wearin' that dress. But if'n you want clean things to put underneath, then that's different. I could ask for it. But you know, this is dangerous talk. I'll help you if'n you help me!" She put a third bill in his hand and he went away, seemingly satisfied.

Next morning under the tray Jeb had a tight package. Her clean things. Also three notes: one from Charles, Valerie and Lucy. She thanked God for delivering her husband home. His note said little, and the others too. Maybe they didn't trust Jeb. Anyway, she felt it a wonderful beginning. She was happy all that day. Then, at four o'clock, the keys went rattling at the door again. It was sour-faced Gus Wheatland coming with her dinner.

"Afternoon, Margie. How you doin'?"

"Oh, I'm all right, Sheriff. How much longer am I goin' to be here?"

"Now don't you worry about that. You're safe in here while there's a war goin' on. The wheels of justice are turnin'. Richmond knows about you now. It's jis a question of time, Margie."

She wondered why this new twist to her name. Then she saw his agate eyes staring into her face while she ate the black-eyed peas and fatback. Lucy's note mentioned Mrs. Bowne. Maybe this was why he was actin' nice. Maybe Mrs. Bowne was doin' something. She didn't think he knew about her plan with Jeb.

"You got enough blankets?" he asked, looking at her colorful one she had stretched on the wall.

"Oh, if you have another one, I could use it." She regretted her words as soon as they were out of her mouth. She didn't want favors from this man. His blotchy fat face still frightened her.

"Well, I'll see what I can do about it."

There was something in his tone she didn't like. She still couldn't be sure that he didn't know about the money she had given Jeb. Something in his voice even suggested he was looking for money. She only had about thirty dollars more. She had to be careful. She could write a note home asking for more money. It would be so easy if they had a code language established. Poor Charles was not so good at writing. His letter just said that he was fine, that he had put Elias in his grave and put the house back in order. She was wondering if somebody had come in and wrecked it before Charles got back from Cobb's Creek. Well, anyway, he was safely home again. But the next morning what Jeb told her was shocking.

"The Confederate Army has taken over yo' house," he insisted at breakfast. "They made yo' husband get out. He an' that slave girl went back to yo' brother's—"

"Then Carrie is free," she gasped. "Oh, how wonderful! You

mean the brown young slave girl?"

"No, an old yaller one. Her name is Celeste."

"What happened to Carrie? The one they picked up with me?"

"Oh, she's out at Camp Edwards where they lock up all the runaways—"

"She's no runaway! Oh, Jesus, Lord, how can these things happen?"

"The darkies got bettah food than here," Jeb told her. "You want me to bring you food from home? From yo' brother's house?"

"I-I really don't know, Jeb. I don't want you to get caught. Maybe some tea or coffee, Jeb?"

"Yankee coffee smells. The Sheriff would know. Maybe a li'l tea. Jis a little." He waited for her handout. She put another two dollars in his hand. Then quickly she pencilled a note home on the back of Charles' letter. She mentioned Mrs. Bowne and the Walkers in Alabama. Lucy would understand.

Luckily Marg had a few bible verses in her purse and she took comfort in reading them every evening. The noise upstairs always stopped at nine p.m., and she assumed lights went out at that time. The Negro man next door usually sang on till about ten, then all was quiet. It was then that she enjoyed her reading by candlelight snug in her bed. This night it was cold so she did not take off her dress. The stays were uncomfortable and she bent a few of them. Just as she was getting comfortable again, the keys went rattling in her door!

"It's me again," called Gus Wheatland in the dark. "I finally got that blanket for you."

"Oh, Sheriff," she gasped, pulling the covers up to her neck. "I didn't know you were comin' back."

Now he lit a candle, setting it on the tilted tabletop between their two faces. "You know I wouldn't forget you." He put his hand quickly on her wrist. Marg twisted out of his clutches.

"Now, now, you settle down," he drawled, warningly. She knew he was a very strong man. His fingers, like steel, had twisted her hands down to the tabletop. Then he moved to sit on her bed. The springs groaned as his body took up the main space.

"Please, please," was all she could say. At the same time she was praying to Jesus to deliver her.

Wheatland had his right hand around her waist. Where she had twisted a stay, it was now sticking painfully in her ribs. She moved to get more comfortable and Wheatland did the same. "Sheriff, you must leave me alone!"

"Come on, you know all about white men. An' you don't want me to stay ignorant, do you? You li'l quadroon wenches fascinate me. Come on, one little kiss."

Marg was panting as he pushed her head down into the covers. She had a small pair of pinking shears in her purse, and that was under her bed; if she should reach it, she could stab him. Marg cried out; she didn't want to stab anybody. As he wrestled with her dress, she could hear the material ripping and she cried out again. Maybe loud enough for the man next door to hear her. Now she was embarrassed. She stuck her fist in her mouth and bit down on it, letting Gus do what he wanted to do while she fought down her voice. She could smell him now. His foul smell, and liquor on his breath. *Oh, God, help me*!

Soon it was all over. Gus got up and took his candle. He looked back at her as he was leaving. Now she was crying audibly. He laughed a little and left.

The next morning Marg was up at daybreak trying desperately to fix the several big tears in her dress. They were unsightly. She could not be seen by anybody looking like this. Her petticoat still was neat but she couldn't be walking around in that. Maybe she should just stay in bed until they brought her new clothes from home. She decided that was precisely what she would do.

Jeb came in looking worried. "What's the matter? You sick?"

"Yes, Jeb. I have a sore throat."

"Then this soup will do you good." He moved the table up to her bed. Then she burst out crying in front of him. "What's the matter?"

She threw off the covers and showed him the rips in her dress. She didn't have to explain. It seemed that he understood. "Now you have to bring me new clothes."

"Oh, no! I'm not gittin' into this. I think it best you ask the sheriff for new clothes."

"Do you think he'll listen to me?"

"Now he will." There was a look in Jeb's watery eyes. She knew that he knew. "I got yo' tea. You have to drink it cold. Okay?"

"Thank you, Jeb. I don't know what I'd do without you. Is there any news from my family?"

His blue eyes looked into her grey ones. "They didn't write no notes. Told me to tell you Mrs. Bowne is comin' today."

"Coming here? With me looking like this?"

"Don't worry," said Jeb, whispering now because the boss and others were in the office. "If she sees you an' understands the situation, maybe that's what you need!"

175

Jeb was right. Jessica Bowne came at three o'clock and she was horrified at the way Marg looked. "Gracious, they're treatin' you like an animal! I'll send my wagon right off to get you some decent clothes. Sheriff! Sheriff, let me out of here! You really must have some big rats in this place. I'm sendin' off for new clothes for Margery, an' you need some more fire in here. It's cold!"

Right away the sheriff went tending to the big stove out in the hall. He was chewing on his cigar. Marg noticed the smirk on his face. She hadn't said a word to him all day, and he hadn't to her. Just as he started to come into the room, Jessica was back. "My dear, I think it is really a shame for a decent citizen like you to be locked up in a filthy place like this. Sheriff Wheatland, what is yo' explanation?"

"Mrs. Bowne," he whined, "you know I can't discuss the deposition with you—"

"She needs a lawyer! Have you a lawyer, dear? Sheriff, I'm bringin' my lawyer tomorrow. Do you heah?"

The sheriff walked away, in fact, outside. He came back in fifteen minutes with puffy Judge Barlow. By this time Marg and Mrs. Bowne had discussed all the facts except his debauchery. They had agreed that a message should be sent right away to Mr. Leroy Walker in Alabama.

"I'm as guilty as you are," said Jessica, offering a peppermint. "Yo' lieutenant friend heard about you and sent a secret message to me across Confederate lines. You know what he said?"

"Lt. Waverly?"

"That's right. He was then at Macon but now I don't know where he is. He says that when his troops came into town he was right down here at Town Hall, an' when he asked about renting a big house, it was Gus Wheatland and Rayford Innis who suggested yo' home, the Simpsons and the Korners—"

"Oh, Mrs. Bowne, is that true? You must confront Mr. Wheatland."

"I will in court. He's too slippery a man for me to deal with outside the courtroom. I'm goin' to bring you Bill Cahill, a young lawyer friend of mine—"

"Visitin' hours are over," said Wheatland standing at the door with Judge Barlow. "An' in the case of this prisoner, you won't git the chance no more."

"What do you mean," screamed Jessica.

"She's a federal case," offered Judge Barlow. "She's goin' to be transferred out to Camp Edwards."

176

"Well, I'll certainly see her out there," screeched Jessica. "I get along very well with the Army brass—"

A surprised Wheatland was ready with new words. "That'll be next month. Right now, we're preparin' the local case an' she can't have no mo' visitors." Now he grinned.

"And a lawyer, Sheriff Wheatland?"

"I'll be her lawyer," said Judge Barlow, wizardly.

"No, no," protested Marg, freely. "I want Mrs. Bowne's lawyer. I don't want Judge Barlow!"

"Leave it to me," said Jessica with equal freedom. Then she huffishly swished her skirts at the two men as she left. Femininity was her power over them, and she knew it.

Chapter 19

Jessica Bowne did many things for her friend. The local boys had to stop all action on Marg's case. Jessica had gotten word up to Governor Brown in Milledgeville. She had wanted to see him. However, she had forgotten about the war. Atlanta now and all of that area was firmly in Union hands. And General Sherman had many prominent citizens get out of town. His army, burning and destroying, had marched through Savannah and on up the coast, heading for Columbia and on to Goldsborough. Moreover, the January thaw had rivers swollen and impassable. In desperation, Jessica decided to write the whole mess about Marg in a letter to Governor Brown. Army brass out at Camp Edwards got it through the lines, and quickly into Brown's hands.

Marg, still in that pitiful jail in town, was allowed to have her new dresses. Finally, they let Lucy and Charles come and visit! She thought she'd be angry upon seeing her dear Charles, for his staying in Cobb's Creek, but he explained it simply: he had a longing to be with his retrievers, and she believed him. His familiar, dreamy-eyed, handsome, ivory-colored face brought only joy. That warm, little-boy kiss was wonderful. It brought her tears and Jesus thanks. Jessica's young, curly-headed lawyer, Mr. Bill Cahill, came explaining that Marg had to go into Superior Court for a preliminary hearing. He put a new twist to it. He wanted the court to find out who the third man was who had come on Christmas Day to arrest Margery Spence and her maid. He felt it important to stress that the third man had made off with Marg's wagon, her horse and her Christmas presents. The crime was not Marg's running a hotel; it was harassment and robbery. Some expensive articles from her house had been found in a local pawnshop. Strangely, neither Gus Wheatland nor Rayford Innis would say that they knew the third man. In fact, they claimed they had come alone, that Margery's wagon and horse were left on the road. Then Cahill decided to try a delaying tactic; they had to try to get hold of Carrie so she could support Margery's testimony as to what actually had happened. By local law, a black slave couldn't testify, but he now would prove she was free. Marg remembered that her father had said: the white man could weave a truth from a great lie to retain his racial superiority.

Now both armies, North and South, had had to take colored soldiers, and they were found to be excellent fighters as well as loyal to each side. When in February 1865 the Union finally seized the great city of Charleston, it was the truth that colored troops of the 21st Regiment were first to enter the city. Both the town's near-whites and full-blacks were proud of these energetic fighting men of their own blood. While Missouri abolished slavery that January, and Tennessee that February, two border states, Delaware and Kentucky clung to the dying institution. By late February the Union's Gen. Schofield, having assumed command of the Twenty-third corps, now had captured Wilmington and Goldsborough. Joe Johnston was still fighting hard for the South. Little did Sherman suspect that he had twenty-two thousand men to cut off his junction with Schofield. The South put up a most courageous fight at that last big battle in the Carolinas, and just as it happened, the beauties of spring 1865 came into view.

Marg was still in jail as April broke forth. She could hear the white geese squawking as they raced across the unseen heavens. She could smell perfume-dripping lilacs in the air floating down from those high windows. She was weary now of all the delays, and of Gus Wheatland coming almost nightly to violate her body.

By now she had become friendly with the Negro man in the next cell. When he asked her her name, she told him Mary. And she called him James. They would talk every night just before bedtime. But neither could trust the other. She never told him her race or family circumstances. Merely that she was a wronged person who had rented her house to Union soldiers when they were briefly in town. James told her his predicament: he was first a runaway, then he got forged papers and became a free man. Then they arrested him for stealing chickens. He had had no trial because the white man who accused him drowned in the river. They looked for signs of murder but could find none. That was why he was kept so long in jail, while they manufactured evidence!

"You a mighty brave woman," James told her one night. "I knows he's comin' ovah dere, gittin' at you. If'n you kin, git his keys an' toss 'em to me."

Marg laughed. "Oh, James, I've never been that lucky. I'd probably drop them."

"Trust in de Lawd," James told her. "Dat's what you say to me, an' now I say it to you. We gotta break out of heah, ma'am."

Marg thought a lot about James's words, but she couldn't see herself trying to outsmart Gus Wheatland. She had never been quick or athletic. Actually she had thought about sticking her shears into his body, but she didn't know where to put one blow to kill him. And Jesus knew that she didn't want to kill anybody. So, she'd go on suffering her misery. Now she was coughing. The dampness was getting to her lungs.

One beautiful morn in that first week of April Jessica and Cahill came to her smiling. "We've done it," he said, shaking her hand. "The charges of treason have been dismissed, Margery. Did you hear me?"

"Then I'm free?" screamed Marg.

"No, not exactly. There's still this local matter, this nonsense of runnin' a hotel without a license."

"They have to release you on that too," sighed Jessica, looking weary. "I've offered bail, while they talk of a hearing. You see, everybody thinks the war will be ovah in a very short time, so you can't get anything legal done. It's a shame, my dear. But at least we can bring you a good meal!"

Jessica now revealed a big basket covered with white linen. Marg was delighted to have roast chicken. It was the first chicken breast she had seen in three years. The drumstick somehow reminded her of Wheatland. "This I want to give to my neighbor," she said. "Is the road clear? Are they in the office?"

Cahill wagged his finger. "They don't go out when I'm here. They know that sooner or later I'll get you out."

"They set his barn on fire," Jessica told Margery. "Can you imagine, such evil people, in official positions?"

"Now, Jessica," laughed Cahill. "You can't prove what you're sayin', so you might as well forget it . . . like Margery here has to forget her wagon, horse and Christmas presents."

"An' my slave," Marg added, eating scrumptiously.

Jessica gleamed. "I told Cahill to get into politics after this war. It allows you to create a magic truth!"

"Ah could agree in part," whined Wheatland standing at the door. "You certainly have the magic of pull, Jessica Bowne. This nigra woman may git free in a day or so, thanks to you."

"Rascal, you call me Mrs. Bowne," shouted Jessica. "An' it can't come soon enough. She's suffered enough under yo' filthy command."

In view of the gift chicken, the jail brought Marg no food that afternoon. She waited patiently for the boys in the office to leave. It was nine p.m., then she began passing across the cold stone floor the good food she had, calling to James. He went crazy over the drumsticks, potato salad, ham and cornpones. Marg enjoyed the happiness in his voice. Through cell wall they said goodnight at ten, then she lit her candle and read a bit. By ten-thirty her light went out and she breathed nervously, waiting in the darkness. It was his time now.

At 10:37 Marg moved tensely in her bed. She thought she heard him with his keys. Yes, he was there, pulled the barred door open. This night she had gotten up enough courage to put her pinking shears under the mattress. A tear came because she felt this would be her last night as an untried human. God was testing her. She'd have to pay her dues on earth. She told Jesus she just couldn't take anymore of this vile man riding on her body as if he owned her. The choices were few. Forgive me, Jesus!

The evening started with Gus, in candlelight, squeezing her hand. Then he slid through the covers, throwing his big arm around her waist. She'd move a little, with her back to him. They didn't talk anymore. There was really nothing to say. He wasn't there for talk. As usual he took her small hand and made it stroke his fat beardy cheek. "My, yo' hands are cold tonight," he whispered, with mock sweetness. Then he blew out the candle.

She was shivering. She had promised James she'd try, for the both of them. Gus usually kept on his clothes, just in case he had to move quickly. He'd put his gun on the table and slip out of his shoes. Doing the same this night, he didn't know of her shears under the mattress. As she reached for them his batch of keys slipped out his pocket, making a jangling noise. He left them on the floor! She started to call this to his attention. Just at that moment she heard James next door clearing his throat. He wanted her to grab those keys. Quick! And she did. She squeezed them as Wheatland's big arm went around her body, and he was breathing through the hair in his nose. Her heart began thumping like the booming guns. Now what would she do? Just as quick Gus was finished, and he slid over to leave her bed. He'd reach for his keys! No, he wrestled with his shoes, and was starting for the door. She decided to get up and talk sweetly.

"Tonight was my birthday," she told him. "I'm grateful that you came."

"Oh, Margie," he whispered in the black-dark room. "How nice to know it's yo' birthday. Shall I stay longer? Give you another present?"

"No, no." she said, standing over him as he reached to tie his shoes. "You should go on home, to yo' family. I've had a nice birthday."

"Well, I'm glad you had," he said, rising and hugging her close. As he kissed her lips Marg broke away, but then she made herself catch his hands and squeeze those stubby fingers. Then, like a crazy person, she ran to the iron bars, and threw the keys to the right, to James. "James! Come, James! Quick, take the keys! Get us out of here!"

"Why you little—" In the dark Wheatland grabbed her hard and swung her around. Marg reached for his pistol. When the smooth thing was in her hand she reached up in the dark and hit his head. He wasn't out; she hit him again. Hard! Yet, he had strength to grab her skirts ruthlessly. She swung again at his head. He was reeling this time.

Marg had thrown the keys too far from James' celldoor. He was there yelling, but he couldn't reach them. Then, breathing hard and seeing the problem, she turned her back on struggling Wheatland, reaching for the stove's poker right by her door. Straining, she could grab it, while Wheatland came on his knees grabbing at her skirts. Yes, with the poker she could push the keys closer to James' door, feeling death behind her. "Quick!" she yelled as his black fingers curled and stretched. A cold blast knifed her shoulders, as Wheatland ripped off her gown and petticoat. She still had the poker in her hand and brought it quickly through the bars. She jabbed at his groin as the corridor's light made him visible. He yelled. She jabbed again. Big black James was out in the hall now, fumbling with her door. Wheatland snatched his gun out of her hand and began yanking out her hair, big chunks of it. She tried not to scream, realizing all their noise would soon arouse someone on the second floor. She bit her lip each time the painful blows hit her head. She went down. Her lip was bleeding. Her head felt cracked.

Feebly she reached out for the bars, and James swung them open. Wheatland lunged for him like a crazy man. The two wrestled hard out in the corridor. Marg slid along the floor, watching and sliding. When she saw the black man reach for the sheriff's gun she began screaming again. "No, James!" she cried.

Just then, sure enough, the guard from upstairs came running down the stairs. James, upon seeing the white official with gun drawn, began moving quickly, like an animal. Pie, pie!! Shots rang in the air. As James and Wheatland stood up wrestling along the wall, they both looked as if they had lost their senses. Arms plowed out like octupus tentacles; smoke came from the guard's gun and James' gun. Marg sank back into her dark cell as both men were shooting. Now it seemed Wheatland had the gun. Pie, pie!! Then it was quiet again. The guard from upstairs stood over the two figures sprawled out on the stone floor. He was breathing hard, and watching Marg too. She saw blood oozing from both Wheatland and James. Now more people came through the front doors. She staggered back, grabbing her rent clothing, then soon swooned on her bed, realizing that the nice Negro prisoner next door was none other than Big Jim, fugitive from Edgewater Plantation. Dead now, as was her persecutor, Gus Wheatland.

END OF PART TWO

PART THREE

1865-1866

Chapter 20

It was still early April when Marg got out of jail. Those icy cold chills in her shoulders suddenly disappeared as she stepped into the morning's sunlight. People in the square were all staring. Her mind was on God. She was praying her thanks. And she was grateful to family and friends accompanying her. She had dreamed of going home to Malcolm House with its big bay windows and pecan-colored woodwork bathed in God's warm light. Actually she could only go to Valerie's house with its wrap-around porch, octagon-shaped rooms and cemetery view. Even this was a blessing. They passed a little brook with clear blue water and rolling waterwheel. So free of violence! Seeing it was like seeing God Himself.

The Confederates were still in Malcolm House, and they hadn't offered a penny's rent. Had either Marg or Charles gone near the place, it would have caused pandemonium, since many townsmen still thought of them as traitors. Also, she had become notorious for being involved in Gus Wheatland's death. Her lawyer Bill Cahill put two private armed detectives at Valerie's door, and advised Marg to stay close to the house, at least until after her court appearance. Yes, she and the jailhouse guard were to appear before a Grand Jury. She was to tell how Gus Wheatland had been killed, and how Big Jim did it. Marg told her lawyer she wasn't sure who began shooting first. At least, the guns were never in her hands.

The children suffered all the time their mother was locked up. A handsome blond John, now at fifteen had a different view of who he was. His father said it was better if the boy thought black, since he had begun to behave as if he were a pure white. And Beth at 12 was also snooty. Poor little Meg, at 9, wouldn't allow the gossip to faze her. She was interested in butterflies, and in butterfly dresses, and butterfly hairdos. With smiling Irish eyes, she enjoyed being a very beautiful child, dressed up to celebrate her mother's return. When people made ohs and ahs over her beauty, she repeated what her elders had told her: it was God's work.

The real gossip in town was not Margery Malcolm Spence's doings at prison, it was the surrender of General Robert E. Lee at Appomattox. General Lee met General Grant on Sunday, the 9th of April. They say Grant was carelessly dressed while Lee kept his perfect military bearing to the end. The Confederate officers were allowed to keep their sidearms and horses. Richmond had fallen and President Davis and his cabinet had left the Sunday before, on 2 April. As soon as Union troops took over Richmond, the downtown district was burned to ruins. Davis had a temporary capital at Danville, then he moved on to Washington, Ga. where he dismissed his cabinet. Thus, there was no Confederate government to try anyone for treason.

In all the big cities Negroes were holding victory parades, and the whites were flabbergasted to see black associations of carpenters, coopers, masons, teamsters, bakers, blacksmiths, wheelwrights on parade. In New Orleans the Daughters of Zion had a fancy float of perfect beauties. The white man himself had no better examples of Anglo-Saxon charm or physical perfection. It confused him to see this orderly, intelligent, white-to-black Negro on parade, so much like himself, and, so organized for freedom. In Georgia now the white newspapers were reporting Lincoln's speech of April 11th where he spelled out his reconstruction approach. Nobody cheered nor scolded the many white deserters now coming out openly in Maple. Out of the woods (like sheepish niggers).

It was on April 14th that the Confederates finally gave up Margery's house. A private came with a note saying they could come back home. Just as she hitched up Gregory's wagon and got her gang together, a horde of people came running down the street. They were all excited and screaming. Charles and Marg thought, for sure, it was a lynch mob. Scurrying for cover, they wondered what had happened now. Then their friend Dr. Lou Simpson came again telling the news. General Forrest had been holding off Yankee troops in the low waters of the Chattahoochee. Union General Wilson who had been down in Selma now had crossed the Chattahoochee on horseback. He rode his cavalry right into the heart of Maple. It was a Union prize again! The remaining Confederate troops there had to surrender. The soldier who came to Marg was actually a Union private. He brought the colonel's note to Gregory's house without explanation. Marg got all excited, now thinking she would see Lt. Waverly again, but he never came. His outfit was elsewhere.

They found Malcolm House to be a total wreck. It was as bare and dusty as a stable. All Marg's good furniture, linen, draperies, cutlery was gone, or, nothing was beautiful any more. The bare sandy floors looked terrible. At least the doors were still stained and on their hinges, to knock off the cool April breezes. She right away had sticks crackling and blazing in her fireplaces; she put her gang to work making comfortable beds. Celeste and Mamie, who had come back with Charles from Cobb's Creek, made a delicious cabbage soup. Mamie had married a tall lanky, brown-colored individual, Larry, who wore overalls and a keen-shaped haircut. The children and Larry got along fine. Little Meg was interested in the tight charcoal-black curls of his negroid hair. Beth liked the way he played harmonica. And John loved his skill in carpentry. Together they started repairing all the broken glass, the windows, the mirrors, even one magnificent china pot.

The first day of freedom was really an excitedly busy one for everybody. On that second day news reached town that on victory eve somebody had shot Abraham Lincoln, as he sat relaxing in a theater, and that he had died the next morn in Kirkwood Hotel, Washington, D.C. Southerners were saddened by this news, because many thought of Lincoln as one of their own. Naturally all the blacks were shocked because now their future would be uncertain. Marg too worried about this, thinking of freedom-minded Matilda, still out there somewhere in Cobb's Creek. Yet, the good side of Lincoln's death was her secret. She didn't want to tell people that kin on her mother's side, Andrew Johnson, was now President of the United States.

Mr. Leroy Walker now was also dead. Lucy decided to walk back to Montgomery. The stagecoach was not yet running again, but with so many people on the road, walking, she felt she could make it. Marg gave her greenbacks, and offered a dogcart, saying she didn't want the children to suffer so. They hugged each other as sisters. Lucy too had grown stronger. She would survive. Marg promised to keep the school going, but right now none of the children were learning in these days. They too were upset by Lincoln's failure to stay alive and become somebody real in their lives.

Marg discovered that her bone china dishes had been stolen, along with expensive figurines, European vases, clocks, and oriental umbrella stand. She and Mamie found the secret room under the chickencoop still chocked full of goodies, including Ezra Spence's table and

her big family Bible. She thanked Jesus, knowing it was His interces-
sion.

After three days of scrubbing and polishing Marg moved her silver
and antiques back into the house, to her mother's attic. She would not
put them on display yet. Many of the items would have to serve as
banknotes, the money they needed. With the loan of Gregory's wagon
she and Charles went Uptown looking for food. Ned's blacksmithing
business was still intact, but new faces were there, the Innis brothers.
Charles was pulling together his activities out at Cobb's Creek, now
mostly a Negro town. Marg glanced at her eighteen rental houses
where Negroes now lived; they had paid her nothing and she told
Charles she'd put lawyer Cahill onto them. She had matured enough
not to worry about what people would think. Jesus was on her side, and
she did not feel guilty about her thirst to be whole and one's self again.

She knew that in one respect she'd never be the same. When Charles tried to make love to her that first night, she put him off. That was
not her interest any more. In fact, she wanted separate beds. She had
heard that he had been seen out in Cobb's Creek with Laurie and her
brown baby. Charles carrying the baby!

After a week of solid work, the children needed a holiday. Marg
packed a picnic basket and again with Gregory's big wagon, she and
Charles drove them out to Cobb's Creek twelve miles away. Charles
wanted to retrieve some of his horses and Marg was going to buy a new
wagon. Actually not new, and that was why she took Larry along. He
knew all about repairing wagons. They'd buy something on sale at
Claremont or Edgewater.

Both plantations had suffered great damage in the last days of the
war. Most of the slaves now were gone, or wandering at a distance,
while the owners were trying to patch things up, and to earn some
money as well. At Edgewater, where the roof had burned, Marg didn't
see any wagons she liked. Abigail was still in the kitchen, happily at
her chores as if no war had happened. Marg brought her a cheaper
ring, and accepted a spot of brandy. She didn't want to see any of the
pure white Malcolms, not even Miss Wanda. None of them, not one,
had come forward to help her during those dreadful three months she
was in jail. Sticking together was their Christianity.

At Claremont Mrs. Bowne was away in Atlanta with her brother,
Mr. Lance Folsom. The new overseer, Mr. Andre McGill, was polite in
showing them what was available. He of course knew Charles; and
Margery's famous name was naturally known to him. He had never
seen Negroes so near white. This excited him, so he wasn't bitter at all
about doing business with them.

Marg bought a surrey with leather top. By begging Mr. McGill, she was also able to purchase a sack of corn and a side of bacon. And to please him she also bought a batch of canning bottles, a wash bowl and pitcher, some tools and nails. Her smile made it possible to get five blankets, a quart of molasses, and some hay. Larry told her what he needed. He had been a slave right there at Claremont, and now he was out there doin' business. It made him real proud.

Marg felt a yearning to see Matilda, but she was nowhere around. Rumor was she was off somewhere helping some former rich whites sell off their goods. Marg knew she was good at business. She wouldn't be a burden to anybody. Marg thought back to her teen years when Matilda suddenly appeared at Edgewater asking to hold her doll. Marg said no. She didn't want her blond beauty handled by black hands. Next thing she knew, Matilda had made her two dolls, from scraps of material. Marg was thrilled at the gift. Aunt Bess told her Matilda was the better Christian, and Marg never liked that. Then Aunt Bess went back to China and died, sealing her prophecy. Judge Edward gave Marg Matilda thinking it friendship when it really had been jealousy.

Nowadays talk was that slaves roaming around were destitute, and molesting white women. On the road you could see poorer whites, very angry at the turn of events, frowning and cursing. The black man to them was undeserving of freedom. They had all benefitted from the free labor of blacks. But no one would ever admit that. He'd be their criminal now. Marg could see the hatred in their faces; she knew that the war wasn't really over. Even those who had never owned a slave would not now give up blacks so easily.

Cousin Sue and Jeeter now had a son, a little blond toddler, and a curly-haired infant daughter. Marg was amazed at what changes the short time had brought. It seemed only yesterday that they had married. Sue now was fat: a big square white-faced woman with beautiful features, light-brown hair and dimpled smile. In spite of war, their one-room house was a dream. Jeeter had built a special alcove for the children, and another for Sue's piano, now that Amy, her mother, had died. Her brother Mitchell occupied the big family house and younger Albert was building his own. They were part of the prosperous in Cobb's Creek. Their village seemed normal; its people knew how to cast off the sufferings of war by hope and hard work. Marg noticed their good nature.

One more chore: she had to find Carrie. She decided they'd go home by way of Camp Edwards. There, she felt a little glorious seeing the Union flag again. The soldiers looked a little better than Confederate troops. At least they weren't haggard or raggedy. Charles watched her as she eyed the officers, looking for Waverly. Some day she'd have to tell him how she felt with Lt. Waverly. Her man had never complimented her for beauty or care, and now she felt it was something she needed. She shook her head and bit her lips, thinking what a sin the friendship had been. And Poor Jesus also wanted her to love that brute, Gus Wheatland.

Carrie wasn't at Camp Edwards. All the runaways sent there by Maple authorities had been released, to go out and find life on their own. None had been given a dime or directions! All the northern troops did was release them, like animals. As Marg questioned the Union people, she realized they were no more concerned about the wretchedness of black people than the southerners had been.

Now Marg was trying to feel differently about the institution of slavery. She had been a slaveowner, a generous person of color, one who never deeply questioned the rights or wrongs of it. Like others from good families, she accepted it. She had never been in a slave cabin. Today she had Charles stop so she could look at one. A broken log cabin with smoky, crumbling fireplace. Several filthy pallets on an earthen floor, cracks in the shredded walls, animal smells. Outside a wretched ragamuffin about seven was struggling with a gunnysack and a mule. As she moved to help him steady his load, she realized the boy was terrified at her attention. She didn't look like a friend! Clutching his piece of bread, he ran off leaving his load, scratching his rough flax shirt, and frowning at this strange woman who had entered his world.

Back in town, the endless parade of beggars, white and black, were mostly in rags. Naturally they came to Malcolm House because of its outward beauty. The only way the Spences got any peace was to drape the whole front with dusty tarpaulin, as if the house were not occupied. It stayed that way for weeks. Poor Bubber was still next door, caring for an ailing Mrs. Muggeridge. Mr. Muggeridge had disappeared with the Confederates, defeat being too much to bear. Bubber still ran messages, and he gave what money he earned to his mistress who had wickedly been selling him his freedom ever since the Emancipation Proclamation. Now Marg wanted Bubber for her own, but she kept telling herself this was wrong thinking. She could help him without owning him.

Only few Federal people in the South after slavery realized the depth and tenacity of the class and caste system. Marg was disappointed they didn't come to her. Instead, they went to Dr. Fred Bowman, a brownskinned Free-colored who lived opposite Marg on Plum Avenue. He had for years a thriving practice serving plantation masters and their slaves. In spite of his deep brown color, he was wealthy, having been free all his life. His grandfather, Percy Bowman, had earned his freedom by being an excellent brick mason, having built Maple's Town Hall, its courthouse and several of its most magnificent churches. Yet, Fred Bowman's whole family had suffered as black people. All they were allowed during slavery was their big immaculate house, their servants, their carriages, and their privacy. Dr. Bowman didn't like Margery Malcolm Spence, none of her kind. They were too white. Now he could proudly look down his nose, because the Federals had come to him and not to the Spences.

In those first post-war days the real problem was feeding the people. The troops got the railroad tracks back in order and one train a day would back in, bringing grain and staples from Atlanta. The Malcolms' Peachtree Drive house was still a hospital, and medicines and bandages were needed there. Another crew of soldiers were repairing the Chattahoochee docks, so the steamers could land again. Already the pedestrian bridge connecting Alabama was back in service. White men who had for years looked upon labor as being beneath them were now crossing, carrying loads, glad to have them to carry. In many respects, it was not easy to detect a difference in carriage of the ex-slave and the man who had been ruler of slaves.

All along, brave slaves had helped the Yankees, giving them food and directions. Others had steadfastly served their masters with honor through the last days. This had been as individuals. Now things were happening in groups. There were loud singing sessions on streetcorners. All the whites who had never owned a slave were manufacturing stories of blacks, claiming surly viciousness, when the real culprit was fear. The free ex-slave was everywhere! Composed, he displayed no bitterness. And in the evenings he went back to his cabins. A lot of planning had to be done. And some were even consulting their old masters on this.

Pretty soon, one evening a knock came at the Spences' front door. Marg was thinking about her brother Anthony and Lt. Waverly. When she got there, with a careful light, she found none other than Carrie. Coming home to Malcolm House! "Bless you, angel," cried Marg, reaching to hug. "Looks like you've been walkin' for days!"

A tattered Carrie stood back proudly. "I's been to Macon, to see my folks. An' my name now is Carol, not Carrie. Carol St. Matthew. Papa picked it. He's always liked dat book in the Bible."

Marg was amazed to learn that Carrie had a family. Charles when he bought her had learned nothing about this. Others came into the foyer and greeted Carol warmly. Marg then fixed her some supper, while Celeste brought down some fresh clothing. Mamie announced that she was going to change her name to Maggie Mae. And her husband would be called Lawrence, not Larry. Lawrence Brown. It was time for celebration. Drinking parched corn coffee, they teased Celeste because she wouldn't consider changing her name. She'd be known as Celeste Malcolm, and Marg liked this. It made Celeste in a way a real relative. After all she did have a son by Marg's father.

At eleven, Marg went up to bed feeling satisfied. Then Charles came with his announcement: he wanted to bring Laurie's baby, Jason, into the house. He claimed the baby's mother was suffering from tuberculosis and couldn't care for him anymore. Frowning, Marg wanted to know if it was to be for a short time or long time.

"Forever," laughed Charles. "We'll call him Jason Spence, as I am his father."

Charles' classless mien vexed Marg. She complained she couldn't take in the baby's mother.

"I guess not," sighed Charles. "Anyway, Mrs. Bowne is tryin' to get her into the hospital down at Valdosta. An' if she doesn't survive that, you raise him as my son an' yo' own."

Marg had had no experience with brownskinned babies. She knew that his life would be different. She didn't want to make any promises. It would be more appropriate to give the baby to Mamie and Larry, now Mr. and Mrs. Lawrence Brown. Of course, she wouldn't tell Charles this. Maybe with the baby, and his fatherly role, maybe he'd get sense and stay home more. Marg hoped this, and told Jesus so.

Chapter 21

As the dreamlike festivities of the summer of 1865 gave way to hard work and new lives, the near-white Malcolms had a family meeting to plan their future. The rednecks still controlled the blacksmith and the produce business, and nowadays, they'd make no room for cashew-colored people. If the family was to remain in either line, they had to map it out and be aggressive to get money in their coffers. The first task was to help Mitchell and Albert plow the land for vegetables and flowers. Somehow, Charles would start up his vegetable business again. Marg declared that this time it would have to be in a store. In their search they found a good place, but the pure whites wouldn't rent to them. Frank and Phyllis Korner owned two buildings and they had room for one tenant, but neither Marg nor Charles would go to them. The Korners now were pure whites, and there'd be no contact whatever with their former near-white friends.

They had heard Frank was back from service with Gen. Hood's courageous army. Some said he looked older. Now Phyllis could go home; she didn't have to keep the counter any longer in their jewelry store. The picture-taking business was brisk too, while families said tearful good-byes and began moving to new parts of the country. The rumor was that most of Maple's fifty near-white families had moved away, some to New Orleans, some, up North. They had suffered too much, squeezed in the middle of a strange, dishonest caste war.

Laurie, the ex-slave, died of tuberculosis over in Valdosta. Marg grabbed Jason's brown hand and promised to teach him what she could of life. As the hot summer months nestled in, she donned gingham and sandals and went out to Cobb's Creek to help in the plowing, planting, weeding and watering. It was so good to be out in the sun again! Her coloring grew hard like the rednecks, but she didn't mind. Mitchell and Albert had managed to get enough seed to put eighteen acres under cultivation. They'd mainly grow food crops. Charles had never liked cotton, in spite of the money attached to it. He decided to grow a few acres of peanuts on his own land. For the most part, Edgewater and Claremont Plantations were idle. There simply wasn't the labor force or the capital to run them on the grand scale of old.

It was rumored that the Malcolm family wanted to sell out. Mrs. Bowne had lost a considerable amount on the land, and in Confederate bonds. Now she was trying her best to renew her reaper contract, and to raise funds from her railroad ventures. But she was a proud one, and never invited Marg out to the house so long as it was in shambles. Whenever she came in town she'd stop by for tea, claiming she came to see Jason. She observed the medium-brown curly-haired toddler, thinking Marg or the servants had done pretty well with him.

The three white-faced Spence children did not like their new black brother. John with turned-up nose, wearing his blond hair in a bloused curve, wouldn't go anywhere near the chocolate-colored little boy. Beth was curious but she was always laughing when she pinched the baby's brown cheeks, legs or hair.

"He looks too black to be our brother," cried Meg, until she got smacked for it by Celeste.

Marg made a point of sitting with the new child at breakfast. She let him call her Mama, and she referred to Charles as his "Papa". She had consulted Cousin Don before accepting this burden. He told her to go along with Charles' desire. She had nothing to lose. The world of the secure and fair mulatto class was fading anyway. It had been a false world, the minister told her.

Lucy wrote from Montgomery that she was in temporary quarters, waiting for husband, Kenneth, up in Chicago to send for her. He was a porter up there. Well, better than being a porter down South.

In late July Marg received unexpectedly a letter from Mr. Tom Haney in New York. He claimed he had good news for her; he wanted her to come to New York as soon as she could. She wondered why he wasn't specific in his letter. It either had to do with her stocks or her brother. She was afraid to urge him to write the details. Anthony might be dead and she did not want to learn it by letter. Somehow she found the money and began planning her trip.

While there was no need to stop at Charleston or Raleigh, she did want to see Louise and Lydia, if they were still in Washington, D.C. While she was no longer friendly with Phyllis Korner, she did write a note to her kin Angela in New York. She seemed a decent sort one would want to keep up with. At the last minute Marg decided she could not travel alone. The rails were too unsafe. She urged Gregory to make the trip with her. When he hesitated, she promised good news. She could almost feel it in her bones. With her intuition, Jesus had not let her down before.

The August train ride was hot and uncomfortable, and a real education. Marg had had no idea of how extensive the war had been. She was completely shocked at seeing Atlanta flat and burnt to cinders. And Charleston too, and all the big cities straight up the coastline. And the people were still suffering. Throughout Carolina and Virginia, the public met the trains, for handouts. Gregory gave soap, cigars, socks, and several extra shirts and underwear. He made his donations equally to whites and Negroes. But some rowdies in the coach had him disgusted with the white man. They were racists to the core. They were cursing the black man for all he was worth. Gregory started to go back and tell them he was black, but Marg said no. They couldn't afford any infractions. She had sold Lilian Simpson some of her jewelry, to raise funds to make this trip. They had to go quietly and modestly. And she had used creams on her face to get back her white color. She knew it was as important as money in America.

In New York, it was again the fancy Fifth Avenue Hotel. Marg realized this was a mistake; it made her glum, thinking of Anthony. She had herself a big dish of juicy red strawberries and whipped cream, and this had her thinking of her dear father and his last Sunday of life. Quickly she got dressed and took a cab to see Mr. Haney. He had a new office, with name on his door in gold letters. His cheeks were still pink, but fatter. "Well, now," he said with a little kiss. "The war didn't do so badly by you. Mrs. Spence, you're as charming as ever. And now, Mrs. Spence, you're a rich woman!"

"W-what do you mean?"

"I mean, I've re-invested over sixty thousand dollars in your name! That's what you've earned in four long war years. Congratulations!"

"O-oh, I don't know what to say. Mr. Haney, a-are you tellin' me I have sixty thousand dollars?"

"More than that. All your items paid off handsomely. The Copp Steamship Lines, Sparks Textiles, and even our family's copper mine. Are you sorry you listened to me?"

She sat back and fanned herself. "I-I simply can't believe it. I don't know what to say other than thank you. We need money so badly. The South is devastated, you know."

Now he turned serious. "And will be for quite some time. I would advise you to go slowly on plans. In fact, I would say just re-invest the money again with me. Some striking things are about to happen. Look here."

He took them to a table with a display under glass. A small squarish machine. "This is a typographer, invented by Mr. Austin Burt of Detroit. Now, next to it is the Fairbank's phonetic writer. And, over here, we have the Alfred Ely Beach ribbon typewriter. Mrs. Spence, this is the way to go. In a few years, these machines will revolutionize the world. My family are working with a man called Densmore. His machine writes twice as fast as the human being, and it makes print just like a printed book. See?"

She was impressed, but she had to disappoint Mr. Haney. "I'm sorry, but I think I will simply cash in. We need the money so desperately down in Georgia."

"Not all of it! What are you planning there?"

"My husband, Mr. Haney, is trying to rebuild his business. We have to because it's the only way we can make a living. We do not have office jobs like you do in the North."

Haney laughed. "Okay, but for God's sake, don't take all your money. Just a little bit of it. I swear, I can make you rich if you leave it mostly with me."

Marg looked to Gregory for advice. He was hoping she would refinance his tailoring shop. "Mr. Haney, isn't what you're doing like gambling?"

"It is, Mr. Malcolm. But all of life is a gamble. I'm telling you we're in for some great times. You must remember I make my life at studying the trends, and moving appropriately. I'm sure the railroads are going to grow, the copper industry, the steamships, just as they did during the war. Only this time it's transcontinental. The whole country will be involved. You're on the ground floor."

There was a twinkle in Gregory's brown eyes. He was a bit more of a gambler than Anthony. He nodded toward Marg. She knew what he meant.

"All right, Mr. Haney," she said, sitting back. "I'll merely take ten thousand. The rest I'll leave with you."

Haney was satisfied. As he brought papers for signing he asked questions about the slaves and about the southern white man. The South had been conveniently narrowed down to just these two groups. Marg preferred to change the subject to her lost brother. She asked if Haney had any word from him, any knowledge of where he was.

"Anthony did go into the army. Yes, late in 1861. He came to see me once on furlough. Then he was a lieutenant with General Schofield.

198

He looked fine. Last I heard was Christmas 1863, almost two years ago. Well, you can always write the War Department. And, as you say you're going to Washington, you certainly can find out while you're down there."

Marg and Gregory were grateful for this suggestion. They stood and shook hands again. It had been a very refreshing meeting. Marg bought a few dresses and she arranged once again to see Angela Baker. This time it was easier. Angela no longer lived in Brooklyn. Both Jerome Brothers were now millionaires with new brick mansions in Madison Square. Marg went there in a rented carriage, and as before, she went to the servants' entrance. A smiling young black-haired girl of twelve admitted her.

"I remember you," cried the girl. "You're Mrs. Spence from Georgia. I'm Jennie. Remember me?"

Of course Marg remembered Mrs. Clara Jerome's second daughter. She kissed her, smiling, remembering too the talk of Indian blood which Angela claimed as their only unwhite heritage. The proper girl now knocked at Angela's closed door in a black-dark corridor. Soon a cautious inch of light appeared. Seeing Marg, Angela opened up revealing a drawn face, full of despair. It didn't look like the same Angela. She had aged so.

"I'm in a state," confessed the ivory-colored woman through blotchy eyes. "They're dismissing me. But I've been expecting it for some time. You see—" She went and closed the door properly, making sure nobody was listening outside. "You see, as the Jeromes move up in society, they don't really need me. In fact, I think I'm a burden—"

"Oh, Angela, how can you think that? You've been with them for years, an' they've been pleased with you."

"Marg, you don't understand. It's more than that. This question of 'kin'. You see, Mrs. Jerome, the two of them, they cannot afford any problems now that they're on their way to the top. They want the best secure world for their children, an' you can't blame them. I must go! No poor cousin is needed here on the staff, especially one who—"

"My dear Angela, is it really so bad?"

"Marg, they move around with the *best* people. Understand? Mr. Frank Griswold, the Belmonts, all the millionaires! They're in the smartest clubs, the Coaching Club. When the Atlantic cable was broken, they offered their yacht, which also raced the Atlantic for a trophy, and they were guests of the Queen of England! There's simply too much risk with me around. Actually, the risk is for their daughters. For them to do well in America—"

"Angela, why don't you come with me? We're digging out of the war, but I think you'd love it down South. Maybe for a short change?"

Angela stood up and kissed Marg. "Oh, that's so wonderful of you to invite me. No, you see, I know many prominent people. I have my pick of good jobs. It was just such a blow to me that I could be discarded just like that."

They avoided the real subject. Marg at this time presented her little gift, a box of Irish handkerchieves. Angela was delighted to have them. Next she asked about Phyllis and Marg told her frankly what had happened, about Frank's war duties and the family's choice.

Angela sat silent for a while. She was smiling a bit and her eyebrows went up and down as certain ideas came into her mind. "We're all persecuted people," she finally said. "Even the Jeromes with their racetrack and prized horses. The Bible tells us about horse-trading among people. My mistake was thinking family all the time. Catherine knew this and it petrified her. It was as if they were living with a blackmailer. Can you understand that?"

"Yes. I could see it in my relations with Phyllis."

"Marg, I shall be glad to go. I don't want to be a burden on anybody. The thing is, we shouldn't give up dignity. Keep moving with positive people. Those who withdraw respect, while aiming for material success, they'll stumble. Margery dear, that's what the war was, a stumble from economic heights. All that killing, just to put right somebody's chessmen and their greedy dollars."

Marg thought about Angela's remarks when riding with Haney, so proud in his new carriage, and to be among those reviving four-in-hand driving. She saw dressed-up lackeys: flowers in buttonhole, white gloves, gold-plated harnesses, black coachmen and two white footmen. The rich in New York could put on shows like the southerners. They were alike!

On the trainride down to Washington, her thoughts had softened. If America was money-comfortable people, maybe she and Gregory, Charles and Mitchell could make enough of it to be included in that world, or, maybe God wanted her to give it to the poor, or to her children. John, Beth, Meg and Jason. They'd need something more than religion. And she'd certainly send some of it to poor Angela.

"Gregory," said Marg, grabbing her brother's hand. "Don't tell Charles about the ten thousand dollars. It's not that I don't trust him. Jesus made him a down-to-earth person. I'm more devious. I have many plans for that money an' for them to work, I have to do it alone. Understand?"

Gregory smiled his handsome smile. "If you've got me in the plan, sister."

200

Chapter 22

As the neat and cozy New York train pulled into Washington, Marg listened to two men behind her discuss politics. The question of whether President Johnson would confiscate the land of rich southern planters and give it to the Negro. The fat man claimed this was Thaddeus Stevens' idea, that of pulling down the aristocracy both in the North and South. He mentioned a friend, Henry Winter Davis, who was writing an article against Johnson, calling for the enfranchisement of liberated slaves, without touching wealth. The little man, who seemed to be a newspaper correspondent, said the plan was to keep pressure on Johnson in the press, that Johnson was sick and would soon have a stroke.

Marg was alarmed. "Gregory," she whispered, "do you think we should try to see him?"

"Who?"

"The President. Mr. Johnson."

"Oh, no. We shouldn't intrude."

"Maybe if he's sick, Gregory. He'll know who we are. If we just show up, he can't refuse us."

"What's the point of it?"

"Well, it may help us. You know he's appointed James Johnson of Maple as the Provincial Governor of Georgia."

"Yo' father's cousin," whispered Gregory, "Mr. James Johnson, is a pure white. I don't think the President wants to see the likes of us."

"Gregory! We're human beings. And, Americans of substance. How can we harm him just by shaking hands and sayin' hello?"

"Well, if that's all you want to do, okay. But, Marg, don't go begging any kin favors."

"Don't worry. Hah! I'm sure he'll caution us as he did Lucy: *don't tell a soul we're related*!"

Louise Johnson met them at beautiful Pennsylvania Terminal. She had on a stylish hat, but its purple made her look older, and much more negroid now. Once again she took Marg to fashionable Willard's Hotel, there to separate and not speak. The Willard was still an all-white hotel.

Marg's first business was to visit the War Department and to ask them to find Anthony. She did this the first morning. Now, relieved, she felt a little devilish. She wondered if Lydia Farley Smith could get her into the Executive Mansion. Over lunch she composed a note to Lydia and sent it off. That same afternoon a note came from Lydia saying Mr. Thaddeus Stevens would look into the matter, but she must come to dine that same evening.

At 7:00 p.m. a powdered Marg was all nerves as she greeted cashew-colored Lydia at the beautiful townhouse she was keeping for Mr. Stevens. She relaxed upon learning that just the two of them were there. The clam chowder was all Marg would eat. It was excellent. Then over wine, Lydia spoke of a possible visit to the President's mansion. She advised Marg to have some special visiting cards printed immediately that evening. On the way home Marg stopped by the printers and waited for her order. She had decided her special calling cards would read: *"Margery Malcolm Spence, householder of Maple, Georgia, second cousin of Frances McDonough of Raleigh, North Carolina"*. She only had a few printed, for she would never need such a calling card again.

Sure enough, on the second morn Mr. Stevens sent a message to the hotel through Lydia, that it was all right for her and Gregory to go to the Executive Mansion that afternoon. Marg was ecstatic. Louise helped her to get her face and hair perfect, then she got into a handsome elaborate frock of soft blue velvet trimmed in white lace. When they arrived at the sprawling Executive Mansion the gatekeepers thought she was a celebrity and did not question her in the least. After her grand entrance she hadn't expected a long dry wait on a public staircase, but that's exactly what happened.

This particular corridor of the Executive Mansion was filled up with coarsely-dressed men, some of them obviously ex-soldiers there to seek pardons. A few women there were to appeal for a father or a brother. The place smelled of stale tobacco and body heat. More important people came another way, and they were ushered right into a plush ante-room. The doorkeeper kept her and Gregory with the motley crowd but he promised to present their card to the President soon. It was getting near three o'clock and Marg was worried because she knew Mr. Johnson only gave audience from nine till three. In her nervousness, she dabbed expensive French perfume all over her wrists and neck. It seemed to fight the smoke and smell of the corridor. The next time the doorkeeper came to them, he smiled, and breathing the scent, moved them closer to the front of the line.

"The President has your card. He said he will see you."

Marg was delighted. Now she didn't know what to talk about. They certainly couldn't discuss relatives; she didn't know any of them. Maybe she could remind him of his having met Lucy. That would be enough. And tell him what help the people of Georgia needed. She was sorry now that she hadn't brought her pearls. She could look a bit more like an aristocrat, or the rich girls of New York.

It was ten minutes after three when they were invited into the cool, deeply-ornate office of the President. Seeing Marg, a beautiful woman, Andrew Johnson made a half-stand from his desk, offered his hand, then sat down smiling. Two aides stood close by, and the doorkeeper stayed at the far end of the room.

The President studied her unique calling card. "Well, Mrs. Spence! And I presume this is Mr. Spence?"

"No sir, Mr. President. This is my brother Gregory. Gregory Malcolm."

"Do you know the source of that name Gregory?" he asked them both.

Neither Marg nor Gregory knew what to say. The President continued: "It's humble, an' it comes from Carolina. Yo' good mother wanted to remember her roots." Next, in his soft musical voice he asked how Lucy was and how Maple people were fairing in the aftermath. Next, he took out a gold watch and glancing at it he said: "I'm sorry, I must leave for an appointment. Actually an excursion. They say I don't get enough exercise. Today they're takin' me on a drive to Rock Creek and Pierce's Mill. May I drop you on the way?"

Marg looked at Gregory, too flabbergasted to speak.

"Where is your hotel?"

"We're at the Willard, sir."

"That's right on our way," said the President, leading the way.

They all left through a back door. The President of the United States led them across the soft carpets of the East Room, and into another corridor. None of the mob outside his room had to be encountered. At the wide staircase carpeted in red Mr. Johnson's secretary came forward. There waiting was a very presentable man of Anglo-Saxon face, and a severe-looking stoutish man. They were introduced as Mr. Preston King and General Ben Butler. Mr. Butler had no words to say to Marg or her brother. He greedily stepped in close to the President and began talking politics. Downstairs and outside, the President said a few words in private to Mr. Butler while the carriage was coming up. Next Mr. Johnson smiled handsomely at Marg and Gregory, inviting them into his plush carriage.

The President's secretary began a commentary for the three guests in the carriage, explaining about some plantings in the ground near the White House. The President leaned close to Marg and whispered: "Mr. Butler was inclined to suggest execution of Mr. Davis and Mr. Lee. What do you think about that, Mrs. Spence?"

That evening Marg had to go again to the residence of Mr. Thaddeus Stevens. He had wanted to meet her. Besides, she had to report on the visit he had arranged. She wore the same outfit she had had on at the White House. She hadn't expected him to look so old, but he had a strong face, and a twinkle in his blue eyes. Lydia had said it would only be a brief visit because he had another engagement. Even so, she brought out French cakes on the best china and the best wine, for Marg. The thin-lipped congressman was indeed interested in this fair quadroon who had been put in a Dixie jail for having Union officers in her home, and had survived it. He was impressed. He asked her offhandedly about her talk with the President, and when she told him, he made a wry smile and declared: "They can't try Davis for treason. They knew in the beginning the belligerent character of southerners. All I want them to do is give the vote to the Negroes, and seize all that plantation property to pay the national debt. It's over three billion dollars! And don't worry about those aristocrats. They'll survive, like Robert E. Lee, who is now a college president."

On the third day, Marg was on her own. She noticed some changes in Washington. It did not have the lordly leisure or aristocratic elegance it had had on her first visit. Now, Louise told her, many of the finer houses had closed; society had gone elsewhere. Mobs of poor Negroes were hanging on the streets. The very distinguished looking people who used to sit in the lobby of the Willard were not there this August. The loud laughter of the ex-slaves sometimes came through the door. Some soldiers were in the streets, gamblers and con men too. Some women of indifferent morality were also around.

Marg was supposed to have another visit at the Stevens house but he was rushing off to Lancaster and had a last-minute meeting with Chief Justice Chase. So, Lydia instead came to the hotel to have dinner with them there. This created a stir, because Lydia, by Washington standards, was obviously Negro. The town was full of half-caste people, and the only way one would know that they came from the inferior side was if they dressed or talked that way. Lydia had a loud Negro way of talking, and this made them spot her immediately. She didn't care. She was famous in her own right. The hotel people had to serve her. They did it grudgingly, and after she left Marg and Gregory were suspect. They could not get room service or a boy to take down their luggage. They had to bring it down themselves.

Lydia met them again at the railroad station, with Louise, where people were more apt to be civil.

"Don't think racism is dead," she told her friends. "These white people are just as silly and just as stupid as they were before. An' just think of the half million who died in this struggle. That's why my Mr. Stevens wants to make sure it's all settled properly. Naturally he wants Negro suffrage and some restitutions from the former slave owners. Hah!"

"Mr. Johnson has accepted the Lincoln reconstruction policy," Louise put in. "There has to be gradual change."

Lydia spoke up. "Those who have misgivings about Mr. Johnson think he's too much like Lincoln. Had to learn to read from his wife. From a slave state. A southern Democrat. From the poorest white origins. His father was a porter. Now they whisper about his Indian-like swarthiness, sayin' too that the President is the illegitimate son of a gentleman of some distinction. Hah! Marg, we should get *you* to lobby for us."

"On, no," screamed Marg, walking faster. "I was glad to meet him but I would in no way bring embarrassment to the poor man. He's got enough troubles."

"You could blackmail him," hissed Lydia, leading them towards the train.

"I'd *never* do that," said Marg stoutly. Then she stopped walking. "Mr. Johnson is a pure white. Nothing can change that. And you must remember I'm American first. I would never do anything to hurt this country, or the President. I think all racial things, family or not, take second place."

"Amen," said Louise, setting down Marg's bag.

Lydia was confused. She just reached out and bought a batch of newspapers for her departing guests. "I don't know when I'll get back down in Georgia, honey. But what I'm sayin' to you, don't let those people walk over you again. You heah?"

"Yes, Lydia!" said Marg, taking her own bag, as the steam from the train billowed around them.

"If they come to put you in jail again, you shoot them. You heah?"

"Yes, Lydia!" said Marg, grabbing Gregory's arm and kissing her friends one last time. She then accepted a little bouquet of violets from Louise. It reminded her of Matilda and her first return to Maple. The tears came freely.

Chapter 23

While in New York Marg made arrangements for all three of her children to come North to school that September. John was the first to leave. It was all so sudden his Uncle Gregory had to rush to complete two serge suits and one broadcloth and Aunt Valerie made him shirts as well, so that John would be handsomely well-dressed up at Lawrenceville, a select school in New Jersey. Beth and Meg would go to a Friends' school in Concord, Massachusetts. Two ladies from Maple's mulatto clan had been there and recommended it highly. It was certainly a strain getting the children ready, particularly the girls. They had to borrow luggage from Dr. Simpson. But everybody was cheerful about the event, even the girls. Mainly Marg was happy she could now afford to send her children off where they'd have civilized surroundings and where they could eat as normal people once again. The South was still struggling with its food problem, and the problem of civility.

That autumn she kept busy not to feel the loss of her three angels. Walking in town she saw lots of strange northern white people. Some said they had come to manipulate the freed ex-slaves. One well-dressed stranger came up and asked Marg if she could take in three roomers. This time they would not be white people, but northern colored women who had come South as missionaries. Many now could be seen in Maple, well-dressed, polite and intelligent, a credit to their race. These three colored ladies were to teach in newly created schools for ex-slaves. Marg was happy to help out in this instance. Now that Confederate paper was worthless, she was glad to see some more northern money.

First, Miss Fanny Boulware from Indiana arrived. She was a prim, cookie-colored woman with coarse reddish hair and a few blotches in her complexion. She was given Lt. Waverly's big room. Next came Miss Hortense Teasley from Cleveland. She was short, pleasant-faced, with thick lips and hips, warm eyes, nice black hair and a brown skin. She was given the back bedroom shaded by the fig tree. Next came vivacious Josie Timms, from Chicago. She was thirtyish, with a full bosom, round yellow cheeks and flashing eyes. Marg didn't want her near Charles. Instead of giving her the front yellow bedroom, she claimed that had to remain her guest room. She sent poor Josie up to the attic, to her mother's rooms. Josie didn't mind because up there she actually had more room; it was more like her own three-room apartment, what she had had in Chicago. Only better.

During their absence in New York Larry now Lawrence had done a beautiful job in transforming the side green bedroom into a nursery for young brownskinned Jason. The baby was boisterous in there, and Marg was happy to see him pleased. She also liked that John and Larry had made twin beds for her room and had placed a wide pink damask canopy over both beds. She promised Larry she would get him some better tools. This made her think again of Edgewater and Claremont. It was a nice October afternoon so she decided to take her surrey and go out to Cobb's Creek.

On the way she saw wrecked homes, sculptored chimneys standing naked in purple ashes. Walking past the blackish heaps were some well-dressed speculators from the North. She thought about the talk of politicians in Washington. The plan was to confiscate every estate worth ten thousand dollars and containing two hundred acres, to give forty acres to every adult Negro. They'd sell off the rest of the South to satisfy the three billion dollar debt. This would make 70,000 homeless whites. Some said this would unnecessarily punish women and children. The *New York World* said: "Mr. Stevens is no fool and knows better than to believe this stuff." She liked the *New York Tribune* best and had started up her subscription again. Now she smiled thinking of Lydia and her spry Mr. Stevens. It was nice knowing important people in the world.

Just south of Cobb's Creek the road forked and Marg took the left mud road which led into Lain's Corner. This was a community of poor whites. Today she was going there first. She wanted to talk to her lawyer, Bill Cahill. His cottage was one of the neater ones. Once painted yellow, now it looked like something dry and very thirsty. Behind it Marg could glimpse the crushed skeleton of his burnt-out barn, which citizens had given him for fighting her case. The picket fence out front was leaning and weatherbeaten. The chickens roaming there within picked at the sandy soil belonging to the young couple.

"It's not much," laughed Bill, a bit self-conscious, "but it's home! Ain't that right, Birdie?"

"That's right," whined his blondish wife, in typical southern fashion, showing bare ankles. "Bill's father gave us this place, Miz Spence. An' we thought we'd only stay here a year, then war came. I said, 'My God, I'm stuck here forever.' Do you think folks will evah get prosperous again?"

"I think so," chirped Marg, standing prettily in a new cotton dress. "I've got a job for yo' husband. If he wins me this court case, it'll be somethin' new if not much."

Cahill now got businesslike, waving for his barefoot wife to go inside. He offered Marg Birdie's broken chair while he propped himself against a rusted water pump. Marg, sitting, told him it was true the Malcolms were getting ready to sell Edgewater. She dug out some papers from her purse. It was her father's final will, the one showing that she and her brothers were to get 300 acres of Edgewater.

"I want you to take this into court an' get me my share of Edgewater."

Bill studied the papers. "Gee, that's a tall order. Judge Barlow has already ruled on yo' father's will."

"That's to be overturned," said Margery, stoutly. "If you're the spunky young lawyer I think you are, you can win my case."

"Gees, Mrs. Spence, that'll take a lot of research. An' you know there are feelings involved."

"Of course there are. My feelings! These are new times, Mr. Cahill. The old methods of Judge Barlow and company won't hold with the military governors. Mrs. Bowne thinks I'd have a chance now." She handed him a Yankee ten-dollar note.

"Oh." Cahill grabbed the bill, showing white teeth. He scratched his curly sandy hair. "Well, I'll think about it. Might give it a try."

"I know you're on the side of honesty," said Marg, getting ready to leave.

"Am I?" he smiled. "Since that word changes like a stream, we'll strike while the tide's right, huh, Miss Margery?"

He hadn't called her that before. It sounded all right coming from him. Marg had long wanted to be less formal. Now she'd go and see Jessica, whom after all these years she still called Mrs. Bowne.

Mrs. Bowne's big house was a mess. Reddish bricks were crumbling down the right side like fallen gingerbread. Artillery fire had scarred the neat white front. Arched windows now were blown out and

209

free of architectural beauty. So far the front yard had been put in order with smooth grass and flowers. Some brickwork had been started. Claremont, lacking agricultural activity, looked deserted. Only a few of its many Negroes remained.

Mrs. Bowne still owned much property in the main business section of Maple. Most of her Broad Street stores were rented. Marg wanted her to make room for a vegetable store Uptown. Mrs. Bowne didn't agree. She thought Charles should stick to his blacksmithy shop outside of town, and build it up.

"We were in vegetables before, Mrs. Bowne. I think Charles feels better in that line."

"I know he's afraid of Ned's bunch. The Innises, an' the Wheatlands. While the military people run things many oldtimers, like possums, will crouch back in corners. But they'll dig themselves out. Hah! They'll be back!"

"That we fear, an' I don't want any more trouble. Life's too short, Mrs. Bowne. We feel it would be peaceful for us in vegetables again."

"Not on Broad Street. The whites don't want you up there."

"Phyllis and Frank Korner are there."

"They're white people."

"No whiter than I am!"

A zap of sunlight took hate from Mrs. Bowne's eyes to her wrinkled skin. She adjusted her glasses. "Margery, you've got black folks in yo' house. Even a black baby. Yo' husband's. How can you live as a white person in a white community?"

"Forget it," sighed Marg, exasperated. "At the upper end of Broad Street, near Rose Hill, you have some property. I'd like to buy it an' build my own building there."

"Nothin' doin', child. That still would stir up the whites. I do have an old building out on Post Road near Buena Vista, if you want that."

"There's not much business out there, Mrs. Bowne."

"Child, the city's growing that way. Just think what it will be five years from now. Right now, no niggers or white folks around. Just right for you."

"We'd starve there!"

"Not if you're good at business. There's an acre in back an' two acres out front, for parking the wagons. An' you could even grow yo' tomatoes out back. Soil's good for tomatoes."

"Well, I'll talk it over with my husband," sighed Marg, about to leave.

"Don't you want to know the price?" asked Mrs. Bowne slyly.

"Didn't I ask?"

"You didn't, which means somethin' else to me. You went up North an' got yerself a lot of money. Isn't that right?"

"Oh-h, Mrs. Bowne, you're funny!"

"No, I'm not. You see, girl, you haven't learned to be shrewd enough to deal with me. I'd nevah let a cat out of the bag like that. That way they charge you a fortune. Hah! I'll give you the place for one thousand dollars. Yankee cash, my dear."

"I still have to ask my husband."

Marg got into her carriage. Mrs. Bowne was right. She should have played poor-mouth. But one thing she learned. Mrs. Bowne herself was suffering. The old biddy's mouth was watering when she said one thousand Yankee cash. Marg had herself a good laugh. She'd tell Charles and he'd tell her how to match Mrs. Bowne's brains. Charles wasn't really a dummy. No-sir.

When Marg got home she was delighted to see a letter from the War Department. They had found Anthony. He had fallen with Schofield's forces at Franklin. He was in a hospital at Nashville. The complete address was given. Marg sat down immediately and wrote to her beloved brother. The Government's letter did not say the nature of his wounds. She was apprehensive. She wanted to catch a train and ride up to Nashville, but something she had learned from Mrs. Bowne: she had to be more stingy with money. A letter would do for now.

Charles drove out and looked over the Bowne property on Post Road at Buena Vista. There was a large weatherbeaten wooden building in a sandy forsaken lot. It had two floors and two separate stores. It was very brown, full of splinters, and huge. He had no idea of operating a building that large. There was actually room for three families in addition to stores. He mentioned this to Marg when he got home.

"Nowadays," she replied, "you cannot be certain what kind of people come rentin'. I'd rather keep the upper space as part of our business. Maybe we could give Larry a workshop there. He doesn't have enough room here to be cuttin' wood for furniture."

"Are you plannin' to support him in such a business?"

"No, Charles, we'll just give him a start. I think he's smart enough. He and Maggie Mae offered me rent for their room. I told 'em no, not until 'I get you on salary!' Ha-ha!"

Charles scratched his little pinkish pug nose. "Offer Mrs. Bowne $900, Marg. With the one hundred we spare we'll get a lathe an' some saws for Larry. Isn't that the way?"

"It sure is," laughed Marg, kissing her husband on his boyish lips.

Mrs. Bowne with smile took the nine hundred dollars cash for the property. Then she explained to him that the double store was not all her own. She only owned half of it. The left half belonged to another family, the Wesley Giles. Charles knew them. He'd ask Mr. Giles about the property. However, as it turned out, the Giles had gone off on an extended trip to Europe. They were not expected back before the spring of 1866. Charles couldn't wait that long. He'd go on with his business deal with Mrs. Bowne. He, Albert and Mitchell worked like zulus, nailing new boards, painting old boards. Happy because soon they'd open their own fruit, vegetable and flower shop.

Uptown on Broad Street the Federal Government built a beautiful structure called Freedmen's Bureau. The long white building quickly became the center of activity. Long lines would stretch from its tinroofed veranda, waiting for food rations. Some black troops from the North worked there. Right along with the whites! Doing the same jobs! This aggravated local people. The diehard pure whites of Maple would not be outdone by the military government using blacks this way. Mrs. Callie Jones had a meeting in the Presbyterian parsonage among twenty-four key people from the old government. No, they couldn't control city or county administrations just now, but they could control the hiring done in private businesses. So, all the banks, stores, the factories and offices in Maple would take a position: no Negroes except for cleaning jobs.

The seat of this underground government would be Harry Hannibal's newspaper, the *Maple Star-Journal*. Red-faced Harry was there at the meeting. He agreed his paper would publish no news about black people, unless they were criminals. There would be no news about the mulattoes either, for technically this meeting considered them black. The group felt confident it could restore the South, the integrity of pure whites. They called themselves the Maple Standing Committee. They'd be diligent and belligerent. They'd meet every two weeks, completely secret. They'd be the underground for the South. They'd die for white supremacy.

There was a scandal at one of the plantations near town. A fifteen-year-old girl was beaten with a whip because she talked surly to the mistress. Twenty young Negroes got together and left that place. Then on the road they were harassed by white men who took their money and their horse. The law enforcers would do nothing. The blacks had to walk on, hungry and empty of everything. More and more, whites were stealing from blacks. Whites who owned farms urged Negroes to stay there and work for them under *contract*. They said they'd protect them from bad white men. Yet, they'd only give the black one-fifth of all he'd make, or some, only one-twentieth. When blacks asked for oats they had cut, the white man said no, that he hadn't been free when the oats were planted.

Blacks were attacked on the roads by whites who kept asking who they belonged to, and when they said nobody they got a stick in their faces. Some dictated to blacks that they still had to say 'master' and 'mistress'. One Negro was shot in Maple for not giving up the road to a white man. But as the months grew, more Union soldiers returned to Maple. They lived amongst the well-to-do Negroes and befriended the poor ones. The Freedmen's school started in the black Baptist church in town was a success. Children and adults came for miles to attend. Other poor ex-slave children, in rags, had a delight every afternoon watching the retreat parades, with all the army fanfare of drumbeating and bugle blowing.

Dr. Lou Simpson and his wife went on vacation to Savannah, and wrote back an interesting letter to Marg and Charles. It read:

October 17, 1865
Our dear Friends, the Spences:

We certainly have been enjoying our stay in Savannah. Lilian has had me in church every Sunday! There are five huge black churches here. They are the center of activity in the Negro community. Beautiful buildings, seating one thousand people, each one. And with magnificent organs. I was surprised to see all this culture among brown people (just freed!) whereas in Maple it mostly exists with fairskinned people. The Negro in the South can truly be proud of what he has done outside of slavery.

We've made some very good friends among the darker people. Twenty of the city's black leaders met last January with General Sherman and Secretary of War Stanton. One of them, Rev. James Lynch, a northerner, stood alone in telling the commission that the colored man should be living interspersed with white people. The rest of the group followed Garrison Frazier saying blacks would prefer living by themselves. Washington listened to them and allowed self-governing black communities to be established in the islands off Georgia's coast. Today, seven months later, more than forty thousand ex-slaves live in such settlements in coastal lands from Charleston down to St. Johns River in Florida. While the talk of forty acres of land for each freedman was based on a firm promise from Sherman and Stanton, the U.S. Congress backed down. This was told to me by my friend, Rev. Ulysses Houston, one of the committee, an ex-slave, now written up in newspapers here as an example of the rising brain power of the new South. He's brilliant. I like him and his record. He was a nurse, a minister of God, established the Third African Baptist

Church and a settlement at Skidaway Island. Has also been a butcher, a cattle salesman. Learned to read from sailors. And is only forty years old. Was ordained by the white Baptist association. I've learned a lot from Houston, I hope I can apply it when I get back to Maple. The seafood here is delightful. See you soon.

Love,

Lilian and Lou.

The person who really enjoyed this letter was complacent Cousin Don, now white-haired but not too tired-looking from his singular struggles. Out at Cobb's Creek, his St. James Methodist, the mulattoes' church, had suffered. Too many of its congregants now had moved away. After hearing Dr. Lou's letter Cousin Don called his vestry together and it was decided to welcome those ex-slave blacks who wanted to come there. In a matter of weeks the church had more than one hundred new families. Many wanted to be remarried with the rites and ceremony of the church. Many wanted to send their children to Cousin Don's school which had heretofore only had lightskinned children in its classrooms. Marg encouraged her kin in his dilemma. She even went out daily to help with the teaching.

She secretly was having a time getting used to poverty and black faces. The three ladies living at her house were intelligent, but somewhat not quite dignified. None of their fathers had been white, or aristocrats. They could not talk about events like she, Valerie and Lilian talked. The North had given them determination and charm, but socially there was a rather vague listlessness. Marg didn't think they were religious enough. She could not see that vibrant knowing quality one finds in good southern people who love Jesus. Mainly, Marg didn't like the several brownskinned men knocking at her door, asking for these young ladies. Her strict rule, they could only be entertained for a half hour, in the parlor, and never more than one day a week.

The three female servants of Malcolm House, Celeste, Maggie Mae and Carol, took care of cute and very brown Jason. While Marg allowed him to call her 'Mama,' she felt guilty since so little of her time looked after his needs.

"Celeste," she called one December day, "do you miss yo' children? Do they ever write you from New Orleans?"

Fair Celeste tucked at her neat white hair. "No, ma'am. I figgers they're happy. Otherwise I'd hear a thing or two. You know, you bring 'em into the world to lose them. I did all I could for Effie and the boys. If I was younger, an' their father alive, I might venture to New Orleans. Hah!"

"You still could go! The railroad's back workin'. I'd give you the money."

"No, ma'am. Let 'em come to me, if they wants to see me. Likely this black-white business has confused my children. Poor things. Don't know who they is."

"When Jason's mama died, I agreed he'd stay here. But how can he grow up thinkin' I'm his mother, with white skin?"

"The truth is, Miss Margery, we're all brothers. John, Beth and Meg have white skin too, but their father and dis chile's father is the same man."

Marg didn't want to dispute it. She went back to her reading of the Thirteenth Amendment. She didn't like the wording of it. It seemed to say that involuntary servitude was still okay, as a punishment for a crime. And she knew from her own experience that the lawyers and justices determining crime were crooked men.

That Christmas week of 1865 Marg went to the post office several times. Once she found herself standing right next to Phyllis Korner. Their skirts were touching. She was certain Phyllis had seen her out of the corner of an eye. *Dear Phyllis, speak to me!* Marg pleaded under her breath. But neither woman spoke nor acknowledged that they were any more than strangers. Phyllis wanted to be pure white in Maple and it was paramount that she act the part completely and at all times. Marg left that place confused but also relieved. Her friend was alive and in good health. Phyllis still had the pink of youth in her cheeks, and the hands of an aristocrat.

That Christmas the Spences were delighted to receive a letter from Marg's brother, Anthony. He was still up in Nashville, claiming he was in fine physical shape, except for a few pieces of shrapnel and a damaged left arm. If he continued to heal he expected the hospital to let him go early in 1866, and he would come home for a short spell. He claimed he wouldn't go back to studying medicine, but he did want to live in the North, somewhere.

Marg quickly wrote a cheerful letter to her brother, telling him how much they missed him, and to keep praying to God. She then rushed to the post office in a chilling rain to post her letter. With umbrella raised she bumped into a man and quickly apologized. To her great astonishment, it was Lt. Waverly.

"Charles, what on earth are you doing here in Maple?"

Tall and elegant in his uniform, he replied, "Still fighting the war, Margery dear. We came back in late October."

"You've been here two months an' haven't said hello to us? Not a word!"

He blushed a bit and ran his hand through his long curly brown hair, now glistening from the rain. "Well, I thought about it, an' I inquired about you. I'm glad you're back in your nice house, and that your husband's back home."

"Oh-h, so that's it. Well, I'll assure you my Charles wouldn't bite you. He understands common courtesy. Besides, I've already told him you were my friend."

"Did you? Marg, I was really worried about that mess with Gus Wheatland. I'm sorry I couldn't be here to testify."

"I know, I know. Mrs. Bowne brought me yo' message. I was most grateful to have it. I'm sure it helped out in the end. I really don't know how I got out of that place alive—"

"You're looking wonderful. Can we stop for tea? I'm staying at the Ralston Hotel. They have a nice dining room—"

"Heavens, we never go in there! Thanks just the same."

"Oh, come on. This is Christmas! A year to the day. I told you I'd see you again."

"It was all Providence's work. You never would have come by to say hello. I'm disappointed in you, Lt. Waverly."

He kept smiling down into her comely face. "Come on have a tea. For Christmas' sake."

She stared back at him. The elaborate Ralston Hotel was just across the square. "Well, for five minutes," she replied warmly. "My family's waiting for me."

They sat there, in the big window, looking out at the rain. The glow of the room's comfortable fire showed in their eyes. She had told him all the important things about jail and about getting a family back together after such a catastrophe. He had told her about the terrible fighting he and his boys had experienced outside Macon. Marg was upset upon hearing that the young blond corporal, Sweeney, who had played her piano was now dead. She closed her eyes and could still hear his delicate Chopin. Charles went on telling about his duty in burnt-out Atlanta, and now back in Maple, repairing the bridges over the Chattahoochee.

"Have you seen yo' folks up in Ohio?"

"Oh, yes. I was home briefly at the armistice. My brother Bob was killed at Gettysburg."

"Oh, no! I'm really sorry to hear that. He was the religious one."

"That's right. You've got a good memory."

Marg caught Charles' hand across the table. "I remember something else from our discussion. When I was in jail, for a brief moment, like Bob, I decided to be my own God. I was ready to kill that man molesting me."

Charles looked right into the fire spot that glowed beautifully in her grey-blue eyes. "I suppose you were greatly hurt by that experience, knowing what you told me."

"What did I tell you?"

"That you would only know one man in your life, your husband."

"Well, Lt. Waverly, what do you want me to say now? That I am an unchaste woman?"

"No. But I was thinking. Did you and your Charles get back together again?"

"What do you mean?"

"You know. Together."

She slammed her fist on the table. "How can you dare say such things?" She got up to leave. He tried to help her with her stole, then stood there patiently while she got into her gloves. "I'm sorry, Marg," he said quietly. "I thought we could talk about it, friends as we are. And also I figured, as we've matured, maybe now there's room in your heart for me."

Looking down, she reached for her umbrella, and marched to the door. When he opened it for her, she looked him squarely in the eye. "Had you come to me like a gentleman, in late October, yo' very first day, maybe now I would believe you. I think you've got yo' priorities all mixed up, lieutenant."

She left him at the hotel's door. She almost ran back to her carriage, as the rain and wind tugged angrily at her skirts.

Chapter 24

Marg worried all the Christmas about her treatment of Lt. Waverly. She knew she should have invited him to the house for a homecooked meal, but her pride was too much with her. She made up for it by being very friendly to the servants. Celeste was very happy because she received a letter from her youngest son Joey in New Orleans. It read:

December 21,1865

Dear Mama,

Happy Christmas and all that. John and Effie send love and kisses too. I've been teaching out at Baton Rouge. Oh, I should tell you first, I came out of the army okay. I first enlisted in the Confederate army then switched to the Union side when they liberated New Orleans. I was at Brashear City and hitched a railroad ride down. I think I had a touch of yellow fever. Anyway, they took me upon learning I was colored. I had been learning French. I speak pretty good now. Effie and John speak it like a native. Well, the union people got me teaching school to the ex-slaves. I teach them both in English and French.

When Gen. Butler was here he treated the ex-slaves like "contraband", property of the enemy. Then he got tough on women walking the streets. The clergy got him out. Now the northerners are okay but the local whites are hostile. They shot at us up in Lafayette Parish for opening a school. They don't want blacks to have nothing. But eating is pretty good now. Plenty of sugar, corn and cotton. Negro people are saving their money to buy homes.

Effie has a beautiful Spanish mansion. I used to go there every weekend but now Claude (her husband) thinks otherwise. Since I identify with the colored, and teach with them, Claude fears it would cause him trouble in his banking business. So John and I stay away. We see Effie and her little boy, David, at church. She misses you. Wants to know if you kept Miss Wanda's jewel she sent you. Since it's Christmas we enclose some money in this envelope.

Love,

Joey.

Celeste was most delighted to have the fifty dollars from her children. She told Marg to get her some new dresses, but what she really wanted was a pair of glasses. She thought she could read again if she could see. Writing a reply would be a problem; she was almost too shaky for that.

As January 1866 started, Mitchell and Charles had their business going at a good clip. The first months had been hard because people in Maple simply had no money. They kept bringing by things to trade for food, and Marg let them have what they wanted, taking whatever trinkets they offered. As it turned out, the upstairs room over the store became like an antique shop, and customers came up there to see what interesting things they could buy or take home on barter. So Marg's upstairs store really got started on its own.

She let the boys operate their business downstairs and she and Larry took care of the upstairs mélange. He would repair chairs, tables, and clocks. She'd take over when they wanted to buy cuspidors, oil lamps or draperies. Her girls were making pretty curtains at home. Marg was quick to share the profits with them. Meanwhile, she became well-known in town for her unique specialty shop. Whenever she got items of silver or jewelry she'd call over Jeb Hunter. He was the white man from an indentured family who had been her only friend at the jailhouse. Now Jeb dropped by often to see her, and they had an arrangement whereby he'd secretly take silver things to the Korners' store to see if Phyllis and Frank wanted them. Now a lot of items in Korner's Jewelry, Photo, and Gift Store were straight from Marg's place, and neither Korner was any wiser. Marg gave Jeb twenty per cent on the sales, and he was happy doing friendly business for this wonderful woman, Margery Spence.

Haney in New York wrote her good news about her stocks, also enclosing some literature about stock futures. His footnote said he had heard from Anthony, who was coming to New York and wanted Haney to find him a flat. Marg wrote to her brother immediately, reminding him of his promise to come home. In two weeks' time there was a hollowed-cheeked, ivory-colored Anthony, looking much older, sitting before her, with his left arm in a sling, hiding the stump where his hand had been.

"My dear," cooed Marg, "I know you can't think of surgery or medicine now. You can't play the piano. But you certainly can go back to school and finish yo' degree. I'll support you. In fact, some of our New York money is yours anyway. Have you seen Mr. Haney? What do you plan to do in New York?"

Anthony sighed deeply. "I plan to go into business."

"In a big city like that? It takes loads of money, Anthony. Why don't you come home to us?"

"Because the type of business I'm interested in simply doesn't exist down here. I'm thinking of becoming an art connoisseur, an' have my own gallery."

Marg remembered now how he used to keep the walls of his room full of pretty pictures. "Well, that's nice but I was just thinking what Dad would say." She recalled how J.J. Audubon's famous birds were Anthony's treasures, this mainly being because their father, Judge Edward, had stressed to him that Audubon was a mulatto, although no history books would tell you that.

"Marg, the world has changed. Dad would not know this post-war world. We can't go on being bastard children of white aristocrats."

"That's a cruel way to put it. We are Americans. A good class of Americans. Don't talk us down the way the greedy new whites do it."

"Well, realism is moving us out of focus. I think our class will die out quickly. And I don't want to be an ex-slave with all their trappings. The new tan and brown community is surface deep. New York's classifications are less severe."

Her face had settled. "Think seriously now."

"Listen, I met some carpetbagger on the train, and when he learned I was colored he had an endless bunch of foolhardy plans for me. His stupid schemes for making money. I said 'no, I have my own life to lead'. And they think they're more intelligent than you are! Hah! I could never again fit into this southern atmosphere."

"It's yo' home, Anthony"

"America needs people to break out of this caste system, Margery. I'm a pioneer just like Paul."

Now she sat up straight. "Let me tell you about yo' brother. We had to contact him in California because of my court case on Edgewater. Well, I got back this fancy vellum letter from his lawyer. It seems Paul is well-off now, in real estate speculation. His lawyer wanted to pick to pieces what Cahill and I have set up as our share. I said 'no, I won't have it'. I finally got his signature on the papers. The case comes up next week. I think Paul is on his way here. But I hope he doesn't arrive in time. Remember, in youth he was never able to share anything."

Anthony smiled, looking like his father. "We once had the same girl. Is he married now?"

"Oh, yes, to some white girl named Daisy. He let me know that they wouldn't be staying with me, that they'd take a white hotel."

As quite a few people in town were whispering about Marg's court case against the Malcolm family, the gossip blew sky high when a private Pullman railroad car was docked down at the Central of Georgia railroad station. Paul Malcolm had come home in grand style. The poor whites were the first to discover the handsome and plush private car. Paul had hired two of the poor whites to guard it all the time. And Daisy, the wife of the mulatto, looked like a full-fledged white woman. A northern white woman. Paul brought her to the house that first day. She wore frilly fur and a sneer. She and Marg immediately disliked each other. They were certainly a different class. Marg called her a hungry tramp putting on airs.

Luckily now all the family were together for the first time since her mother's death—Anthony, Paul and Gregory. They went out to the white cemetery and put a large bouquet of Mitchell's flowers on their father's grave. Then they went to the colored cemetery and did the same for their dear mother. They had one big meal together at Margery's house but that was all. Paul had promised to sit quietly at Marg's trial. And luckily, maybe because of him, she won her case. These four would by terms of the recently-disclosed will share in the fortunes of the late Judge Edward Malcolm. It was big news, but not a word of it appeared in the two local newspapers.

Harry Hannibal of *Maple Star-Journal* was leading the way and sticking by his promise to Callie Jones. There'd be no news whatever printed about niggers and mulattoes, especially when they were successful in some business deal. Red-faced Harry did have type all set for another story: BLACK WOMAN LOSES IN CONTESTING MALCOLM WILL. His wife frowned at the headline. She really couldn't see how he could refer to fair Margery as a black woman.

"This is what we're fightin' for," stormed Harry destroying the type. "We've gotta make 'em black enough to stay black. The written word, honey, can be as powerful as slavery."

On the fifth and final day of Paul's visit Marg was invited down to his private Pullman car for a Valentine's Day luncheon. Everything inside was red and gold velvet. Daisy tripped through the plushness like a princess. She had curled her brownish hair in "nigger curls" and tried to look southern in a gingham dress. Marg and Anthony sat across from them while a black man served filet mignon. They drank their champagne without a toast. Marg spied two good-looking blond children in a photograph and assumed it was their children. Daisy saw her looking and volunteered their names: Kathy and Harvey. Marg asked their ages and tried to remember the details, to write in her father's big Bible, the one he kept for the colored family. There was another one out at Edgewater for the white Malcolms. Marg felt this was where Daisy wanted her family recorded.

At court, only Jack and Edward had come. All the slew of Malcolm women didn't show. They claimed the reason was that Mr. Tom had just died. Marg got this from her lawyer. There was no need to walk across the room to offer any condolences to Jack or Edward. They'd understand her behavior. It was the Malcolm way.

When Marg and Bill Cahill went out to Edgewater Plantation to survey the 300 acres they had won, they were to learn that the rest of the huge estate had been sold to a Worth family from Jackson, Mississippi. They would cut it up into small sharecropper plots, selling to blacks or whites. Unfortunately most of the blacks who had loved Edgewater, and had worked so hard for its success over the years, they couldn't afford the $300 the Worths were asking for the plots. The mansion house, still in disrepair from the war, was to be torn down.

"I'd love to buy it and restore it as a fancy hotel," Marg told Bill Cahill as they rode by in her surrey.

"You could but it would take a heap of people to fill it up. Maybe you could discover hereabout some mineral springs like at Warm Springs or Ashville. Or, maybe you could have the army officers here from Camp Edwards—"

Marg didn't like the tone of his voice. There was a teasing quality about it, as if he knew of Lt. Charles Waverly.

Anthony actually left with his brother Paul. The fancy Pullman car would go first to Washington, D.C. before heading west. It never had come from California, only from St. Louis. Paul wanted people to think grand things of him. Anthony wanted Paul to come up to New York to meet Tom Haney but Paul disdainfully declined, claiming he knew as much about high finance, stocks and bonds, as any of his brother's white friends. So they parted in Washington, and neither one would see Louise, Lydia Smith, or President Johnson.

Hearing the news about the private railroad car, Jessica Bowne summoned Marg to lunch out at Claremont. It was the first official invitation she had received since the war. A cozy little round table had been prepared with glowing white linen and dishes, set out on the side terrace, where they could catch the fragrant breath of lilacs and other spring blooms.

"What a pity I didn't meet yo' brother," sighed Jessica as distant hens cackled. "You Malcolms soon will be the only ones left in town. Did you know, the white Malcolms are moving to Atlanta?"

"Really? Miss Wanda and Jack too?"

"All of them. They're building a big house there on the road leading to East Point. I hear it's lovely."

"Well, with Edgewater gone, and the slaves, I did think they'd move back in town. But the house is still a hospital."

"They'll keep it so, says Miss Wanda, but I doubt they'll ever come back. Yo' stay in jail had something to do with that decision, and yo' taking them to court."

"You flatter me," smiled Marg dreamily. "I certainly didn't make any dent in their fortune. I'm sure the million my father left them has been well-invested."

"Yes, in railroads and power plants. That's one reason they're going to Atlanta. Both Edward and Jack will have corporation board jobs. Aren't you proud of yo' kin?"

Marg laughed out. "Three years ago you would never have acknowledged that they were my real kin. Jessica, you believe in that southern twist of the truth, I know!"

The white woman hit Marg playfully on the sleeve. "How dare you call me Jessica! Margery, my dear, there's something I want you to do for me. It's a business matter so don't say no too quickly."

"What is it, Mrs. Bowne?"

"I don't mind Jessica, from you. Try it again."

"Yes, Jessica?"

"Fine! Well, I have this housekeeper. Ida Winston. She's helped me tremendously, you know, with all the war damages. The house finally is looking like a house again. Since we don't entertain much, I told Lance we could let her go. She's interested in business. A black woman. You could help her, Marg. Let her learn all she can out at yo' shop. That's precisely the kind of business she wants to operate eventually."

"Well, I suppose I could use an extra hand, provided you're giving me a good worker—"

"Oh, she's excellent. But, mind you, she's got a mind of her own. Hah! But that's no harm in this new age for black people. Now, she's to spend four hours a day workin' at yo' place, an' I'll pick up the tab."

"Jessica, absolutely no. You don't pay her."

"I said this was a business deal. Wait till you meet Ida." Jessica went to the door of the house and called inside. Soon there was a black arm pushing on the screen door. Marg looked that way with a horrified expression on her face.

"Matilda! What on earth are you doin' here?"

"This is Ida," said Jessica, making the introduction. "Do you know this girl?"

"This is my Matilda," cried Marg, reaching up to hug a plump, smiling, still fat-faced dark-brown Matilda. "Angel, how good to see you again! Do you really want to come and work with me?"

"I told Miz Bowne I'd sho like to try my hand at business. As a free person, if'n I don't like it I can walk away."

Same old Matilda, telling her mind. "Of course, angel," said Marg, making room so that Matilda could sit with her on the white iron settee next to the refreshment table.

"Ida will still live here," explained Jessica, still standing. "She's not my slave but she still belongs to me, so no funny business, Marg. When she's trained she comes back to me. I have several good plans in mind."

Mrs. Bowne wouldn't be explicit. And Marg, feeling charitable, didn't press. The fountain out on the green rippled with its silvery rain as Marg held that leathery hand. In her heart she felt wonderful to see Matilda once again, and to have another try at making amends. Now they were breathing the same perfumed air, but she did feel she owed Matilda something. They never should have parted as they did, almost as enemies.

Chapter 25

Poor Cousin Don. He had trouble with his new black members. He had wanted to love them so much, but they never accepted him. He was a white man in appearance and in spirit. They wanted a black man to lead them. A gospel type of preacher. They wanted to sing spirituals. They wanted to shout. Cousin Don had always operated a quiet dignified church. Well, when he finally decided to give it all up, to retire, he offered to help the trustees find the right type of minister. He suggested guest speakers and made a list. They wrote and invited preachers from all over Georgia. This was the democratic way. Some even came from Alabama, all that spring. Then in June they decided on Ulysses Houston from Savannah. He was the one mentioned in Dr. Lou Simpson's letter. An important trailblazing man in Georgia. St. James would be honored to get him. But Houston told them he wasn't coming to stay, that he'd still keep his Baptist church over in Savannah.

While Lou and Lilian were strongly pushing for the church to accept Houston, the membership was ready to split over the incident. They were Methodists; how could they take a Baptist preacher? Dr. Lou got up in the pulpit to explain it all; he was of the same race, the same protestantism, the same God. Parishioners with their religious experience still felt otherwise. So, after an exchange of letters, it was agreed that if Rev. Houston kept the title "guest speaker" and would come for a limited stay of three to six months, it would be all right.

Maple whites heard about the controversy and tried to get into the middle of it, but the hierarchies of the colored churches had completely separated themselves from the white folks. The whites never had wanted them in their churches or cemeteries, and now the black Baptists and the black Methodists had their own conclaves. If this strange St. James Church decided it wanted to take a Baptist preacher into a Methodist pulpit they could get away with it. It was their world.

So, on that last Sunday Cousin Don came to his church wearing a new grey suit Gregory had made him, along with his quiet, carefully-dressed wife, Amelia, and their three grown white-faced children. He introduced Rev. Houston, telling of his brilliant record in Savannah and of his commendable work with the Federal Government, to bring the good Christian life to so many. The church was packed, and the choir in their new robes (also made by Gregory) sang beautifully. Finally, at the end of it all, Cousin Don got up, blinked his tearful eyes and tried to compose himself to make his farewell speech.

The rumor was that the blacks had taken over his church, but as he stood on his rostrum for the last time he saw a nice American balance—his congregation had about twenty per cent Anglo-Saxon faces, with white color and light hair; equally, twenty per cent were black African types with rich color and strong noble features. The most of them were neither extreme, just a mixture of young and old, yellow, tan, and brown faces, some attractive, others less so, but all looking eagerly and pleasantly at him, expecting something from Jesus's world. Most of all he remembered that *these were all the enemies of America*. Yet, without them America could never have been rich and endless as it was.

He looked about, adjusted his glasses, then with relaxed hands resting on his open Bible he began saying:

"I've been coming here since this was a lonely patch of pine trees. I'm speaking figuratively. Actually where this church was built, up on the knoll, there were maple trees. But who in America is precise in naming things? Well, I want to be precise about one word. I am a Christian. God sent me to do what I've done. We together have built this little chapel, and the school next door, in a spirit of love. We have heard in the 15th Psalm of David that those of us who dwell in this tabernacle dwell as one, with no malice to our neighbor. We must consider that God has blessed us all these years. We have had luxuries in spite of war. We have already had all the promises made to Abraham. If we have abused the power and the prosperity, then God's second coming means He will take the rule away from man. So, the keepers of the laws of human government, beware. You have brought war and pestilence upon yourselves. All the suffering poor and wretched, all the solemn young men in uniform who did their duty and died, God allowed them to serve you and God took them away.

"Peace has not yet come to America. It may take decades to settle and calm the pushing, shoving, the hating by color, the unChristian suspicion, judgment and punishments. Peace will only be here when one man does not see himself superior because he is white. The wisdom America needs is an understanding of the joining which has already occurred. We are one people by spirit and by blood. No power-hungry separatists can change the fruit of America having blossomed from diverse seeds—the little children—a strong permanent fruit, a creation of God.

"He has also given you the privilege of darkness which commands you to see with special vision. You have, my children, a duty to fear the Lord, to walk upright, to speaketh the truth and not backbiteth; a duty not to take reward against the innocent. Through the privilege of darkness your sight will allow you to lead them out of the money tunnels, on beyond their cruel weaknesses of classifications, words, vanity and false vanity, on into the light of Christ, the salvation of the world."

He took his seat shivering a bit. Marg's soft, aristocratic fingers reached out and patted his shoulder. With her approval he knew that it had gone well. He trusted her judgment, and respected the fact that she had suffered like Christ.

***** ***** *****

From Christmas to June Marg had been going weekly to the post office, sending letters and packages to her beloved children up North, and also to her dear brother Anthony in New York. Each time she looked around hoping to see a friend. Each time she wore her very best gowns, and took the shiniest carriage of the five she now owned. One morning by surprise she saw her old red wagon right out in front; that wagon which had been stolen from her that ill-fated Christmas morn. She decided to wait and see who its driver would be. As she waited, Lt. Waverly, in dress uniform, came out of the hotel, walked directly across the square, headed her way! She kept her eyes on him; he didn't look up. Trembling, she started to avoid him by going inside. What she did was get into her buggy, and turn the horse direct in his path.

"Hey, you tryin' to run me down!" he called cheerfully. She wasn't sure he knew that it was she. He probably flirted terribly with young pretty girls. But she was no longer young. Still, she tried to smile as if she were.

"Lt. Waverly, you should watch where you're going!"

"No more lieutenant. I'm Captain Waverly now. Hi, Marg! How are you?" He jumped up and sat next to her, taking the reins.

"Where're you thinkin' of going?" she asked sharply, as the horse moved off.

"I'm taking you home. Isn't it a beautiful day? Nothing like the rain we had the last time."

"I want to forget that day," she told him. "I treated you terribly. Did you have a nice Christmas?"

"Of course. I went home to my dear old Mom, to celebrate my promotion!"

"You mean you had it then?"

"Sure." He looked at her with handsome squinting eyes. "I wanted to tell you that day, but you were mighty hufty!"

"Well, I had reason," she blushed. "You know, you've upset my plan. I just saw my stolen wagon. I was waiting to see who has claimed it."

"Aw, let the crooks be," he frowned. "They're a dime a dozen here."

"Where *are* you taking me? Home?"

"Why don't we go for a ride? It's such a beautiful day."

"You've said that before. Do you know the way to Post Road and Buena Vista? I'll show you my business."

"Great! I'll bet you're doin' wonderfully well out there now that Edgeworth has caught on."

Edgeworth was a brand-new post-war town. It started when the Worth family began selling off Edgewater in eight-acre plots to share-croppers. Now more than one thousand people had built small homes in groups near their land. To the surprise of Maple town-fathers these suburbanites were liberally mixed, with blacks and whites next to each other, like on a checkerboard. However, the little business communities did take on racial lines. Wentworth Village became the white center on the north side, and Blackworth on the south became the Negro ghetto-town with its grocery store, owned by Dr. Bowman, Mel Young's blacksmith shop, and a barbershop and pool parlor which Lou Simpson had an interest in. Marg's business luckily was not in this quarter. She was up around the well-to-do people in Wentworth. The whole of the farming areas were referred to as the town of Edgeworth, and it was the people here, both black and white, who had the money to buy what Charles, Mitchell and Marg were offering.

"Well, here it is," she called cheerfully as they parked among some twenty wagons.

"My goodness," he exclaimed helping her down. "Somebody here is getting rich."

"Does that make me less desirable?" she asked coyly.

"It depends. Are you going to introduce me to your husband?"

"If he's here," she continued, still lightheartedly.

Charles was in his white apron whacking at a big bunch of yellow grapes hanging over his head.

"Charles, honey, I want you to meet Captain Waverly. We ran into each other at the post office. Do you remember my speaking of him?"

"Of course," said Charles, smiling through his little reddish moustache and offering his hand to the army captain. "I remember your calling him Lt. Waverly. Well, captain, it's good to know that the army is taking proper care of its good men. Marg told me you're an engineer. Are you still on the Chattahoochee? With our bridges?"

"Still at it," smiled Charles Waverly, amazed that Spence knew so much about him. "But it's winding up now."

"Does that mean you're leaving us?" asked Marg with astonishment.

"Oh, by the end of summer. We can't stay here forever. There's plenty of work for us all over the South."

"I gather then," said Charles, "that you plan to stay in service, as a career?"

"Oh, perhaps just a little longer. I haven't really thought about it. You seem to have a good business here. How do you do it?"

"Lucky, I guess," laughed Charles, offering his guest some grapes. Captain Waverly took a few, offering Marg some, but she walked away.

"Come, I want to show you *my* business." She led him to a narrow closed staircase. She went up first and he followed, resting his hand on her haunches. She paid him no mind. Upstairs, she shook her skirts and looked him in the eye. "Maybe you also remember Matilda at our house?"

"Oh, Matilda!" screamed Charles Waverly, rushing to hug the black woman.

"She now calls herself Ida," said Marg, tartly. "She's learnin' my business an' doing wonderful at it."

"It's sho good to see you again, lieutenant," called Matilda. "An' I don't mind if'n you call me by my old name. Now I'm free I got a new name, an' a new mind. For makin' money! Ha-ha-a!"

Marg now was giving orders to Larry who was sawing wood in a far corner of the big raw room. He was making her two more counters. She introduced him to Captain Waverly, and Larry stood at attention, in respect of the uniform.

Then Matilda took Waverly away to show him shelves of dishes, pots, lamps. In a corner was a cot loaded down with drapery material.

Over it, he was most impressed seeing Army surplus barbed wire, rope and fencing. "Somebody knew how to deal properly to get this stuff," he told Matilda.

"Oh, it was easy," snapped Marg, walking up. "With enough Yankee dollars you can buy anything!"

"I'm very impressed," he told her frankly.

"I'm glad," she said, satisfied. "Now I've got to get busy sharpening some spades I've promised for five o'clock. Larry'll drive you back. Do come again, captain!" Just as she was shaking his hand a stout and reddish Mitchell came in with an exuberant brown child.

"This is my son, Jason," Marg told Waverly. "And my cousin Mitchell."

Captain Waverly spoke to both, taking particular notice of the child. "Your son?"

"My . . . my husband's. Oh, by the way, Captain Waverly, if you're free Sunday, how about coming to dinner? It's homecoming for my three children in northern schools." Graciously he accepted.

John, Beth and Meg arrived by train on Thursday, all looking wonderful and more grown-up. None had changed too much, except John who was taller, with hair now a chamois yellow, less blond. His voice had a frog in it which meant he was becoming a man. Beth's darker hair framed a beautiful face. Marg was proud of her young lady of thirteen whose manners were excellent. Poor Meg was a bit nervous; school marms had scolded her about so many habits, she was inclined to be shy and clumsy. All three got kisses from their mother, and Charles was overjoyed as well.

At seven a.m. that Sunday Marg greeted her mirror, pleased to see sparkling eyes and glowing complexion. She'd have thirteen for dinner, her biggest sitting since the war. She had invited the new pastor of St. James, Rev. Houston and his wife, her first brownskinned couple. She had wanted Cousin Don and his wife to balance the table but they already had an engagement, with the new schoolmaster. Both Gregory and Lou Simpson couldn't come. They'd be out chasing politicians. Houston had strongly urged Gregory to try out for the state legislature. Gregory was getting himself ready for the November elections.

"Jeeter's now working in the city," exclaimed Cousin Sue, looking overweight yet handsomely dressed, arriving with her two kids. "At the Freedmen's Bureau. We're makin' good northern money, Marg."

"It's the only money now," Marg told her. "Forget the Confederacy. It's dead!"

Houston laughed, politely holding on to his little brown wife, Essie. "The lady speaks the truth. We're now a part of America. Mrs. Spence, this is simply an adorable home! Lovely!"

"Thank you, Rev. Houston. As to its history, my father and his father built it, after he finished law up in Massachusetts. He lived here as a judge almost thirty years."

Houston smiled over his claret. "A white man, I presume. You know, we have lots livin' like this in Savannah, also in Atlanta, New Orleans, Washington and Charleston. And it's a pity, without equal political influence!"

"I'm readin' all about our new leaders," Marg told him. "Francis Cardozo, Alonzo Ransier, Henry Hayne, Pinchback, Emmanuel Fortune—"

"Those are all Near-whites," Houston replied. "We black men have leaders too."

"We're all the same!" shouted Marg, wanting to believe it.

"Not really, Mrs. Spence. Men like Richard Cain, Jonathan Gibbs, Robert Elliott, Mifflin Gibbs, they all had it much harder. As black men and ex-slaves. Do you realize that this time two years ago I was a slave? Don't you wonder how I learned to talk, to write, to wear clothes?"

Marg was embarrassed. She was certain this wise man knew that she herself had had slaves. "Rev. Houston, how can we do more to help the black men in our midst?"

"Forget that you're white," he clipped, following his smiling wife into the dining room.

Captain Waverly was already there with Marg's three handsome children, Cousin Sue, Jeeter, their two, Jason. The only person missing was Charles and they'd go on without him. Marg asked Rev. Houston, seated at the head of the table, to say the blessing.

In his rich preacher voice he said: "We beseech Thee, Oh Lord, to rule the hearts of those who bear the authority of government in this and every land, that they may be led to wise decisions and right actions for the welfare and peace of the world. Amen."

Essie Houston said "amen" after her husband. Meg snickered into her napkin, and Marg gave both girls a hard look. "Are you enjoying your stay in Maple?" she asked the Houstons.

"It's a magnificent small city," the reverend replied. "I had heard so much about it, that's why I accepted the pulpit. We wanted to see for ourselves if the streets were paved of gold."

"Oh, you flatter us," cried Marg. "We're poor! We've always been poor!"

"In comparison, Mrs. Spence, Maple is a seat of prosperity. In many areas Federal agents act like slave brokers, sending the black man in as cheap labor, back to the same ole plantation bosses. Washington now is takin' local rednecks as its civil agents."

"Really?" gasped Waverly. He'd speak as a white man. "I know there are abuses on plantations, this business of selling provisions on account. It's wicked and the ex-slaves don't always know they're being cheated."

"Let's talk about something cheerful," cried Marg, raising her crystal wine glass to say a toast. Just then Charles came in. Being reasonably well-dressed, he seated himself at the foot of the table. He gave a toast to the ladies, then to the guests from Savannah and finally to Captain Waverly. Charles Waverly in turn toasted his host and hostess. The Houstons ate in silence, remembering that Marg didn't want to discuss race or politics. Soon Charles felt it was too quiet and opened up a subject himself.

"Jeeter," he said with a smile, "why don't you tell everybody about yo' good luck."

"You mean my job?" asked Jeeter, drawlingly, touching his curly brown hair.

"Yes, son. Tell them that you're the only colored local employed there."

"They've got two others," explained Jeeter, "but they're from the North."

"I helped him get hired," said Charles, proudly. "We now have locally a Civil and Political Rights Association. Our goal is to get rid of the Freedmen's Bureau's incompetent chief, a racist West Virginian ex-colonel."

"That's a common complaint," Waverly put in. Then he turned to Houston. "We hear Maj. Gen. Saxton over on the coast is having troubles because white planters are coming back to lands already given over to colored. The colored groups complain right to Washington—"

"They have to," stormed Houston. "With game-playing local generals treatin' the black man with contempt. Now our Tunis G. Campbell, he's a northern black who came South to help organize our schools. Excellent, but he had to petition Washington to get even a pencil. You see, the transfer of feelings here has passed over from slaveowner to northern petty chiefs. Anybody in charge of the Negro will abuse him. I think only Christianity will solve the problems."

"Up in New Jersey," said John in fine voice, "I went to the Episcopal church with a brownskinned boy and they threw us out, wouldn't let us sit in a pew."

"We have a lot of good men on these problems," said Waverly defensively, "But perhaps not enough for the whole country."

"Captain Waverly," called Rev. Houston, "what are your own feelings? Do you think the black man should live in separate quarters? To seek his freedom away from white men?"

Waverly turned a bit red. "Well, I've been giving some thought to this. I think it will take a long time—"

"How long, Captain?"

"Oh, maybe fifty years. That's just a guess. The generation after the next one should not know the problems."

"Mrs. Spence's son has just told you what he's experienced, an' he's blonder than you are. Admit it's a solid and lasting caste system, Captain."

Just then the three colored lady-schoolteachers came into the house, laughing and chattering, not knowing of Marg's dinner party. "Thank goodness, we can leave this subject," said Marg standing up to invite them in. "Gentlemen, I forbid you to talk of this any longer! Some intelligent and handsome ladies will join us, and my Cousin Sue will play us some beautiful music. I have rum-raisin cake for dessert, or would you like more wine?"

"I'm all for a party," called Waverly, raising his glass as the three comely ladies walked in. Sue and Jeeter went to the piano in the next room while the children excused themselves from the table. Marg noticed particularly that her husband was grinning only at that Chicago wench, Josie Timms. Marg went over and encouraged Waverly to go outside with her children, to see the new croquet set Charles had bought them. Waverly left while Marg sat back down to watch Charles' behavior among the black people. The girls, she knew, would soon be talking about food and dancing. Already the preacher man's eyes were popping too. If she could keep his wife well-fed, she was sure there'd be no more political talk.

Chapter 26

Marg was satisfied with her dinner party. Captain Waverly had gotten on famously with her children. Somehow, Sue as well liked him very much. To everyone's surprise, he sat at Marg's piano and picked out "Dixie". Then they all sang a few war tunes. Next, John sat down at the keyboard. Up North he had learned to play classics quite well. His Bach was strong and beautiful, and he played Chopin with as much nuance as his former teacher. She was most impressed. His parents, looking amazed, didn't know what to say. It made Marg proud and comfortable all evening.

Charles and Waverly sat drinking brandy, and smoking cigars. Jeeter and Larry (the ex-slave) compared notes on furniture-building. The party didn't break up until eleven p.m. Marg happily said goodnight, apologizing to a still-rigid Rev. Houston for stopping the political talk. He understood. He had met women like Marg before. He knew that she was richer than the white man, and that Captain Waverly had a little special feeling inside, for her.

The next morning, bright and early, Jeb Hunter came by to borrow a few dollars from Marg. She didn't mind lending to him. He now had a job weighing cotton. This too was a white man's job. He had seen too many blacks beaten up at the jailhouse. This new work was better but he stayed broke at it. He came with his cute daughter, Cindy, and it was obvious that she needed some clothes. They were whites who wouldn't feel outdone by taking hand-me-downs from the near-whites.

Marg went upstairs and made a big bundle to give him. Meanwhile, John and Cindy sat in the kitchen, talking about school. She knew he was up North at a rich man's private school. She'd tell her poor white friends about it. She wanted to tell John about the niggers they had forced in her class, but she knew it wasn't a fittin' subject. Then she told about the Edgeworth farm her father had just bought. She had been a town girl all her life. She didn't know if she'd like the country. John told her it was getting to be about the same. She could hitch a ride into town, any time. Cindy with big brown eyes asked if he would come out and visit. Of course, she was teasing, because the caste system wouldn't even let poor whites be too friendly with rich niggers. These blue-eyed ones could be anything they wanted to be! Like magic, or people on a stage. She sometimes wished she were a fairskinned colored person, with lots of money.

"I have to hire some more servants," Marg told Matilda several weeks later, as they worked together in the shop. "With Larry here with us, there's no man at home. I need a gardener, a coachman and a cook. Celeste is too old to do much. She keeps tryin', an' I guess that's what keeps her alive."

Matilda was smiling her little impudent smile. "She's too proud an' prissy to do much, Miss Margery. If'n you want me to find you some good black people, I have to know how much you're gonna pay."

"Oh-h, you won't hang me up on that one! It depends on their references an' their work. These are tough times, Matilda—"

"Ida is my name!"

"All right, Ida. I was readin' the other day that lots of black people don't want to work with their hands any more. They all want to be preachers or schoolteachers, or just dandies. An' some are even gettin' fancy, thinkin' speakin' French is more important than speakin' English. Freedom has gone to their heads."

"Not everybody, Miss Margery. You know dere's lots gettin' abused a'plenty. Out here a'piece, one man's holdin' wives and chillun, jis to get mo' contract work from the cullud man. Like slavery times! Well, I got me a shotgun, an' I'll use if'n I have to."

"Mercy! Don't bring it around here. Oh, where are the white lady's chairs? With the green velvet cushions? She'll be here any minute now. If I'm downstairs get four dollars from her. No promises to pay. If she doesn't have greenbacks, tell her we must hold the chairs."

Matilda laughed. "You're a hard business woman, Miss Margery. Ha-ha-a! Dat material didn't cost us but fifty cents. Remember!"

"Ida, we lose on some things. We have to make it up on others. Oh, I'm so happy to have you workin' with me again! When you left me in the middle of those hard days I could have died. Why did you do it? Had you been fightin' with Elias?"

"No. Elias never gave me no trouble. I jis knew you'd have trouble with those Yankees in yo' house. Sooner or later, it had to happen. An' Big Jim died to save you."

"Why do you say that?"

"'Cause it's true. He died to save you, like Humphrey died to save you."

"Oh-h, Matilda. Ida! How can you keep such thoughts in yo' system? Don't you love me, baby? Haven't I been right by you?"

Matilda's lips were firm. "I worked many years with no pay."

"So did all the . . . Matilda, how much money is it that you want me to give you? Not that I approve of this kind of talk. I think you've got some nonsense in yo' mind that I owe you somethin'. Every now and then it comes up. All right. I'm givin' you the chance to name yo' price. An' after that, young lady, I don't want to heah any more talk like this. You upset me terribly."

Still wearing her smile, Matilda went off to her little corner where she polished silver. Marg picked up her skirts and started downstairs without another word. She banged the screen door going out back, to the tomato patch. She had to balance the ledgers, but she just needed some air. The sun was hot but the wind was blowing. The brownish air felt soothing. Dust made the tears sting as they hit her cheek. Feeling them evaporate, she asked God what she could do to keep on an even keel with people. She knew she could never satisfy Matilda. The dollars would never be enough. Actually, Mrs. Bowne had the right idea: train Matilda to think and to appreciate. If she were in her own business, and it were going well, she wouldn't act so villainous. Marg was willing to give some money to Mrs. Bowne, but she didn't want to give it directly to Matilda. Ida.

"Hello! How are the tomatoes?"

"Oh, Charles! Captain Waverly! You startled me. Did you come here on foot?"

"That's right. I was over visiting with Jeeter and Sue an' they told me you were only four miles down the road. It's my free afternoon so I walked over."

"I'm glad you did," she said, catching his hand. "I've just had a fight with Matilda. She's tryin' to blackmail me. Wants money for the time when she was a slave."

"Why don't you give it to her?"

"Because there would be no end to it. She thinks I was responsible for her brother-in-law Humphrey's death . . . and the death of Big Jim at the jail."

He put his arm around her shoulder. "That was cruel, wasn't it? Come, shall we walk a bit?"

"How late is it? I have to get back to my journals."

"Aw, a moment for a nice leisurely stroll will do you good."

"You should be tired after comin' all the way from Sue's."

"I have on good shoes. An' in good company. I'm enthusiastic. An' I'm young, angel. Real young!"

She ignored his teasing conceit. They just walked along swinging hands. She listened to the mockingbirds in a pillow of shade trees. Their song was beautiful.

"Margery dear, what you should realize about Matilda is that she thinks you're an easy touch. Now, if you refuse her money, what harm can she do?"

"Today she told me she has a shotgun."

"Do you think she'll shoot you?"

Marg laughed. "Some do it. The wounds from slavery can be very deep. I know she's not afraid of me, an' she doesn't respect me any more—"

"Why is that? Could it be me?"

"Hah! What does she know about you? Nothing. Simply nothing."

"But she may be imagining, huh?"

"No. I don't believe she's that wicked. It could be my Charles. When he an' Laurie had their baby, maybe that's when it happened. On the other hand, I know mankind is fickle. When you're on top, they envy you. They even like you. When you skid, they hate you for skidding."

"When did you ever skid?"

"Well, Charles, not to be shocking, but let me speak plainly. If a woman allows herself to be abused . . . you know what I mean? . . . well, if she does, they lose respect for her because she's broken the code, the ideal."

He squinted as the sun's burst of daggers edged a black cloud. "Marg, you shouldn't be afraid of anyone in this town. That ideal woman was not the instigator of trouble. Society can't blame you for what unpleasantry happened without your sanction. Marg, let's sit here on the grass. Now listen, dear, I think the trouble is you and Charles. You would not feel so insecure if he loved you."

"Oh-h, Charles, my husband loves me!"

"He runs around. You know it. He's been doing it for years."

For a while she just sat there, unperturbed, fingering the tall dry glassblades. "Are you perfect, Captain Waverly?"

"No, but I'd darn try to be, if I had a lovely person like you in my life. Marg, it still could happen." He leaned over, letting his shoulders shadow her own.

"No Charles," she said, pushing him away. "I don't seek any new happiness. My children gave me so much joy when I saw them—"

"And Jason? Every day. Doesn't he remind you of your husband's sins?"

"No. The poor thing needs me. We're beginning to love each other very much. Charles, when you leave here I hope you find a nice girl. One who will appreciate your sensitivities, an' make you a good wife."

He reached to hold her hand. And a big drop of rain plopped on his wrist, then on her wrist. They were noisy big drops. He stood up smiling. "I appreciate your good wishes. Come on! *Hurray, Hurray, Hurray for Jubilee!*" He sang in a beautiful tenor voice.

"You sing so nicely, Charles."

"It's a catchy tune. Hey, it's really raining! Shall we run?"

Just as they started running, the rain came pouring down. They were in a sloping meadow without a stitch of shelter. It got very dark, then lightning flashed across an opaque sky. A cool breeze ran with them to a soaking tree. When they realized they too were soaked, they just ran on, laughing a bit. Cold water hugged their clothing, trickling inside like glue. Soon they were back at the black-earth tomato patch. Soggy shoes moved towards the parking lot which was now empty. Not one wagon at the store. Oh, yes, one was there. Her buggy. She rushed to take her gelding up on the porch. Charles gave a hand. The vegetable store was deserted. Not a soul was around. It was after four. Mitchell had closed up early. She'd take Captain Waverly upstairs to her pine-smelling shop. Big globs of rain water trailed the stairs as they walked up.

"Oh, it's running all down me!" she screamed. Finding an oil lamp, she lit it and began taking off wet things. When Charles did the same, she realized she had to go to her small office up front. He followed, and she did not stop him. Still panting, they sank down, leaning against the dry cot of draperies. Together.

Flashes of lightning stabbed angrily at the darkened room as rain falling on the tin roof made its considerable racket. Once again Charles started singing the Jubilee song, "Marching Through Georgia". When he finished he reached a wet sleeve across her breast and kissed her on the lips. She said nothing the first time. Then when he did it again, she quietly said: "I'm a married woman, Captain."

"It matters not," was his confident reply. And he kissed her again.

"I'm a colored woman, Captain."

"Oh, for gosh sakes! That's nonsense! Marg, perk up. I love you, angel."

It was as if they were waiting for daylight to come again, but as the thunder snarled and the rain calmed down to a steady pitter-patter, darkness took over. She lit a kerosene stove and asked him if he wanted something to eat. Charles just sat there with spongy face, kneading the pile of dry draperies. He crossed his legs, completely relaxed. "Quit sputtering around an' come back to me."

"What if my husband came up those stairs?"

"Well, my dear, I'm not a prophet. Don't you love me a little bit? A risky little bit?"

"Charles, this has become an embarrassing moment. Remember what you said, I live for appearances. I cannot wait for the rain to stop. I feel like getting into my buggy and riding home."

"What about me?"

"You've got to walk back to Sue's. Didn't you tell them you were comin' here?"

"I did. But the rain could have changed things. Camp Edwards is only a couple miles from here. Why can't you drive me out there?"

"It wouldn't look right. I'd rather you go back to Sue's."

"Soaking wet? Just for an alibi?"

"That's right. But you can dry a little bit more before we go."

He grabbed her down to his side. This time it was a real kiss, and Marg gave in, as the lightning flashed with a thunder roll outside.

Chapter 27

The children went back North in September. John had been hunting and riding several times with Captain Waverly, and Beth and Meg had been with him to a parade out at Camp Edwards. He had asked Marg to come to a dance but she had refused, wanting very much to go. Her Charles was busy getting placards printed up for Gregory's election bid. The dance would have been a good way of saying goodbye to Waverly; he was leaving the very next week. The sight of him at first made her very nervous. He had asked her to come to the Ralston Hotel for dinner, but she had refused. Finally she agreed that perhaps another buggy ride would be all right.

She made up a few of his favorite sandwiches and brought along some bottles of his favorite wine. Their spot was the high point over the Great Meadow at Edgewater Plantation. A new road was going through which would make Camp Edwards four miles closer to town. As the road cut right through the middle of the former cotton fields of Judge Edward, it was decided to name the road Malcolm Road. Marg was ecstatic.

"At least something of Daddy's struggle will remain here," she told Waverly, feeding him a piece of her lemon cheesecake.

"Now don't get offended but doesn't it make you feel a bit funny calling him Daddy?"

"He was my father! Listen, you're as bad as these rednecks. You don't conjure up a new truth and force it on me. I'm not a stupid darky!"

"You told me yourself you're a colored woman."

"There's a difference. Lord! Now, stop, Charles! I don't want any more of this talk. Go back to Ohio an' leave us be. You northerners are makin' a mess down here."

"I'm sorry. We're only human. Listen, the next time you go to New York will you tell me?"

"Why? For you to come waltzin' over to make a mess of my marriage? Charles, I don't love you and this time when we say goodbye I think it should be for keeps."

He scratched his long straight nose and twisted reddish glistening lips. "That's why you've been so tense today. You really dread saying goodbye to me."

She tapped his head. "Aren't you the conceited one! Tell me, Charles, what is it you see in me? I have to know."

"Well, for one thing, you're pretty. For another, you're very smart an' honest. I think most of all, it's your devotion and dedication that wins. You're like a busy ant, doing so much and not knowing why."

"I don't like the way that sounds. Are you saying I'm stupidly wasting my life?"

"Some of it. You see, life is people. I've noticed there are very few people in your life. You should have many more friends."

She thought of Phyllis. "Our group has never been large. I've tried to make friends with the Free-colored but somehow it doesn't work out well."

"Would you have liked to have been a pure white woman?"

"Yes. I think so. I'm almost there, why shouldn't I feel that way?"

"Well, you can be, with me."

"Now Charles, this is the last time! In fact, we should start back now. I think I'm going to cry."

He wrapped his arm strongly around her shoulders. "Well, we can always write. Would you like that?"

"I don't know," she moaned. "I really don't know. Maybe after you're gone I can tell you better how I feel. Shall I leave you at the Camp, or are you goin' to your hotel?"

"The hotel. Wanna come up?"

"No thank you. I'll say good-bye at the door. In fact, I'll stay in my wagon. It's been nice, Charles, having a good friend like you. At first I used to think of you as a brother, but it became more. You're a sensitive good person. Had my mother met you, she would have liked you. And I would do whatever she advised me to do."

"When your little girls' turns come, don't make it hard for them. Say yes if the guy's worth it."

"Are any of them worth it?"

He reached over and kissed her on the mouth. With taut reins, the horse paused. Waverly slapped the ropes. "Come on, you black devil! Move out!"

Marg smiled and caught his arm. She was thinking of her father's attack on Lydia Farley Smith.

St. James' Church under Rev. Ulysses Houston had a fiery summer. In fact, the church split at its seams. One group of the congregation went off to Edgeworth, building itself a brand new church. This was the group wanting to remain St. James Methodist. They found themselves another mulatto preacher and returned to quiet dignified services, in their new location. The old church by its people became St. James Baptist. While Houston wouldn't stay, they found themselves a country parson, a strong political Baptist. This one's loud and colorful pleadings put ladies in the aisles throwing pocketbooks at him. Young dark Rev. Amos Moore called it the spirit of the Lord. They also bought him a house and many expensive gifts.

Moore, a friend of the Simpsons, fell right in helping Gregory to become well-known politically. Valerie really wanted to switch to the new mulatto church but her husband said no. He had to play the game and remain with the Baptists, at least until after the elections.

November came, and luckily Gregory won over his opponents! He'd be going to Milledgeville as a state representative. The blacks, in fact, won most of the seats in Muscogee County. Vicious angry whites simply could not understand it. Callie Jones and her Maple Standing Committee decided it was time to organize with out-of-staters. It was whispered that a strong secret lodge did exist, and that soon it would start keeping niggers in their places.

Marg was happy to have a brief letter from Angela; it read:

October 29, 1866

My dear Margery,

I'm working for the Mellon family and very happy in my new job. I have a sitting room, a bedroom and a lovely bath. I still see the Jeromes. Catherine has invited me out several times. Now that I'm not in the house, the meetings are more relaxed. And Clara's girls still enjoy me. We sat together at the gala opening of their new racetrack on September 25th. Loads of celebrities were there including Gen. Ulysses Grant, Adelina Patti, Fanny Ronalds. The track seats 8,000. There's a luxurious clubhouse, dining rooms and facilities for sleighing and skating.

I'm going home to Palmyra for Christmas. A few oldtimers enjoy seeing me.

Love and best regards,

Angela.

P.S. Jennie's birthday is on 9th of January. I thought you might want to know. She'll be thirteen.

242

Visits now to the post office were rather sad. There was no Captain Waverly over at the Ralston Hotel, and no letters from him. Marg wrote her children but this year she didn't really miss them. She had been feeling poorly. That old hacking cough she had had in the jail. She allowed Matilda to open the shop while she lingered in bed. But hard work was still a part of her routine. When Mrs. Bowne offered pears, she went out and picked several bushels full, and carted them herself for shipment North to her children. A few she gave to old Mrs. Muggeridge next door who had had a stroke. Bubber had run away and she had no servants now. Her husband too was ailing. He had come back, never accepting the defeat of the South.

Some of the whites on Plum Avenue had moved away. Now the new black well-to-do people were all over town. Marg smiled at them but she didn't want them in her house. It wasn't a question of color. She simply did not like people who gossipped. Dr. Fred Bowman was leading them. One day when the Bowmans had a tea party one of their guests parked his wagon in her driveway. As he sashayed across her lawn she felt like getting her shotgun. That same afternoon Marg got irritated upon seeing another black man on her lawn. Then she realized it was Mr. Wilkins coming to pay the rent. The old devil had behaved shamefully until she got Bill Cahill to take him and the rest of those squatters in her rental houses, to court. Now she had no respect for the man. He had forced her to think of him this way. But he still had good manners, and talked smoothly to find out what he could from her. "And Mr. Gregory's already gone to Milledgeville?"

"That's right," she cried in a false cheerfulness.

"You tell him they's holdin' back funds from our schools. We need a state or national education bill. Can you remembah that, Miss Margery?"

"Yes, I heah you, Mr. Wilkins."

"An' the market people always give us buzzards an' no turkeys! That should stop, Miss Margery."

"I'm not the mayor or the military governor, Mr. Wilkins. Just Mrs. Spence."

"You're a good Christian, Mrs. Spence. One with influence. Now you know what happened over in New Orleans? The Union people have allowed the locals to refuse Negroes rides in city cars. They'll only take us in star cars. So our people sat down on the Chief of Police, and got him to issue an order that we can ride in all cars! Now here in Maple, we have no transportation! Unless'n folks are rich enough to have their own. Mrs. Spence, why don't you get us some omnibuses, or city cars?"

"Mr. Wilkins, you are free to start any business you wish. By the way, what do you do for a living?"

He grinned. "I'm the jackleg preacher at Spruce Street Baptist. Oh, by the way, I'm collectin' to get started a new firehouse for the colored company. We're takin' donations."

"I'll give fifty dollars," said Marg resolutely.

"Could you make that one hundred, Mrs. Spence? The Lord will bless you!"

When he went away, Marg thought about the farce in religion. As she turned to go in the house, another visitor came up. It was Uncle Vincent, Lou Simpson's father. "Well, I'm glad to see you!" she cried. "Don't tell me you've been on another world trip?"

"That's right, Margery dear. Africa this time. I don't think I'm goin' out any more. I'm sixty-two years old. Now there's a bit of racism even on the high seas! I've got a plan or two."

"You've alway been a busybody. Would you care for some brandy?"

"No, child. I want you to try something I brought." He pulled a silver flask out of his hip pocket.

"Mr. Simpson, I couldn't be drinkin' spirits here on my porch!"

"Easy daughter, ain't no spirits. It's a cola-nut drink I made. Try it! In Khartum they chew this seed. I jis soak it, mix it with seltzer, add a li'l sugar, an' see whatchu got. You like it?"

"M-m, I think it has possibilities. It should be cold, Mr. Simpson."

"Exactly." He smacked on toothless gums. "Idda make us rich!"

"Now don't tell me you want my money in this venture?"

"Naw-w," he smiled sheepishly. "It's jis one thing I wanna talk over with yo' brother Jack. Heah the family's moved away to Atlanta, huh?"

"That's true," chirped Marg, smacking too. "An' we have no more contact. Just as if our paths had never crossed."

"What a pity," he sighed. "I was hopin' I could see Mr. Jack."

"You still can. Go up to Atlanta. An' let me know how they're doing. Abigail used to keep up with Matilda, but she's dead now. Poor Daddy. This separation business would worry him. He was really a northerner, never understandin' how vicious these people want to be with their caste system."

Vincent stood up and pocketed his flask. "They still love money, Margery. That I know for sure!"

244

The rest of that early November day went quickly. For Marg it was a humming day. A tune had been on her lips. She did not deny the happy feeling. Maybe that evening she and Charles could enjoy a glass of wine together. It tasted better in good and expensive crystal. Just as she was getting down two prized Waterford glasses, in walked Cliff Redberry, in moccasins, at the back door.

"Cliff! Of all people!" she screamed as he swept her off her feet. "My you're a sight for sore eyes. Where in the world have you been? Lucy said you were no longer in Montgomery."

"I'm back in Girard," claimed the Indian man calmly. "The peckerwoods give me heap work there. Remember, I'm not a rich man like you. I have to work for my living."

"Oh, any man handlin' guns could be rich if he wanted to be. You know, that night you left here you must have known the troops were comin'. We had all kinds of trouble."

"So I heard," he exclaimed, allowing her to pour him some brandy into a pretty crystal glass. Remembering his nature, Marg got down a plain glass, and Cliff liked that better. In fact, he went over to the cupboard and got Charles' plain whiskey, for a chaser. That suited him fine.

Marg eyed him. "What have you been doin'? It's a wonder some pretty wench hasn't got you married, a handsome guy like you."

"Oh, I've had my chances. Ha-ha! Won't pick a wife in Alabama though. Too few of my people left. Would have to mosey on out to Oklahoma or Texas. Since the white man means to exclude us from these parts—"

"Oh, it's not that bad! Plenty of half-Indian people left."

"I wanna pure-Indian squaw. You know, Marg, I'm like you. I'm fiercely proud of my heritage."

"Am I that way?"

"Strongest part of yo' personality."

"Gee, thanks, I'm glad you told me. What else do you know about me?"

He looked at her with warm suspicious eyes. "That you'll soon have a baby—"

"Cliff, what on earth are you sayin'? I'm too old for children! Besides, me and my husband, we've got other things on our minds just now. Wait till you see our new store. Oh, it's a wonderful business. I like all this hustlin' around dealin' with people."

"An' you're makin' paper gold! Marg, I want to put some money into a coal mine up near Birmingham. Think you could loan me fifteen hundred?"

She was in a good mood. "Cliff, angel, why not? You've been our good friend for years an' years. Only thing, what I've learned from Mrs. Bowne, even among friends, it's to be businesslike. You put it in writing. Cliff, let's say with interest at six per cent for five years. Okay?"

"Don't be greedy, ole friend! Make that four per cent. An' I don't need five years. Four's okay. You agree?"

"Why not," she laughed. "If you're stayin' a few days, tomorrow I'll have my lawyer, Cahill, draw up the papers. At four per cent. But there has to be a clause that if you default, everything comes to me."

"Good gracious," he laughed. "Okay, Marg. An' I'll volunteer to be godfather of yo' child. Li'l rich rascal will need somebody like me to watch over him."

"Cliff, quit yo' kiddin'. There won't be no child. We're old sensible people."

"An' I'm old sensible Creek Indian."

Several days later Marg woke up at five a.m. Charles had just left and she felt as if she had talked in her sleep, or he had kissed her and said something. She couldn't tell him she had missed her period for three months. She couldn't go to her doctor or to any of the locals. She knew it was a baby. She didn't need Cliff Redberry telling her such things. Captain Waverly's baby. It made her sick and hopeless to think about it. She had been such a fool. She should have kept him out in the rain. God had the horse there waiting. There was no excuse for her mistake. She was old enough to know better. In fact, age was the trouble. She had thought she was much too old for this, and now, Providence had her paying for her mistake. Her sin.

This morning as the rooster crowed, she lounged in satin sheets, deciding with humiliation to consider all possibilities. She could find some midwife, the ones who had hatpins and potions. That would be against her religious convictions. She could tell Charles, but it would shatter him. Now he was gaining a reputation among black people. If they laughed at his wife, that would be like sticking a knife in his ribs. No, she couldn't hurt Charles by telling anybody in Maple. She'd simply have to go away.

Maybe to Alabama, to her Cousin Lucy, or to Cliff Redberry and the Indian people. No, that was just like being in Georgia. Gossipers everywhere! Strangely she thought of Angela Baker, up in New York.

Phyllis Korner's cousin doing domestic service with rich white people. Angela would be a perfect mother for her baby. No, it would be burdensome for her. And too far away. The wrong world. She knew Tom Haney would help her if she asked him. And she'd probably have to pay again for her mistake. Oh, Lord Jesus!

Her husband would hate her; her children would hate her; the town would hate her. If they knew. Suddenly God stepped in. A letter arrived from Cousin Lucy saying she was leaving Alabama, that Kenneth had finally sent for her. She and the children would start out for Chicago next Thursday! Marg sighed; her baby seemed to move. She wanted this baby. Just within a few moons she could have a beautiful whiteskinned baby. She would not treat it as she had treated poor brown Jason. And all this still didn't make her feel that she loved Charles Waverly. Yet, her own Charles could be mean and spiteful. No, she'd never tell him, just as she had never told him about all the money they had sitting in the banks up North.

This day Marg was nauseous. She sent word by Lawrence that she wouldn't be coming out to Wentworth. She had to get this thing organized in her mind. Maybe she'd have a miscarriage. In the fourth month it was possible. Or, soon she'd start looking fat. She went to her mirror. Maybe already the wise ones were suspecting, like Cliff. Right away she began tearing her frocks apart, padding petticoats, making the stomach lines look normal. She had stupidly been too confident. She should have done this several weeks earlier. *Lucy, why have you picked this moment to go running off to Chicago?* You owe me this! Oh, Lucy!

By nightfall she was dead tired. Carol, Maggie Mae and Celeste were training two new girls in the kitchen. And they had a new coachman, Adam Hinds. Marg didn't want to see any of them. She rang to have a tray in her room. Roast chicken and a salad. That's all she wanted. Celeste kept trying to fuss about her illness, but Marg wouldn't have it. At times she had to speak firmly to Celeste. Some of her obstinance was almost as bad as Matilda's. They had all been abused. But when you're paying money for service it's not like the old days. You want your peace. Celeste in her retirement had too little to do, and no personal life. If she had any loyalty there'd be no room for playing wise fool. Marg told them all she simply wanted to be left alone with her cold. It was true; her chest didn't feel right.

It was after eleven p.m. when Charles came in. She was still awake in bed, right where he had left her that morning. The servants must have told him how sick she was. He came in calling. With closed eyes she played completely knocked out. She didn't want to talk to Charles. She was making up her mind what she'd do.

She would go to Washington, D.C. She'd tell Louise Johnson everything, and Louise would have to take her. In fact, what she had in mind was to give the baby to Louise. Poor thing didn't have a spot of close kin anywhere in the world. And since Louise could be contrary, she had to make it an attractive offer. She'd send greenbacks as well. All this for ten minutes' indiscretion!

END OF PART THREE

PART FOUR

1866-1870

Chapter 28

Surprisingly Louise was delighted at Marg's ultra-secret news. Marg had told her not to breathe a word of it to a soul, that it was a life and death matter and that she didn't want any one any where in the world to know, other than Louise herself. It had not been told that the child's father was a white man. Louise suggested Christmas time for her arrival. By then she'd have her little house ready to hold two more souls. Marg had sent her five-hundred dollars and that was more money than Louise had ever had at one time. She was going to get new blankets, new pillows, new stove, new drapes, a new bed and a lot of baby things. Marg had told her that she didn't want to inconvenience her in any way and that she could well afford to hire a nursemaid to look after the baby while she herself was in Washington, and after she had left town. Marg didn't talk about adoption papers. She really didn't want to give up her baby permanently.

The big problem was telling Charles something plausible. Marg began fixing his favorite Creole spaghetti, with beef and green peppers. Next, she read to him from northern newspapers. She claimed wanting to go back to school, that she was tired of the store, that she might make herself a woman doctor. This was strange talk for a Georgia woman, but up North it was possible. Surprisingly Charles took it nobly. The one stipulation she made: the three brown schoolteachers had to leave her house, immediately. She didn't want any roomers there while she was away. How long? She didn't want to say nine months. She told Charles four or five months. This would be one semester in school.

She even wrote to Georgetown and Howard to secure admission papers. Everything fell together two weeks before Christmas. Charles was very sad now to see her leave. He thought she was doing it because of his philandering. He promised to be a better husband. She made him feel all right by giving him money to run the house. It was a good sum. Enough for him to open another store.

She told him she would first go North to be with the children for Christmas. Marg didn't get to New Jersey or Massachusetts. It was all a lie, like the rest of her story. Distant cousins in Concord (white) took care of her three while she went to Louise's dumpy house in D Street, Northwest, and enjoyed being made a fuss over. New cottons donned her bed, and she read her newspapers there.

Just then in Washington Thaddeus Stevens and Ashley of Ohio had gotten the House to pass a resolution to investigate accusations against Andrew Johnson, i.e. that he had preknowledge of the assassination plan against Lincoln. Marg sighed, everybody was having troubles! And she herself did not escape a scolding. Louise, with serious face, told her that she was not a common woman, and never should have allowed herself to get in deep with a man who wasn't her husband.

"He was a Union captain living in my house," Marg confessed. "In war times it is not always prudent for a girl to refuse—"

"You're no girl" snapped Louise. "Marg, he didn't abuse you like in jail?"

"No, nothing like that. Louise, I must admit, it was a bit of a romance. I suppose I was getting even with Charles for all the runnin' around he's done over the years. But I'll assure you yo' little baby will be a beautiful child. His father is simple gorgeous."

Louise looked worried, and a little bit undecided. She certainly would like a child to brighten her lonely life but she was also a duty-bound careerwoman. Seldom could she take a day off from her job. She told Marg she didn't know what she could do if the child got sick. Marg assured her if anything serious happened she would come back up from Georgia. The railroads now were getting magnificent in frequency and mode. Marg had had a private bedroom all the way; she was almost as fancy as her California brother Paul.

While Louise strictly promised not to tell a soul, somehow, Lydia Farley Smith when they met knew everything. She began offering the names of several prominent doctors who were discreet as they were famous. The birth certificate could be made out in Charles' name or in name of the Prince of Wales. Marg wouldn't have to leave her bedroom. The doctor would come at anytime, and a private nurse would be on duty twenty-four hours that first week. This sounded like the kind of thing Marg wanted. On Thursday she donned her new furs and went with Louise to the office of Dr. Sidney Greenblat.

Marg had never before known any Jewish people. She liked Dr. Greenblat. He seemed warm, kind, sympathetic, as well as expensive. She told him she didn't want to discuss the baby's father just now, that she would give him the information he needed after the baby's birth. The good doctor merely shrugged his shoulders, smiling. He had heard that story before.

Marg made Lydia promise on the Bible that she wouldn't breathe a word of this to Mr. Thaddeus Stevens or to the President. She didn't even want them to know that she was in Washington. Thus, she would not be coming to Lydia's house. This was all serious business. She was not interested in socializing. In spite of her strict words Lydia still managed to get Marg out for lunch at one fancy hotel or another. Marg had secured in Georgia an entire new wardrobe and was dressed like a princess. Many senators and high-level politicians stared at her, wanting to be introduced. She met a few.

The dreary days with snow and ice fascinated Marg. Louise's house was warm and toasty and she enjoyed being there, reading her many magazines and books. She was to learn that the President had just finished a grueling whistlestop bit of campaigning to get a better Congress to support his reconstruction policies. He had been heckled and booed at many places. Mr. Stevens' Radicals were still going strong and a new conservative group of Republicans including Mr. Alexander Stephens of Georgia was making trouble for Johnson. Moreover, the President's friends had been defeated at the polls. The Senate refused to confirm his friend Senator Cowan of Pennsylvania as minister to Austria.

It seemed Mr. Stevens' Radical group was stronger than ever; they made up two-thirds majority of both houses. And Lydia was busy as its First Lady, giving parties for her boss. The newspapers were full of Mr. Stevens' words and plans. Some even included a nasty racial note about Lydia. Most conveyed that he wanted new and severe measures against the South.

The Fortieth Congress would arrive in Washington to commence its extra session on 4th of March. Thaddeus had submitted his own reconstruction bill to compete with the one of John Sherman. Keeping his hands in the pie, he had made Federal commanders to be stronger than state governments, with greater power in making arrests and in running trials. Marg liked this, because the new local rules were really hurting her people. Where states permitted Negroes to vote they could move ahead having their representatives in Washington. Benjamin

Wade of Ohio was the only one vocalizing that a destructed South had to be sewn together again, and he was as strong and as active as Stevens.

On the first day of spring, that year of 1867, Marg received a short thank-you note from Jennie Jerome, for her birthday present, a pink satin scarf. The poor child spoke of her parents' impending divorce, that her mother was taking her and her sisters off to Paris, to live there permanently. Marg thought of answering but she felt it was no use. The child would be in a new world—a war world. Marg went to her window, pulled back her curtain to look at the little birdies who had been cheeping since early morning. A little rain had fallen in the garden. It was peaceful. It reminded her of the peaceful look of cemeteries, the final resting place of all men, of her dear parents. While at Gregory's she had been bewitched by that view. As if they were trying to get to her, to help her rebuild her life.

Spring always seemed to stand for fresh life. Yet, her memory of winter, the leaves falling, the summer blooms before that, made her realize it all was fleeting. She was now thirty-eight, almost thirty-nine. Her vision was suffering; she had these hacking coughs; her skin and legs were not their old selves. Just then she got a sharp pain in her side, then in her belly. Oh, God, it's time!

Louise wasn't home. Slowly Marg got herself into some garments and a shawl, and made it to the front door. In the porch's icy air she rang for Mrs. Abrams next door. She would help her; she'd fetch Dr. Greenblat.

The baby was a beautiful plump, round-faced little girl. White, with a dusting of blond hair, and a little nose as red as a beet. Her dark eyes were alive, already squinting and fighting the daylight. With nicely-shaped head, she looked like any other baby in a near-white family. She would not suffer because of her appearance. And Marg decided to call her Justine. Justine Waverly Spence. Charles would never have to know her middle name. In fact, he'd never have to meet her. And if she ever came to Georgia she'd be a Washington belle, visiting for a short time. Oh, she was cute! So cute!

Marg thanked God for a safe delivery. She felt fine, except for some coughing. She still had a bug in her chest. Dr. Greenblat told her to stay in bed two days. Mary, the nurse, would help her later in the week to walk around the house a bit. He said that if she took care of herself she could go home to Georgia, by train, in early April. Marg looked at herself in Louise's ivory handmirror. She looked pale and drawn. Like a sinful woman! There was no point in going back to

Georgia before the color was back in her cheeks. She did not want to leave her baby so soon. Maybe she'd stay on till June. Then go up to New York to fetch her children. That was an idea. Then Charles could gaze into all their faces at once. In that way nobody would notice the way she had changed.

A nurse's aide was hired just to take care of Justine while Mary looked after Marg and her needs. It was better having two girls. They'd chat and laugh together, as brown people do. Washington had a way of writing race into birth certificates. When Dr. Greenblat asked Marg what did she want it to be, she said "white." Not for the baby's gain but for the needs of the United States. They needed many more white people who would be gentle and kind across race lines, and that's what her Justine would be.

Louise was thrilled to see and touch her new baby. Already the baby was many shades lighter than its foster mother but that would be no problem because it happened all the time in the colored community. Louise went along with the name although she was disappointed Marg had put none of her name on this child whom she'd have to care for. Marg told her she could go to court and add a name later, but now Marg talked as if she'd want Justine back when she reached her teens. She claimed since Louise was older she could then become the grandmother, and they could share this beautiful person together. Justine could take train rides and come to Georgia as often as she'd be in Washington.

"Lord, who knows what will happen to us in fifteen years," sighed Louise mournfully. "Dis chile may be out there on the streets, hustlin' men."

"Never!" screamed Marg. "You make the character of the child, Louise. Remember this; it's very important. She'll know nothing about race or low-class people unless you let it get into her life. In Georgia we have always carried ourselves as if we were the cream, the most dainty, the most god-like creatures. I want my Justine to be that way. No mingling with street-people, ever!"

"Well," smiled Louise. "If I'm her mother she should take after me, an' I've always been a plain homebody. No pretense. But as you know, this is a fast town, especially where beautiful young ladies are concerned."

"Louise, darling, you don't have to live in Washington. You can go anywhere you like. All over United States. Remember, I shall send you a monthly stipend. If you save it or spend it, it does not matter. Justine will have her own money when she comes of age. You don't seem to realize how lucky I've been in life. An' God wants me to pass it on to my four children—"

"Five children, now," put in Louise, shaking her baby. "You don't want to forget Jason. Or maybe you can just send that li'l rascal up here to me. I love children. This li'l girl already is making me very happy."

Louise Johnson's house on D Street stayed a hectic place for several days. The professional nurse Mary left after one week; and just Lavinia, the practical helper, remained. She was good to the child. Only seventeen herself she had a way with children. She knew just what to do to stop the crying, or to get the baby to eat. They both were pleased with Lavinia who had been a slave just two years earlier. She lived with her two aunts. Her mother was dead. She didn't mind living in with Miss Johnson, and Mrs. Spence. They paid her well and she was making many plans to do things with her money. Mainly she wanted to go to school, to learn how to read and write. Marg promised to help her get started but she was too confused to do any teaching in Washington, D.C. Instead, she began planning a new wardrobe. Louise's seamstress, Mrs. Burke, was called over. Marg simply had to have some new formal gowns before the party season ended in June. Now she was ready to sweep some senators off their feet.

Marg's first social engagement after her ordeal was a small candle-light dinner party at Thaddeus Stevens' house. She had been invited before but this was the first time Louise was invited as well. This meant it would be a colored party, because those high up in Washington seldom made a bi-racial mix, knowing how terrible some white congressmen were with their airs and prejudices. The colored high-ups preferred not to mingle with them, to suffer their gibes and stupid remarks. Nobody knew this better than Stevens with his beloved tan-skinned paramour, Lydia Farley Smith.

"They mean to scandalize yo' people forever, "Stevens told Marg, as he finished froglegs in lime sauce Lydia served on expensive china plates. "This status war could last for centuries!"

"Gracious," chirped Marg through white-powdered cheeks to which she had added a little rouge. "Could Americans be that hateful?"

"Oh yes," continued Stevens. "The hateful ones have the stronger will and the stronger pull in the halls of Congress. The only way we beat them, we had the stronger army: our two million men to their seven hundred thousand. And we had better supply lines. The good generals, however, were all with the South. An' we demobilized too quickly. The mess down there now is poorly-trained bureaucrats with too much power. And I don't mind if the carpetbaggers keep firing their behinds!"

"Then, Mr. Stevens, you do not believe as people say that it's because the colored race is too much in command now?"

"Of course not. Your people are not savages. In Carolina I heard that young Elliott fellow, better speaker than Daniel Webster. The colored race, just out of slavery, is doing magnificent things. For America! An' some did splendidly even before emancipation untied their hands. The Free ones! You see, Mrs. Spence, good men are apt to forget your kind. All the capable, wealthy, fair . . . the vicious will make you nothing. They want to bury you! Making their myths true!"

A handsome youngish tan-colored man also at the table raised his delicate hand to make a point. He was the world-renowned concert pianist and composer, Louis Moreau Gottschalk, America's only great one. His following at all the great concert halls thought he was a white man. His father was Jewish and his mother, a Negro. But coming from New Orleans he certainly could be a white man. "Mr. Stevens," said Gottschalk finally, "I think your point is well-taken, but I must ask you who are behind these rabid congressmen who still want to foment racial dissent?"

Stevens made a groan, then he twisted his big body into a more comfortable curve. "Naturally, I could say the Democrats, but there are devils on both sides! Some in both parties regard me as a vindictive partisan but I'm a fighter for right. I keep telling myself that the late lamented Andrew Johnson, blessed in my memory, never heard a word I said."

"Why do you refer to him as 'the late'?" asked Lydia with a smile breaking at the corner of her purple lips.

"Because, my dear, he's finished. He'll never carry out what God wanted him to do. He'll never understand that the economic power of the former slaveholders still is *the* issue. The Union party has to wake up and do the right thing, to save the nation."

"Then the war isn't over?" asked Moreau, pointedly.

"It certainly is not," snapped Stevens adjusting the black wig he wore. "An' the Copperheads up North are just as much traitors as the southern white scoundrels."

"I was once called a traitor," Marg told him. "The thing that frightened me was that they could have gotten away with the charge, through all their courts and fancy legal proceedings, if the war had not been breaking up at that time."

"I doubt that," said Stevens poking out his lower lip. "You were a southern aristocrat, a lady, much more than you were a negress. It would have played on their conscience—"

"No, Thaddeus," yelled Lydia. "How about that white school-teacher up in New England? They were ready to hang her for having colored pupils."

"New England isn't Georgia," he growled. "Like I say, this whole darn game is a play on conscience. Now these black codes have been adopted! The South'll crown Johnson king before Congress meets again. Freedmen have not been violent enough! Some want to Africanize them, not Anglicize them. I say America is as America does. We cannot afford to have a beautiful ideal on the one hand, and behave like scoundrels on the other."

Next, Mr. Gottschalk was asked to play something on the piano. He played *La Bamboula* for Stevens, *The Banjo* for Lydia, and *The Dying Poet* for Marg and Louise. Marg's mind ran from John to Justine. When guilty feelings persisted, she told Louise that she wanted to go home. After a cordial good-bye to Mr. Stevens and Mr. Gottschalk she told her hostess she had to write letters to her husband and children. Back home, Louise made a comfortable fire in Marg's room. Marg had her French brandy, then wrote Charles saying she was attending college at Georgetown. She did get to a few lectures, but mostly she wrote a lie. Another lie.

Chapter 29

In June when the hot humid heat came to Washington, Marg got all dressed up and tearfully said goodbye to her beautiful Justine. The train was taking her North to New York where she'd have conferences with Mr. Haney. Her brother Anthony was away in Paris making some art purchases. She'd meet her children at the Fifth Avenue Hotel. The girls would come down from Massachusetts and John would be over from Princeton. He had been there getting his admission papers to enter the College of New Jersey. His father had wanted him to go to the new college for colored, Howard, in Washington, D.C. But Marg certainly didn't want John in Washington, to discover her great secret. No, he'd have to go to Princeton. And John wanted now to study music, not medicine. She was toying with the idea of having him meet Mr. Louis Moreau Gottschalk who was now in New York for a big concert. But no, she didn't trust the fact that he was from her Washington group. She had to keep the two worlds separated.

On the other hand, Marg had heard from Lydia in confidence that Gottschalk had an illegitimate child by the famous actress, Ada Clare. She and this charming man could be close friends, but she put it out of her mind. That evening he came to her hotel he was all engrossed in the long tour he'd soon make to South America. He was, in fact, going the very next week. With courage, Marg refused his invitation to dinner. That look in his expressive eyes was more than a look of mulatto kinship.

She did have lunch with Angela Baker who now seemed very happy, still working with the very rich Mellon family. But she was fully a domestic worker. It made her feel different than being in the house of kin. Marg told her to forget the Jeromes. But she just couldn't. They had been too much the wick of her candle. Yes, she still wrote to the children, to Jennie mostly. And Jennie, she said, would be sorry that she missed Mrs. Spence of Georgia who had come to visit again.

Marg and her children spent several days buying clothes. Things had gone well in Wall Street. She was a much richer woman now. Haney had a list of things he wanted her to invest in: a new lawn-cutting machine called "mower," a shoe-sewing machine, a transparent product called "celluloid," and of course the typewriter, still waiting for patent office approval. Marg said she wanted nothing just now. Maybe next year. What she really wanted was to start something in manufacturing herself. She envisioned bringing a northern-type business to Georgia. But as yet, she didn't have enough money for this. The Korners had begun marketing a viewing apparatus called stereo-scope and it was making them rich. Mrs. Bowne had a glob of mercerized cotton stocks as well as her reaper, sewing machine and railroad stocks. The white Malcolms had money in the Bessemer steel process, as well as in power plants and railroads. All Marg knew was that northern white people had much more. They were very very wealthy.

Haney liked the idea that she had come alone this time. He kept speaking of her beauty, her *mature* beauty now, and he suggested dinner at several fancy restaurants. She kept refusing. All she would agree to was a carriage ride to look at the new art gallery her brother Anthony had started in East Eleventh Street.

Marg was in for a bit of excitement on June 26th. She had read that morning about the President's visit to Boston where he had laid the cornerstone at the new Masonic Temple. It mentioned he had stopped in Philadelphia on the way and had experienced a greeting of wild ovation. Then he was coming to New York. He came that day, riding in an open barouche drawn by four horses from the Battery straight to her hotel. Men and women crowded out front. Everyone was in a festive mood. With curiosity she and the children stood back in the crowd. She had no intention of getting close. But he spotted her in the crowd and raised his hands. The bodyguards made a path straight to Marg.

"Mrs. Spence, what a pleasant surprise!" said President Andrew Johnson.

"How do you do, Mr. President. These are my three children," said Marg proudly and somewhat embarrassed.

He made over them, showing great approval in his eyes and manner, of their looks and deportment. He even had a few words with John. Then he turned back to Marg and invited her to dine with him that evening. She unfortunately had to decline. They were taking the four o'clock train South.

The ride South was hot, dirty and boring. The children enjoyed looking out the windows at the fleeting ever-interesting American landscape. They passed Washington at twilight, on down to twinkling lights in Virginia. The kids slept through North Carolina but sunrise brought South Carolina and tumbledown cabins and poor people waving at them. Marg felt happy seeing the sunlit cornfields, the giant rivers with their clear, pristine waters. It was a great land. A big land. She had a feeling these days she was communicating with the Spirit World. Her dear father was pleading with her to do something for him; he wanted her to make a big impression on America, for his sake. He felt she should have stayed in New York to take advantage of the President's invitation. Her mother was saying no, that there was no greater gift than motherhood, and religion. Marg had to learn how to deal with this tug-o-war spiritual advice. These ideals from Mother and Daddy. There was only a thin line between good and evil. Her mother warned that she was balancing herself dangerously on a precipice. She'd be dead soon, said Alice, long before her time.

Charles, with his little reddish moustache, was waiting for them at the Central of Georgia station. Bless his heart! With Carol, Maggie Mae, Larry and Matilda. Matilda, bless her heart, carried deep-blue violets. The occasion was saddened by the fact that Celeste had died the night before. They'd have a big funeral for her out at Cobb's Creek. At St. James Baptist. Celeste had been a Methodist but she loved the original church, that simple white chapel with its beautifully-colored stained-glass windows. And Cousin Don, once again, would perform the service from the pulpit he had built. Again some Negroes were arguing. They didn't want him back there, even as a visitor, puttin' some yalla woman in her grave. How can people be so vicious! thought Marg, as the story was being told to her.

She ordered lots of flowers from Mitchell's interest, and an expensive headstone for Winston and Celeste, together at last. John, Joey and Effie were to come from New Orleans to bury their dear mother. In the end only the boys came. Effie and Claude could not risk the exposure. They had to remain true to the pure white community. That was the most important thing, for continued success in their lives. Effie did send a lovely burial dress. It seemed to express her heartache over the miles. Lawyer Perkins came to the funeral as a sanctimonious white businessman, not a loved one. Marg looked at him thinking of America's hypocrisy, its false racial stand. *God, what will come of it?*

As the July heat cooked them to toast, Marg lounged out back, making a breeze with her mother's tan-colored palm fan. Among her mail she was happy to have another letter from her child's guardian. It read:

July 27, 1867

My dear Margery,

The baby's fine. When she sits up and does pretty things I try to teach her to talk. Lavinia just loves her! And for me Sundays can't come soon enough. As you know, Congress had this July session and the hotel was packed. I even went over to hear Mr. Stevens make his speech on the Military Bill. The gallery was packed with fancy ladies from the diplomatic corps. He's feeble now. And talking impeachment. He thinks President Johnson has made a mess of things. Some say Stevens himself wants to be president. But seeing him tottering on his cane, I feel sorry for the man. He was so vigorous until recently. But he won't give up!

The Radicals really don't have any evidence to impeach A. Johnson. Stanton is the devil behind the scene. He should resign as the president wants. Gen. Grant may step into his shoes. He's all primed and ready. Rumor now is Ben Butler has detectives on Grant's trail. I was talking to Mr. Montgomery Blair who's writing an article for *New York World* suggesting Grant might be presidential material! Well, that's the Washington game. I do think you might live with us longer. I believe you could be influential here. Mr. Stevens too!

All the best,

Louise.

As 1867 moved through its hot and dry summer a reflective Marg read newspapers and wrote letters, always sitting alone on her screened-in comfortable backporch. Her eyes spotted the chicken-coop's need for paint. She recalled how its cache of silver and antiques saved them in lean months of war. Now she thought of Captain Waverly who never wrote, and her dear innocent baby, Justine. At times the want to hold that child was too much. Whenever she had crying spells, Matilda would hold the shop together very well. Now she talked of starting her own little shop in Blackworth. Marg gave her five hundred dollars when she finally agreed to surrender Miss Wanda's brooch, so that Celeste could be buried with it.

Lo and behold, with the five hundred dollars, the first thing Matilda announced was that she was getting married. To none other than that Free Negro rascal, Henry Wilkins. Marg made some pretense not to go to the wedding. She didn't want to see that man who for several years had cheated her out of money at her rental houses. No, she didn't have to socialize with the likes of him. Matilda felt for

262

certain Miss Margery didn't come because of the caste system. She knew those near-whites had little real feelings for the blacks or the ex-slaves.

Matilda left the store just as the heat of August came under the roof. Marg got a local black girl to take her place. Polly had no interest in antiques or the bartering business. She liked store-keeping for the money. Marg tried to train her to be sharp in handling people and money, but several times some slick-talkers gyped Polly out of extra change. Disgusted, Marg put her mind on helping Larry introduce a new item to the store. He liked to work with wood. He had been rebuilding many outhouses for people but Marg got him away from this degrading foul job. She wanted him discriminating about his own talents.

Together they went slowly through Malcolm House looking for some catchy item they could reproduce for profit. They finally decided on Marg's beautiful English walnut Queen Anne lowboy table in the front foyer. The one that held the family Bible. It had magnificent lines as well as sturdiness. Marg felt certain that if they reproduced this table in numbers, they could make money. She was sure the whites would want it, perhaps a bit smaller, a table for the bedroom. They could call it Malcolm Table, or, the Spence Table. And she had a Chicago firm sending down sixty gorgeous hurricane lamps to go with the sixty tables Larry was to make. With this scheme, she felt she was getting closer to her manufacturing goals.

Husky Mitchell and Albert helped with the rebuilding of the second floor. Another layer of wood was put on the ceiling to keep the heat out. Where Larry's corner had been a fenced-in area, now they put up a new plate glass wall, to attract customers to his talents. They really needed more space. The strange ghost store next door was still vacant. The Wesley Giles family had come back from Europe and had gone off again, this time to California. Charles had not managed to see them, to buy the store, although he heard it had a price now, five times what he had paid for his store from Mrs. Bowne. Inflation was creeping into the American scene. They noticed it in other matters.

Handsome John, now a full-grown young man, some times would come out to the store to help Marg with customers, or downstairs, with his daddy. He really wasn't interested in their little businesses. He had become sophisticated up North. Like his mother he read a lot, and he'd practice Bach and Mozart at Marg's piano. With his fondness for music he'd spend much time out in the country at Sue's farm. They had good times together. It was he who brought the news home that Jeeter and

Sue had a note from Captain Waverly. He was a civilian again, out West in Oregon, doing engineering work. Marg was delighted to have the news, but why hadn't he written her? Marg thought of telling him about their little girl, but Sue had no return address.

As the summer moved along, John had his own horse and his own carriage. He went many places in the valley, looking at all aspects of southern life which he deplored. He even went out to the new plot of the Jeb Hunter family. He and Cindy began seeing each other weekly. Jeb didn't mind, but this upset Marg quite a bit. She told her son that there was no future in the friendship. The Jeb Hunters were poor white trash; that was the beginning and end of it. He should not be wasting his time that way. John argued back that she still did business with Mr. Hunter and treated him kindly whenever he came around the store. John didn't believe in hypocrisy.

Poor Marg was caught off guard when Jeb came one day asking for a thousand dollar loan. Marg gave it to him, remembering John's words. She had also just received a loan payment from Cliff Redberry. She felt like a banker, making a little interest this way. White people had been doing it for centuries.

Chapter 30

As soon as the autumn leaves began to appear in the pasture the children got ready to return North to school. Both Beth and Meg were beautiful young ladies who attracted attention. Their mother didn't want them traveling the rails alone. So she'd pay someone to accompany them North. This time it was a brownskinned woman named Chism. Once in Massachusetts Beth wrote her mother immediately about some discomfort they had had on the trip, with a terribly rude white conductor shouting constantly at Mrs. Chism. Marg didn't know what to say to this. The racial anger in the South was beyond appeasement, or understanding.

One day in late September a shiny new carriage drove up. It was Matilda paying a social call at Malcolm House where she had worked as a slave. Marg was sincere and cordial in welcoming her. She gave a belated wedding gift, a set of crystal glasses. Matilda was most pleased to have them. She had her own home now. The $500 had gotten her started in business in Blackworth, and she was very happy there. Marg complained that her new girl Polly wasn't good at much. Matilda offered to train her. Marg laughingly agreed if Matilda herself would come back and do inventories. Surprisingly, Matilda said she would. She also wanted some of Larry's tables to sell in her barter store. Could the blacks afford such an expensive item? Matilda assured her they could. Marg agreed four or five could be taken on consignment. It was a business talk, of equals. Matilda departed happy.

The bright sun lasted into October. Marg spent a whole Saturday morn digging in her flower garden. Just as she was ready to leave it for a bath, a handsome blond young man walked up the walk. He wore khaki and a knapsack.

"Excuse me," he said, fingering his goatee. "Are you Mrs. Margery Spence?"

"I am. How do you do?"

"I'm George Cable. A friend of John Malcolm."

Marg frowned a bit. Why would her half-brother Jack be sending anyone to her? "Oh. Are you from Atlanta?"

"No, ma'am. I'm from New Orleans. John is there too."

Now she knew who he was talking about. Celeste's oldest boy. "I'm surprised to hear from that John. How is he doin'? And Joey? Effie?"

Cable smiled through his blue eyes. "They're all fine. I'm a young writer, Mrs. Spence. Makin' my way across Georgia. John said . . . well, he thought you might oblige me with lodging for a few days."

"Why, by all means," chirped Marg to the white-faced youth. "We'd be happy to take you in. I see you're English-speaking. I thought they all spoke French."

He followed her into the neat, rich-looking foyer. "Some of us have British antecedents. A few of us, Mrs. Spence, admit a li'l touch of Africa. Like you!"

"Oh, how nice! You're so white I took you to be a pure white."

"My father insisted that we are. But I knew otherwise by the age of twelve. I was fourteen when I finally got up nerve to let him know what I knew. This almost shocked him to death. I promised not ever to talk of it . . . but I do keep it in my writing."

"How interesting." Marg led him into Lt. Waverly's bedroom. "Is this all right for you?"

"It's a beautiful room," said Cable. "May I ask the price for three days?"

"Oh-h, you're a guest! I've never had a writer in my home. Dinner's at six, Mr. Cable, an' I expect to hear all about you then."

Marg went off to start the water for her bath. First she brought up a bouquet of chrysanthemums for young Cable who was spreading out his belongings on the bed. Marg liked blond young men, she couldn't deny it. It was her father's blood and she saw nothing wrong in her feelings.

She had been eating alone since the children left. This evening Charles came on time and she hadn't expected him. She found herself explaining that George Cable was a family friend, a friend of Celeste's boy, John. Charles would not turn away a friend of Judge Edward's boy, John. He saw no harm in the young man being there. She was thinking too that Captain Waverly had said that she didn't have enough friends. "Charles, we're so blessed to have George with us. I've learned so much about New Orleans. He's twenty-three an' a newspaper writer on

266

the staff of the *Picayune*. George, during the war we used to read yo' paper whenever we could get our hands on it. Charles, Mr. Cable served in the cavalry of the Confederate army, but he's from our group, more or less."

"Some of my Virginia ancestors were from yo' group," Cable explained as he and Charles shook hands across the table.

"An' now you're white and workin' in the white world," said Charles amicably.

"That's right. You know it is getting very difficult for people of color. At one time, they had considerable rights in Louisiana but slowly they've mostly been taken away."

"I remember," said Charles, having a go at Marg's French wine, "my father used to speak of a rich Louisiana colored farmer named Andrew Durnford. He had a plantation and nearly a hundred slaves. Some sugar refinery people offered him $50,000 to use his slaves to test a new procedure an' he refused, thinkin' they'd corrupt his rule."

Cable smiled. "I know that story. Actually, the inventor-engineer, Norbert Rillieux, was a Free Negro himself, and his vacuum process for refining sugar had financial backing, but the white planters were jealous and didn't want to deal with him. Did you know who Durnford's good friend was?"

"Who?" asked Charles, turning bright-eyed.

"John McDonough, a wealthy white New Orleans philanthropist. Durnford used to go North to Virginia, to buy slaves for McDonough. Actually he felt more white than colored. So you see, there cannot be preciseness of black an' white even on the morality issues. Durnford's son, Tom, is a neighbor of ours. He was educated in the North, but was never one for emancipation of slaves. By the way, I see in your Bible in the foyer the name McDonough—"

"Oh, you've looked at our Bible?" gasped Marg, with napkin to her lips.

"Yes'm," smiled Cable, apologetically. "It's such an impressive big and beautiful volume. Those McDonoughs in yo' family, from Carolina, could they be the same as the New Orleans ones we know?"

"Oh no," laughed Marg. "We don't know of any relatives in New Orleans. Surely not rich philanthropists." Then she thought again of Celeste's boy, John. "Well, let's say America in time will be one people. Is that too radical for you, Mr. Cable?"

"Not at all. I agree with you. You know, when Toussaint L'Ouverture led the rebellion in Saint Domingue, many French-speaking colored flocked to New Orleans. Pure whites always feared the rule of the lightskinned colored. In Louisiana we had a magnificent Free Negro militia and, as in Cuba, the separate *pardo* units were for the fair, an' the *moreno* units were dark people. They were used when the United States went to war against Britain in 1812. An' Claiborne needed them to put down slave rebellions. In 1788 Free Negroes with their military class were one-third of New Orleans. They became reinforced with refugees from West Indies and Cuba. So-called whites, deeply jealous, went to Government seeking controls over darker brothers who helped make America."

Charles smiled. "The colored were even earlier fighters. My friend Redberry tells me the Natchez Indians were largely put down by whites using Negro troops."

"Do you know why Spanish and French populations remained hostile to Free Negroes? They were more secure in business, the shopkeepers, the artisans, skilled laborers, the property owners. The white man only had his caste. In time he'd make laws to keep the Negro a lesser man."

"They weren't really Negroes," put in Marg, passing a beautiful roast to her guest. "Most of them were as fair as the whites."

"True. Because the Frenchman came without his women. He had many children by colored mothers an' declared them his natural children in the parish registers. But pure whites as a group continued to nibble at the freedom of these mixed families."

"I don't understand it," called Charles, having Crawdad. "If Free Negroes had power, skills, militia, how did the scoundrels take it away?"

"Government edicts, legal stuff! When USA took over Louisiana in 1803 the fair Free-colored were as high up as they ever would be. By 1810 their numbers had increased fourfold, whites barred them from political gatherings! They went to Claiborne and he put them off. Then later the Secretary of War, Henry Dearborn, told Claiborne to use his own discretion in trying to disarm them. The colored militia had won decisive battles an' even the British were prepared to use them. Yet, white locals remained hostile. When Louisiana became a state in 1812, the Federals recognized the Negro militia, but now they had to have white officers over them! They were limited to four companies, an' had to own land valued over $300. This made them more elite than the whites. They had to fight to get equal pay, an' inclusion in the Federal ranks. When the New Orleans City Council became white, they slapped a curfew on the whole Free Negro community! In this century little pockets of influential whites have enacted new laws state by state keepin' Free-colored just as close to slavery as possible. I stress in my writing that they had been higher people under Spanish rule. The Federal government now works for the caste system, always makin' pure whites superior!"

Charles scratched his greying curly hair. "We were the buffer caste. Now that doesn't exist."

"Right," yelled Cable. "Just like a Creole no longer has Negro blood. Now they say the mixture just means French an' Spanish. Heavens, what next?"

"These recent Latin American refugees still have Negro blood, now they'll be white, while America's older colored'll be punished as solid blacks, an' unworthy!"

"It's a disease," Marg told them. "George, you keep on writin' about it. Maybe that's the medicine."

Cable laughed, and quickly took up his napkin. Marg was glad to see that he was well-bred. "Mrs. Spence, if you give a disease a diet of yams, historical yams, a few people will improve. I'm a romanticist after their conscience. I write about love. Very often my heroines are lovely an' beautiful Creole girls who've been smitten by Yankee types who have accepted them as individuals but scorn them as a group—"

Charles shook his head. "George," he chuckled, "on deep moral issues, what kind of southerner are you?"

"Transplanted!" laughed Cable. "My father's from Virginia an' my mother, New England. That's the medicine!"

"Interesting," said Charles, impressed. "An' you know Louisiana history so well."

"You have to, to be a good American. You see, Pop died when I was fourteen. I had to work to support the family. I read in place of the schoolin' I didn't get."

"Wonderful," cried Marg, really liking him. "Our group produced Pushkin for Russia and Alexandre Dumas for France. We need you next. Have you been published yet?"

"Not yet," confessed George. "Only newspaper stuff. I show what I write whenever I can. My mother tells me I have to be more aggressive. I have a friend who really writes well; he now calls himself Mark Twain. We met in a saloon. Sam's idea is that you must travel. He's runnin' a press in California now. So, I'm beginning my travels by seeing Georgia."

"Very good," laughed Charles. "The two of you should continue encouraging each other. And bein' aggressive, you'll get yo' foot in the door! But as I understand it, yours is like ministry work; you'll never make much of a livin' at it."

"Well," sighed Cable, a little dejected, "it should serve another purpose than money. I really want to let the country know how people feel. You know, nice people, *like you*, whom they forget are Americans . . ."

"Splendid," smiled Marg, grabbing young Cable's yellow-haired arm. "Have I got some stories for you!"

"Oh, yes. My wife should talk to you." Charles was encouraging the friendship. He was really thinking about an engagement he had out in Cobb's Creek; some young almond-eyed thing who didn't believe that he was 44 years old.

Chapter 31

There was trouble brewing in Washington. In March of 1867 Congress had passed the Tenure of Office Act to limit the President's ability to remove any high officials without the Senate's approval. Edwin Stanton, Secretary of War, was giving Johnson so much trouble he let him go in August, and laid steps to put General Ulysses Grant in his place. For people like Thaddeus Stevens this was the straw that broke the camel's back. He wanted Johnson condemned, and Congress to soar as the country's gold apex. But Congress was peppered with partisan fights. Politicians raced across the country shouting views to be remembered in the November elections. Some sly ones, like Rutherford B. Hayes, would run for office side-stepping the issue of Negro suffrage. It could make him governor of Ohio. Poor Thaddeus Stevens took a brief rest; it was said he was suffering with dropsy of the chest, thought to be dying.

As elections grew near, graft was rampant all over the country. The various state conventions had cost thousands of dollars. Alone among southern states, South Carolina had a legislature with a Negro majority. The state had 80,550 registered Negro voters and only 46,880 whites. Their free public school system meant mixed attendance. The big shock was the talk of dividing land among freedmen. In Louisiana, public conveyances were thrown open to both races—the theaters, schools, and the university as well. The disfranchising schemes meant that state conventions had to concentrate on writing laws. In Georgia, the document framed was considered reasonably conservative and sane, because of the wise influence of Governor Joe Brown. While conservatives stayed away from the polls, a majority vote was required. Georgia's Ben Hill thought they'd be short thirty thousand votes, so he urged they adopt the constitution by default. In Arkansas conservatives gave a hard fight to Radical leaders. Where the Union League had its

agents sweeping into plantations and into Negro cabins, white southerners had race-haters at work as well.

In November, Democratic gains were achieved everywhere. They
triumphed in California, and nibbled at the normal Republican majority of Maine. Even in Thad Stevens' town of Lancaster, Pa. they
gained. The angry old man yelled "Impeach, now!" While Negro suffrage was defeated in Ohio, and Johnson was glad, Jay Cooke, deeply
disappointed, blamed Radical Republicans with all their bitterness. The
Congress met and Stevens crawled into his seat with a grim determination to destroy Andrew Johnson.

Marg decided to have her children home for that Christmas of
1867. Some of their classmates would be coming partway South, and
they could travel together. Actually Marg didn't fear for her children
being alone, since they were fair enough to be pure whites. But the
atmosphere was always terrible wherever colored people moved freely
in public. Hateful whites were determined to deny courtesy to dark
people, and they'd show off wherever laws and customs allowed them
this freedom.

The house now was too dead at holidays, and poor Jason of course
needed to get to know his kin better. The boy was doing very well in
kindergarten, at the Claffin School, in town. It had a mixture of students: the black ex-slaves, the yellow ex-slaves, the Free Negroes and
the Near-whites who were not rich enough to get away. The three colored ladies who had lived at Malcolm House were among its teachers.
They loved Jason, and protected him from the rowdies and jealous
older boys who'd push him down, saying he came from a family of
slaveowners. Marg was hoping people could forget the past and live
together, but Maple was getting to be a belligerent town. Whites who
had never owned a slave were now dictating to every darkskinned person. Since there was nothing Christian about their behavior, dark people had to be ready to protect themselves.

Her three children had many questions once they got home, and
were riding around the city. There were many strange and biting new
laws, called black codes. The military authorities let them happen, and
were not resisting the new rabid local administration. Now, colored
were never served in stores until every white face was served first.
They could not enter the same railroad station with the whites. They
had a separate waiting room, with a sign marked "Colored". Marg
took her mob right through the center of the old waiting room, as if
they were pure whites. Yet, when the children were alone she told them
to obey the new laws, to go where colored were supposed to go. She

didn't want a hair on their pretty heads harmed. John now was her particular worry. He still went out with Cindy Hunter.

The new St. James Methodist was in Wentworth, a so-called white town. It had remained independent of the AME diocese. They had bought land, and as before, built a religious school next to the new church. Cousin Don, although ailing with a stomach disorder, went back to preaching and schoolteaching. At old St. James, now St. James Baptist, Cobb's Creek had its biggest congregation. No longer an intellectual haven, the spirited countrified service drew them in. Yet another new minister, Rev. Moses Coates, strengthened the spirit with good hand-clappers, and politicians too. Five members held top jobs with the occupation Army. Waving his hands angrily, Coates denounced the meddling whites who had come at midnight to scar his doors and break his windows. The sexton now would live in and carry a shotgun. He told his congregation that the war had not ended.

More than a year had passed since Rev. Houston had gone back to Savannah. Yet Charles still missed him because they had become fast friends, fishing the creek together at least once a week. He had just gained a seat in Georgia's senate, but he and Charles still exchanged letters about every four months. Houston's last letter dwelled on the troubles of Savannah's Freedmen's Bureau with its inept and hostile staff. While he didn't mention it, he had become known in Washington by telling the Johnson administration that the whole colored community throughout the South was suffering abuse from angry local whites and pompous Union people in the Bureaus.

This was also being said by new black leaders in the North who were getting heard in newspapers. However, they all knew the real problem was a self-centered, anti-Negro Congress, which felt the Negro should have nothing until every white man had everything! Illiterate Europeans were coming in. And with immigration at high level, trade unions grew strong and lily-white. Negroes could not get the skilled jobs they had done for decades. The post-slavery caste system was letting new white Americans take their place! Where the poor Irish had served as indentured servants close enough to the Negro to bear his children, now they were separated and superior. Even the new dark Europeans were regarded as superior. The position of the Negro in USA was slipping down, down, down.

At dinner conversations the children were also learning from Uncle Gregory who told about his work in the Georgia Legislature. Marg quietly fumed, remembering all the bigshots she now knew in Washington. Looking at Charles turning grey right in front of her, she decided she was still young in spirit. She'd accompany the children back North, at least as far as Washington. And she'd spend a few weeks with her dear, secret Justine.

The real problem was getting somebody to run the store. Valerie had volunteered but she was much too busy keeping Gregory's tailorshop operating with its two black apprentices. Lilian Simpson too wanted to help out, but she still had nurse duties arising from Dr. Lou's patients, many still white. Marg decided the only thing to do was to ask Matilda, but when the black woman flatly refused, Marg was hurt. Actually Matilda didn't refuse outright; she made her price so high Marg couldn't afford it. She wanted one hundred dollars to watch the store for two months. Marg considered making it one month, but she did want to study at Georgetown, and her course would not be over until March. She talked her problem over with Charles and he naturally suggested Cousin Sue. She could ride over with Mitchell and Albert. Marg felt gleeful. She wondered why she had never thought of her dear, northern-trained Cousin Sue.

Sue, square and strong, now with short blond hair, came to learn the business several days before Marg was ready to leave. She had never been around a place where people came in wanting things. Marg told her how to behave if they were surly whites, or angry Negroes. Larry would be there to back her up, and the shotgun was in his office. Actually peaceful Larry was disappointed. He had wanted his wife Maggie Mae to have the job, but Miss Margery never thought of her. None of her girls had enough fight in them, except Matilda.

That January and February of 1868 Washington was tense. Grant and Stanton were still fighting over the War Department, and newspapers were interfering. Stanton, while posing as an ultra-Democrat, had been double-dealing with Buchanan and Charles Sumner, and now, Johnson. It seems even Grant too was differing with Johnson whom he accused of holding too much power and control. The Senate went into pandemonium when it received the White House's notice to remove Stanton. The poor man was served at a masquerade ball at Marini's. In the morning, citizens rushed to the Capitol, fearing the President's overlooking of Congress, and the rumors of a new civil war. Thad Stevens was there, haggard and quiet, ready for the killing. The enemy had played into his hands. Today, he'd offer impeachment resolutions.

Marg sat cooing with her baby until Lydia arrived by carriage, urging her to get dressed. They were going to the night session of Congress. It was Washington's birthday. Holman of Indiana got up and asked for the reading of the Farewell Address. The clerk began. Bang, went Colfax's gavel. The Farewell Address was out of order. They were there for current speeches. The voting would now be on Monday. The elegant citizens went home. Washington buzzed with excitement that whole week-end.

Monday broke dark and stormy. Again Lydia came for Marg. Snow was falling. They both were dolled up in woolens, perfume and furs. As they conspicuously entered the House, they found the galleries brilliant with gay colors. All the elegant ladies of Washington were there. Marg met a charming Mrs. Kate Chase Sprague, the Chief Justice's socially-prominent daughter. They in fact sat in the same fragrant row of seats. Then there were seven long hours of debate. Through it all, down below, Thad Stevens, sick and half reclined, sat resolutely. His great hour had come. Finally, with cane and helping hands, he got up to speak his impeachment resolution. The roll was called. Colfax then had to name a committee to prepare the articles of impeachment.

The next day, the committee worked feverishly preparing the articles. Some people wanted to quarrel with Stevens on the legalities; he gave them some profanity. Finally there were eleven articles, nine to remove Stanton, the tenth concerning Johnson's speeches, said to have disgraced Congress, and the eleventh, a catch-all designed by Stevens to get to a sensitive Congress, to capture votes to get rid of Johnson. In New York, some nitroglycerine mysteriously disappeared, and additional guards were stationed about the Capitol, and Stanton himself summoned more soldiers for his protection.

Horace Greeley in New York claimed that the politicians knew that Wall Street and Fifth Avenue were not with them. There was a mass meeting at Cooper Union; the big talk and clamor was about the 'law'. Ben Wade, heir apparent, sat at home by his Washington fire, in dressing-gown, waiting for his call to power.

Johnson, calm and dignified, went on with the business of ruling and living. He came with his charming daughters to a reception given by Chief Justice Chase. The rumor was that detectives were watching senators and soon would be watching the Chief Justice. Privately Johnson was discussing his selection of lawyers. He first chose the distinguished Jeremiah S. Black. Then mysteriously Black's name was dropped.

It seems Black had requested a man-of-war be sent to Haiti when some clients of his had a million-dollar claim to the island of Alta Vela. This request was rejected. And now his plan for Johnson's acquittal was rejected. Johnson felt the scheme proposed was dishonest, and against his conscience. Black, realizing the President was sore, had second thoughts and apologized. But Johnson didn't want him now. Radicals had tried to misrepresent the incident; Johnson now was advised to be a silent man from now on.

Marg didn't go anymore to the Thaddeus Stevens' house. The man was much too busy and too ill. Lydia claimed that she was constantly trying to strengthen him, and to keep life simple at that little brick house on B Street. But all kinds of politicians, businessmen and newspapermen came there, trying to see the congressman who was shaping history, and the country. Two Negro boys had been hired to carry him in a chair to his office at the House. He still kept his humor. One day he turned to the blacks carrying him and said: "What am I to do when you boys are dead?"

Lydia had him in a fine sable suit on the day the trial opened, on March 30, 1868. His black wig was neat and a pillow softened his chair. Marg was there. She had written home that she was staying on, for these important events. Actually she could call them a family matter although she had made no effort to see the President. She listened as Butler gave the opening argument for the prosecution, not knowing if she were on Mr. Stevens' side or the President's side. The country was in a mess, but she felt it was the people's fault and not any one man in government. In fact, Andrew Johnson was being made a scapegoat. She couldn't tell Lydia this, for Lydia was one hundred per cent behind her man's point of view.

William Evarts made a speech in the President's defense, showing that all the paper activity had not hurt Stanton in the least. He said to violate an unconstitutional law is no crime. Johnson had done no more than Lincoln. Meanwhile, letters were pouring into the White House, men wanting to enlist in the new civil war. Newspapers printed gossip; the country's focus was off but it basically remained calm. Johnson went about unguarded. He met his Cabinet in his library, because the Cabinet room was now being used by lawyers preparing his defense. The trial resumed and a regular fashion show was in the galleries where beautiful ladies in most gorgeous apparel, who came to be seen, tried to get a mention in the press. Marg's name was twice in the Washington papers. Once for attending a party at Jay Cooke's residence, and again for being in the company of the sociable Kate Chase Sprague. She was glad nobody had discovered her connections with Andrew Johnson. That would be enough to kill the man.

Outside the Senate Chamber where some entertainment prevailed, the Charles Dickens readings were stopped, because of the impeachment trials, and the fact the novelist was ailing. Fanny Kemble was giving dramatic readings to packed houses. Others were going to Dan

Rice's Circus. Marg herself went with Louise to see Joe Jefferson in "Rip Van Winkle", and another time they got to hear the spiritualist, Mrs. Daniels, at Harmonial Hall. It was springtime in Washington and nobody stayed at home.

Anthony had come back from Paris and he wanted to ride down and visit Marg in Washington, but she flatly refused. She was not ready to deal with the issue of her family knowing about the baby. Even dear Anthony could not be trusted. She told him she had chest pains, and this was true. She gave him some duties with Mr. Haney and these, fortunately, could be handled in the mail. He sent his sister a clipping from the *New York Herald* of April 26, 1868. Everybody liked minstrels and black jokes. This was a suggested new plantation melody. It went: "Old Andy's gone, ha, ha!
And Old Ben's come, ho, ho!
It must be de kingdom am a-comin'
In de year of jubilo."

Charles wrote Marg to come home. He was lonesome. She promised she would as soon as her college exams were over. She did go to Georgetown two days a week. Actually she was waiting for a big speech Lydia had told her Mr. Stevens was preparing. They would go one last time together to the House gallery. In pearls!

The day was April 27th. Just as the hour struck, the Negro chairbearers bore the ailing old man, like an ancient pharoah, to his seat. Soon he was reading his speech. For thirty minutes. Then he turned pale and handed it over to Butler to finish. Marg found it a bitter warning for any senator who'd vote for acquittal. It was not a good speech. As William Maxwell Evarts got up to speak, Marg decided to go home. She had heard enough of Washington. She'd pack and start home the next day.

The train was bearable this time because she insisted on Pullman service. But it was taken off at Atlanta, and once again she had to ride in a crowded dirty coach. They were practicing Jim Crow throughout Georgia! The Negroes were not allowed to sit near white people. Conductors were making them get up and move, all bunched together at one end. While Washington played theatrics!

Marg felt like talking up, but she was thought to be a white woman. She sat back enjoying it, asking Jesus if this was sinning.

Charles shocked Marg by saying he wanted to go to Savannah to become a high official. Houston had gotten him the offer of Commissioner of Ports and Waterways. Charles wanted this job. He felt they could rent a house in Savannah and stay there half the year. He wanted the experience of being a government official. Marg tried to talk to him about the needs of their store, but he wasn't interested. Now she realized that his enthusiasm was no longer out at their Wentworth establishment. Besides, he claimed some new people had bought the vacant store next door, and soon would open some kind of business.

What Charles didn't say, Marg had to discover for herself. The new business neighbors were an uneducated bunch of blacks! She didn't know how they had gotten the money to buy the place. She criticized Charles for not knowing ahead of time that the building was being sold. They could have bought it. Now, with uncouth blacks there, making noise, what were they to do? Mainly, they did not know what kind of business next door would have. There was a lot of wood going in. A lot of hammering. Somebody said they were building rooms, to make it a hotel. Marg decided to go to Mrs. Bowne again, to pressure her to give up that land on Broad Street. Marg wanted to build her own building. Charles said he wasn't interested now. Either he'd go to Savannah or get out of business. Poor man. She never had thought of him as a government official. But it was a matter of respect. She knew that.

Back in Washington, her erstwhile poor kin, Andrew Johnson, was suffering also in a matter of respect. Senate voting on the impeachment articles began May 16th. At the final roll call on May 26th, all was intense drama. Ross of Kansas voted "Not Guilty", and the contest virtually closed minus the one crucial vote they needed for conviction. The Methodist Church at its general conference had had an hour of prayer beseeching God to help senators toward truth rather than error. Marg knew that life was controlled by people acting out little prejudices. As soon as news of the results reached her she sighed in relief, thanking God, then she sat down and wrote a note to President Johnson. And within a few days she received back a personal reply, which read:

June 12, 1868

My dear Mrs. Spence,

I am deeply touched to have your kind letter at this time. You know I shall treasure it and continue my service with strength from God, and with the faith of the people.

Yours sincerely,

Andrew Johnson.

Marg felt wonderful, mainly because the cheap white man delivering her mail had seen the beautifully-embossed envelope with "The Executive Mansion" in strong black letters up in the corner. Now he had more respect for her. Just an envelope had done it.

Chapter 32

This time Mrs. Bowne relented. She'd sell Marg the property she wanted on Broad Street. Marg was ecstatic. She'd hire an architect-engineer and plan a fantastic place. It would be the most modern business building in the city. Meanwhile, they'd continue selling in their splintered wood Wentworth building. Business was brisk both in the green-grocery and upstairs. The new blacks next door had opened a dancehall. Actually it was some kind of clubhouse. They only were there on week-ends. Marg didn't meet any of them but she decided this was all right. Then, lo and behold, they had some function one afternoon. Carriages took over all of Marg's parking lot. There was a loud band playing, and all kinds of fancifully-dressed Negroes going in. Her white customers didn't like it. They all wore sour faces.

Sure enough, in two weeks' time, Marg's business had dropped off considerably. She tried to put her mind into the new place where the ground was being broken. If they could get some newspaper publicity, all would be fine. But the *Maple Star-Journal* still had a policy of publishing no good news about mulattoes or blacks. Now Maple blacks were more than fifty per cent of the population. And many of them would vote, come November. After her building was up, she'd pressure civic authorities to do better by the black population. At least they should have equal use of the press.

Marg was so busy that August drawing plans for her new business building, that she stopped all reading of newspapers and journals. Thus, she had a real shock upon receiving a letter from Louise Johnson saying Thaddeus Stevens was dead. The letter read:

August 23, 1868

My dear Margery,

    I'm sure you've read the news that poor Mr. Thaddeus Stevens died on August 13th. I saw him a month earlier when he was trying to help the lady artist, Miss Vinnie Ream, get back her working place in the Capitol Building. He was deeply hurt when Mr. Buchanan died. You know they had been old buddies back in Lancaster, as well as political cohorts. The Senate adjourned when the news came. The House too was to adjourn but Mr. Stevens wanted to offer a resolution. When he got up he really wanted to talk about his own impending death. He asked his colleagues to fling ambition away. I think his last vote was for the Alaskan Purchase.

He went home to B Street late July, too feeble to return to Lancaster. Lydia wanted him to go straight to bed but he refused, staying on his feet, paddling around the house until about August 10th, when he had to go to bed. He was two days in bed. Wouldn't talk to anyone. I took flowers over there. He just relaxed in the covers, looking as if he were sleeping. The doctor came to change his medicine. He opened his eyes and said grimly—"Well, this is a square fight". Lydia had sent for two colored Sisters of Charity who were attached to Providence Hospital, which Mr. Stevens had helped to found. And then she got two colored ministers to come. They prayed at his bedside.

Mr. Evarts and Mr. Sumner were among evening callers, but Lydia made it a colored folks' evening. He was sinking. Doctor asked him how he felt. He said: "Very mean, doctor." Sister Loretta then asked to baptize him in the Catholic faith. Lydia agreed. She got down on her knees. Mr. Stevens died holding Sister Loretta's hand. That night, the colored company of Zouaves came and stood guard over his body. At noon, next day, about fifty of them accompanied the body to the Rotunda of the Capitol. Lydia said he remembered your praise of rosewood, so she got him a rosewood coffin. He lay in state there till midnight. Many visitors. Mourners. Next morn, a black hearse dawn by four white horses moved his casket to Pennsylvania Station. He left Washington to be buried in Lancaster. I didn't go. Lydia wrote me that he lay in state again in Lancaster, again guarded by Zouaves. In the procession they had 15,000 people. Now here was a man baptized a Catholic, with burial service read by a Lutheran minister and a sermon by an Episcopal clergyman, although the only church he cared about was the Baptist, church of his mother.

The will allows Lydia to occupy the house for five years. She'll get $500 annuity for life, or five thousand cash. His nephew is to get the rest of his fortune, if he abstains from liquor for fifteen years. But this is doubtful. He's buried in the colored Catholic cemetery. There is a place for Lydia next to him.

Justine is fine. Lovely. I'll tell you more in my next letter.

Love,

Louise.

Marg had to have herself a bit of brandy to digest the sad news from Washington. Poor Mr. Stevens. He had been such a help to the country. She knew some would be cursing Lydia for treating him like a colored person. Well, that was precisely what Mr. Stevens wanted. He wanted to shame all those bigots who thought themselves too good to be next to niggers.

She told her children. They had been home close to the house all summer. Rather listless, all three of them. Maybe it was the terrible Georgia heat they were not enjoying. Like Marg, they didn't have many friends in Maple. She encouraged them to get to church to meet people. Once they went all together as a family. Cousin Don was proud to introduce them to his congregation. After service, Marg saw a lovely blond girl with a beautiful face talking with some young people on the church's meadow. Right away she felt this one to be the perfect young lady for her John. She went over and introduced herself. The girl's name was Hattie Clark. Her people had recently moved to Maple from Dothan, Alabama. Her father was a doctor. No, her parents had not come to church this Sunday. Marg was a bit forward and anxious. She invited the girl to come visit at Malcolm House. And bring her family.

Sure enough, one afternoon early in September a fine carriage drove up with the Clark family. They were very fair people, just like the Spences. Marg was delighted to meet Dr. Irwin Clark, his lovely wife, Edna, a son named Edward, and to see once again lovely Hattie. John too thought Hattie with her lank straight blond hair was all right. He sat next to her at lunch, and they talked about schools. She was at a nice swank seminary in Atlanta, for colored girls. Soon after eating he excused himself. He had a date with Cindy Hunter out in Edgeworth. Marg felt now he was too much like his father.

The Clarks had built a huge new house not far from the old mansion area of Walnut Street. Dr. Clark was from an old Alabama family. Mixed like most rich southern families. Clarke County was named after the white ones. He was born in Thomasville, but began his practice in Dothan to be independent. They had moved from Dothan because of the new black codes down there, which were worse than slavery times. They had been stoned and their lavish house had been burned by vandals. Dr. Clark blamed a new group of local officials who relied on poor whites, and a vigilante group called the Ku Klux Klan. He said the latter, for white supremacy, were spreading hate all over the South. Wearing masks, they'd undertake beatings and even lynchings, to terrorize blacks whom they claimed should stay away from voting booths, guns and white jobs. A free Negro, to them, threatened the fair flowers of white womanhood. Marg knew this to be the thinking of diseased minds. She had heard similar talk from Gus Wheatland when he was doing his devilment.

"They're here in Maple too," said Dr. Clark, finishing his cordial. "You see, the plan was to intimidate poor Negroes who might take the sheets for ghosts. But devilment grows, an' they wanted a bigger laugh intimidating the well-to-do colored man. My trouble in Alabama, I had to speak to their leader, General Clanton one day, when some of them were around. So, I became their target."

"You mean you did nothing to arouse them?" asked Marg, alarmed.

"Nothing at all. When they found out I was rich, oh, they harassed me every day, an' more so when they saw that I had a fair wife and an Anglo-Saxon blond daughter."

"What in the world are we goin' to do?" asked Marg, finishing her own drink. "Dr. Clark, have you opened yo' office yet in Maple?"

"Not really. I've got a little makeshift office at my home."

"Well, I've got a deal for you. I want you in my new building. It will be ready in five months. Absolutely the finest business building in this city."

"Well, that sounds great," said Clark, looking at his wife for her approval. "That should boost me way up."

"It may be a risk as well," Marg warned him. "But I think you're as much a pioneer as I am. I think we have to give these bigots a fight. Don't you agree?"

Clark agreed, and Marg was very happy about her new friendship.

The next day she drove out to Wentworth to have a word with Cousin Don. When he wasn't preaching he was reading and collecting facts about the country's race problem. She was sure he knew something about the Ku Klux Klan.

"Sure, my dear, I've heard of them. They started in Tennessee back at Christmas 1865. Six young boys, looking for some fun. The original idea was to have a few laughs frightening the Negro. Then they found strong support, lots of people wanting a southern outfit to offset the so-called harm being done by northern Union League people. Now it's caught on seriously, even in Maple. They have some of the best military men as their leaders. Gen. John Gordon heads the Georgia group. Yet, they've been involved in ugly, anti-Christian acts. Terrible lynchings."

"Does the government care?"

"Oh, Washington knows about them. One of Mr. Stevens' Radical Republicans, Governor Holden, helped them get popular by a newspaper joke. A little article suggesting Negroes go after white women. It inflamed the Klan and got them into politics."

"Do you think they'll do us harm?"

"Pests can grow to do harm, my dear. When I first read about KKK I was thinkin' it wouldn't get anti-Negro, because the Lowry boys of the original six, in Tennessee, have Scotch-Irish ancestry, yet really are from our people."

"No! Cousin Don, we don't have that kind of hatred among us."

"Scot-Irish, Indian, German, Negro, it's all American hatred, my dear. The country's one grand mix, whether or not the people believe it. Why should any of them be hating the next one?"

Just as Marg was leaving she asked her relative's advice about Charles' plan to go to Savannah.

"Let him go," shouted Don. "Will do him some good. I'm sure you're strong enough to stand on yo' own feet for a while."

"He wanted me to go to Savannah with him."

"I can't advise you on that. I'm sure by now you know duty and loyalty. A wife encourages a man to those higher attainments he may feel fit to pursue. Frankly, I like Charles, sinner that he is. Sure, let him go to Savannah. It's all in God's plan."

That night Marg told Charles word-for-word the advice from Cousin Don. Without comment, Charles went off to write his friend Houston. Meanwhile, Marg sat at her bureau with a letter. It read:

September 24, 1868

My dear Margery,

Justine is finally walking! Like an angel. I'm so proud of her. Her hair is silky, turning dark, but we don't mind that. I'm reading story books to her, *Alice in Wonderland*, just now.

Everybody in Washington is talking about Anna Dickinson's book "What Answer?" which is about a rich young white man marrying a colored woman. I read it. I thought it a sincere little story. Well, here, they've made it a political football. They say the authoress is a Radical and was dismissed from her factory job during the war, for demonstrating against Gen. McClellan. The *New York World* calls the book literary mess, like Sylvanus Cobb's editorials for the *Tribune*. They say the book couldn't occur in certain countries. "And what treason to the Radicals, too, to make the heroine but three-fourths black!" They say Wendell Phillips should look after this straying sister—"educate her up to the full glory of the wool head and the tar heel."

It seems the *Tribune* took the opportunity to get out a story on the savagery of southern whites, tying blacks to trees, whipping them, and murdering. A New Orleans writer, William Chandler, used the occasion to bring out the lawlessness and violence of that city. Some think Mr. Grant can stop it all. Lydia tells me the soldiers are marching again in Philadelphia. In New York, Tammany has

staged a pre-election spectacle featuring a bosomy Irish girl as god-
dess of Liberty, audaciously wearing red cap, carrying pikestaff in
one hand and broken chains in the other. Greedy white people don't
know what they're demonstrating for. Lord, help us!

Your cousin,

Louise.

She was going to answer right away but Charles came back into the
room. He said he'd be leaving for Savannah within two weeks. Marg
wanted him to delay it a while. She wanted to give a big party out at the
store, a way of saying thanks and good-bye to all their good customers,
before their new place opened. She wanted Charles at her party. He
told her to put it late in the next month and he perhaps could get back
by train. In fact, he liked the idea of a party after his appointment. As
commissioner he'd have a uniform and all their friends and customers
could see him in it, see how far he had gone from a vegetable cart to a
big job in government.

Charles was gone by the first of October. Marg got busy planning
her party for the third week in November. She wanted it outdoors, a
barbecue in the yard, and that would be about as late as they could have
it before cold weather. She'd get Larry to build a big open charcoal
stove with turning spit. Jason's three schoolteachers from up North
could get her a dance couple and some musicians. Maybe Mitchell and
Larry could build a grandstand and she'd get her girls to decorate it in
beautiful colors. And the children could have balloons and a maypole
with crepe streamers. They'd have great fun.

She thought of inviting the whole colored community, but since
her business had been interracial, it was proper to invite both colors.
Without mixing them. She put full weeks on all this and didn't feel
lonesome for Charles way off in Savannah. Before long she was writing
the invitations.

One night there was a knock at her door. Larry bringing up a hot
cup of tea, for her. She was surprised because he never did household
chores, now that he was wood specialist out at the store. He had come
to talk. Reaching for her robe, Marg invited him in. As in slavery
times, he stood and she sat down.

"It's about dem new people," he said. "Miss Margery, I found out
who the store belongs to. It's Ida Winston's place, although she's got
her husband's brother runnin' it."

Marg frowned, not remembering who Ida Winston was. Then it
came to her. This was Matilda! "Larry, are you sure?"

"Yes'm, indeedy. Dat's why I'm tellin' you. All dem parties dey holds at night when yo' store is closed. All neighbors know 'bout it. Miss Margery, it's a loose place. A broddle—"

"A what? You mean, brothel? Oh no, Larry! We can't have that!"

"Yes'm, i'tis. Dey pay off the Sheriff. Dat's why you ain't nebeh seen 'em out dere."

Marg now stood up. "Well, thank you, Larry. I appreciate the information. We'll do something about it."

She went back to Cousin Don. He listened, adjusting his glasses and frowning. His whitish eyebrows made him look like an albino these days. "Well, Marg, if Rev. Moore and Rev. Coates will go in with me, I'll request an injunction. But this will take the cooperation of the whole community—"

"And Matilda will be angry with me."

"You shouldn't be afraid of her. There are laws to protect the serenity of the countryside. Any anti-Christian behavior must be stopped. I'll talk to the ministers."

As Marg left, she toyed with the idea of keeping the old store running. And she'd ask Larry not to talk of Matilda's place with people in the store. Of course she told Mitchell and Albert. It was their business as well as hers. They smiled, accepting human nature. They wanted to stay on running the two stores: the new one Uptown, and this favorite original store.

"Let's not make any fast decision," said beefy Mitchell still looking like an adolescent. "Out here in Cobb's Creek people respect each other, even though some may be doin' wrong, keepin' it on the quiet. We won't have no trouble in daylight!"

Marg wrote Charles all the details, then tried to forget the matter. Charles' reply did not comment on Matilda. He told how very pleased he was with his new government job. He had to attend many official functions, and the Savannah people were treating him very cordial. He had a lavish apartment over the Merchant Seamen's Building. Three servants to take care of his every need. A brougham carriage with proper coachman and footmen. His dress uniform was much like a Navy officer's outfit. He was traveling in style and liking it. He said he'd be home on November tenth, to be in time for Marg's party on the twelfth.

The weather was still beautiful that year. The pecans were falling in sunlit patches where squirrels crouched, enjoying a feast. Marg got carpenters out to build the bandstand and a dance floor. On the morning of the party merchants began arriving with their wares, one after the other. Larry and Mitchell's brick oven smoked artistically, with barbecue meat from Maple's best butcher. Albert's daisychain of flowers made the yard look wonderful. Guests began arriving shortly after noon. Some brought food, others brought going-away gifts for Marg and Charles. He really looked handsome in sparkling uniform. Marg was sorry Frank Korner couldn't be there to take a picture of her man.

Sue, in linen and lace, arrived with musicians from the public school. While she was getting the boys set up, Jeeter took the children to try some barbecue before the crowd arrived. Jason hung on to Sue, who looked gorgeous with white woolen shawl that had belonged to her mother. A prized antique—something made by skilled slaves.

The dancing began about two p.m. The whites in their corner, and the colored in theirs. Everybody knew how to smile, and the warm weather made it relaxed fun. Soothing music filled the air, as did the smells of chicken, ham, ribs and barbecue sauce. Both groups raved about Maggie Mae's tart and spicy cole slaw. The drinking was sociable. Little party cups. No drunks.

Towards late afternoon, they heard doors slamming next door. Marg was apprehensive. Some whites were still there; she didn't want to hear a lot of commotion from the dancehall. What she heard was loud female laughter, coming from upstairs. Perhaps Larry was right in speaking of prostitution. With the windows up, it sounded just like that. Marg thought of how not to disturb her guests in the yard, and the children too. Her band could play louder. Then she went out to her parking lot to survey the happenings. Lo and behold, the dancehall people had wagons all jammed up against her people's wagons. Wheels touching wheels. Nobody would be able to get out. Marg decided to knock at the door and complain.

Who should answer but short, fat, happy-faced Matilda. All powdered and brown, in lacy pink dress. She carried a glass of whiskey in her stubby little fingers. "Oh, Miss Margery," she called with bright eyes. "You comin' to my party?"

Marg ignored the question. "These wagons in my lot, some of them will have to be moved. They're blocking everybody."

"Dat's my lot too," snapped Matilda, losing her smile. "You graded it all over, but Mr. Giles told me half of it's mine." She was about to close the door on her former mistress when Marg's hand went up to block the move.

"Just the same, Matilda, they have to be moved. As it is, nobody can get out. We don't want the horses to panic."

"God-dammit!" shouted Matilda, coming out with hands on her hips. "Don't you go givin' orders to me. I owns as much of dis land as you do!"

"Matilda, there's no need to shout at me."

"My name ain't Matilda, God-dammit. You address me like you should. I'm *Mrs.* Wilkins. Mrs. Ida Winston Wilkins. Do you heah what the hell I'm sayin'?"

"Matilda, don't you curse me. Now if you want me to fetch the sheriff, I will."

"You fetch him," screamed Matilda. "Call him!"

"Matilda, don't shout—" Just then, Matilda grabbed the bow of Miss Margery's party gown, giving it a pull that turned the wearer around. Marg steadied herself by grabbing the four-by-four wooden post. Her foot went out, and Matilda's foot met it. A hard kick, then Matilda grabbed her by the hair and pulled her off the porch and out into the yard. Now a number of people from both parties came out to look at this spectacle, a black-and-white fight.

"Didn't I tell you my name ain't Matilda," Matilda kept shouting. Her hands were flying as she beat on Marg and ripped at her clothing. "You have respect fo' me. You call me, damn it, by my right name! You're not goin' to abuse me any longer. Do you heah? Do you heah?"

Marg was thoroughly embarrassed. She didn't know what to do. But other than a sense of propriety, she had to have a sense of survival. So she put up her hands and pushed Matilda away each time the angry dark woman came at her.

"All dem years you abused me," yelled Matilda with angry eyes and hair now all wooly and disarranged. "Hittin' me with newspaper. Hittin' me with whips. No, God-dammit, I don't have to take no more. You white-faced hussy. Git out my face! Git out my face!"

Next thing, they were both down on the ground, in the dusty sand of the parking lot, rolling over and over. Some boys in both groups were yelling to keep the women fighting. Pretty soon Charles, in his fancy uniform, came out and separated them. Matilda was carried away by her half-drunk husband. And as Marg too now lost her temper, she cursed back and threw a stone, just as undignified as that slave bitch.

Soon all was quiet again. The sheriff had arrived and he was walking up with guns shining at his hip. Naturally he came to the party that had white guests. Marg, too upset to tell him anything, went to her office upstairs. Maggie Mae came with her, and put a cool wet rag on her forehead. Now the chest pains came. Marg felt awful. As she looked out the window, on all the festive colors in her backyard, she began to cry.

"Don't cry, Miss Margery," cooed Maggie Mae, quietly. "Everything will be all right."

Marg was thinking about her reputation. The Clarks were down there among her guests. Pretty Hattie and Dr. and Mrs. Clark. How could they ever believe she was a decent woman? And she had so much wanted to make a good impression, for her son's sake.

Chapter 33

Marg's tiff with Matilda was all over the front pages of the *Maple Star-Journal*. Moreover, the article slyly spoke of her stint in jail, her implication in the death of Gus Wheatland, and in the death of Judge Barlow's slave, Humphrey. All they knew, Humphrey had been seen at her house, and had received some money. Nobody knew for what, or about Marg's blackface nights. All this travesty of justice sickened her. Charles stayed, and tried to calm her down. He made her realize that nothing would be gained by pressing charges against Matilda. They'd just drop the matter. Both she and Matilda were fined by local authorities, for disturbing the peace and for operating parties without proper permits. The money would go to the vacation fund of the sheriff's staff.

Nowadays Cobb's Creek and Wentworth were served by the City of Maple's new police department. They had many uniformed white men, as in northern cities, walking around giving orders. They carried nightsticks and would beat on citizens, on all kinds of black people. Black preachers were complaining but so far nobody was listening to their complaints.

"It will come to a showdown," said fairskinned Dr. Clark as he visited one December afternoon at Malcolm House. "We all know, Mrs. Spence, that you were a victim and not a perpetrator."

"Even so," she claimed, nervously, "each time there's such an incident, you win a few more enemies. I don't want black people around town hating me. No matter what Matilda says, there's no reason for them to hate me."

Clark smiled. "Why don't you show the community your benevolence, by doing something especially for them. Make a donation to one of their causes."

"Dr. Clark, I don't believe in buyin' friendship. Anyway, the black hospital has always had our dollars, ever since my dear mother was alive."

"Why not make it a li'l more spectacular? Why can't you give them a school, a church, or even a new hospital?"

Marg's eyes popped. "You think I have that kind of money?"

"So it's rumored," he continued, pleasantly. "With yo' children in expensive northern schools, an' you putting up a $35,000 office building here. It's worth it, Mrs. Spence, to keep the good rumors flowing."

"Maybe I will," said Marg, standing. "I'll think of something spectacular. Maybe I can do it with yo' dollars helping." She gave him a knowing look. She knew now that he too was a very rich man.

In spite of the death of Thaddeus Stevens, the Radical Republicans were still in power in Washington, and now leadership went to Oliver Morton of Indiana, John Logan of Illinois, and Ben Butler of Massachusetts. Some regarded their procedures for adopting the fourteenth amendment as strong and unconstitutional. To be restored, southern states had had to establish Negro suffrage, create a constitution on a Radical pattern, and elect legislatures conforming to the new requirements. Southern states did not get back in the Union until redeemed by Congress. And the reconstruction act of March 2, 1867 had provided that no person excluded from office-holding by the proposed amendment could be eligible to election as a member of the state's convention to frame its state constitution.

Carpetbag legislatures did ratify the amendment in 1868. While Secretary Seward declared the amendment in force, Congress fought him and passed in haste its own resolution declaring the fourteenth article as part of the Constitution. Congress talked of 27 states in the Union, whereas Seward's version included 37 states. The question of whether states were "reconstructed" and back in the Union made the country on shaky legal ground. Moreover, there was a question as to whether Congress itself had the power it had assumed in this matter. So, in the presidential campaign of 1868, cocksure Republicans glossed over their glib acts of power in admitting or excluding southern states. They had narrowed down their roster of candidates to Chase, Colfax and Grant. Democrats in their July 1868 convention had declared the question of slavery and secession as settled, and moved for amnesty. The question of franchise to them belonged to the states. They also wanted the abolition of the Freedmen's Bureau. The powerbrokers of Democrats also had their keen, greedy eyes on Chase, but his own Ohio didn't support him enough. Smoky pow-wows among them even considered Andrew Johnson as their candidate. But Pendleton outstepped him in the first ballot. Horatio Seymour, former New York governor, was president of the convention and he got his chance in the fourth ballot, and remained till the twenty-second ballot.

Finally, in the election, the popular vote brought Seymour 2,703,000 votes while Grant got 3,012,000. In electoral votes Grant got 214 to Seymour's 80. It was said that a half-million Negroes voted for Grant, and only 50,000 for Seymour. Many northern states had refused to let the Negro vote. So, as that year of 1868 ended, the public knew that northern sentiment would not support nation-wide Negro suffrage. The Radicals would keep the issue open.

Sumner had pressured to have the Negro vote in the District of Columbia. Johnson had vetoed early in 1867 the suffrage bill which had passed both houses. Congress subsequently passed the bill over the President's veto. But as for the territories of Nebraska and Colorado, who had the voting privilege only for whites, there was some dilly-dallying. Nebraska got through whereas Johnson's veto of Colorado stayed. The real issue in the aftermath of the election was that Republicans were taking the vote as a mandate for enfranchisement of the African race.

Marg thought about it, and forgot about it. She had never been able to fit into the kidglove politics made for people. It was Christmas-time, and she sent her usual messages of good cheer in many directions. She thought of writing Charles Waverly at his Ohio address. Her Bible spoke of the need to take initiative in friendships. But she still had not forgiven him for sending a note only to Jeeter and Sue. Instead, she sent a message to Tom Haney. In fact, on a whim she'd also send him one of the Malcolm tables. He loved beautiful things, and he had been a very good friend.

Along about the end of January 1869 Marg finished buying materials for her new stucco and brick building. It would be a magnificent edifice—three stories high, in Spanish design, with red tile roof and big arches and arched windows. She had seen such a building in a photo Mrs. Bowne had shown her of Mexico. Hers would have a similar courtyard. For six retail stores, each with patio in smooth red terrazzo. There'd be benches so people could sit down, and palm trees. Bill Cahill got a young Atlanta friend to do the drawings, for twelve hundred dollars. They were all excited because, for sure, it would be the most attractive building in Maple.

Marg thought of naming it "Spence Building", but decided, thinking of her father, Malcolm should be in the name. She wanted both communities to feel at home coming there. Little did she realize that racial feelings were too strong for that.

The building was first to be finished in April, then May. By June she still did not have her water connected. Rayford Innis was supposed to approve the site for occupation, but he kept finding things wrong.

Each time Cahill would hand him a ten dollar bill, on the side. The contractors, McDowell and Son, were the best in Muscogee County, but the workers laid down on the job, purposely, knowing she was a rich colored woman. After delays and cost overruns, Marg got in Negro workers, paying them extra to correct the bad work done by the whites. Then her white contractor came back, behaving better. He explained that the cost of materials had been under-estimated. Finally she agreed to buy most of the major things herself. In his supply of mere nails, cement and labor, he charged a fortune. She knew she had to pay it to get the building finished.

When the grand opening came in September, Marg only had two tenants, Dr. Clark and her old friend, Dr. Lou Simpson. Gregory and Valerie were supposed to take one store for their tailorshop, but considered the rent too high, and they really liked their old place in the black neighborhood. Marg's location, next door to the city's leading shopping area, was basically a white area. So far, the whites boycotted her fancy place. She hadn't expected that. When Mitchell and Albert soon opened their greengrocery there, many thinking they were white flocked to their store. Then news got around that they were "quadroons", in Marg's family, and the new trade slacked off.

"I'm not goin' to lower my rent," Marg told Dr. Clark one morning over coffee. "The place is well worth what I ask. I'll just be patient. Oh, did you know, the Union League asked for offices up on the third floor. I'm afraid to let them in my building."

"That's right," laughed Dr. Clark, in a singsong. "They're regarded as carpetbaggers an' that's the best way to have the Ku Klux Klan pestering you. How about the darkskinned colored people. Don't you want them?"

Marg sighed. "Well, a few of everybody. That's what I had in mind. My friend, Mrs. Bowne, promised me a white doctor and a white lawyer. She's gone up to Newport for the women's suffrage convention, and I think they got cold feet. Hah!"

"Go visit them. You have to be a li'l aggressive in business. Or, let me do it!"

"You want to do it for me?"

He smacked his lips, finishing his coffee. "Well, I'm gettin' a pretty good reputation in this town. I'm workin' with both sides. Cautiously. Yo' old friend Korner even talks to me."

"Oh, Frank! And Phyllis. How are they doin'?"

"Very well. I can't imagine why feelings are so strong between you. This place would be excellent for their shop. You want me to talk to Frank?"

"No. I'm not begging. If they want to come, it's on their own. Phyllis knows she's been hateful to me for no sane reason. You don't let a bunch of rednecks dictate to you how to treat friends. I think they realize they made a mistake, but they have too much pride to turn around and say so—"

"And so do you. This is precisely what the war has done to people."

"While President Grant lounges at Long Branch, we're sinking," said Marg, pouring more coffee. Edna Clark, returning from shopping, joined her husband. He passed her coffee and continued talking.

"I know that Washington scene. It's busy with knaves. Grant's bewildered by the scope of his office. He's just lost his secretary of war, Rawlins. I'd met General Rawlins, a remarkable man. A very good judge of character. If the Cabinet has any other that good it's Hamilton Fish."

"You mean the secretary of state? I met his wife in Washington. Yes, Mrs. Kate Chase Sprague introduced us."

"Those are powerful ladies. And elegant too. Mrs. Fish does much for the arts. We go to Washington now and then. My wife's brother lives there. Julian Hemings. Do you know him?"

"No, but the name sounds familiar."

Clark smiled. "They're all in the family of President Thomas Jefferson."

"Really? Oh, Edna, how fascinating!"

Edna threw her hand and made a little face. "Honey, don't put too much in that."

"It's something to be proud of," continued Marg. "Who were your forebears?"

"Well." Edna smiled serenely. "My paternal grandmother was Critta, Sally Hemings' sister. They all lived at Monticello. My father, Jamy, was born in 1787. He was one of the runaways. He ran off in 1804 to be a carpenter. He could have been a white man, but he didn't choose to be."

Clark cut in. "You see, two others who ran off, Harriet and Beverly, a man, they went off as white, married white and remained white. An' Tom looked so much like Thomas Jefferson, everybody knew, and Jefferson loved them. But those who ran off really could make a new life, bein' fair enough to be white. It's not like blacks runnin' off."

"My father went because of the law," Edna put in. "Mr. Jefferson freed most of 'em, but he never freed Sally. He promised to when they were in Paris. She didn't want to come home. Mind you, none of the history books tell about these kids, as if they don't exist. They just talk about Martha and Maria, who had the white mother, as his only children. It's all so false, Marg, I don't pay it no mind!"

"But it's yo' heritage, Edna!"

"My wife doesn't talk about it," Clark exclaimed. "These southerners are so resentful of well-connected colored people. What about yo' John, Marg? Does he intend to come back here to live?"

"I don't know. I hope so. He likes Princeton, but meets so few of our people up there—"

"We're up there! But you're right. My Hattie will go to Atlanta U. within a few weeks. Has John seen the place?"

"No, he hasn't."

"Well, let him come up with us. A nice one-day visit."

"He's supposed to go back North Tuesday. I'll talk to him."

"Yes, you do." Clark got up to go back to his offices. Marg realized if the Clarks ever went to Washington they could find out about Justine. Now she was panicky until they left. Closing the door, she quickly got down on her knees, in her new little office, and asked Jesus to spare her any further embarrassments. For her great sin, she thought she had paid her dues with people.

That afternoon, among beautiful autumn leaves, she rushed to the post office on her way home. Just as she had expected, there was a letter from Charles. She stopped to read it at the counter. It read:

September 10, 1869

Dear Marg,

It's been hectic! I've moved to a bigger place on Victory Drive. Like Washington, we're having scandals of corruption. The whites here are suspicious of everybody. They feel the voting last year was irregular so they, the Democrats, are cementing themselves in important jobs where they can get them. My post is not in jeopardy yet. Through Houston I'm friendly with all the Radicals. I've got a new bridge to put up over to Hutchinson Island. It will cost almost a million dollars. We canvassed for bids. Boss Tweed in New York heard about it and had some of his Ring apply! I've gone over all the bids carefully. I'm going to surprise you—I think a friend of yours could best do the job. After working West, he helped finish the transcontinental railroad last May. I'm really pushing for his bid at our budget meetings. Will keep you advised.

Savannah still fascinates me. I love the palm trees and the ocean. Whenever I can, I go out on my sloop at dawn. The fishing's great.

My basic salary's been raised to $3,800 per annum. If you need any money, let me know. Love to you and the children, especially Jason.

Charles.

First thing to cross Marg's mind: he didn't talk about his girlfriends. While he seemed secure in his work, something he said was too frightening to think about. Dr. Clark was right. White America would squeeze them out. Jefferson's tan children would never be known by the country. Her poor children too would have to fight to be recognized. She tried to visualize her John with lovely Hattie. They'd make such a beautiful couple. Theirs could be a blessed American family, God's example to the rest. But the castes of Man, that imperfection, was there.

At home, John had left a message that he'd be staying the night with the Hunters. Again Marg thought of deceptive Spence blood, then of Irwin Clark's discussion about northern schools, then about Edna's connections with President Jefferson, and finally about the Korners. With superiority the game, pure whites North and South imagined their separation from blacks, and in that false supremacy, they'd wickedly rewrite history. They'd construct it like a bridge!

She'd not fight the Hunters because they were poor white trash. She could like them for knowing what they were. Yet, within the next ten years Jeb no doubt would be going up in the world. Faster than her John! He still had not paid her back the money he had borrowed back in 1867. She could put Bill Cahill on to him, or the courts. And that would also break up that friendship between her John and his Cindy.

Chapter 34

When Jessica Bowne returned to Maple in October she was ecstatic over Marg's new building "Malcolm Spanish Court", which was still more than half empty. Jessica right away began attending to the matter she had promised. However, the white lawyer no longer wanted to rent. The doctor came reluctantly, saying since he had some Negro patients, he'd use this office for them. As a replacement for the first, Jessica found a white woman who dealt in the spirit world, Madame Sylvia. Marg frowned at the profession and the ratty young woman with reddish, crinkly hair. Her clients were all types, strange lookers, thought Marg, but she didn't mind so long as Madame Sylvia paid her rent.

The North had improved Jessica. She spoke with clarity and confidence. There was a healthy glow about her. Now Claremont was solvent again; Lance Folsom had them in the farm implement business. They had loads of success with new little farmers all around. In town, the Eagle and Phoenix Cotton Mill prospered, with Jessica on its board of directors. She decided one day to take Marg to lunch at one of Maple's fancy (white) restaurants, Stonewall's, also on Broad Street not far from Marg's new building. Both of them dressed lavishly for the occasion. A few rednecks, with toothpicks, stared at them.

"Newport was like a regular fashion show," said the elderly woman, stylish in red and grey. "They had all come to hear Harriet Beecher Stowe defend Lady Byron whose noble lord turned out to be a degraded incestuous wretch. Theodore Tilton denounced her in defense of his fellow poet. Mrs. Stanton was vigorously defending Harriet. My, it was quite a day."

"I read something of it in the New York papers. I hear you-all agreed to fight for the vote, now that Grant's in power. Do you think he'll support you?"

"Lord knows! I can't imagine he goes to Long Branch solely to eschew fast horses. He bows to the ladies passin' Stetson House. Mind you, he doesn't lift his hat. I think he's a drunken beast, just like the rumors say."

"Now Jessica, you told me never to believe in rumors."

"I still say it. Marg, are you in love? It shows, in yo' pretty pink cheeks!"

"Oh, come on! With whom could I be in love? Other than my husband."

Marg didn't reveal that she had had another nice letter from Charles. When she got home she curled up in bed and read it for a second time. It read:

October 15, 1869

Dear Marg,

     I meant to write you Tuesday but I'll confess, I was out drinking. It was a nice reunion. To start with I should tell you that a Cleveland Company, Waverly Engineering Company, got the contract for the Hutchinson Island bridge. I felt so happy being able to pull that off. When your Lieutenant Waverly arrived he was just as handsome in civilian dress as he had been in uniform. He was most surprised to see me in a big official position. He couldn't get over it.

     I helped him get an apartment for himself and three of his men. They're young and kind of wild but they do excellent work. The authorities are all very pleased the way things are going.

     Once in awhile Chuck (I call him that) comes by for a beer and we go out as oldtime friends. The way he talks about you, I think he was in love with you at one time or another. Did you know that? Well, he's got a Cleveland girl now, but she's not down here. While he's here working maybe you should take the train and come over to visit us. Like old times. Or, I could bring him down to Maple. Savannah people, though, are not so strict about this race-mixing. It's like a Spanish port in many ways. Well, you let me know.

Love,

Charles.

Marg thought about it. She could never visit them in Savannah. If she stayed with her husband in his house, it would be uncomfortable. Probably with Spanish girls coming all hours of the day and night. If she went to a hotel, she would be uncomfortable, because there, the so-called handsome Lt. Waverly would be bothering her. Mrs. Bowne was right. She was in love, or, she felt like a young girl once again.

She'd stay home, and let them pine for her. Whichever one came to Maple, she'd accept him. That was her present mood.

Early in November Marg received two letters from New York. Her brother Anthony's mentioned that he was having problems with his landlord and he proposed to buy a building in Eleventh Street. It had eight apartments as well as two stores below. He wanted to know what Marg thought about it. Poor dear Anthony. She wrote him right away. By all means he should buy the building. In fact, she wanted him to look out for one for her. She didn't want to be putting all her money in Georgia, or in Mr. Haney's schemes.

The other letter was a surprising one from Tom Haney. He was belatedly thanking her for the very nice little walnut table she had sent him eleven months earlier, as a Christmas present! Like Charles Waverly, pure white men, she surmised, were terribly slow at writing. Next, Haney spoke of his friend James Densmore who was getting his typewriter into shape to market it, and he wanted somebody to make wooden platforms for it. Haney asked if she would be interested. If so, he wanted her to come immediately to New York!

Marg felt too tired to be taking that long, dreary two-day ride up North. She didn't even want to see Justine just now. Thinking of the naked reality of God, she sat by a warm fire, writing a nice letter back to Haney. She thanked him for his offer, and forgave him for his long delay in acknowledging her Christmas gift. She mentioned if he could negotiate the contract for wooden platforms, she'd be glad to make them in her shop. She hadn't even discussed the matter with Larry. She didn't believe Haney was serious.

One December day as she was helping her girls pluck chickens, she received from Haney an Express letter, a very thick envelope. It contained a contract for her to sign. She ran to Cahill. He looked at it two minutes, said it was all right, then charged her an exorbitant thirty dollars for his time. He had seen where Marg was to get $4,500, that is, nine dollars apiece to make five hundred wooden platforms for an experimental typewriter Densmore had designed with a Mr. Christopher L. Sholes. She couldn't even remember what the machine looked like! Attached to the letter were some drawings, mostly dotted lines with span figures. She gave them to Larry to see if he could make anything out of it. He wasn't too good at reading. He showed them to his wife. Maggie Mae, somewhat confused, gave her idea of the drawings. Thinking benevolently, Marg suddenly said:

"I think the two of you should travel up to New York an' investigate this for me. You think you'd like to go?"

298

The two ex-slaves' eyes popped. They had never been outside the Maple area. They had done no railroad traveling. "H-how could we make it, Miss Margery?" asked Larry, dumbfoundedly.

"Well, other people manage. You'll have to manage too. I'm sendin' you both up to New York for Christmas!"

Marg, through Mr. Vincent Simpson, found another colored man who would be traveling North. Plans were made for the Browns to go along with him. Marg had a long talk with Uncle Vincent. He gave her names of two modest small hotels runned by Negroes. She didn't want her couple being baffled by staying at some place much too fancy for them. She also sat down and wrote a long letter to Tom Haney, explaining exactly Larry's talents and asking that he be shown everything. *Haney was always askin' about slaves; this would fix him.* The decision to go to contract would be Larry's, and Tom's. Marg would sign her name at the appropriate time, making whatever small changes she'd deem necessary. Now she felt giddy, treating Mr. Haney this way. But life should be hilarious, sometimes!

All Maple's colored community talked seriously about Marg's great generosity. The story even got to Matilda who just stood with her hands on her hips, saying evil words about "dat woman". She wouldn't call her 'Miss Margery' any more. But she was glad for Larry and Maggie Mae.

Marg also wrote a note to be hand-delivered to her brother Anthony. He was to take them sightseeing, and to a good restaurant. Marg wrote down all the New York sights she wanted them to see. Giving was a wonderful feeling. It made her Christmas of 1869 something with feeling. Good feelings.

Just about this time Marg heard again from Anthony. He was in a better mood. His letter read:

December 17, 1869

Dear Marg,

It was good to hear from you. I've moved right ahead on my purchase and I'm very glad about it. The building does need some repair. I think I should be able to move in by April. That's a good time because I have a gallery showing of the works of Samuel Colman. I'm very excited about his beautiful water colors and oils. By the way, I'm getting some customers from Washington. A few diplomatic ladies have bought from me, and now their friends are coming. If people can regard me as a specialist for American painters, I am happy.

There's a little scandal here. A guy walked into the *New York Tribune* offices and shot down Albert D. Richardson, the Radicals' big journalist. It seems Richardson was living with another man's wife. Well, she was divorced. The guy doing the shooting, Dan McFarland, was condemned by Henry Ward Beecher, a friend of Richardson's. Beecher rushed to his dying friend and performed the marriage ceremony to join Richardson and Mrs. McFarland before he died. Beecher was assailed from the pulpits of the country for taking sides with an adulterer. And Vice President Colfax got into it, as he too was Mrs. McFarland's friend! So you see why I'm a little bit cool to religion/politics just now.

My arm is better. It aches me sometimes, but I don't want to wear a false hand. People have to accept me as I am.

Love,

Anthony.

P.S. Of course, I still believe in Christmas. Sorry I couldn't make it home this year. All the best to you, Charles and the children, and for 1870!

By surprise, Marg also received a Christmas letter from George Cable, the young New Orleans writer friend of Celeste's John. It read:

December 18, 1869

My dear Mrs. Spence,

Just a note to wish you a Merry Christmas. I enjoyed my trip through Georgia very much. But I came home to New Orleans, and got married two weeks ago! To a lovely girl, Louise Bartlett. John Malcolm introduced us, so you see the world is small. I still keep at my writing. I'm now working on a very respectable quadroon lady, Madame Delphine, who worries about her daughter's future in this political-racial world. You gave me a few ideas for it. Thank you.

I see Effie quite a bit now. My new house is near them. She always asks for stories of Georgia. I would give you her address, in case you want to send a Christmas greeting, but people are so frightened. I really don't think this war of brother against brother is over yet.

My lovely Louise sends her warmest greetings to you, saying she hopes to meet you some day. I am very happy. John sends regards, and Joey too.

Love,

George Washington Cable.

Marg felt wonderful having Cable's letter. She wrote him immediately, giving him all the encouragement she could, and wishing him the best in his marriage. She went into Phyllis Korner's shop and picked a silver compote, and sent it to the Cables. Unfortunately, neither Korner was there. She had become bold for Christmas. She was willing to say hello to them.

That same afternoon a sad letter came from Louise. It read:

December 20, 1869

Dear Margery,

I know it's Christmas time, but I must give you some sad news. Louis Moreau Gottschalk, our fine pianist-composer, just died in Rio de Janeiro. He was only forty-four. He had been having tremendous concerts down there, and he loved the people, saying they were mostly mixed. The cause of death is not clear. Some reports say yellow fever; others say peritonitis. I've even heard that it was assassination, by some jealous husband. I'm glad Miss Ada Chase has their son. He should grow up proud of his father, who was America's most celebrated artist.

Justine is enjoying immensely the tea set and doll you sent her. We're both sorry we won't see you this Christmas. I hope you have a nice peaceful holiday, there in your lovely home. And thank you, Margery, for giving me such a blessing.

Love,

Louise.

Charles arrived on the twenty-third, with a beaming Captain Waverly! No longer captain; just a fine-looking civilian. Marg thought he looked simply gorgeous in his black broadcloth. He still had twinkling brown eyes, wavy brown hair, and his towering youthful look. She put down her work basket and took him upstairs, to his old room. Charles would be next door, since Marg now had taken down the twin beds in her own room. Waverly shook his head, marveling over the restoration of the house. He said it looked better than any general's house he had been in.

Charles went through the rooms, spoke to the servants, had himself a bath, a drink, then took Adam the coachman and went out to Cobb's Creek. He didn't suggest that Waverly go along, and Marg felt strange about it. Almost embarrassed. Waverly noticed it, and said: "The weather's good. Why don't we go for a buggy ride?"

Marg smiled. "Now you know, Charles, I'm a married woman."

He grabbed her arm and ran his fingers through hers. "And I'll bet you were worried to death about my coming here, sleeping in this house."

"Yes. Now that you bring it up, let's get one thing clear: there'll be no sleep-walking. Understand?"

He just grinned, and tickled her chin with one long finger. "Didn't your husband tell you, I'm engaged?"

"No! Charles, I'm happy for you. Congratulations!"

"You don't sound like you mean it," he exclaimed, hugging her as they went out the front door. "I think, Margery Spence, you do love me."

"As a matter of fact, Charles, I've come to that conclusion myself."

He stopped in his tracks. "Then shall I break my engagement to charming Miss Charlotte Stone of Cleveland?"

"Rascal. If she's charming, you'd better grab her. Nothing will ever happen between us again. You know that, Charles."

He said nothing. They got into Marg's shiny new black buggy. The horse was young and spunky. Waverly took over as Marg wrapped a soft blanket around her shoulders. It was the same blanket she had taken that Christmas Day Wheatland came to ruin her life. She didn't talk about it. They both kept silent with their thoughts. "Where are we going?" she finally asked.

"To the Great Meadow. Out Malcolm Road."

She smiled. "Think you remember the way?"

"I remember everything that's happened to me in Georgia. You know, I matured down here in Dixie. Oregon and Utah was all work, but this place—"

Marg was thinking. She felt like saying: "Charles, we have a daughter." But somehow, it didn't seem right. He might really quit that girl he had up in Cleveland, and she could promise him nothing. No, she decided she would not mention sweet Justine.

"Charles, I forgot the sandwiches!"

He laughed. "It's wintertime. What would we look like eating sandwiches in the cold."

"Well, why are we going then?"

He turned right into her face. "Maybe for a kiss or two."

"You can do that here."

"I will." He reached over and kissed her on the cheek, then on the mouth. As their warm lips met, she let her kid gloves touch his neck. It was so relaxing! The new young horse stumbled into a ditch, and they both laughed. "Why didn't you tell me this guy was stupid?"

"Now, Charles, Skid is nice. Don't laugh at him. He's givin' his whole life to us."

"Would you ever do that for me?"

"Charles, I'm not an adolescent! If you matured in Georgia, you certainly don't show it."

"I'm still young at heart, Marg."

"But you don't feel the way you used to about me. I can tell."

"Marg, I feel the same. Believe me. You know what it is? Life must move on. I'll probably marry Charlotte, and we'll be very happy, but it could never be like you and me. Marg, I think tonight I'll tiptoe into your room."

"You'd better not!"

That night, Marg put two chairs in front of her wide oak door. She didn't fall asleep, thinking she heard someone out there. But Waverly didn't show, and her Charles likewise didn't come. She felt like half a woman. She cried herself to sleep.

While they had eaten in, at home, the first night, after that there was a round of parties: Gregory and Valerie's, Sue and Jeeter's, then Dr. and Mrs. Clark had a very elaborate feast for them. Two days after Christmas they were invited out to Claremont by Mrs. Bowne. She broke her policy about entertaining black couples. Charles was invited to share the dinner table with his wife and friend, Waverly. One thing in southern tradition still observed, Mrs. Bowne didn't have any other guests while they were there.

"You Yankees really cost me a heap of money," she told Waverly. "I had to spend more than twenty thousand to get my property back in shape. An' yet yo' Yankee governments talk about confiscation. An' the crooks are buildin' three-story brick houses all over D.C. Last summer, on my way North, I stopped in Nashville for a layover rest. I stayed at the St. Cloud Hotel. An' there I heard a so-called retired Andrew Johnson speak of the corrupt Congress he had to deal with. He quoted the Bible. Book of Samuels; I'll have to read it. The poor man lost. He was tryin' to get the Tennessee Senate seat. I saw him again in Washington. We both stayed at the Metropolitan. The scandals took his thunder."

"Any scandals in particular?" asked Marg, sweetly.

Jessica sighed. "Well, to begin with, the husband of yo' friend, Kate Chase Sprague, Senator Sprague, has always played second fiddle to her. A dissipating man, one day in April he attacked another senator on the floor. It had something to do with a business deal in Rhode Island. Anyway, he said that many senators were in the employ of great corporations. Hah! Did they attack *him* after that! Then he read letters to show how good he was. That night, workingmen came to their mansion to serenade him. The Spragues have cotton money, and theirs is a fine old house at Sixth and E Streets. Well, Chief Justice Chase came out instead; he took the honor! Next, at Congress, Sprague was attacking Senator Abbott . . . called him a North Carolinian carpetbagger, a puppy. Abbott threatened to horsewhip him. Everybody thought there'd be a duel! The gossip of Washington could make it happen. Well, Sprague actually went home to his library. Through Sumner and John Sherman, the peacemakers, the story got to Greeley that Sprague was demented. However, Greeley thought he was ready to go over to the Democrats. Well, Sprague continued attackin' all summer, even up in Rhode Island where I was. Do you know what happened? There was a mysterious withdrawal of his credit, the collapse of his business. He knew Black Friday was coming."

"What's Black Friday?" asked Marg's Charles.

Waverly sipped his claret. "Some New York boys, Jay Gould and James Fisk, tried to capture the gold market and there was panic last September in the Stock Market. Many innocent dealers were ruined."

Marg looked serious. "I wonder if I was ruined. Shall we leave our money in the stock market? Is the corruption that bad?"

"There's always been some," said Jessica, having her brandy in one gulp. "You see, people like Gould and Fisk can manage to escape loss by simply repudiating their contracts. They should have been punished, but the Government looked the other way. They are friends of the President! Grant goes steamboatin' with Fisk while he's milking the Erie Railroad—"

"I have some stocks there," screamed Marg.

"Be sure yo' broker knows when to move. Do you let him act for you?"

Marg didn't want to tell Jessica that she had Larry and his wife up in New York at this moment. Mr. Haney couldn't be dishonest. She was sure of that.

Jessica relaxed a diamond-studded arm on the next chair. "I think their conspiracy to corner gold, to force merchants to pay exorbitant rates, was known by the President. You see, Gould's close contact was a speculator named Abel Corbin, and he is the husband of Grant's sister! A scalawag General Butterfield of that Union League group was to tell them how the Treasury would move. Word was Grant had decided against the sale of gold. Gould an' Corbin gave an editorial to John Bigelow at the *Times*, claiming it to be Grant's financial policy. The financial editor was suspicious, but it got published anyway. Gould bought heavily. Others were assured there was no possibility of loss. Corbin told Fisk Grant's sister was in. You see, Grant had instructed the Secretary of the Treasury not to sell. He was impressed about the marketing of crops. Also this bull an' bear business, and Government should not interfere—"

Waverly broke in. "Johnson when running for the Senate hinted that Grant was taking gifts."

Jessica waved her hand. "Even as a loser, he gave a dinner at Stacy House for Cooper an' all that gang. So much for Johnson! Well, Grant told Secretary Boutwell to move on without change on gold until the present stock struggle was over. That was on September 12th. I was on my way home. Next night, Boutwell dines at the Union League Club, an' on the 15th, Lawdamighty, Horace Greeley publishes a leading editorial charging a gold conspiracy, an' demandin' Boutwell act. They all screamed: 'It's the Secretary's duty to sell gold when the market is highest!' I was told to buy bonds as fast as he sells gold. The greenback situation would get tight. You know what happened in the end? The women got together. Mrs. Grant wrote Mrs. Corbin about the President's distress over Corbin's speculations. Gould saw the message. He knew his game was up! Hah! He'd save himself but he neglected to tell Fisk who was still buyin' while he sold!"

"How do you know all this?" asked Waverly, serious enough.

Jessica smiled. "Mr. Fisk's lady-friend, Lucille Western, is a friend of mine. You know, James Garfield is now investigating this for the House. The President shouldn't be so confident that his hands are clean. Butterfield's resigned."

"Well, I try to be honest in my money-dealings," said Marg, just a wee bit tight from the wine and whiskey. "Little as I have. Charles, baby, I guess we should just live it up. Have ourselves a ball. Look, why don't we all go to Europe? I've been dyin' to see Rome, an' Greece, an' England, an' Germany—"

"Why not Africa?" said Jessica, equally tight.

"Oh, you make me sick with that Africa talk! Are you still tryin' to tell me my place? That old-fashioned stuff?"

Charles Spence could see things getting out of hand. He laughed a bit, and pushed back his chair. "Easy now! As you always say, let's not talk race."

"Let her talk it," yelled Jessica. "If it weren't for me she wouldn't be in such grand shape. That new building, Malcolm Spanish P-Plaza, was a mistake. You know the nigras aren't ready for that."

"I didn't build it for nigras," shouted Marg, rising. "Come on, Charles. It's time we got home. Well, Mrs. Bowne, thank you for a lovely evening! I sho enjoyed myself." Marg was talking in a deep stilted drawl.

Jessica got up, a little feeble in her sparkling skirt. "Well." She hesitated a bit. "I'm sorry, my dear, if I upset you. You know I have a wicked tongue. But I still love you." She reached with sagging chin, and hugged Marg to her chest. "Merry Christmas, baby."

Three days later, Jessica Bowne was dead. Died in her sleep. Lance Folsom called at Malcolm House and gave details of the funeral. Waverly and Charles were still there and they promised to come to the funeral with Marg. Folsom, who had always been something of a bigot, seemed not to be this time. He told the white man that the Spences had been good friends to his sister. As good as any white people.

Chapter 35

Folsom came again to Malcolm House on a rainy afternoon, 12th of January. He wanted to tell Marg that she was mentioned in his sister's will, she and Charles. They would get the Pear Orchard, all ten acres of it, provided they'd use all the proceeds from the sale of pears to help colored people. Jessica specifically spelled it out that she did not mean mulattoes; she wanted Marg to deal with the pure blacks. The proceeds were to go to African types only, and ex-slaves only. Marg asked if she could give it to St. James Baptist Church, and Mr. Folsom said no. There still were too many mixed people there. Jessica's will had been precise; she meant jet blacks only. Marg thought again. This meant nothing for little Jason.

As she went about her quiet house sipping tea, she thought about her many hours with Jessica. Mrs. Bowne had always tried to be strong, and Christian. Marg knew that she was deeply hurt when the town fathers named the new road Malcolm Road. Now she wondered if she could get to the right people to have a road named after Jessica. She talked it over with Dr. Clark.

"That's a marvelous idea," he said, now calling her Marg. "I think Frank Korner is on that committee. Why don't you talk to him?"

Marg flushed red. "Now you know, Irwin, I don't deal with the Korners. You have to come up with a better idea."

"Well, there's Rayford Innis down at Town Hall. Or, you could let me do it. Let it be my suggestion."

"Now that's a good idea. And I thank you. I don't believe you understand how my hands are tied when I try to do things in this town. Now that I have my typewriter contract, I tried to get permission to use the Cobb Creek sidetracks for shipments, and they turned me down."

"You should join some committees, Marg. You have the time. It's very important when you want to be recognized in civic life. In fact, I think you should run for mayor."

"Me? Mayor of this town?"

"Why not? You'd make an excellent mayor."

"You forget I'm a woman. They'd never vote a woman in."

"Well, pick something less conspicuous. You like books. Why don't you try to get yourself appointed library director?"

Marg frowned. "Oh no, Irwin. I'm much too busy for that. I have to get my manufacturing business started. Larry and I are very busy with paperwork, as well as the actual making of typewriter platforms. He did splendidly up in New York. Mr. Densmore was very pleased with his suggestions about the shaping of the wood. First, Larry says, they were skeptical, thinkin' him a dumb ex-slave. Then when he started sketching things, they saw he had talent an' a good mind. Densmore even took him out to an inventor, Edison's, place in New Jersey. They're making a talking machine, an' maybe there'll be work for Larry on this."

A smile of admiration crossed Clark's broad, cashew-colored face. "I think what you're doin' for that boy is stupendous. Everybody's talkin' about it."

Marg walked proudly to her window. "Dr. Clark, I've never been concerned about the talk of people. If that interests you, and you had been here a few years ago, you wouldn't be my friend now. Gossipers have control over most people. I know what they say about me. Both sides. I'm happy to be in the middle."

He laughed. "You'll have to lean over a bit to give away the pear money."

She made coquette eyes. "That you're goin' to do for me."

He came to her frowning. "No, Marg. This is yo' chance. Make them like you!"

A comforting letter came from Louise at the end of that week. It read:

January 12, 1870

My dear Margery,

Justine is fine. Growing by leaps and bounds. We're sorry you couldn't come up for Christmas. She simply loves that beautiful satin blanket you sent. It's lovely. I didn't know whether to say "It's from Aunt Margery" or "Mama Margery". You have to advise me on this. I want to do the right thing in teaching your darling child. Her father really must be a good-looking man. She has a lot of you, but there is something new in this child. Lovely!

They're paving the streets, all the way from my house to Judiciary Square. Washington is prosperous once again. You see diamonds in the hotel lounge, equipages on the Georgetown Road.

There are the state dinners and formal balls. Before the war the best-dressed went to Mrs. Gwin's balls. Now it's these intimate little parties for the society of I, J and K Streets. Mrs. Kate Sprague chooses her guests with great discretion. She rather snubs Lydia now that Mr. Stevens is dead. President Johnson was here. We had a brief chat. He was on his way to dinner at Welcher's. He's glad to be back home, away from all this. I think he's relieved too that nobody knew about us.

I saw Julia Ward Howe with a bunch of old abolitionists and Radical friends. She thinks Lafayette Square is society. The rich are building new areas, near Chief Justice Chase's country place, Edgewood. Kate with all her gowns and jewels is still attracting the foreign boys. They've got forty servants out at Edgewood, and I hear their house at Narragansett has eighty rooms. Well, this atmosphere will give Justine a lot to think about, above these gambling street characters. I think she should study music, because the entertainers get in the best places. You said medicine when you were here, but that would be such a waste of her exceptional beauty. She's really a doll.

Love,

Louise.

Chapter 36

Along about Eastertime, Front Street by the Public Market became Bowne Avenue. A front-page article, and picture of Jessica, was in the *Star-Journal*, but no mention of Margery Spence. At the same time, down on Broad Street, at Courthouse Square, men began to gather daily. You'd see as many people there as you would at Public Market. It seems the Negroes grew to habituate the place, making speeches. Whites in groups would hang back and curse them. During the Grant-Colfax elections they grabbed a nigger carrying a gun, right there. He said he had it for squirrel-hunting. Somebody yanked it off the nigger, and shot him in the arm. In Maple, these days, many whites were taking weapons from Negroes. One thing, they had heard about black Hiram R. Revels taking oath of office as U.S. Senator from Mississippi. In the grand sendoff parade, the white fire companies all left because a black regiment was allowed in line. By the time Revels got to Washington, the whole country knew that he was northern-born while representing Mississippi. Of the three senatorial vacancies, the colored people had insisted that one should be filled by a Negro. White Republicans made it the lesser post, the fractional vacancy of Jefferson Davis, which would mean the black taking it could only serve a term of about one year.

On January 31, 1870 the *New York World* had said that dignified Revels could take care of himself, and he would "not suffer himself to be browbeaten even by Sumner". He had come with Mississippian Adelbert Ames (white) soon to marry Ben Butler's daughter. Upon seeing Revels, Pig Iron Kelley said he found Negroes in the South to be intellectual superiors of the whites! Amidst the corruption (senators and congressmen now selling cadetships to West Point), the new Mississippi Senator became the center of attraction. A venerable journalist, Major Poore, made a grave social error. At John Forney's party early in February, General Grant dropped in and Poore arrived late and he

310

turned to dark-brownskinned Revels and ordered him to get him a glass of wine. To the mischief Revels merely answered by telling the man they had met at Sumner's.

When it came time for Revels to make his maiden speech, the galleries were packed. His diction and grace were beyond reproach, and somewhere in the corners of America were bitter whites declaring that every Negro now in a high post, by virtue of reconstruction, was some kind of fool or ignoramus.

Homesick, John had come home for Easter. At the dinner table the usual political topics prevailed. He told what he had learned at Princeton. He claimed that Revels, older than most, had surprised white congressmen by being so astute, so capable. On the Senate floor he got to his argument in no uncertain terms. He told them not to admit Georgia senators until blacks were guaranteed protection in the state. Ratification of the Fifteenth Amendment was soon to follow. Radicals then made orators of their new Negroes, knowing they had a struggle to regain Delaware, Maryland and New Jersey. One of John's teachers had gone down to Arlington to the Union League convention. He reported the organization's finances were secure, and that they'd move South again to get more Negroes voting. Revels then appointed a colored boy a cadet at West Point, which soured white congressmen. John read a clipping where Godkin of the *Nation* called it a foolish thing, injurious to the colored race.

John had heard Godkin speak at Princeton. In spite of his acclaim at the *Nation*, John did not think him an unbiased or liberal northerner. Marg agreed that power alone was often the only good of some people.

As spring flowers took power coming out of the ground, Marg got back to her reading, making herself comfortable in pillows in her couch on her lovely screened-in backporch. Now she had a soft grass rug out there, and a table for sipping lemonade. She read where the nation looked towards the Caribbean, some expecting to purchase Santo Domingo for $1,500,000. It seems Grant's interest in this quasi-black republic came through speculators and gamblers. Also President Baez seemed eager to sell his country. So, acting for Grant, General Orville Babcock had sailed on his diplomatic mission with a warship for moral support. Secretary Hamilton Fish became disgusted that such proceedings had gone forth behind his back. In February 1870 at the Haitian capital Admiral Poor had given public notice that any attack on Baez would be considered a declaration of war against the United States.

Back in Congress, Morton, who had taken Thaddeus Stevens' place, was cracking the party whip, and Senator Wilson admitting that nine-tenths of the people were against the treaty. The *New York Herald* claimed that Morton had a large collection of Santo Domingo products on his desk, including a block of salt. The paper said that among many statesmen gathering around to taste the salt was none other than the black man Revels. Marg smiled; she knew the eyes of the press would be on him! Louise had written her that, in this matter, Hamilton Fish had tried to dissuade Sumner by offering him the post of Minister to England. Eventually, when the treaty failed, Grant went trout-fishing.

That spring Marg got several letters from her brother Gregory. The Georgia Government was about to move from Milledgeville to Atlanta. Gregory was not altogether pleased to be working under fat and pleasant-mannered Rufus Bullock, Governor of Georgia. Some said the state was running under carpetbaggers protected by the sword. In truth, Bullock's less than two years in office had showed an administration reeked with corruption. He had H.I. Kimball, a man who craved no office, distributing posts for retainers. Kimball's only asking: one hand in the Treasury. Seats now in the legislature could be had for a price. Thinking an opera house an edifice of wanton waste, Kimball bought it, remodeled it and sold it to Georgia as a State House. And, since a fine hotel was needed, he built Kimball House, which was paid for with state bonds. They were also building railroads with the state's money. Kimball became a partner in the Tennessee Car Company. Government money was also used in the Bainbridge, Cuthbert and Columbus Railroad, the Cartersville and Van Wert Railroad, and poor Mrs. Bowne had some money in all three of these companies.

When Lance Folsom went up to Atlanta, he was supposed to see Gregory, but Gregory avoided him. He was in fact on a committee studying the looting of the Brunswick and Albany, all the claims of war debts. One line which had brought in regularly $25,000 a month before the war, plunged the state into debt now at the tune of $750,000. Gregory felt it advisable to tell Charles something about corruption in government, so he wrote to him in Savannah, talking generally about unsavory deals in the building and maintenance of state roads, and also in the collections at ports.

However, as a Republican, Gregory was somewhat at home in Georgia's state legislature, largely Republican. Governor Bullock was so fearful that the Democrats might gain, that he went to Washington to plead for support. Some in Congress disdainfully thought of the 1870 Georgia Legislature as a cross between a gambling den and a colored camp-meeting. Washington needed Georgia's vote to ratify the Fifteenth Amendment. However, what had happened, a sickening race war had broken out among the Georgia team. All of a sudden, the twenty-five Negro members of the House, and the two in the Senate were expelled. It was not Democrat against Republican, but race against race. At first they had looked over Gregory, thinking he was a white man. Then somebody from Maple whispered the truth, and Gregory had to get out along with "the other blacks".

When Bullock got to Washington the matter had already been discussed between Grant and Sumner. It was decided Bullock could stay in power but the state would be remanded to military rule. Bullock and his associates were appalled. This would mean an election to be held in the fall of 1870. The Democrats might win, and they also might begin investigations to see what needed cleaning up.

While Gregory was home, looking sad, Marg got an urgent letter from Charles. He wrote that Waverly had been hurt in a black powder explosion of sodium nitrate. Spinal damage was feared. Charles suggested that Marg should come right away, to cheer him up. Marg arrived in Savannah on a very hot day in mid-May. She took a room at the Davenport Hotel, rather than disturb Charles at his house. She also wanted to be close to the hospital on Gwinnett Street where a pale Charles was semi-conscious, resting under sedation.

He recognized her with shiny, blinking eyes. "Angel, I-I didn't know it was s-so easy for life to change from good to bad. E-everything was goin' so well with my job."

She patted his cheek. "Don't worry about it. The main thing now, we want to get you well." She had brought a picture of Justine. It was in her purse. To show it to Waverly could upset him. She decided not to.

"M-Marg, I think my hands are cold. Can you feel them?"

She grabbed a hand he had resting on the white sheets. It was cold. But she would not tell him this. "I have yo' hand now. It'll warm up soon. They have you in the shade. I'd let some light in this room."

Just as Marg looked towards the door, three plainly-dressed fair ladies were ushered in. One was short and elderly, thin and scrawny, with glasses, looking a bit like a countrified version of Jessica. It was his mother. Marg could tell. She rushed over. "Mrs. Waverly? Oh, how wonderful you came. I'm Mrs. Spence. It's dreadful what happened. He's resting well." Mrs. Waverly smiled a bit. Quietly she introduced her daughter, Ann. Blond like Marg; a bit more severe.

"I'm Charlotte Stone," spoke the third younger woman. She too was rather blond, and German-looking, with a plain round face and little grey eyes sitting in saucers atop fattish cheekbones.

"How do you do," replied Marg. Now she was embarrassed. "I'm just leaving. If there's anything I can do, please let me know. I'm Mr. Spence's wife."

"Yes, we know," said Charlotte, a little stiff. "We're getting another doctor for him. A military one. There's talk of an operation. A blood clot."

The next day, Marg came and sat quietly with his family. She felt Mrs. Waverly liked her, accepting her tidbits and water. Marg preferred to be with him alone. She asked a Negro nurse if it were alright if she came late in the evening, perhaps at sunset. The woman said it would be all right. Marg now spent the daytime walking around the quaint town. She also visited Charles at his office and at his house. It was a beautiful old place with period furniture. Even an Ezra Spence table! The housekeeper was Spanish, an elderly woman. Marg was convinced there was another Spanish woman around. A younger one. She saw things that only a young woman would use. She did not ask Charles about them. She did ask for his friend Houston, only to learn that he was one of the expelled senators, now back in Atlanta.

Going back to the hospital at night, she dreaded to enter Waverly's room. For several eerie days they all remained suspenseful. He had begun to sink, in and out of a coma. Hot, humid heat gripped the atmosphere, yet, he was cold. Marg sat alone at twilight, holding his hands. Some days she'd feed him a little soup; other days they'd manage to talk a bit. Often he'd be so sleepy she wouldn't bother him with words. They'd just look into each other's eyes. The more she thought of it, he should know about his daughter. There'd be no other. Yes, she had a feeling he would die. What she kept asking God for was strength to help her northern Charles in these his last hours. She did not want to talk falsely about living. And she saw no point in reviewing the good times. Maybe if there was a Hereafter he'd feel comfort in shared beliefs.

"Jesus has always been very good to me," she said quietly, that Friday evening. "Whenever I needed strength I would ask Him and He would give it to me. Charles, in jail, I lived many days on my prayers alone. Then when it was all over, I came out thanking God. You know what for?"

He looked up with a little boyish smile in his bright eyes. He shook his head.

"Well," she continued. "It was my children. I had not been the best of mothers. I had selfishly put so much time into my own projects. God made me realize that they were important, the extension of my life. An' my duty was to prepare them . . . love them more."

"T-they're not like you," he feebly whispered.

"In a way, you're right. But in mood, anxiety, hope, they're me. That force of living, exactly me. I know because I now have a fourth child—"

"Jason?"

"No. I mean someone else. Charles, *we* have a daughter. You and I. She was born three years ago. She lives with my friend Louise in Washington. Her name is Justine." Marg put the photo right before his eyes.

He looked at it with a little smile in his lips. Then a serene brightness came into his deep-brown eyes. "M-my d-daughter, huh? Swell. Her n-name?"

"Justine. I guess, after justice. I liked it. I felt you'd like it too. I wanted so much to tell you Christmas. Forgive me for not . . . sooner."

"Y-you gave me. Yours and mine. Swell."

"Then you forgive me?" The photo went back into her purse.

He reached out and took her hand. "Y-yes. F-forgive. An' take c-care our daughter. J-justine." He died. The room made itself quiet, with only the clock ticking. She closed his eyes. Elias raced into her mind. She pulled her fingers out of his, then folded his beautiful hands. Standing, tears began to bubble out. She rushed to the door not looking back.

Out in the dusty-yellow hall hot globs of water streamed down her cheeks. Her handkerchief did its job. Then she glanced towards the window at the hall's end. She could see far out a strong blotch of bright orange sunlight, pushing through a blue-black sky. Like a Baltimore Oriole, she thought. An eerie blackness stretched in front making it impossible to know where earth and sky divided. That black mixture of sky, ocean and sand captured her thoughts. Life comes out of blackness, and goes back to blackness. She walked towards the window feeling its hot moist tropical air, soon hearing the cheeping of night birds just beyond. With all the tall doors around, it was like a wooden coffin, closing in on her. No, they were stationary, hiding her Charles, in there in his supreme stillness. His honor guard.

At the breeze, the orange became silver, then orange-purple. Finally, deep purple gobbled it up. Now she could imagine foam in the secret-hiding black. The ocean was taking over. Noisily pulsating. The ocean of life.

END OF PART FOUR

PART FIVE

1870-1877

Chapter 37

Arriving home, Marg was listless for several days. She couldn't believe that Waverly was dead. Her dear secret love. She thought of Poor Justine who would never see her father. There wasn't even a photo of him. Marg decided to write Charles about this. Maybe somehow he had gotten a picture of her child's father. Poor Charles. She'd never tell him the truth. If she were anything like Matilda, she'd be screaming at him saying he was responsible for Waverly's death, by inviting him to Savannah. Now his family and that poor Charlotte Stone certainly must have some hard feelings against the South. Poor Mrs. Waverly. Both her sons now were gone.

Marg felt poorly, but she had to snap out of it. It was June and she had to take a trainride North, to attend John's graduation from Princeton. She had persuaded Charles to come, and they'd meet in Atlanta, taking a Pullman North. And, she'd not see Haney this time.

This big family occasion was Charles' first trip out of the South. The new world did not surprise him. Standing in his uniform next to his tall son he looked like a cashew-colored Asian prince. Quite a few northern people stared at them. Statuesque Marg was beautiful by anyone's standard, and pretty Beth with soft white cheeks, big grey eyes, long brownish hair, and no bosom. And shorter Meg, a dishwater blonde, had her mother's cheekbones, Malcolm greenish eyes, and a cashew-colored face like her father. Southern whites were more used to the beauty of fair colored families. Northerners stared in disbelief that children with a drop of Negro blood could come out as fair as John, looking like their ideal, the pink-cheeked blond Irish or Germans. Some classmates remarked that their own white fathers were darker than John's Latin-looking dad. A few with twisted noses gossiped that these were "three-quarter Celts", or, Negro people.

John didn't mind. He was proud of his parents and his sisters. Now he would go to Harvard, to study medicine. Dr. Clark had finally convinced him that a trained medical man could get rich and respectable, and still keep music as a hobby. Marg was so grateful for her friend's intervention that she told Charles she'd take the Clarks a very nice present. They went to the brand-new Stevens department store in New York. There she ordered a most expensive set of Wedgewood china, the likes of which she had seen in fancy Washington.

They would of course go no where near Washington. Charles, John and the girls were eager to see the capital but Marg was firm in stating her objections. They had to get back to Georgia to start picking pears, out at their new property inherited from Mrs. Bowne. Some squatters otherwise would steal them. Charles worked the Cobb's Creek land spending a few days with Jeeter and Sue. Meanwhile, John and his mother entertained lovely Hattie Clark, whom Marg had encouraged her son to invite to Malcolm House.

Hattie, always slinging her long, luxurious flaxen hair, usually wore a serious expression. She did not know music but told John she was interested in it. They dressed her old-fashionedly, in lace, and she wasn't allowed to use scents. She and John would sit at Marg's piano; he'd play until she got bored. What Hattie liked to do was play dominoes. She knew how to win and that brought a smile to her soft round face. When John teased about a broken front tooth Dr. Simpson was working on, she'd push him and he'd grab her pale hands and kiss them. Marg watched all this from a distance. It wasn't warming up fast enough to suit her thinking.

When they got back to Maple Uncle Gregory had gone back to the pow-wows of Atlanta. Louise wrote that Governor Bullock's expensive suite at the Willard had been charged to the state of Georgia. The rumor was he had taken a bill to Grant to sign without reading, and then he became host at a lavish feast at the Café Français. He wanted Ben Butler to prolong his term two more years. Some congressmen were angry at Bullock's effrontery. A desperate Bullock turned to the press. The *New York World* of March 18, 1870 had said he was using "female body" to get what he wanted. For a public plea against the Bingham Amendment he paid Forney's paper nearly five thousand dollars, charged to Georgia. However, the Bingham Amendment was passed and Bullock had to rush home to get ready to stand election.

Since autumn of 1869 the power of the Ku Klux Klan was growing all over the South. In Tennessee an anti-Klan law was enacted; soon Brownlow's militia was getting about the state committing outrages of its own. In South Carolina, Governor Scott was employing a militia as well. North Carolina had an interesting case with Holden's militia.

Born in poverty, Governor W.W. Holden, a follower of Clay, amazed Whigs by being engaged by the Democrats as editor of their *Standard*. He claimed Democrats were friends and supporters of equal rights. He pronounced himself a Jeffersonian and later to be under the influence of Calhoun. He was for secession. His 1858 try for the governorship was prevented by the Whig aristocracy. Then he turned around and became against secession, voted for Breckenridge (as did Johnson). He opposed Lincoln on using force, and two years later was opposing Confederate policies while Georgia troops burned him in effigy. Faced with a race problem shortly after the war, he was for colonization, saying the races could not live in harmony. He declared himself to be of Johnson's persuasion, and party, then became president of the Loyal League, fighting Johnson. An opportunist veering with the weather, he controlled his clever Senator John Pool who had an art of inflaming Negroes. Whites too were inflamed. Soon after Holden's paper went too far suggesting Negroes should cultivate "the women", Klan activity and great uneasiness rose in his state.

In the spring of 1870 General M.S. Littlefield who had plundered Georgia was in North Carolina still controlling railroads, and manipulating bonds. With election-time not far away, North Carolina's legislature was to investigate the frauds. Holden got Grant's okay to have a private army, to deal with the Klan, and others. His John Pool was to set up the papers for their army; it was to protect the people, and save the party at the polls. They were to be guided by what Powell Clayton had done in Arkansas. They'd have a judicial officer with the troops, in case a habeas corpus writ had to be answered. Pool said this plan had the President's agreement. Holden was reminded he was a Reconstruction acts governor, just as Smith in Alabama was. He had to control Klan activities. So, as commander of his troops he'd have Colonel George Kirk, a tough man who had lived in Tennessee.

Martial law was declared. Kirk's army, a raggedy bunch of mostly poor whites, 700 strong, got its guns. Four hundred were under age and two hundred not even citizens of the state. They began making arrests indiscriminately. North Carolinians complained by petitions. Kirk waved aside the writ of habeas corpus the Chief Justice served on him. Josiah Turner of the *Raleigh Sentinel* charged Democrats were being terrorized. When there was a mock hanging of Holden, he grew unhappy. The *New York World* realized Grant was in on this. The *Nation* claimed the soldiers were mostly black!

When North Carolina went to the polls in August, the Democrats swept in. Kirk was arrested but permitted to escape by a Radical sheriff. He got to Washington where the Capitol police protected him. Poor Holden was impeached. Marg read all this while she was trying to advise her disillusioned brother Gregory what he should do. She had a feeling similar troubles were coming to Georgia.

Summer was kept bright by the young people. Marg's girls of course were now seeing some boys. Since they were talking proper New England English, the boys attracted had to be similar top mulatto types. A fine brownskinned boy came, but Marg didn't encourage him. It was politics, and she hated it! Then September came, and her three eagerly got ready to go back North.

She was trying to think up something for poor Jason. But with his brown skin he'd not have it so easy up North. The Yankees too were full of bitterness by color. While she was glad the older children were not in Georgia in these terrible times, she'd keep Jason a bit longer, close to her, and teach him all she could about mankind's folly. Yes, the Lord wanted her to care for Jason. That's why his name had been on the lips of dear Charles Waverly as he was dying.

After John's leaving late in September, the quiet of Malcolm House made Marg feel depressed. She also felt physically run-down. She started to visit Dr. Clark but there were more important things to do. To fill the vacancies in her building she had advertised through black churches. Now she had coming: a barbecue enterprise, for the first floor, a laundry establishment, then up on the floors: a fledgling weekly newspaper called the *Maple Clarion*, a ladies' hairdressing shop, a male barbershop, a tailor, a herb medicine place and a photo shop. She had lowered her rent, so they could carry on in proper business fashion. She had rules about noise and cleanliness, and had hired Bob Jenkins as porter. Conscientious, he'd keep tabs on them. He was in fact Bubber's brother. Poor Bubber. He had set out for Chicago, and nobody had heard from him in two years.

The Muggeridges next door were both ailing. They now had a young black couple living there. The man kept the lawn looking fine, and his mistress was always busy at the black kettle in the yard. She hung out beautiful laundry. Marg began speaking, praising it. The sepia lady one day told her, with glum face, that Mrs. Muggeridge had just died. White Georgians came by the dozens to pay respects to their rebel sister. Marg recognized some of the family people, but she didn't go near the place, just sent flowers.

The carriages stayed around for several days, then all grew quiet again. Marg wondered if Mr. Muggeridge wanted to sell the place. He had indicated so in the past. One day she went over there, knocking cheerfully. She was surprised seeing the way he looked, like a ghost. Hardly recognizable with his wrinkles, watery eyes, wispy white hair and tottering stance. War had aged him twenty years. He said he'd think over her proposal. Meanwhile, she wired Haney in New York to transfer sixty thousand into her Atlanta bank. She had a strange feeling about things, with the election coming.

While colored had not customarily voted in Maple, now they were, and whites would gang together at voting times, and go witch-hunting. They'd beat up on Negroes here and there, warning them not to vote the Radical ticket. One black girl she met at Public Market said they had come to her cabin in the night, had dragged off her husband after tarring-and-feathering him, then all three of them relished her body out by a tree. She was so upset by the experience that she cried out there all night long. In morning light, she got herself together to go home, only to find her house in ashes.

The voting booths were in the various schoolhouses. The whites now would take over completely, bringing poor ignorant country people into town by wagoner, making them march in to "Vote". It was a shame, but so far, Republicans had managed to keep in power.

Poor Gregory was back home again. Doing tailoring. Waiting to see whether the coming elections would give him back his job as legislator. St. James Baptist was really busy for him. He told Marg he wanted to drop out, to return home to job and friends. But everybody urged him to stay on in politics. Cousin Don said his being there was important to the future of the colored race in the South.

When election time drew near, late in October, the Ku Klux Klan rode through Maple. Their big parade was aimed at intimidating Negroes. They drove by Gregory's house, with many running through the cemetery in sheets. They were mainly down on Broad Street where white gangs would run up quick, and beat a Negro down to the ground, then run off just as quick. Negro businesses were ramsacked, especially the prosperous ones. The sheriff and the town authorities would turn their heads. There was no protection. Marg now wished she had rented to the Union League people. They were doing much useful work. More than the Freedmen's Bureau people. Grant's troops, in town to keep order, were not so helpful. Many had anti-Negro feelings now. They could laugh at all the goings-on.

On that election day, many brave Negroes went out early to the polls, washed and looking dignified, wearing their Sunday best. They came in groups, usually church groups. The preacher would lead his numbers in an orderly fashion, then as soon as they'd reach the portico, the white man would scream at them, curse them, disperse them, sending some off running and others into the booths. The white watchers looked for ignoramuses, people they could tell how to vote. There'd be a pile of clothing. They would force the dumb Negro to go in one time dressed a certain way, then grab him and send him back in, dressed another way. The whites even had shiny black top hats there, to cock on a nigger's head, and get a good laugh. The intelligent Negro got chased away. Some people living near the polls came out hourly to pick up the wounded. Their children too were trained to offer first-aid to victims. With so many beatings, people were courageous to go anywhere near the voting places. Bob Jenkins, Bubber's brother, led Marg's group to the polls. She was proud of them, but wondered how they voted, thinking they did not know enough about civic affairs.

Governor Rufus Bullock was defeated. Georgia's legislature mostly became Democratic. Whites did not worry about it being fraudulent. They were relieved and saved from the Radicals and the niggers.

Chapter 38

Luckily Gregory and his friends got re-elected. When, however, they got back to Atlanta, the white bigots in the legislature still would not let them take their seats. Federal investigators came immediately to straighten things out. They leaned heavily towards the Democrats, accepting their view of all the irregularities. They didn't even want to see the affidavits of proof of abuse. However, by pressing, the colored men were able to get their seats back. The Government of Georgia now had a Democrat majority, and the Ku Klux Klan was an accepted part of society. White people on the streets grinned, but they continued to abuse Negroes. They'd snap at them like dogs. Marg watched the pushing, cursing and rudeness wondering why they didn't realize they were ruining their own personalities.

They passed a local ordinance that Negroes could not own guns. The sheriff's staff went raiding at people's homes, looking for guns. They'd steal whatever the nigger had which seemed of value. Colored people had no protection from Washington. What gains they had made in the few years of freedom were quickly stolen or destroyed. The poor colored farmer without guns would have to let his crops be taken over by birds and beasts. Moreover, by the whites crossing his land in hunting parties. Their horses could eat whatever they wanted of Negro farmers' crops. It was a shame. So much hate and abuse.

Vincent Simpson, Dr. Lou's father, bought the fledging black newspaper, the *Maple Clarion*, which had offices in Marg's new building. He claimed the Malcolms up in Atlanta gave him eight hundred dollars for his beverage formula. Marg asked about her white family. They were all well, rich and chic, moving around in society, with the best people. They had completely forgotten about her!

Where Georgia's small communities grew more oppressive, intellectual Negroes continued to complain to Atlanta and to liberals up

North. Finally, in Maple, to pacify the stevedores and the colored community, Washington relieved the white colonel who had been running the Freedmen's Bureau. They then appointed Dr. Fred Bowman in his place. Some people on Plum Avenue felt like celebrating, but Marg was apprehensive. She felt she knew the character of her neighbor. He wanted to shine as an important man, with titles and the like, but keep bitterness against certain people. She did not think he had the courage to deal with the problems, or with the white man.

Stealing and abuse remained the major problems. The politicians and the white collar officials got to all the provisions being sent down from the North. Negroes were conveniently blamed for theft. But the thirsty white man, quite visible, was vile and had his mind on getting rich. Marg wondered how they could call themselves Christians.

At her own church she surveyed what was needed, deciding to donate an elaborate pipe organ, new carpeting, and a stained-glass window in honor of her parents. Cousin Don was very pleased with her generosity. He now had given up his leadership in the school; a younger man was running it. They had problems like in the public schools. The fountain of northern Free Negroes as teachers was drying up. And their own were not yet trained. Books coming in from the North often were stolen or destroyed by whites down at the post office. The children had to be trained to take good care of everything. In Maple, the white schools got their salaries and operating funds, but not the black schools. Luckily a few were able to exist on gift funds from the Quakers up North. Local donations were few. Marg was thinking about giving a handsome sum. Haney had written that while her investments with him were valued over $100,000, it would take him more time to liquidate things to get the $60,000 she wanted at her Atlanta bank. Even intelligent local whites were jealous of well-to-do Negroes. The Klan had burned crosses in front of the houses of several successful families. Not a word of this in the *Maple Star-Journal*. The brutalizing of colored people was common practice among the rabid bunch gaining leadership in America's South. To treat them like mere animals was popular.

One Thursday in November Marg had just returned from the post office where she had mailed a sweater up to John in Cambridge. As one of her new girls, Irene, rushed to get her a cup of tea, Jeeter and Sue came in looking greatly disturbed. "I've just been fired," Jeeter told Marg. "I've lost my job at the Freedmen's Bureau."

"Oh no," she exclaimed. "How could it happen?"

"Dr. Bowman's cleaning house, makin' room for his own team. My job was given to one of his friends."

"It's more than that," said Sue, taking two of Marg's chocolate candies. "They accused Jeeter of stealing sacks of rice, an' Jeeter's never stolen anything in his life."

Marg adjusted her glasses. "What connects you to the accusation then?"

"Well," sighed Jeeter. "I'm in charge of the distribution to the old folks' asylum. It goes out by wagon every Tuesday an' Friday. My records show exactly what we've given. Inventory stores are also double-checked, an' I can't be held responsible for what happens on the way, or faulty records at the other end."

"Of course you can't. Is that all he's got against you?"

"No. He claims I've systematically refused some black families who want to get in at yo' eighteen rental houses."

"Jeeter, he must be kiddin'! That's my private business. The Government doesn't run my houses!"

"My boss says Dr. Bowman said this his first week. His mind's against fair people. The other guy too is on his list of incompetent people."

"Don't you have a recourse committee?"

"No," said Sue, sitting down now. "All one can do is write to the Governor, or to Washington. I think the real score is Dr. Bowman has some grudge against you, Marg."

"The ole devil has many grudges against me. Well, Jeeter, I'll fight for you, but I've got to think this out an' see whom we should get to back you up."

"Jeeter doesn't want to go back," offered his wife. "He's had enough of the corruption—"

"If somebody is stealing rice, it's still our concern, isn't it?"

"Oh, most definitely," he uttered. "But they're goin' hop up an' blame the man keepin' the records. They have the power to do that. Cousin Margery, why can't you get me in high politics, like yo' husband and Cousin Gregory?"

Marg smiled. "That arena is more corrupt. Besides, they're older men. You'll be there when you reach their age. Jeeter, honey, to fight for yo' future civic life, there must be an erasure of this charge. I'll talk to Dr. Clark. He can clear it up, get you back, or into a better job."

"I've heard a lot about him," said Jeeter. "Not all good. It seems he's working with the Democrats."

Marg herself had a chocolate. "Jeeter, you have to work with people. I dare say, if you went to Dr. Bowman an' explained what you've told me, he might see you as an individual, look into the matter, an' give you yo' job—"

"Cousin Margery, you know he's never liked you, an' I'm in yo' family."

"No, we can't prejudge people. Face him, Jeeter, an' see what he says. Then, after you've told me what he says, I'll talk to Clark."

Her suggestions seemed to make sense. Meanwhile, Jeeter went home to Cobb's Creek and reluctantly took up farming again. He wanted Cousin Marg to offer him something big like she had given Larry. Maybe management of Malcolm Spanish Court. Sue told him he was too shy, because he didn't have much education. Jeeter was shy, and completely without the aggressive thirsts of others. But once having been bitten by the white-collar setup, he didn't want to go back to farming.

Carrie, Marg's faithful servant, suddenly quit. She said she was going back to Macon to do dressmaking, near her family. Marg was sorry deep inside. It was like losing Matilda all over again. And why shouldn't she equally get a little money? Marg made it two hundred dollars, and Carrie nearly had a fit. Now she could ride the railroad. She had planned to walk the eighty hard miles to Macon, as they had done in slavery times.

On the day Marg got herself pretty to go talk to Dr. Clark at his office, she dressed warmly because there was definitely a cold wind outside. At her wardrobe she started coughing, and went into the bathroom. She spit up blood. When she mentioned this to the doctor, he began asking questions. He suggested a thorough medical examination. He even took samples of sputum. Several days later he called her in to talk about it.

"I'm sorry to tell you this, Marg. You have tuberculosis."

She kind of smiled. "Well, I've feared that for some time. What do I do now?"

"You'll have to change yo' lifestyle. Rest is very important. I want you to stay in bed every morning, till ten o'clock. An' go to bed at nine. And drink lots of milk. And keep warm. Do you have a place to sit in the sun during these wintry months?"

"I could move my bedroom down to the first floor. The conservatory is the brightest room in the house. It gets sun all year-round."

"Well, is it warm enough?"

"Oh, it could be carpeted and made very pretty. I need a change, doctor. I think that's the first order for me."

"Why don't you go off on a long vacation?"

"With Charles and my children gone, every day is like a vacation. Maybe I *am* lonesome."

"You and my Edna should get together. Have friendly visits. These are stressful times. People need to relax. I'll write you a prescription, but the main thing you need is to slow down."

Marg went home to an empty house. There was no one to hear her sad news. The servants had Jason, and she didn't feel like crying. Dry-eyed, she recalled God's telling her many times that she would die early. Or was it her dear mother visiting from the Spirit World? Suddenly Marg thought of something. She'd consult Madame Sylvia. Have her horoscope read. Madame Sylvia was one of the three white tenants at Malcolm Spanish Court. She had a brisk business. Many whites as well as colored. Gossip had it that she could influence people as much as the Radicals, or the Ku Klux Klan.

"Oh, my dear landlord," shrieked Madame Sylvia, a rather faded twenty-seven-year-old redhead, wearing big earrings and heavy makeup on pallid cheeks. "Do come in! I've been wonderin' when you'd come see me."

It was not rent time, so the woman knew that Marg had come for a chat like other customers. They talked about the weather, the changes in town, and a little of politics. Suddenly Sylvia asked her zodiac sign, then they were off on the right track. She had cards and she could also read palms. Marg preferred the latter. Sylvia made a few gasps, but she didn't say much that was shocking.

"See this? This is yo' life line. It's long, but it's been broken and rejoined. You're Aries, now under influence of Leo. A bad period ending, you're goin' to have lots of good luck. Mrs. Spence, you think I'm a fake?"

"Oh, no," Marg laughed out. "I see you read a lot. Anybody who takes his profession serious can't be a fake."

Sylvia decided to change the subject. "I'm glad you rented to those blacks. I knew these devilish whites wouldn't come to you. They love your building. It's the prettiest thing, but they're goin' to keep on bein' onery. When did he die?"

"Who?"

"The love in yo' life. I see it here."

"Oh-h." Marg was embarrassed. "Some time ago. My father."

"No, I don't think it's yo' father. I see passion. You lost him, didn't you?"

"I guess so. Madame Sylvia, I have a feeling of impending danger. I want to know what it is. What I have to do."

Sylvia was quiet for a long time; she kept rubbing her slender fingers across Marg's palm. "Well, my dear, you should always be with somebody; not so much moving around on yo' own."

"Does it mean I'm goin' to be attacked?"

"Who knows," said Sylvia, raising her voice. "I must warn you there are some crises yet. Come to me whenever you need help. I mean that."

"Thank you, Madame Sylvia. Are you a southerner?"

Their eyes met. Sylvia seemed amused. "I'm surprised that you asked. No, dear. I was born in Cincinnati. Got to talkin' like this up there. 'Course, they ain't no angels! How about a cup of tea?"

Marg said "yes, thank you", first wanting to settle the bill for the palm-reading. Madame Sylvia wouldn't take anything. She insisted it was her pleasure. A good strong cup of Orange Pekoe followed. Marg wasn't supposed to have it. The doctor had put her on a diet of milk. Oh, well, it was Christmas again, she told Sylvia, and they had a good laugh.

There was something about this strange young woman she couldn't figure out. She kept reminding Marg of a wise old witch. Was it expectation, or that alive look in her tight little eyes? Reddish veins at her chest had her looking like an alcoholic, an uncouth woman. Yet, with a warm, full depth of character. Marg had never met anyone like her. What it was, you couldn't put a class tag on Madame Sylvia.

After a few complimentary words about her tea, Marg questioned again. "Do you have much of a family here?"

"No one, my dear. I'm what you call a Lone Eagle. I settled in this town by accident. To me, life is yo' food, yo' house, yo' job. I liked my surroundings, so I stayed on. I've been here five years. Before that I was in New Orleans."

"Mercy, I'm meeting loads of people from there," said Marg gleefully. Then she told briefly about the celebrated pianist, Louis Gottschalk, who died in Brazil, and a little bit about George Washington Cable.

"Nope," said Sylvia, taking out a cigar. "Don't know either one. I was only there about a year. I came to get my husband. He was on the *Sultana*."

Marg looked confused.

"Don't you know about the *Sultana*?"

"I'm afraid not," said Marg, apologetically.

"It was that big troopship that sunk in the Mississippi just at the end of the war. Fourteen hundred lives lost. My Joe was one of them."

"I'm sorry," was Marg's quiet answer, as the cardlady looked to her lap. "The war was so cruel. I have a brother who lost his arm below the wrist. He was in the Union army."

"So was my husband," said Sylvia, taking another puff. "This doesn't disturb you, does it, dear?"

"No, I love the smell of cigar smoke. My father used to smoke them." That's it; this girl was acting much older than she is. An act.

Sylvia's beady eyes looked right into Marg's face. "Was he nice to you?"

"Oh, yes. Very nice."

Sylvia made a sigh. "Well, I don't trust but a few of these southern whites. Did you know about my father, Theodore Weld?"

"No, I don't believe I know that name."

"Famous in his day, thirty years ago. Hah! They had a price on his head. That's when he was with the American Anti-Slavery Society. For years, he acted as an agent, trainin' young guys in how to work with runaway slaves."

"How wonderful!" cried Marg, really liking this lady.

"Mostly he taught school, even little colored children. But he's known best for his books. One of them sold more than a hundred thousand."

"Then he really is famous! Is he still alive?"

"Oh, yes. My mom too. They're back an' forth, between Coxsackie, New York and Belleville, New Jersey. Now, you might know my mom. She wrote too. And lectured. She was the southerner! But at fourteen when she got a slave girl for a present, she refused it. Said, no! She didn't want no part of slavery. She and her sister left Carolina an' went up North to Philadelphia. That's where they both became famous."

"Really?" Marg was impressed. "What were their names?"

"The Grimke sisters."

"Oh!" screamed Marg. She knew this family. She knew Sylvia's people. Actually, it was the Negro part of the family she knew about. "Archibald and Francis!"

"That's right," laughed Sylvia. "Now you wouldn't connect a scrounger like me with that class, now would you? Did you think I was from such a distinguished family? Huh?"

"It's a real surprise!"

"Well, you see, the women in my mother's family have always been rebellious. An' my father's always been like a backwoodsman . . . itchy feet! You know!"

Marg sat back and admired her hostess. "It's such a small world," she said. "Your mother, which one is she? Angelina or Sarah Grimke?"

"Angelina. I see you know us very well."

"My mother knew about their work in women's rights as well as slavery. And years ago, we heard publicity about yo' grandfather. Wasn't he a distinguished South Carolina judge who treated his slaves as human beings? Then when one of his sons had slave children, they were accepted by the white family! We read this great story in the *Liberator*. My mother showed me the article to make me have courage in my own life." Bob Jenkins walked in to announce that Marg's carriage had arrived. She had to go. She rose, tugging at her wraps.

"I'm impressed," said Sylvia, dousing her cigar. "Had no idea a backwater town like this had enough culture to know about my people."

"You move in the white circles," Marg told her. "The educated colored class know about you."

"Colored or white," yelled Sylvia, standing up. "I don't worry about that nonsense. People are people. Now you think I'll get my head blown off for sayin' that?"

They had a good laugh. Marg realized she had made a new friend.

Chapter 39

As 1871 started, Marg obeyed her doctor and spent long morning hours in bed. She did not move down to the conservatory. The big leaded windows made that room a bit drafty. She stayed on in her favorite bedroom, the pink one, which had originally been Miss Gloria's. It was perfectly warm. For sunlight and fresh air, she would go down at eleven o'clock and have milk-tea, or a late breakfast, lounging in a new chaise lounge she had put near the conservatory windows in the direct path of sun rays. Her schedule now after waking was to do her reading first, in bed, on the second floor. This morning she had a big batch of newspapers and magazines, plus a few books.

Since meeting Sylvia Weld Sharkey she had ordered from New York Mr. Weld's *Slavery As It Is*, published in 1838. She found it fascinating. She could see how Lyman Beecher had called the man "logic on fire". Next, she read Angelina Grimke Weld's *Appeal to the Christian Women of the South*. It asked for more Miriams to lead captive daughters to the light of liberty. Not knowing Miriam, Marg had to search in her Bible. She was impressed to learn that Sarah Grimke was a Quaker. Perhaps her own two daughters knew this. She saw where Mr. Theodore Weld had had many New England poets as his friends, and, most great poets except Edgar Allan Poe were abolitionists, or sympathizers. Marg hadn't realized how many good people were on the Negro's side. Poor John Greenleaf Whittier got mobbed four times! She read that William Cullen Bryant had tied the fight to despotism and anarchy.

She wrote a list. She'd order: "The Branded Hand" by Whittier. This could have helped her during her prison days. But, in a way, wasn't she still in prison? Also she wanted Henry Wadsworth Longfellow's "The Slave at Midnight", and some Ralph Waldo Emerson books. He had been her father's favorite. Now she was tired. She'd get up and have her tea. Yes, of course, with lots of milk in it.

Just as she got downstairs, Irwin Clark came in blowing and puffing from the late January weather. "How's my dear patient today?"

"Cold," exclaimed Marg, going to her second bed, the chaise lounge by the conservatory window. The quilts on it were beautiful silks and satins. "I'm thinkin' about putting central heat in this house. I saw it up North. I think we need it."

"It's very expensive," said the fat-faced, cashew-colored man, sitting nearby and also having tea. Irene dutifully put the good cups around on Miss Margery's mahogany table.

"Oh, Irwin, I don't worry about money any more!"

"You're one of the lucky ones. Remember that, Marg. So many colored people work hard an' have nothing. They're frightened daily about havin' enough greenbacks to meet their needs. Now, up in Washington, this Legal Tender bill will soon get passed. We don't want a repeat of the panic of 1837 or 1857. Some say this is an age of prosperity, but just look at the numbers who are completely left out!"

Marg sipped her tea. "The white man calls them the lazy ones."

"No. Absolutely not."

"Of course not. Look how that Tweed gang is robbin' the coffers of New York. My brother says poor people there have less than ours, robbed by clever well-dressed crooks! Forced to disorder, squalor an' crime."

"Well, New York's problems relate to poor immigrants continuing to pour in. Here in Maple we have a closed li'l society. A man should have a chance. Yet, it's a continual fight where stealers live off another man's work! Marg, I want you to join our club."

"What club?"

"The Maple Historical Preservation Society."

"Irwin, I'm bored with historical questions."

"Hah! Don't go by the title. It's a stimulating think group. Colored people who want to turn things around. We put our minds together an' come up with new ideas."

"Without squabbling? I can't believe it. All right, what do you want me to do?"

"Just come to the meetings. Every Tuesday night. At Spruce Street Baptist Church."

Marg frowned. This was the church where that rascal Wilkins, Matilda's husband, was an assistant pastor. "I don't go around ignorant people."

"Listen, ours is not a church group. We just use the building. Come, I think you'll learn something, an' you can make a contribution too. And bring yo' coachman too. It's not safe out there at night. Eight o'clock, Tuesday."

Marg got herself dolled up that coming Tuesday evening. Then she went back to her wardrobe and put on something less elaborate. She'd be among sensitive low-class colored people, raucous or raunchy. Jason had told her how they think of the Spences as slaveowners. She got down a simple frock, and no jewelry.

It was a stuffy wooden room, with a cabbage odor, scratched-up benches and chairs. A good fire was roaring in the pot-bellied stove. As she came in, with Adam Hinds, they all looked around. She nodded a smile. She was going up to sit near Dr. Clark, but decided to stay in back. On her own.

They were discussing the school situation, the fact that no funds were coming down from Atlanta, and the Maple authorities were giving little. One yellow woman got up and told of the taxes they pay, insisting a delegation go to the mayor and complain. A brown man got up, talking loud, saying it was no use complainin' unless you knew what you were complainin' about. What they needed was a look at the records. Marg smiled, remembering her courthouse days. The honest records would show what was going to the white schools. Dr. Clark agreed the comparison would help; he volunteered to take a small group to the mayor. About four people of the thirty present raised their hands to volunteer.

Next, they got to the business of voting irregularities. A deep-brown lady named Mrs. Blake claimed the Union League watchers were not at the polls. The law didn't mean for white bigots to chase away watchers. She wanted Federal troops to be there, making arrests if white people misbehaved. Others agreed the voting problem was a Federal problem, a failure of the occupation forces. A lightskinned man got up and said in a nice tenor voice that sooner or later the troops would leave and they'd have to live with these same whites. You have to shame them, to make them behave properly, or, try makin' them friends.

"Ain't none of 'em goin' be a true friend," shouted Mrs. Blake, seating herself next to Marg. "I know 'cause most my neighbors on Plum Avenue is white, an' dey's not goin' change in the least. Mornings, none of 'em speaks, even if'n you gives a nice Christian greetin'. You can't go in they churches. An' I don't wants befriendin' them jis fo' handout junk. So what's to be done? Nothin'. We live in our world, and they in theirs! Maybe we should ask Federal guv'ment give us separate votin' days, an' votin' places." She sat down hard.

"A pretty good idea," said Clark, rising. "Folks, we have with us this evenin' Mrs. Margery Malcolm Spence, who's been on Plum Avenue for years. Suppose we ask Mrs. Spence to form a committee, to go around neighborly, to see if'n there's a project which might interest both black an' white neighbors—"

There was a mumbling around the room. Marg sat tight. Soon Mrs. Blake got up again. "I motion we elects Miz Spence as leader of the group to get people mo' neighborly . . . not only on Plum Avenue but all over town!"

Somebody seconded the motion, and the chairman pounded his gavel to indicate acceptance. Marg sat tight as the room got quiet. Clark looked to her; the others also. They wanted a speech. She had to say something. She rose slowly. "Ladies and gentlemen, it gives me much pleasure to be here this evenin' an' I accept yo' offer to lead us in this canvassing of neighborhoods, to create harmony and work-together possibilities. As I was listening to the speakers, it came to mind that we need cooperation in settin' out garbage neatly. With both peoples served equally! Whereas this is a meeting of colored, the others might also be asked to be involved—"

There was a stir in the room. Had she said the wrong thing? Several got to their feet; Marg couldn't hear what they were saying because Mrs. Blake, sitting right there, had grabbed her arm, yelling congratulations for her sane suggestion. "I agree! People have to learn to work together," she beamed.

After the meeting, Marg offered to drive Mrs. Blake home. She lived in the next block up from Marg's house. The deep-brown woman was delighted to be offered a ride in the elegant carriage of rich Mrs. Spence. At her house, Adam got down to guide the heavy brown woman to the ground. She leaned on him, but didn't say thank you. He smiled, knowing his mistress meant to show kindness in every way. Marg thanked him at home, and asked what he thought of the meeting.

"Miss Margery, I sat dere thinkin', dey talks a lotta words. If'n people wants to do somethin', dey should jis up and do it. Why life always got dis talkin'?"

"You're right," said Marg, starting upstairs, appreciating his wisdom.

All that spring of 1871 Marg worked with the Maple Historical Preservation Society. She and Mrs. Blake became rather good friends. She invited her to Malcolm House, showed her all the rooms, the back garden, Beth's old doll house, the new carriage house, the new laundry rooms. Mrs. Blake was flabbergasted. For years she had worked in domestic service for whites; none of them had what this lady had. And she just went crazy over the delicate French plates Marg used for tea.

Marg sat opposite, trying to learn Mrs. Blake's hobbies, what they could talk about in common. It seemed, they both had an interest in pottery and in children. Mrs. Blake had a sixteen-year-old boy, Richard, who did ditchdigging, and a girl, Fanny, who was twenty, who did nothing but sit around home.

"I don't know what I kin do to make dat girl work," said Bonnie Blake.

"Maybe she'd like to work for me," offered Marg, not really thinking it over.

"No," laughed Bonnie. "She don't like no housework. You could neber get her to do what I has to do to make a livin'. Hah!"

"Well, I'll think of something else," Marg replied. "In fact, you send Fanny over here to talk to me, an' we'll get our heads together. Okay?"

This was when Marg was just beginning to have success with the Pear Orchard. Something from Fanny's black mind was to make it even more a success.

When Jeeter lost his job at the Freedmen's Bureau, Marg decided she'd tear down her eighteen rental houses. They had gotten to a state of disrepair, and she didn't want to keep putting money into them, and she didn't want to argue with Dr. Bowman, or people like him, about whom she'd take as renters. Those cottages had been there more than forty years and had served their purpose.

With the job done, she gave a little gift, some fishing tackles to Bob Jenkins, her porter, because it was his friends who did the excellent wrecking job. When the huge sandy lot was all cleared and fenced in, white people came to Marg asking her what she was going to do with the land. She hadn't realized that anybody would be interested in it, but the business area was moving towards Thirteenth Street. When she asked Dr. Clark for his advice, he once again joked about it being an excellent location for a hospital.

Marg had no intention of putting herself in a project which would require a collection of a quarter of a million dollars. No, not until the idea of a new black hospital hit Fanny Blake's ear. Bonnie's lazy child's eyes lit up. She said Marg's pear money could be the seed for this goal. What she meant was that she and some of her friends should be allowed to use all that pear money toward the hospital goal. What they'd do:

take the pear money and give shows, and in that way raise money for the hospital. Marg looked dumbfounded. Fanny sighed, then explained that she had always liked singing. While looking like a surly-acting black misfit, she was in fact a Christian girl. She sang in a group at church. Now Marg liked her idea. She had never thought of a money-raising group of young churchgoers.

What Fanny had in mind, the young people's choir at her church, St. James Baptist, were excellent at spirituals. Fanny wanted Marg to sponsor them, send them off to white churches to sing. Maybe even as far as Atlanta.

When Marg passed on these ideas to Dr. Clark, he was ecstatic. All he said it needed was organization. He asked if Marg wanted to put it to the Maple Historical Preservation Society; she said no. That group was arguing. The ignoramuses and the intelligent people couldn't get together. No. She more or less wanted this a family project. She'd put money in, and Dr. Clark would put money in. Together they'd build the singing group, and the new hospital. They got started, in August, by inviting all the young people to Marg's house to sing. It was a hot sticky night. Marg had lots of fans, perfumed the air, and a paid little boy running her antebellum ceiling punkah. The young people were amazed at the beauty and majesty of Malcolm House. Edna Clark came, and poor Hattie Clark (looking very strange in this group of all dark brownskinned youth), and Bonnie Blake came. The latter was in charge of refreshments and she did a marvelous job making sandwiches in Marg's elaborate kitchen.

In the end, the young people were allowed to talk. Edna had them take a vote on the proposals, and they decided to call themselves the St. James Jubilee Singers. Their twenty voices had good harmony and lots of spirit. They made Marg's house echo like a cathedral. After they left, the Clarks and Mrs. Blake and Fanny sat around in the parlor, discussing how to approach the white people to get them interested in these singers. Marg had thought it out. Madame Sylvia, or Sylvia Weld Sharkey, was a congregant at First Baptist, the white society church. Marg was sure she could get Sylvia to talk to their minister, to invite the group to sing there one Sunday. And, a collection would be taken.

It all worked out. The St. James Jubilee Singers made their debut at First Baptist on the first Sunday in September. John, Beth and Meg came. Marg was nervous about this because colored people were not welcome in the audience in any Maple white churches. They sat with blond Hattie Clark, and Jeb Hunter and his daughter, Cindy, equally strangers at this fancy church of the rich people. Nobody bothered them. Everybody was so impressed at the way the young niggers sang, that was all the talk. The people gave them an offering of two hundred and fifty dollars. This was the first money for the Clark Memorial Hospital.

Of course nobody knew at that time that the hospital would be named Clark Memorial. But sad things did happen that September of 1871. Now that the ice had been broken with the white community, the group was invited next to sing at Grace Congregational Church. Clark got enthusiastic. He talked to Frank Korner who was to get them a singing engagement with the Business Men's Club and also with the Elks Lodge, and at white churches in Macon and LaGrange. In fact, the two men were together talking about it on the fifteenth of September. At twilight, a mellowed and handsome Frank drove his surrey up in front of Marg's Malcolm Spanish Court. Wanting to be nice to the good doctor, he suggested they first have a few beers at O'Brien's Tavern, then go on out to Lain's Corner Baptist (white) where the St. James Jubilee Singers were singing that night.

Neither Frank Korner nor Irwin Clark showed up at the church, or back home that evening. When they didn't return by eleven-thirty p.m., their womenfolk got worried. Edna and her son came over to Marg's asking questions. Marg knew details of the two men's meeting that night, and explained them to Mrs. Clark. Upon leaving Edna Clark wondered if she should not ask the sheriff to investigate. Bonnie Blake and her daughter had returned from Lain's Corner. They were still awake when Edna and Marg went to them. Bonnie of course said they were missed at church, but she didn't advise involving the sheriff just now. She said wait till morning, then she and her brother would drive out to Cobb's Creek and Lain's Corner, checking the roads on the way. And, who knows, maybe by morning they'd be back home, safe and sound!

Phyllis Korner did not come to Marg's house. Instead, she checked with Sylvia. In fact, she went there with her blond son, Mark, who was going to Harvard just like John, and was to leave for school the next day. The only way Marg knew what was going on in the Korners' house was through her servant, Adam Hinds. A friend of his, Jesse, was the coachman for the Korners. Mrs. Korner (Phyllis) had sent Jesse that night scouting on all the highways. And it was poor Jesse who discovered the truth.

Dr. Clark and Frank Korner had been murdered. Coachman Jesse at midnight had turned off on a lonely country road not far from the business section of Lain's Corner. In a pine grove ditch, he found an overturned surrey with no horse. Inside the carriage were two bloodied men: Irwin Clark and Frank Korner: with ashen faces of equal whiteness, joined in Eternity.

Right away the rumor spread across the colored community that this dirty job had been done by the Ku Klux Klan. The sheriff's office did not deny it. There certainly was no clear motive for the crime. They had not been robbed. Clark's expensive gold watch was still on his person, and the hundred dollars cash he carried. Frank was still wearing his German heirloom ruby which had been in his family more than a hundred years. His big camera was still in the wagon. No, robbery was not the motive. It seemed to be racial hate.

The *Maple Star-Journal* wrote up the crime in its strange jargon, in part saying:

> *The Maple community has lost a warm, loving and dedicated citizen in the death of our beloved photographer and businessman, Mr. Frank Korner (white), whose misfortune was to be traveling in the same carriage with a noted black doctor, Irwin Clark, who came to Maple three years ago from Dothan, Alabama, where he had been notorious by taunting the white community . . .*

Marg didn't finish the article, noticing its slander; she did feel some joy for Phyllis, who had long wanted to be regarded as "white".

Chapter 40

Beth delayed her departure for Wellesley College to attend Dr. Clark's funeral, and to be with her good friend, Hattie Clark. The Negro aristocracy throughout the South was shocked by the tragic loss of this capable and valiant fighter for equality. Both Marg and Beth were very impressed by the huge display of flowers that came to the Clark mansion in Walnut Street. And the distinguished friends from as far away as Mississippi and South Carolina.

It was only natural that many of the visitors were near-white, Anglo-Saxon types. One handsome blond fellow, there with his father, caught Beth's eye. He was Theodore Cardozo of Mississippi. He was going to school at Amherst College, also in Massachusetts. They exchanged addresses and Marg was pleased to see her charming daughter act, knowing it was an excellent time to be forward. The boy's father, Thomas Cardozo, was head of public instruction for the whole state of Mississippi. The family was free-born and originally from South Carolina. Marg knew the name of his uncle, Francis Cardozo, who like Thomas, his father, was a graduate of the University of Glasgow in Scotland. Mr. Francis Cardozo had been principal of Avery Institute, a delegate at South Carolina's constitutional convention in 1868, chairman of the Committee on Education, also he served as Secretary of State. Marg had read that their mother, the boy's grandmother, had been a beauteous mixed-blood slave and the father, a highly aristocratic gentleman (white), and she knew too that in all America there were no bluebloods as aristocratic as the Charlestonians (white and colored).

Marg of course did everything she could for the Clark family in their bereavement. She even thought seriously of sending flowers to poor Phyllis, but a force inside of her kept her from doing this good act. Phyllis, she was sure, had plenty of good friends now.

To poor upset Jason she explained that the world is so full of hate, that you can't teach people to change, only help them change. By love. And never be jealous. Don't worry about happiness due you. You carry it around with you. It's inside. Jason nodded, with set brown lips.

Sylvia Sharkey was very dear in coming by to help soothe Marg's nerves. She first came to Malcolm House on invitation, wearing her best silks. She was a rare visitor by not commenting on its opulence or beauty. Marg assumed Sylvia was of less culture until she visited Sylvia's grey, wooden rented house in Chestnut Street, one of the few all-white areas. It was like a neat museum: little miniatures in gold frames, crystal cups, colorful velvet throws draped near marble statuettes or figurines. It was clear that this lady of the cards loved being in her beauteous home.

"You have everything so homey," Marg told her at tea. "One would think you've been here longer than a few years."

"Oh, I'm like the Arabs. I can unroll my sacks from a camel's back an' have a palace. Hah! You know, as little girls we were always on the move, with my parents' crisis-bound occupation, or pre-occupation."

"You say they're still alive?"

"Oh yes. They're soon to leave their New Jersey farm to go up to Massachusetts to start another school."

"That's marvelous. With them, I suppose it's like religious fervor, helping the blacks—"

"It's more than that, my dear. They think American. The things they do are to help everyone! You know, Mom and Aunt Sarah were thrown out of the Quakers. They were impatient with the Friends' moderation on slavery, an' the Quakers were distraught with their progressive ideas. It was unheard of then for women to lecture on a public dias. You see, religious or not, man has this weakness of bein' intimidated by his own laws and customs. My family has its quirks too. When I started doing my readings everybody was shocked. 'How could she? Comin' from a good family!' Well, when I left New Orleans, determined to be independent, I stumbled into my profession through a need for funds. Wonderful, Marg! I learned self-responsibility. An' in my li'l advice to people, I want to create leaders, not followers!"

"Marvelous," smiled Marg, enjoying a sugar cake. "An' I never had it in mind to be a storekeeper or a commercial landlord."

"What was in yo' mind, in youth?"

"Nothing, really. Just to be a southern-type housewife, I guess. Now I'm really going to surprise myself, Sylvia. I'm going to build that hospital for poor Dr. Clark."

"I know you will! It's in yo' sign. You'll raise that quarter of a million dollars, an' you'll get a beautiful building up. But, my dear, to manage it will kill you."

"You don't think I have the ability?"

"It's not that. Whenever you try to do things, people will fight you. I'm Virgo, like a turtle, an' I can fight 'em. But you get wounded so easily."

Marg got up and reached for her shawl. "No, Sylvia," she said, playfully. "You don't know me that well. I'm thinking racial these days. It's something I *must* do for the colored people. Tell me, what ever happened to the two youngest Grimke boys? The Negroes in yo' family?"

A radiant Sylvia rared back. "Well, both graduated from Lincoln University. Archie's just started law at Harvard Law School, and his brother, Francis, is finishing something at Howard, expecting to go to Princeton Theological Seminary next semester."

"Marvelous! You know my son finished Princeton. Now he's up at Harvard. Would there be any harm if I wrote and told him of our friendship, an' have him meet Archie?"

"No harm," chuckled Sylvia. "We don't consider it a sin to know Negroes, or to share blood with them. Yes, I'd like Archie to meet your John. He spends Christmas and summers in Washington with Francis. Has yo' son ever seen the capital? Our boys would love to show it to him. I think every bright youth should see that place."

Marg was apprehensive. She wanted to tell Sylvia about her daughter, Justine, but the time hadn't come yet. She started saying her good-byes.

A uniformed black servant showed Marg in at the Clark's spic-and-span mansion. The floors were a tan glow everywhere, and as slick as glass. Edna came through a curtain of big green plants in the marble atrium. She was smiling bravely. Marg first complimented her for holding up so well at the funeral. Next, she commented on the nice array of visitors, Theodore Cardozo in particular. Edna smiled, saying he was one of her children's friends, Ed and Hattie's. Marg then offered her a check for one thousand dollars, money Irwin had given her to start the singing group and the hospital. "No, I couldn't take it," sighed dignified Edna Clark, sitting now, which brought attention to her lovely black velvet mourning dress. "Thank you, Marg. Irwin would want you to use that money just as he intended."

"But Edna, dear, you have no profession. How will you live?"

Edna smiled. "We'll manage. I know the whites wonder how, but we'll manage." Edna's house had four live-in servants and four others who came on day service. While the good doctor's Maple practice was just catching on, Marg assumed rightly that they both had old family money that stood them in good.

"Marg, fit me into the plan," pleaded Edna, cheerful enough. "While I have no skills, I'm not too old to learn. I hear the group is goin' up to Atlanta. Do you need a chaperone?"

Marg accepted the offer, and Edna Clark became a great asset, a true friend, someone who would work as hard for her as her dear mother.

That mid-October Marg received, by surprise, a sad letter from Lucy. It read:

October 12, 1871

Dear Marg,

We've been wiped out! It was a terrible fire. It destroyed much of Chicago, the business center and many neighborhoods. The children and I were at school, but my poor Kenneth was one of the 200 deaths. God's will. While we still have our home, I am penniless. I should be grateful for whatever you could send me quickly.

Love,

Lucy.

While Marg had not known Kenneth, she felt Lucy's loss. Her grief lightly mentioned meant Lucy was concentrating on survival. Marg thought of the money Edna had refused. That had to go to her hospital. She thought too of the $800 she had raised from the pears. She could send that money, but Mr. Folsom would be checking later. He'd know Lucy, her cousin, was not a "jet black". So, as before, she'd hand this money over to the youngsters in St. James Jubilee Singers. Sylvia had actually flattered her on the subject of prosperity. Just now, she was short of cash. Mr. Haney hadn't sent the $60,000 she requested, nor the check for the typewriter contract. And Larry had spent a lot on shipping and supplies. Yes, she'd send Lucy one thousand dollars. And that rascal, Jeb Hunter, still had not paid her a cent on his loan. Marg thought of writing Charles for some of his salary, but no sooner than it had crossed her mind, here he was, her natty husband, walking in the door.

"Well, I thought you were in Savannah!"

He set down his valise, kissed her cheek and allowed a forlorn look to come into his expressive eyes. "Marg, I've come home. My days in Savannah are ovah."

"What happened?"

"Oh-h, you know office work. There are busybodies an' crooks out there. I simply got tired of it. Nothin' really happened."

"Then you resigned?"

"Yes. And they were glad to have it. My friend Houston is still in jail."

"Really? I thought he got back as senator when Gregory went back."

"Oh, they had many more charges against him. Embezzlement for one. I think if I had stayed on, the same charges would have engulfed me."

"Charles, you didn't take any money, did you?"

He smiled through reddish-brown moustache. His head was mostly grey. "Marg, now you know I've nevah been thirsty for greenbacks."

"Good, then I can have some of those thousands you earned. Lucy's been caught in the Chicago Fire. We have to send her something."

"How much?"

"One thousand, for a start. She's lost her husband. Poor Kenneth was one of the fire victims."

"That's sad. But Marg, I don't have a thousand."

"You should have many thousands. Charles, what have you done with yo' earnings? Not everything to that li'l Spanish wench, I hope!"

"Marg!" he laughed. "How can you say such?"

"Because I'm truthful. Charles, how can we live again as husband and wife?"

He came close and hugged her shoulders. "It'll work. You'll see."

"No, Charles, I don't think it'll work. Too much has happened. I don't think we love each other any more."

"Then you don't want me comin' home?"

"Oh, I'm glad you've come home!" She started to tell him about Justine, right that very moment. Then she threw it out of her mind. "Charles, we're practically strangers, an' I'm not sure I want to be close any more. We must have separate bedrooms."

"Marg!"

"Simply, we must!"

"Daily life is love, angel. Now isn't it?"

"Poor Celeste used to say: *Life is a gift*. But I don't want your romantic words. To speak plainly, I don't feel the same about you. Yet, I'll respect you. As the father of my children—"

"Not as a husband?"

"I've told you what Dr. Clark said. I have tuberculosis. I don't want to give it to you."

"Oh-h, it's like a cough. That's all. My daddy had it. Laurie too. An' maybe poor li'l Jason probably has a touch of it too. If God wants *me* to have it . . . well!"

"Don't be selfish. Charles, what you want of me is not what I want of life. We can't start over. An understandin', yes . . . about my sickness and other things. Otherwise, you'll drive me crazy!" They kissed.

Marg got down brandy, and they sat talking two hours. When brandy bottle was empty, a glowing Charles, with bright hazel eyes, wanted to take her to her room. She said no. They had decided on a cool relationship. They'd both stay ultra-busy at work. And to bring dollars home, he'd go out and help Mitchell and Albert again, and she'd be busy with the two bartershops, the typewriter order, her rental building and the Memorial Fund for Dr. Clark's hospital. Charles was very impressed upon hearing about the latter. Marg decided he could be a chaperone for the Atlanta trip. She didn't want to go. He'd accompany the youngsters with Mrs. Clark. No, she didn't worry about anything happening. Dignified Edna, once a cashew-colored beauty, was now a seasoned matronly wrinkled woman. Charles wasn't interested in her type. He wasn't that foolish.

During the Christmas week Charles gave his fine Commissioner of Ports uniforms to Adam Hinds, their coachman. The servant had never had a happier occasion. Marg sat with Jason and Charles, enjoying the holidays. The children stayed up North, with friends. Marg was glad to receive a letter from Angela Baker. It read:

December 23, 1871

My dear Margery,

Merry Christmas, dear! I know I owe you a letter. Sorry, I've been very busy moving myself back to the Jerome house in Brooklyn. Not Lawrence Jerome's but Leonard Jerome's. Remember, with those three beautiful daughters? Well, he's hired me. His wife, my cousin Clara, still lives in France and he needs someone to look after his household here. The big mansion in Madison Square has been rented to a club.

The girls are quite grown-up now. Studying languages, playing piano duets, and meeting sociable people in Europe. In fact, Mr. Jerome goes over in summer; they rent a house at Cowes, with garden facing the sea. It seems society goes there in August. Even the Prince of Wales! Clara loves the atmosphere. Mr. J. accompanied

346

them back to France, then returned home early November. Jennie wrote me that Paris is dreadful now. Leonie has been sent to school in Germany. Clarita is courting, high up!

I keep the house in readiness, but it is unlikely they'll ever come back. I understand Clara intends to have Jennie's debut over there next summer.

I'm fine. Just a few aches in my shoulder. All the best for the New Year.

Love,

Angela.

P.S. I'm so sorry for Phyllis, losing Frank that way. You two should become friends again. I pray for it.

Chapter 41

1872 started cold and windy. Marg did think of Phyllis, rich now but still in her old family home, the Potters' white, wooden, needing-paint house. Marg was always weary in January. She was glad to see the postman. There were several bills, and a short note from Haney saying that James Fisk, one of their financiers, was dead. He had been killed by a jealous associate, over the showgirl, Josie Mansfield. She couldn't understand why Haney was telling her this, unless it meant money out of her pocket. At least now she had her $60,000 and was miserly deciding how it would be spent. A pleasant surprise was a letter from Lydia Smith. It read:

January 4, 1872

My dear Margery,

Happy New Year, honey! I'm here in Columbia, South Carolina. A delightful place after my absence of ten years. You could say I'm on vacation, but it's really a job. I'm working with Senator R.H. Cain, a northern black, who's here to investigate carpetbag power. Governor R.K. Scott is in his second term. Some say the bayonet gave him his post, but I find him a fine, self-assertive man. He comes from Ohio; was a common gold miner in California, and he practiced medicine too. Here he started with the Freedmen's Bureau. He's very popular among Negroes, but some say he cannot distinguish an educated man from a fool.

South Carolina has 420,000 Negroes and 290,000 whites. Charleston has 26,000 Negroes and Columbia has 5,300. Well, naturally the governor moves around with more Negroes; there are more of them! I must say, the State House has changed. It's a beautiful white marble building surrounded by giant oaks. Now with blacks in power there is no lawn, no pretty flowers. They eat peanuts in the legislature; some government purchases find their way into brothels catering to both races. Gov. Scott is supposed to have signed hundreds of thousands of dollars' worth of fraudulent convertible bonds. You can't get to the bottom of the gossip. The white people are

distressed. Old-guard society dislike that Gov. and Mrs. Scott entertain both races! The famous Madame Roland, a brownskinned
woman, is society now.

I met the equally famous Rollin sisters. Katherine, Marie
Louise and Charlotte—pretty quadroon girls. Their father was
French and they insist on being called 'Mesdemoisells'. Two went to
a fancy school in Boston with Wendell Philipps' niece; Louise went
to convent school in Philadelphia, and Charlotte says she was in
Oberlin with your cousin, Sue. She's the one who is supposed to
possess uncanny power over statesmen, black and white. There is a
fourth sister, Euphrosyne, whom I didn't see because she's married a
black man and the family now disown her. With the three still in
society, we exchanged pretty words. They spoke of Victor Hugo,
Whittier and Mrs. Browning's poetry. I had a feeling they were judging *my* intelligence all the time!

The bar-rooms and dance-halls are crowded with Negroes
and a sprinkling of whites. Catered parties have the best Westphalia
ham, cheeses, buffalo tongue, nuts, cherries, peaches. The stealing
may be as the whites say, but I only see it as a slightly rougher cut of
Washington. Politics, as usual.

Love,

Lydia Farley Smith.

P.S. Mr. Evarts was successful in court, so I can keep my
Washington house.

Marg smiled; she could detect that Lydia was happy, not especially
missing dear Mr. Thaddeus Stevens, provider of the house. Just as
Marg was going for her bath, in walked Cliff Redberry. He had walked
in mocassins across the Chattahoochee, ready to pay off the last of his
loan. He sat through several days, eating Marg's good food, and sipping Charles' whiskey. He told her about his gun business and the
likelihood of another Indian war, this time in California. He was glad
Marg and Charles were back together again. On the day of his leaving
he took care that Charles was out of hearing distance, then he said to
Marg:

"I hope it was a healthy baby. You look fine now."

"I'm not fine," she told him. "I have tuberculosis. It could kill
me."

"Oh, I'm sorry to hear that. Listen, there's an Indian remedy for
consumption. Would you like to try it? Some herbs. I'll bring them the
next time I come."

"Oh, please do. I really want to live a bit longer, Cliff. I want to
finish this hospital project. An' I want to see my three children happily
married."

"Four children?"

"Yes, of course. Jason, my dear. Don't let me forget my angel!" Jason, all brown and skinny for nine, came in and hugged his mother, then went on outside to play.

"He's going to be all right," said Cliff. "You can tell when a young'un has a mature mind. One more to safety, huh?" He touched Marg's bare arm, squeezing it. Then he hoisted his sack, ready to leave. Just then, lovely red-haired Madame Sylvia walked into the conservatory.

"I want you to meet my dear friend," Marg told him. "Madame Sylvia's well-known in Maple for her successful business."

Grinning, Cliff slicked back his salt-and-pepper straight blackish hair, and shook hands. "Madame Sylvia, how do you do! We've heard a lot about you. You know, Indians can tell fortunes too. You want me to see what I see in yo' hand?"

Sylvia slapped him away playfully. "None of your tricks! Marg, this man comes to me whenever he gets drunk."

"Then you know each other?"

"Not socially. Now is the first time. Mr. Redberry, if I really wanted to make money on you, I'd tell you little at a time everything I know about you."

He laughed. "Does that mean bad news travels?"

With hands on her rather broad hips, Sylvia stood akimbo. "I could tell you some things without chargin' a fee."

"Go ahead. I'm game. You'll prophesy, an' I'll prophesy—"

"You'll be in trouble," snapped Sylvia, now growing serious.

"Aw-w, come on, why don't you tell us it's all fakery, all hocus-pocus."

"You see, Marg, he just comes to get my goat. He doesn't believe in it—"

"I didn't say that, angel. Hey, listen, I believe what you say—"

"Well, believe this, Mr. Redberry. They're after you. They think you're sellin' rifles to the ni—, to the Negroes."

There was a silence. Marg looked at Cliff as he moved away. His face had become serious. Sylvia stalked him, still akimbo. "They'll lynch you!"

"They gonna lynch me?"

"Okay, go on. Don't be careful. When I heah gossip, it means the story's gotten around. But I'm stupid, huh?"

Marg interrupted when a servant brought a napkin full of sweets for Redberry. "Now, you-all please! Let's not talk about any more intrigue and killings. The Lord didn't mean for people to get on this way. Cliff, if you want to stay on in the gun business, why don't you make it a shipping business, with nothing sold around here?"

He raised his hands in protest. "They'd still kill each other, whether I'm here, Missouri, Kansas, or Detroit—"

"He's right," said Sylvia, now sitting down and taking a cookie from Marg's napkin. "Rebels will be rebels. I think he's too good a man to be foolin' around with guns. Marg, give him a new profession!"

Cliff held out his palm so she could read it. "Like fan dancin', Madame Sylvia?"

She slapped his hand away. "This is no jokin' matter. The Klan are on to you. Take my warnin'."

Marg knelt down between them. "Cliff, angel, listen to Sylvia. Please. Give it serious thought. We don't want to lose you. Did you know Sylvia comes from a famous abolitionist family?"

Cliff raised his eyebrows. "You mean to tell me she's a northerner?"

Sylvia slapped his head. "When have you met a southern white woman as nice as me? Never!"

"Now I can appreciate you a bit better," he smiled, getting ready to go. "You're a carpetbag witch, gettin' rich off us."

"I wouldn't use that 'us' so freely," she told him, in no uncertain terms.

That February Marg got a letter from Ohio. A legal firm. It seems Charles Waverly had owned a silver lode in Nevada, and had willed it to her. The family had discussed this, and had no objection to her taking over ownership. They had gained Charles' engineering concern. The letter closed by indicating a buyer was offering $8,000 for the silver land. The lawyers would wait for Marg's instructions. She jumped up and raced through the house, stopping only as the slick foyer floor took her down. She lipped at her skinned elbow, thanking Jesus.

"Justine, baby, he must have known you were coming! Thank you, Jesus. Thank you, Charles."

She rushed to her wardrobe and got out her suitcase. She'd go to Atlanta today. Her bank there could send the appropriate letter to Ohio. What she wanted now was to negotiate the loan for the hospital. Her assets were strong enough now.

Returning from Atlanta, Marg stayed close to her fires all that winter. She had already paid a contractor to install central heat. While she was thinking of her tuberculosis, others were thinking of her social position. In Maple, only the very rich had central heat. She had the audacity to want to be classified with them. Marg paid them no mind; none knew how she had to watch her dollars.

The bankers in Atlanta gave her trouble. They didn't want to give so much on loan to a woman of color. They even came to Maple snooping around. She decided there was only one way to handle this. She wrote a long letter to Haney saying she needed a recommendation from a famous financier, like the late Mr. Fisk. That Haney hadn't forgotten a thing. He went straight to Lawrence Jerome! He didn't go through Angela, but to strengthen his hand, he brought her into the picture, telling Mr. Jerome she was Marg's good friend. Jerome straightaway wrote the Atlanta bankers, and they were impressed. When the loan finally came through, it was early March. A happy Marg immediately arranged the ground-breaking. She had planned a big ceremony with the black churches, Cousin Don, the school bands, Uncle Vincent's newspaper, speeches, refreshments. She cancelled it all. It was rainy anyway. She just wanted to get on with the hospital.

In April the sun began to shine, warming up the house with its natural heat. Marg and Adam Hinds, her coachman, had become good friends because now they were equals in their meetings at the Maple Historical Preservation Society. Yet, he'd not let it go to his head. Since the two living-in servantgirls liked to sleep late, he made it his duty bringing his mistress her tea every morning.

"Mornin', Adam," chirped Marg, already up and reading her newspapers. "I think we're gonna have a lovely spring day."

"Miss Margery, I been Uptown. Dere's a lot of commotion at Eagle and Phoenix cotton mill."

"Really? What's the trouble this time?"

Adam scratched his white goatee. "Dey strikin'. Don't want to work with cullud people. Dat's always de trouble. Now all de white workers are paradin' out on the street—"

"When we go to Public Market, stay on Spruce all the way, then turn later at Twelfth." Apprehensively, Marg wanted to see her hospital project in progress. This time she had an Atlanta contractor.

"I don't think we should be goin' anywhere, Miss Margery. You know in dis town, don't take long before people is fightin' everywhere!"

"Maybe you're right," said Marg, taking off diamonds. She had meant to tell Redberry to bring her several of his guns. In spite of law, colored people needed to have them.

She had breakfast in the chaise lounge in the conservatory. Just as Adam brought her second cup of tea, in walked pretty Cousin Sue. "Hi, Sue, honey! You're up an' out early."

Sue didn't answer. She came and sat on the footstool in front of Marg. "Jeeter wants to leave."

"What's that you're sayin'?" Marg's mind was still on the strike.

"He doesn't want to stay here any more. He wrote Dr. Howard at the Freedmen's Bureau in Washington, and they've offered him a job up there."

"In Washington?" gasped Marg, thinking of course of Justine. "You're not goin' to leave yo' home to go up there?"

"Yes, we're goin'," said Sue quietly. "I've never liked this town too much."

"But how about your farm, and your beautiful little house?"

"Oh, we'll probably rent it. Mitchell says we should go slow an' see how we like it up North. We're leavin' next week."

Marg grabbed her cheeks. "Oh, my angel!" She hadn't told Sue about her baby, and for Sue to learn it from others would be terrible. "Isn't there something I can do? I told Jeeter he could work in the hospital, or with Larry on the typewriter project."

"No. Jeeter thinks everything here is tainted. He wants to see another part of America."

"Okay, but first go out on a little trip. The two of you."

"No. His mind is made up on Washington. I think I encouraged him with my Oberlin talk."

"You were happy there, but Washington's different. Sue, for the colored man, makin' a living in America is very tough. He has to be ready for all kinds of abuse."

She laughed. "Don't try to convince me! We've decided. An' I'll miss you, Marg. I'm goin' to miss my li'l house. My piano—"

"Dear, if you need money, to ship yo' furniture, please let me know."

"We first have to find a house. I've written to Louise—"

"Louise Johnson?"

"That's right. She's told me we could stay with her until we get settled."

"Stay with her?" Marg almost screamed. Then she took a sip of the cold tea and swallowed it making a face. "Angel, I must tell you something."

Sue's grey eyes looked right into Marg's. "Marg, I know about the baby. I heah Justine is beautiful."

Marg took another sip of cold tea. "My business has always gotten around," she said categorically. "How did you know? Louise?"

"Oh no. I heard it from South Carolina."

"South Carolina?"

"I got a Christmas letter from the Rollin sisters. Charlotte knew. Maybe from Lydia."

"That bitch! She killed my father!" Marg groaned, hid her head, then came up smiling. She was thinking just like Matilda. "Angel, I want you to look after my baby. See that she gets everything she wants. I had to keep it secret because of Maple gossip. Mainly, I couldn't handle Charles if he knew. He's already drinking, now that he's back from Savannah. He's lost interest in the business."

Sue smiled and touched Marg's hand. "Maybe the two of you likewise should leave this place. Get a fresh start somewhere North."

"No. I'm going to finish my hospital, an' keep Malcolm House. It's a symbol, Sue. A symbol of what colored folks can do."

"Only thing," said Sue, rocking back and forth. "Any symbols, old or new, serve as powder kegs . . . because, I don't believe the war is over yet."

"Oh, these silly people will soon calm down. They can't hate us forever!"

Sue reached over and kissed Marg soundly. "You have such a good heart, I'll miss you."

"Sue, angel. When you go, I want you to take Jason North. He'll soon be ten and I want him enrolled at Friends' School in Philadelphia. Can you do this for me?"

"Of course, angel, and you take care. You're too good to let this place get you down."

***** ***** *****

Birch Cliff Redberry began coming across the Chattahoochee every weekend to see Sylvia Sharkey. They were courting. His gun business didn't frighten her any more. She began dressing tacky, more Indian-like, she called it. In his old age, he wasn't looking for a pure-blood Indian lass. Just some warmth and wiggle.

They got married in November 1872, ten months after meeting at Marg's house. The white preacher at First Baptist married them, but not in his church. His cluttered office could barely hold their dozen friends. The only reason he did it was to show his influence at Town Hall. Usually an Indian, like a nigger, could not marry a white woman.

Marg gave them silver, then put her mind on her project. By the end of 1872 Clark Memorial Hospital was all finished and open to the public. It had four wards holding two hundred, and ten semi-private rooms. The operating facilities were the very best in western Georgia. Many said there wasn't a finer colored hospital in the whole state. The whites were jealous. They had tried in many ways to close down the project; Marg used all her contacts in Atlanta and Washington to keep it going. Now, with Jeeter in a nice job in the Freedmen's Bureau, she had better contact than before. Old nasty Dr. Fred Bowman, she was sure, had helped put the whites against her. He was envious to the core. But she let it be known that as a Christian, she'd welcome him to operate in her hospital, like all the other good black doctors. A couple of whites joined in as well. Naturally this irritated some. One Friday night the Ku Klux Klan burned a big wooden cross on the hospital lawn. It didn't frighten anybody. It was taken away quietly.

Jason came home for Christmas; he wasn't too impressed with the North. As a brown child he still found them prejudiced. Marg told him he had to stick it out, that it would make a man of him. When John came home that Christmas, he urged his mother to invite Jeb Hunter and Cindy over for dinner. It didn't have to be on Christmas day, and it didn't have to be all the Hunters. Just Cindy and her father. Marg reluctantly agreed, not knowing what would happen. To her surprise, and Charles', John announced over dessert that he and Cindy were engaged to be married. In front of Jeb Marg couldn't protest, but as soon as they left, she sat John down for a serious talk.

"How can you do this? How can you think this way? Don't you realize the whites would never let you marry in this town?"

"Ma! I'm as white as Cindy! Whiter! If they won't marry us here, we'll go to LaGrange, or Macon. I can easily be as white as any of them."

"John, right now my hospital has the haters busy. I'm tryin' to hold up. This marriage talk is just a mistake. We have so many good, refined, beautiful young ladies in our own culture—"

"The mulatto culture is dead, Mom. Cindy and I will just be American. We're not going to talk race—"

"They won't let you, son. They will brand you. Mind what I say. The only way you can live with Cindy is to take her up North. An' I would hate to see you leave me. This is home."

"For you. Not especially for me."

"When are you going to do it?"

"Next June. At the end of my semester. I've thought of something nice an' quiet. Here at home. Remember the services we had here in the drawing room when the Union army stayed here?"

"Yes, John, I remember. Do you remember Captain Waverly?"

"Lieutenant Waverly? Oh sure."

"Did you know that he was in love with me?"

John turned purple. "What do you mean?"

"We all have decisions in life. He wanted to take me North. We were in love with each other. Well, I didn't behave badly. He felt I had great courage, taking Jason in. Did you ever wonder about Jason, John?"

"Oh, I knew all along. Everybody knows how Dad plays around. I never wanted to be like that, yet, now that I'm really in love, you deny me my chance for happiness."

"John, I just want you to be sure it's Cindy you love. We thought you and Hattie Clark were hitting it off just fine. John, think about it. Hattie is such a lovely girl. I would be so happy—"

John stood up, ready to leave. "I don't love Hattie. You know that, Mom, it's gotta be Cindy. If you don't want us here, I'll stay up North."

"No, John, you bring her here. Have the marriage here. First, I want to talk to Jeb an' see if it is completely agreeable in his family. I wouldn't want you joinin' them if there is the slightest opposition."

John smiled. "You forget. I've been with them for years. They treat me like a brother."

"And their neighbors?"

John didn't answer his mother. He walked out without another word. He was sure of himself, just like his father.

Chapter 42

Jeeter and Sue didn't get out any too quickly. Agricultural prices began to drop way down in 1873. In Congress they stopped talking so much about scalawags, carpetbaggers and Negroes, and began discussing the country's financial problems. It seems railroads had been wastefully built, greatly beyond the demand for them. The bigtimers were calling in loans long before the public knew of the crisis. John was very impressed with his mother's hospital, and he wrote from Cambridge that he wanted her to give him a big administrative job at the hospital, that he'd take a year out from school. This was so that he and Cindy could start married life in Maple, then he'd go back to school the next year, bringing her North. Marg thought this was an excellent idea. With wife, John should have some experience at making his own living. Her administrator, a Mr. Jasper Fox, was a pleasant brown man who had finished Yale. He agreed to take John on as his assistant, starting next June.

One thing Marg hadn't counted on: Mr. Muggeridge wobbled over one morning, leaning heavily on his cane. He said he was now ready to sell. He'd let her buy the Muggeridge house for six thousand dollars. He wanted to get out in May. She'd have to write Atlanta to get more cash. She told him to draw up the papers, that she'd buy it. For John and Cindy. They could live right next door to her, and things could work out better.

It was on a quiet sunny afternoon in mid-May when the white Muggeridges came to Plum Avenue to pick up their aging relative and his belongings. They left a mess. Marg had her servants over there cleaning up. The bedrooms smelled like sick old people. She raised all the windows and burned some of Sylvia's perfumy incense in each room. When the painters came, things began to smell right. She was going to throw out the few pieces of furniture left behind, but then realized John needed these. Perhaps Larry could do them over a bit. When she was checking the sturdiness of one bureau, she found an old faded picture of Bubber. It was when he was about fourteen, looking lean and pleasant in his cut-off summer slacks. They kept it all this time. *They did love him!*

John and Cindy's wedding in Marg's drawing room was a lovely simple affair. Mitchell had the whole house decorated in fragrant yellow and white flowers. Her sister was her maid-of-honor. John's best man was a school friend from Massachusetts. Ed Clark and another northern white boy were the ushers. Cousin Don, wobbly on his cane, performed the rites. He knew and Marg knew that a wedding across race lines was against the law in Maple. If necessary, like several mulatto families, they could go to court and prove that they were less than one-eighth Negro. By that time the young couple could leave the state, if it looked as if they would not win. So, no one much worried about Dixie legalities on the marriage. Cindy was very pretty, carrying yellow sweet peas and white carnations, wearing short curly brown hair and a long tulle veil, lovely white satin gown, with matching gloves and slippers. She had wanted the society photographer from Korner's to take pictures, but Marg persuaded against this. She found a black man just as good. Sixteen white Hunters came in their Sunday best. They showed their delight at being in such a lovely mansion, and they were excited that it now had a connection with them, that their Cindy would inherit this fancy house. Cousin Sue and Jeeter came back down from Washington. They looked fine. Mitchell and Albert came, plus Cousin Don's family, and Gregory's. With the two families there were well over forty people. The only outside guests Marg invited were: Hospital Administrator Fox, the Lou Simpsons, her lawyer Bill Cahill and his wife, Cliff and Sylvia Redberry, and the Clarks. Poor blond Hattie didn't come. She thought she had captured John. She was sick over the loss. And already Marg was thinking Hattie would be a good catch for her slow brother Anthony. But he too didn't come . . . judging poor John.

During the ceremony, a northern girl played Grandma Margery's organ. Just as it ended Marg saw through the window a handsome white fellow light from a carriage and dash across the lawn with a beautifully-wrapped gift. When he reached the door John and Cindy were there too. They had some cheerful words, and the fellow raced back to his carriage minus gift. "Who was that?" Marg asked her son.

"Mark," he said lightly. "He told me he'd drop by."

Now Marg remembered. Mark Korner. She was glad he and John had kept their friendship up at Harvard. Poor lad could have come in!

"Your Justine is a gorgeous little girl," Sue whispered to her cousin. "She's bright an' pretty and just wonderful."

"Not spoiled?" asked Marg, smilingly.

"Not especially. Louise is tough on her. Oh, by the way, did you know that they've been in court? That her name is now Johnson, not Spence?"

Marg didn't know. Louise had neglected to tell her. "Well, I told Louise to do that some years ago. You reminded me, I owe her a check. You know, I have to send money regularly to all my children, and to Lucy in Chicago as well. An' with this hospital, it's no joke. Hah! But John is bright. I'm sure when he gets there he'll find ways to cut expenses."

Sue realized Marg's desperate struggles with money. "Marg, angel, you should try to keep it charitable. Hospitals have a way of eating up money."

"Don't worry," Marg exclaimed. "Edna Clark is out regularly raisin' money, just for us. Already this year she's been to Nashville, St. Louis and Birmingham. Only thing, the youngsters singing for us have gotten too famous. The St. James Jubilee Singers have now hired a white manager. Not a dime comes to the hospital. Now, it's *their* earnings. They're in show business. Mr. Steinmetz's ideas!"

"He sounds like a carpetbagger, stealin' profits."

"Well," chirped Marg, "I've taken them off my pear money. Now that goes direct to the hospital. I'm thinking of selling some of our Cobb's Creek property."

"Not now," Sue told her. "Everything's too cheap now. Marg, I'm learnin' politics. Iowa corn was seventy cents a bushel in 1864, now it brings only twenty-four cents a bushel. An' we've got to resume specie payments. Don't I talk like a speculator? Ha-Ha!"

"Sue, you look ravishing! Washington's good for you. Have you done any playin' for the people over there?"

"Marg, I've thought of that. You think I could become famous?"

"Most certainly, When you're ready, let me know. I'll send you to the right operators—"

"By the way, Louise has yo' daughter taking piano lessons with me. Did you know that?"

Louise hadn't been telling much lately. Marg had had to cut down the monthly stipend to ninety dollars, and Louise was sore about this.

Now Marg knew she could go to Washington and stay with Sue. She didn't want to lose Justine. Or Charles.

By the tenth of July the Muggeridge house was all cleaned and painted, and John and Cindy, back from a New Orleans' honeymoon, moved in with their few pieces of furniture. Marg gave them loads of things from her attic. She was so happy to have them next door. To save expenses, they'd share the coachman and the two girls working in Malcolm House. Now Larry and Maggie Mae had moved out to a house of their own, in Cobb's Creek. He was still putting out the various wooden items Mr. Densmore needed for his inventions. It wasn't full-time work so they were back to building more Spence tables. Larry too was good at running Marg's shop when she didn't feel like standing at the counter. The store in Malcolm Spanish Court was nice and efficient-looking, but it did not earn like the original store out in Wentworth. So Marg kept the original store going, in spite of all the doings of Matilda's gang next door. Yes, it did seem like a house of prostitution! Now Marg wondered if Jessica didn't plan to punish her by devilishly helping Matilda buy that place. *Life, what mischief!*

When the crash came that September of 1873 Marg lost quite a bit on Wall Street. Haney's wire was depressing. Luckily through Angela Baker she had gotten some of her money into other hands. She didn't have a collapse because Jay Cooke's empire had folded. And she felt happy about this because she read that Kate Chase Sprague was suffering: their Rhode Island business had failed, and all her grand Washington entertaining would stop. Marg felt somewhat secure inasmuch as Anthony had gotten her to buy a small New York apartment building. She had monthly funds coming in. Nevertheless, theirs too would be difficult times; her apartment renters were suffering. The North's people were largely unemployed. More than one hundred thousand in New York City alone. Her hard times were mainly due to the hospital draining her Maple resources. Her shops on Broad Street and out Cobb's Creek way were needed to feed her family and the servants. Edna Clark offered to get some Atlanta doctors to buy the hospital, but Marg said no; she wanted to keep it a local venture, her memorial to Irwin Clark, a great friend.

Larry realized times were tough and he proposed that November that he go back North and talk again with Mr. Densmore. He claimed he had a few ideas for the typewriter and some other invention he had seen there. Marg hesitated. No he wasn't dumb. He was trying to help them. Somehow she found the railroad fare. Maggie Mae wouldn't go along this time. She was expecting her first child.

That Christmas of 1873 was a good one in spite of national money problems. Firstly, a nice greeting came from George Washington Cable. It read:

December 17, 1873

Dear Mrs. Spence,

In case you didn't see it, I attach a copy of my story 'Sieur George, which appeared in the October issue of Scribner's Monthly. It's made Louise and me very happy. I'm now reading my friend Mark Twain's ms. *Huck Finn*, about a black and white boy alone on a boat going down the Mississippi. Almost as controversial as my stuff!

All the best to you and your family, for the New Year!

George.

Marg read it again at the dinner table when Jason, Beth and Meg came home from school. Meg, in her first year of college at Wellesley, was studying chemistry. Beth, a senior, was planning on med school, but she had fallen in love with young Ted Cardozo, and they were talking marriage. Marg didn't discourage it. She was proud of both her girls. They were so neat and friendly. And they liked their new sister, Cindy. To keep the Edgeworth community from exploding, Marg told her children not to go out there visiting the Hunters. Jeb understood. He always brought his wife and children to visit at Malcolm House, or at the Muggeridge place next door. They had many happy times together that Christmas.

The new year started with eastern financiers urging the resumption of specie payment, while those in the West wanted expansion of paper currency. Grant vetoed the inflation bill. Silk workers in Paterson, N.J. held mass meetings to demand a tariff reduction of twenty per cent. Coal miners were organizing; Socialists were marching. With all this, Larry came back home from New York on January 13th. He seemed very excited at the railroad station. He gave his first attention to his wife. They had not been separated before. When he got around to telling Marg of his business success, it was on the following morning.

"I did good in New York, Miss Margery," he said over breakfast. "Mr. Densmore liked my ideas. He's goin' to make a few changes I suggest. Also, he took me out to New Jersey again to see Mr. Edison. He was glad to see me. We had dinner at a fancy restaurant, then they took out some drawings an' asked me to make platforms for his ticker-tape machine, an' some telegraph machine he's got dat splits messages in two parts. So, I got us here another contract—"

Marg was delighted to see the contract from Mr. Thomas Edison. She read it through. It was similar to the typewriter contract. They were to provide platforms for 500 experimental telegraphy pieces. They'd earn $4,500. This time she signed without going to Bill Cahill. She didn't want him raking off profits. That Christmas the Cahills had moved into their new home on Walnut Street, not far from Edna Clark, and the old Bowne mansion. Some said in town that he was getting rich off Margery Spence. She had to laugh at such rumors. They kept her from feeling destitute.

Next day, when she went to the shop and saw what Larry had built for Mr. Edison, she was ready to send the signed contract back to New Jersey. Then with owl-eyed look, Larry told her the worst. "Mr Edison invited me to live up there. He said it would save a lot of shippin' money, an' he could find me a place. I talked it ovah with my wife an' she wants to go."

"Larry, you mean you're goin' to leave me?"

"Well, Miss Margery, we 'ppreciates all you've done for us. So, we'd stay on if'n you say so. But Mr. Edison told me if'n I'm comin', not to give you dis contract, to come on dere, an' he'd give me a contract of my own."

Marg sat down, fanning herself. There were tricky people all over the world. "I'm glad you told me, Larry. I think maybe I'd just bettah go up there with this contract myself. I see, menfolk cannot be trusted. That's what it is. An' Haney didn't speak for me. Now, if you an' Maggie Mae want to live North, please wait awhile. I won't hold you here, but I do think we should get through this contract down here with no changes. Okay?"

Larry agreed, shaking his head. Marg rushed home, sent a telegram, then got herself packed for her trip. She certainly didn't feel like a trip, but this was business. She had to meet Mr. Edison. For Haney, she packed a few fancy dresses.

The trainride North in late January wasn't so bad. The coach was warm, and the sights were interesting. Passing through Carolina she thought of Lydia's letter: blacks cavortin' around the State House, dropping peanuts on the floor, and, those nasty li'l yellow-faced Rollin sisters, playing society and telling her secrets! No, she didn't want to face Louise in Washington, but she did want to see Justine. To hold her once again.

In New York, the hackney cab took her once again to the Fifth Avenue Hotel. One or two of the management's people knew her now, and they were cordial. They gave her an excellent corner suite of two rooms, with a nice view of Wall Street and New Jersey. Tom Haney came as soon as he got her message.

"I don't have my carriage any more," he confessed, looking worn. "It was rough, but we're digging out. I lost a bundle, Marg."

"Well, I forgive you for losing my money as well. Poor thing, you didn't know. But I must tell you, I didn't trust you completely. I had other assets—"

"Oh, Marg, then you're ready to invest again!"

"No, Tom. It was sweet of you, helping with my hospital. Thank you."

"Okay, Marg. It was nothing. Just a letter."

"It saved me! Now listen, Tom, we're very grateful what you've done for Larry. I came up as boss of Spence Enterprises. I should meet Mr. Densmore, and I should meet Mr. Edison. You understand?"

"Yes, Marg," he grinned, reeling back on the pink satin chair in her sitting room. "I'll get in touch with these guys right away. They're goin' places! An' you should make quite an impression. You look ravishing, Marg."

She eyed him. He hadn't changed. So Catholic in appearance, so evil in mind. "Can we see Mr. Densmore tomorrow?"

"He's down at his place in Pennsylvania. I must tell you, he's made other plans for his typewriter. He's no longer with Mr. Sholes. About a year ago he started discussing everything with Phil Remington, a manufacturer from Ilion, New York, and they went into contract on a brand new machine. It's not the one for which you were making the platforms. This one has a foot pedal and all the wood business has been handled by Mr. Remington himself."

Marg stood up looking tough. "Then we won't get another contract?"

"Not likely."

"Why didn't you tell Larry? Or me, *a year ago*? Then, I could have bargained with Mr. Densmore *and* Mr. Remington. Tom, I thought you were goin' to make me a millionaire!" She smiled, and he knew that she had forgiven him.

"Well, it's still a brand new business. They're supposed to go to market this year. Sure, I think you should meet Mr. Remington. He too likes to gaze on beauty—"

She slapped him with her newspaper. Then as he came closer, she wheeled around and got her wrap. They were going out for lunch at Delmonico's. With one more dash of perfume, she was ready to be led to the elevators.

363

On Tuesday, a serious Mr. Densmore came up to New York and had a talk with Marg at his offices. No, she couldn't meet Mr. Remington just now. He was very busy at his plant up country. Densmore promised to keep her name in mind if the typewriter needed any more woodwork. Meanwhile, he'd accompany her and Haney to Edison's in New Jersey on Thursday. Mr. Edison was expecting them.

That first Thursday in February was very cold. Densmore sent a message he couldn't make it. Haney decided he and Marg would go on as planned. That afternoon, Marg in her furs she had purchased in Washington, looked gorgeous. She also wore the elaborate green velvet Worth frock. It wasn't new but still looked fantastic on her. Tom Haney was impressed when he came to take her to the railroad station. Marg didn't know that his new offices in Wall Street were with a solid firm. He looked threadbare after having lost in the Cooke fold-up.

"Maybe if I'm lucky," she said, coyly, "you can join my firm, as my business partner."

"I think you have the luck of the Irish," he quipped. "How are things down in Dixie?"

Marg frowned. "Not good at all. There's still a lot of hate . . . on racial lines. If you say you're colored, people are ready to treat you as dirt. I think the poison will never leave."

He winked. "Maybe then *you* should leave. Really, Marg! A couple of years ago I bought myself a little house in Bayonne. It's near the water an' very nice."

"Then you commute to New York?"

"It's not far. My wife an' kids love it. Would you care to come out?"

"I'm not stayin' that long. Thank you. I just want to see Mr. Edison, pass over his signed contract, an' make an impression on him, so that he doesn't forget me."

He slapped her knee. "Marg, you're a smart girl. Much smarter than I am. I never thought of this bein' a big thing for you!"

When they reached Newark, thick clouds were forming. Yet it seemed warmer than New York. The biting wind was gone. They decided to walk to Mr. Edison's factory which was a few blocks from the railroad station. The New Jersey air was fresh and countrified. She liked it. Mr. Edison, a roughly-handsome blond, met them at the door of his shop.

"Marg, this is the genius who made that ticker-tape that keeps us all crazy on Wall Street," said Haney, shaking his friend's hand.

"Come in," called Edison. "I'm pleased to meet you, Mrs. Spence." He was in his thirties, much younger than she had expected. Clearly Scotch-Irish, she thought, with glowing bright grey eyes. He later told her he was Scotch-Yankee on his mother's side, and Dutch on his father's. He indeed was very impressed meeting Mrs. Spence from Georgia. He led them into a rough wooden room full of tables, glass tubes and metal objects. In one corner, he had a rickety desk, a rocking chair and two other chairs. At this office spot, where a pot-bellied stove was glowing cherry-red, he had hot coffee ready. While Haney sauntered through the long drafty room of inventions, Edison and Marg sat quietly, sipping and talking.

"I was quite charmed with Larry," he told her. "He has a quick mind and his wood work is perfect. Was he your slave?"

"Oh no," Marg replied. "His wife was in our household, but Larry came in by marriage . . . after the war. He loves workin' with wood, and I was so grateful when Tom and Mr. Densmore put us in touch with you."

Edison smiled. "Too bad most of the things I'm making are out of metal and not wood. I do need about eight thousand bamboo slivers, little wood sticks. You think you could handle that for me, Mrs. Spence?"

Marg sat forward. "We can try! Does that also deal with telegraphy, Mr. Edison?"

"No. Another one of my projects. I'm working on an electrical lamp. I want to try bamboo as filaments. You know what I'm saying?"

"I'm afraid not," she said, avoiding his intense eyes.

"Come, I'll show you." He took her to a nearby table. With a pencil he pointed to a glass tube. "I'm making us a new kind of evening lamp; the fuel will be electrical current. In here, you need something that glows, with lasting qualities. Just an experiment right now. Over here is my talking machine. You see, this paraffin-coated paper tape is drawn at high speed through a receiving instrument where a stylus or needle embosses it with dots and dashes. We get sound. Soon the human voice, I hope."

"Oh, it's marvelous, all these things you're doing. I won't pretend to understand it, Mr. Edison." She made pretty eyes.

"Science is for women too, Mrs. Spence. Didn't you tell me you have a daughter studying chemistry?"

She was flattered he remembered. "My Meg. Yes, sir. It all seems so complicated!"

"It's our future, Mrs. Spence. Wall Street has helped me because they see great money ahead, perhaps, like the railroad invention. But I'm after knowledge from the revelations of Nature. And, I'm workin' against time. There are some gentlemen in England and France competing with me at every step. Even here in America! I have so many contractual obligations, but I don't wish to become bogged down in manufacturing—"

"This is what I want to do," Marg spoke up. "If there's anything else we can make for you, Mr. Edison, do not hesitate to ask. Down South we have good craftsmen and our labor is cheap."

"Don't I know," he grinned. "I lived a bit in the South during the war years. I was something of a vagabond telegrapher, goin' wherever the rails would take me. You see, I'm a self-made man, Mrs. Spence. No prominent family behind me. I work hard, and your Larry works hard. We understand what it takes—"

Now she was standing close to him. "If you take him away from me, will there still be enough business left for me in Georgia?"

Edison was surprised that she knew. "Oh, that! Well, you see, I think Larry is young enough to add to his book knowledge. A technical education. His mind will open up. An' it won't hurt his talent. He'll go places! He was so excited about everything he saw up North. Will you let him go?"

She looked coyly into his eyes. "If we have another contract, Mr. Edison."

"You folks still talkin'?" asked Tom Haney, coming back with an empty coffee cup.

"Oh, it's fascinating!" shouted Marg. "Mr. Edison is really a genius. I've told him I'm impressed with his shop. It's a busy place for the future . . . for America!"

Edison was touched by her comment. Then he brought Haney into the conversation. "I suppose you didn't tell Mrs. Spence how lucky I was to get that $40,000 from those Wall Street boys on that ticker-tape improvement I made. Without that, I'd still be at base one."

"That was four years ago," said Haney. "You've been making little killings ever since then. I know!"

Edison laughed. "Well, you should know, Mrs. Spence. I got stung on my first big invention, a vote recorder, in 1868. Nobody wanted it! So, after that, I said anything I make, I'm going to have to have a buyer first. Hah!"

"He's a miserly wizard," laughed Haney. "But we're schoolin' him!"

It suddenly got dark; Marg and Haney decided it was time to head back for New York. In fact, it was snowing outside: big, fluffy flakes of snow. They said their goodbyes, and Mr. Edison promised to write to her about the bamboo sticks he wanted. It was a good meeting. She went out into the falling snow feeling successful and refreshed. Right away, they seemed to be in a blizzard. Tom spoke of hunting a cab to take them to the railroad station, but she protested saying they could still walk the few blocks. However, when they got on the road they realized the fast-falling snow was sticking.

Relieved at finally reaching the station, they learned that the train from Philadelphia was late. They sat in the busy waiting room talking about Mr. Edison. "He liked you," said Tom, holding her gloved hand. "He's usually not so talkative. I think you had the right idea, makin' this trip. This could be far more important than Densmore."

"Why do you say that?"

Haney made a face. "First of all, Densmore has sold out to Remington. Secondly, he's not an inventor, just a speculator like me. Now you've met the man who really appreciates the quality of the work of your factory. Right?"

Marg shook her head. She really was worried about the snow. People coming in were puffing and loaded down with it. Tom wanted to go into a restaurant to eat, but she didn't want to miss her train, late as it was.

"Did Edison tell you," yelled Tom, bringing her back a potato knish, "they've already got him lined up to have a booth at the Centennial Exposition."

"When is that?"

"In Philadelphia, in '76, two years from now."

"You mean such things are planned so far in advance?"

"Absolutely. Now you mention that to him when you write. There'll be plenty of woodwork over there. Marg, if you're smart, you can make your million in Philadelphia!"

She slapped his hand away. Their train had been announced. "I wish I had your dreamer's imagination."

They gleefully ran to catch the train which looked like a huge snow-bound monster. They luckily found seats in the crowded coach. With everyone shaking snow from their coats, there was a holiday atmosphere. After they sat for another forty minutes without moving, Haney took out his silver flask and offered Marg some of his sherry. The trip across the river proceeded slowly. It was almost ten p.m. when they arrived in New York.

"This is terrible," cried Marg, going out into the snow again. "How in the world will you get home to Bayonne?"

"I may not go," called Haney. "If I can get a room at the Fifth Avenue."

The hotel was crowded. They said they had no rooms. Haney came up to Marg's suite to sit awhile. "I don't think I'm going to get home tonight," he said mournfully, as they had sandwiches at her table. "This is the worst blizzard in years. I'm stranded!"

"Well, I think Anthony will put you up if you go to him."

He looked at her with crazy eyes. "You want me to go out in that again? Look, you've got two rooms. Why can't I stay here?"

"Simply, it is not done," she told him. "You know that."

He poured more sherry and went to the window to look out. "It looks bad, Marg. You may be stuck with me."

Sure enough, he stayed on and on. About midnight she excused herself and went into her room. Shortly she came out with blankets for the couch in the sitting room. "Well, if you're staying, you need to get comfortable. I see they've turned the heat down. I'm going to bed, and I'll lock my door."

He mumbled goodnight and acted as if he were dead tired. Around three o'clock Marg woke up. She felt a hand across her chest. She couldn't believe it. How could he get into her room? She moved up slowly, checking what he wore. Luckily he was fully clothed. She got up, went to the bathroom, then got dressed and sat in a chair. When he stirred and opened his eyes, she asked: "How did you get into my room?"

He smiled his Irish smile. "Easy. There was a key in the closet door. It fitted your lock."

"Is that usual, for an expensive hotel?"

"Very usual," he moaned, getting under the covers.

Chapter 43

Angela Baker came over to have lunch at Marg's hotel. Looking yellowish and plain, all she could talk about was the Jerome family. The brothers had lost a lot in the Wall Street crash, but young Jennie was engaged to marry British royalty. A Lord Randolph Churchill. His parents, the Duke and Duchess of Marlborough, at first were cool to the marriage. British society frowned on American matches. There was some talk about Jennie's darkness, but they marveled over her great beauty. When it was all agreed, the Duke took care of the young squire's debts of $10,000, and he'd give them a house in London. The young man was in politics. A Conservative. Didn't have a cent other than what his father gave him, and of course, the dowry Mr. Jerome would provide. Jennie would have the titled family name, and some jewels. An older brother inherits the family estate, the huge Blenheim Castle. It seemed Clara, Jennie's mother, wasn't too pleased. Randolph was the second son, not high enough. Yet, Jennie was soon to meet Queen Victoria. As Angela told the story, her eyes lit up. The wedding would be in Paris, on April 15th. No, Angela laughed, she would not be going. She was only a servant. Marg felt, an accepting Angela lived her role excellently.

Marg spent a couple days with Anthony. He was doing all right, selling a few paintings, even doing some watercoloring himself. Every day a few of his friends dropped in. White persons. He wasn't thinking yet of marriage. On her last day, they went to see Fraunces Tavern, which had been owned by a Negro when George Washington ate there. Then they went out to see the construction of the Brooklyn Bridge. At dusk they stopped at a Chinese restaurant to have a delightful Cantonese dinner. Not telling him anything personal, Marg stoned herself for the dreadful trip back to Georgia. First she got through Philadelphia not thinking about Jason. Then it was all she could do to keep calm as the train passed through Washington. She wanted so much to see Justine! But she kept telling herself she had to let go. The child belonged to Louise.

When Marg got back in comfortable Malcolm House, there was a letter waiting her from Beth. She said she and Ted Cardozo were engaged. They wanted to marry in June. She had agreed to go Easter to meet his people in Vicksburg. Because of the prominent position of his family, Ted wanted the wedding there. June 14, 1874. Did she mind? Of course, Marg didn't mind. Had she known, she could have purchased new dresses in New York. Right now, she had to put her mind back on business.

First thing, Bubber's brother, Bob Jenkins, would be taken from his porter's job at Malcolm Spanish Court, and sent out to Cobb's Creek to learn everything about woodworking. Larry would teach him well. She was confident Bob Jenkins would be a suitable replacement, if Larry should go. Next, she right away wrote a thank-you letter to Mr. Thomas Edison. She praised his shop again, saying they awaited more details of the bamboo sticks he wanted. And as Haney had suggested, she indicated her willingness to do his booth at the Philadelphia Centennial Exposition in 1876.

She talked it over with Charles, and mentioned too Beth's engagement, but he seemed to be in a yellow-fever daze. She was really surprised to find him home. Cobb's Creek's attraction had somehow worn off. He preferred to sit in their billiard room, having a little toddy, or on warm days, out in the small garden by the fig tree. He said he was getting ready for spring planting—in between sips of whiskey.

Early in March Marg received a wire from Sue. Charles Sumner had passed on. His body was already lying in state in the Rotunda. A group of Negroes including Frederick Douglass had led the procession. Marg thought of rushing up to the funeral, but she hadn't really known Sumner well. They met at a party and had shared a mutual love of Emerson. No, she wouldn't go. Six weeks later Sue wrote that the Negro hotel-keeper, Wormley, had bought up the fabulous things put on sale from the Sumners' Lafayette Square house. He'd have a Sumner Room in his hotel.

Sumner's Civil Rights Bill failed that session. It seemed whites feared its call for the mixing of the races in public schools. Also, James Pike's book on the corruption in South Carolina's "Negro Government" had just come out, and it made more people anti-Negro. Marg read it to be well-versed. It talked of Columbia's colored living very well, like Robert Elliott in a most fashionable section. Yet, the writer wanted people to think of them as undeserving animals from a zoo. The real animal was the white man, Frank Moses.

Early in May, Larry and Maggie Mae announced they'd go North, to settle down in New Jersey, to work for Mr. Thomas Alva Edison. Marg wished them well, giving them new luggage and a bonus of two hundred dollars. On that last night she had them out to Malcolm House for dinner. Maggie Mae sat strangely in that marvelous dining room where she had served as a slave. A joking comment hit silence. The girl still treated Marg as if she were another class, another race. Marg liked decorum. Mr. and Mrs. Lawrence Brown had it.

Marg drank a final champagne toast to them and their infant son. The raised crystal glasses had her thinking of Jessica Bowne, and all her prejudice about who should eat at a dining table with whom. She thought too of Lydia Smith's sly remarks about the survival of her children. Beth, John and Meg would do fine in the modern world. They loved each other. Marg had noticed at her church that many colored families fought each other, yet, they'd put on airs for the public. She told Larry and Maggie Mae to have another child, and teach the two to love each other most.

Once in Newark, Larry wrote a letter thanking Marg and saying Maggie Mae was pregnant again. Marg was particularly pleased. This was her urging of life, her successful duty for Christ. Larry's writing was still very weak. She hoped Mr. Edison's genius would work on this.

Early that June Beth came home; she and her mother caught the train up to Atlanta to do some shopping. Valerie met them, apologizing for the look of her house. Gregory was quitting politics in four months' time. The guests didn't notice the boxes. Toward the end of the week Sue and Jeeter arrived there from Washington. Sue was looking trim, down twenty-eight pounds, now weighing 184 lbs. Her face was beautiful. Once again she was playing piano—this time, in fancy salons, for congressmen and society. They all had great times exploring Atlanta together. Hattie Clark was their guide. She too was ordering pretty new clothes. She'd be Beth's maid-of-honor. Since Mrs. Clark wasn't there they were all suggesting and buying things for beauteous blond Hattie, so that she wouldn't remain so old-fashioned. On the last day, Meg arrived from Wellesley and they all started out together for Maple. Marg had hired a special private Pullman coach. She had had enough of nasty white people, and Jim Crow practices.

Mitchell and Albert's wives were lovely local brownskinned girls. Like Jeeter Brown's two sisters, they identified with the Negro race.

371

Marg didn't understand this post-war oneness of the darker Americans. Just as there were different Protestant religions, to her, racial strength was in its varieties. Colored families could have different cultures. These girls did not agree with her. Thinking family, Marg frowned when Mitchell and Albert's children took on bad "negroid" behavior patterns. While the mothers didn't notice the flaws, Mitchell and Albert continually scolded the kids for slovenly language, or any slavery antics. Sue shared Marg's concern and was glad her brothers agreed on attitudes of behavior. Eventually, she felt, the wives would realize the family's strict upper-class dedication. The brown women stood their ground, criticizing Sue and Marg for "actin' white". So, when wedding time came, strangely, Ilene and Sally Barrows did not want to go to Beth's ceremony. Both Marg and Sue urged, but the brown wives said no, knowing it would be a mulatto affair, with near-whites being prominent in attendance. The boys laughed it off telling Marg their wives had to stay home to mind their children. Marg finally accepted it. She didn't blame Mitchell or Albert. They came along and had a great time.

Marg had paid the railroad to take her wedding coach on through to Vicksburg, Mississippi. When they arrived in such style, she naturally was thinking of her dear brother Paul who had left them for the white race. Anthony came down on a fast train from New York. The wedding was a gala occasion.

Marg found all the Cardozos wonderful people. She was both proud and glad that her first daughter had found such a sweet and simple man as Ted, with all his trappings of grandeur. In that elaborate guest bedroom, she thanked Jesus and asked Him to take equal good care of her other two. Poor Jason attracted a lot of attention, by being so brown. So did Senator Revels, now president of Alcorn College. Deep brown as he was.

The Malcolm-Spences took their private coach back to Maple on June 15th while Beth and her husband headed for New Orleans, where they'd get a boat for Haiti, the isle where rich honeymooners went. The white papers in Vicksburg called it a "carpetbagger's wedding".

A handsome, Anglo-Saxon-looking John returned to his duties at Clark Memorial Hospital, while Marg and dear and simple Cindy stayed home and got to their project of sewing up curtains for all forty windows of the Muggeridge house. An optimistic Cindy enjoyed the work. Always cheerful, she thought of Marg as somebody her own age. Several times they got into serious discussion of the race problem, but it didn't go far. Cindy thought Negroes were lucky. She only knew the fair and rich ones. Never had really looked at the poor blacks on the streets. She was, somewhat by choice, very naive. Outside of Vicksburg and her honeymoon in New Orleans, she had been nowhere.

From her lowly group, a proud Rayford Innis was now wealthy and respectable. And he allowed his beefy-red, ruthless brother, Brady, to take over as mayor. Townspeople, like sheep, were indifferent. Late one night, Redberry delivered Marg's guns. He and Sylvia had come back to live in her Maple house. His place in Girard had suffered when spring flooding inundated much of Alabama. The poor Negroes along the Warrior and Tombigbee Rivers were suffering the most. Eighty thousand dollars "bacon money" was made available; Republicans ignored the most needy counties, and put it where it would do the most good politically.

Marg read that the black people in Alabama were demanding more. Of course, in predominantly black counties they were due more representation. Negro preachers were talking up, and the Union League was encouraging them. While Republicans only had four thousand whites, the Klan and the Democrats were plenty strong. They didn't like Morton and Boutwell's talk of mixed schools. Grant, expecting defeat, ordered Secretary Belknap that September of 1874 to have the troops ready for Alabama, as well as South Carolina. Democrats swept in, so the anti-black "normal" South had this state again, along with Georgia, Tennessee, Texas and Virginia.

Early in 1875 Arkansas went through its test. A congressional committee was looking at the corruption. Its chairman was Judge Luke Poland, Republican of Vermont. It was rumored that he was up for a Federal judgeship. But his report on Arkansas showed he was against Federal interference. President Grant met with Clayton and Morton; his Special Message suggested that the 1874 Constitution was null and void. The clamor in the press pointed to Grant wanting to assure his third term. Poland's report was adopted with support of all Democrats, and many leading Republicans. Arkansas, it seems, went Democratic, leaving just Mississippi and Louisiana still supposedly in Negro control.

With the elections of 1872 a mess had come to Louisiana. The conservatives claimed they had elected John McEnery Governor, while the regular Republican nominee was William P. Kellogg. The counting and recounting went foul, and the Federal judge, Durell, was said to be drunk. United States Marshal Packard was supposed to take possession of the State House. McEnery's bunch had a conservative ready to go to the Senate while Kellogg's body had their powerful mulatto, P.B.S.

Pinchback. In Washington the battle lasted many months with Senator Carpenter's legalists cutting the ground from under Kellogg. Morton tried to whip his party together, but in the end, the decision had to be made by President Grant. Morton being stronger than Grant had won presidential recognition of Kellogg, but the fight in the Senate still went on: they didn't want to seat the mulatto, Pinchback.

Meanwhile in Louisiana the Customs House clique was levying taxes crazily. The wealthy suburb of Pass Christian had been taken over by Negroes with its social host being Caius Caesar Antoine, the black Lieutenant-Governor by Grant's decree. Whites, cursing the taxes, called him a coconut-head Congo type, an African tyrant. To meet their debts they had to sell, keeping the auctioneers and the pawnbrokers busy. There were murders (mostly of blacks by blacks), and nobody had been hanged. The press was lenient of the monstrous conditions. In the spring of 1874 the planters were denied their customary spring advances. They got themselves armed and became rather dangerous. The carpetbag regime was determined to disarm the whites; the black militia working with black policemen remained active.

It was said that Packard, a great organizer, was bringing in Negroes from other states to vote in northern parishes. Blacks were grabbed from work in the fields to listen to political speeches. They were threatened if they dare vote the Radical ticket. By June, Louisianans were worried about new gossip which said steamboats were bringing in more guns for Negroes. (Georgians put Cliff Redberry in the gossip.) Determined to capture the legislature that autumn, the whites began early to get ready, with help from the White League. Antoine's Black League was busy too. Clashes were inevitable, so Federal officials finally took weapons away from citizens. Indignation rose in the white community.

One September morn found three thousand white citizens at the Clay Monument, in a revolutionary mood. They demanded Kellogg abdicate. Antoine got his militia ready. The cars stopped running. The streets were barricaded. The night passed and in the morning the white revolutionists were in possession of public buildings. The McEnery legislature was told to assemble. Kellogg went immediately to Grant, and Federal troops were hurried to New Orleans. Kellogg was put back in the State House!

Election day found Kellogg's party protected by eleven companies of Federal troops, plus gunboats on the Red River. Grant sent General Phil Sheridan to Louisiana while Sherman, head of the Army, was ignored. The press considered Sheridan an enemy of the South. The

Democrats somehow got their strong man, Wiltz, elected as Speaker in the House. Then the Army came because five seats were contested. They finally got the Democrats to withdraw. They went underground, while cannon were placed before the State House.

Over in Georgia, Cliff Redberry, definitely rich now on guns, moved his Sylvia into their new Walnut Street mansion. She kept her spirituality, and her friendship with Marg. Dr. Bowman too got richer, a millionaire now for sure. Marg smugly kept her comfortable unnamed position, owing no favors to any one.

It was rumored among conservative Republicans and in the North that 2,500 murders had occurred in the elections. After protests, Grant issued a Message, but debate continued. The *Nation* wanted proof that there were not 2,500 election murders. The Senate argued about troops being in Louisiana, and the poor mulatto, Pinchback, was never seated, in spite of Morton's efforts. Louisiana whites still complained of enormous taxes, and niggers driving magnificent horses, with stylish equipages, and wearing diamond stickpins. Kellogg, so-called reconstruction scoundrel, was to remain in office until January 1877.

Democrats throughout the South were incensed by the happenings in Louisiana; they also knew of a scandal up in St. Louis. There, white profiteers had put big money into the 1872 campaigns aiding Grant. A whiskey racket was alive, and it was rumored internal revenue agents were working with distillers, reaping great profits through the abatement of the whiskey tax. A Treasury agent appeared in St. Louis in January 1874, but the guys all around were told not to worry, that Grant would keep things cool. That autumn, Grant with his aide-de-camp, Gen. Babcock, who had gained notoriety in the Santo Domingo affair, went to the St. Louis Fair as guests of Gen. John McDonald, supervisor of Internal Revenue there. There was a big political gathering. It was said Grant's expenses at Lindell Hotel were paid, and he received a gift of a valuable team of horses, with gold breastplates with his name engraved thereon. Then in April 1875 a Treasury agent mysteriously appears again in St. Louis, looking at the happenings in whiskey taxes. McDonald rushed to Washington but he missed the President and Babcock. He then resigned. In a month's time the distilleries were seized, and he was indicted. People were beginning to wonder about General Grant, the President.

In Mississippi, the so-called Negro race was powerfully in office. The press with its tabs had it that a "mulatto" was Speaker of the House, a "corrupt quadroon" was in charge of public schools, a "dark-black" was Lieutenant-Governor, and "plain Negro" Bruce had been sent to the Senate. The "corrupt quadroon" was Thomas Cardozo, Marg's daughter's new father-in-law.

The white man over it all was Adelbert Ames, Governor. He had been military governor, then gone to the Senate with Revels in 1870. A northerner who had married Ben Butler's daughter, he had fought the popularity battle with James Alcorn, to represent the wealthy and aristocratic Mississippians who might go with Radicals. Here too taxes were too high. Blacks who could barely read were said to be in county offices while whites paying the taxes were excluded. Black militia with loaded muskets and fixed bayonets had Vicksburg whites feeling as if they were under siege. When they nominated a strong Democratic ticket, the black Lieutenant-Governor called for Grant's troops. Ames, away in the North, hurried home, but not soon enough. A revolutionary contest loomed.

When Sheridan's troops arrived on behalf of Grant, the taxpayers' fight still had not been won. A half million acres and four-fifths of the town of Greenville had been offered for sale for taxes. The clamor was against alien rule. It seems a "belligerent" Negro Brigadier-general William Gray, had been put over the black militia by Ames, and this irritated the whites. Democratic clubs became militaristic. Torchlight processions were nightly, supposedly to destroy the Negro's "childlike faith in carpetbaggers". Alarmed, the Republican State Convention notified Grant, fearing revolution. General J.Z. George maintained order, in spite of everybody being armed. While the *Jackson Clarion* demanded Ames' impeachment, the fact that a black was lieutenant-governor was his only protection. But the black was impeached, for bribery. In the end, Ames resigned and went home to Minnesota. Democrats won a sweeping victory.

Marg read her publications avidly, to keep up with events, enjoying her screened-in backporch in summer and her new central heat in winter. She also read all that Beth and Ted sent her from Massachusetts where they were back in school. That 4th of July when she put out her flag on Charles Waverly's fine silvery pole, local whites gathered and called it "the traitor's Yankee flag". She decided to leave it up. Then on July 31, 1875 she received a wire from Louise saying President Andrew Johnson was dead. That March he had once again been a guest at Willard's Hotel, and Louise had heard his speech on Grant's aspirations for a third term. And just four months later a stroke had taken him into Eternity, at his daughter's plantation. The funeral would be in North Carolina.

Louise asked Marg to come immediately to Washington, and they could go together. Marg decided it had to be done. She dropped everything and got ready to take the four-thirty train that evening for Atlanta. She'd get a chance to see her Justine once more.

A nice little white-faced girl of eight, with long luxurious brown hair in pink ribbons, was standing at the station with jiggling knees, a short pretty dress and a small bouquet of flowers for the arriving lady. An almond-colored, aging Louise Johnson stood tense, holding the child's hand. Marg strode down, not knowing which one to embrace first. Louise puckered her lips sternly to receive Marg's thin, pink lips.

"Oh, what a darling girl!" cried Marg, picking up Justine.

"This is Aunt Margery," Louise was quick to say. "Say hello to yo' Aunt, Justine."

In the carriage on the way, they talked about pussy cats, gold rings, school books, taking a bath, eating spinach and washing one's teeth. Lavinia met them at the house and took Justine away, while Louise kept the carriage waiting. She and Marg would leave some luggage, then rush off for the Johnson funeral. Within the hour a special train would be going down to Raleigh. Marg was breathless. The coach was crowded and they could not get seats together. Marg sat with a young reporter from the Louisville *Courier-Journal*. He introduced himself as Adolph Ochs. He asked Marg if she were a personal friend of President Johnson. She said yes, and that was all. She had promised herself never to do any "family" talk. Now she was thinking about poor Justine. Under Louise's strict care, she seemed a bit anxious, a bit harrowed. Marg decided she'd talk this over with Sue. She felt like starting a fight to get Justine back. Charles now was no longer the issue.

At the grave in Greenville, Marg and Louise stood close by while the shiny casket was being lowered into the ground. A serviceman was blowing taps on his bugle. Marg recognized a few of the dignitaries. She nodded to Judge McKnight, her old friend in Maple. She'd tell him he looked the same. Not to think of her father, she put her mind on the simple dignified look of the Johnson women. She felt proud of them.

"Strong men were weeping," said young Ochs, as he shook her hand upon saying good-bye.

"It's wonderful to be young and to have feelings," Marg told him. "You keep that, an' you'll be famous some day."

After three days of Justine and Louise, and some rather tense feelings, Marg decided it was time she go out to Caroline Street to spend the rest of her stay with Cousin Sue. Louise didn't try to change her mind. They really seemed angry at each other. Surely Marg's decision to lower the stipends couldn't be the only reason. She wanted to talk about it but it would have wound up an argument. She decided to say nothing. She brought some gifts for her baby; now she'd leave two hundred extra dollars with Louise. That should have brought a smile, but it didn't.

"Maybe she wants me to take back my baby," Marg told Sue that evening as they sat together eating peach cobbler pie.

"Oh, Louise doesn't know what she wants," exclaimed Sue. "I've questioned her, an' it's all mixed up in her mind. Childhood fears. Says she feels strange sometimes in public because the child is so fair an' people stare at them."

"They stared at me and my mother!" cried Marg. "Louise when younger always liked whiteness. If that's it, I'll take my baby home. You tell her so."

Chapter 44

Shortly after Marg got home she received another heavy vellum envelope, from Washington. It read:

August 15, 1875

Dear Mrs. Spence,

This is to express our deep appreciation to you and Miss Louise Johnson for the beautiful flowers sent at the passing of our beloved father, Andrew Johnson. He mentioned you to us several times; we also had the pleasure of meeting his Cousin Frances McDonough's family in Raleigh.

My mother and sister Mary join me in sending our thanks for your sympathy in these heavy days of bereavement.

Yours sincerely,

Martha Patterson.

Marg smiled; she knew this was as close as any well-bred American could get towards acknowledgement of any kinship across race lines. She'd save the letter for John, Beth, Meg, Jason. And Justine. She had intended going by Bill Cahill's to find out what steps could be taken in Georgia to rescue poor Justine. First she'd send a little thank-you note to Louise, to see if any sensible reply would be forthcoming.

That same first week home Cousin Don died. The family didn't want a big funeral. No wires were sent outside of town. Marg went to clean and proper St. James Methodist in Wentworth. It had finally joined the AME group, accepting "African" in its background. There was no need to stand alone. Life was so temporary. We need each other to get to our graves, thought Marg. She enjoyed the service immensely, remembering the quiet man who had worked continuously in a godly fashion. This service for him was a happy occasion for her, listening to "Amazing Grace", her mother's favorite hymn, on that beautiful organ she had had installed in her memory. And to gaze at her brilliant stained-glass window in honor of Judge Edward Malcolm: Jehovah feeding the birds. She could remember a verse of Isaiah 31:

"As birds flying, so will the Lord of hosts defend Jerusalem;
Defending also He will deliver her; and passing over
He will preserve her."

She'd give another window for Don. She felt proud, following the casket, walking over the soft red carpet her money too had bought. Now she could understand the thirst of carpetbaggers, and of white people in general. And she'd love every Negro who could cultivate a taste for beauty of spirit as well as of manmade things. Larry knew that beauty. She was hoping he and Maggie Mae were doing all right up there in that cold, selfish North.

When she got home from the funeral, Bubber was standing there at her door, looking skinny and brown and adolescent, just as he had ten years earlier.

"My gracious, Bubber! Lawdha'mercy!" She hugged him to her bosom. "Boy, I thought you were up in Chicago?"

"Yes'm, I was, but I decided to come home."

"Bless you. You didn't like it up North?"

He scratched his "coconut-shaped" head, as whites would say. "Well, it's all right. I learned to read an' write up dere. Then Bob wrote me what you was doin' down here. It sounded like I should come home."

"Oh-h, so he told you about our woodworkin' business. Fine! We can use another hand. Do you want to join us? Spence Enterprises?"

"Yes'm, Miss Margery. I sho would like that."

"Tell me, how old are you? Did you get married?"

He stood bare knees as before, there with his cap in his hand. "No'm, I didn't marry nobody yet. I suspects I's twenty-fo', now."

Marg still had her hand on his shoulder. "Well, we'll see about that. You got a place to stay?"

"Yes'm. I'm on Glory Road, at Bob's place."

Marg knew that brokendown shack. It was an eyesore. "You can come here an' live with me if you like—"

"Oh, yes mam!" Bubber was tickled pink to be invited to stay at Malcolm House. First thing, Marg put him to work picking her garden vegetables. Then she had him take the ashes out of all the fireplaces. Next, they went over to the Muggeridge house and put down carpeting in the bedroom. Cindy now was expecting, and Marg didn't want her to suffer any chill as the autumn months approached. Next, he fixed John's toolbox and painted an enamel coat on all the doors. Bubber was so glad to be working, to be needed. Glad to be home.

Cindy questioned him and found out where he had slept as a slave. She gave him back that space with a nice new bed. And Marg gave him the old grey bedroom back by her kitchen. Now he had two bedrooms! Plus the room at Bob's. Marg was even ready to discuss salary with him, but she told Bob they'd wait a week or so, to see how he did with Mr. Edison's order of bamboo sticks.

Usually when she'd go out to Cobb's Creek, Bubber would take her, enjoying his snuff and the snuffbox she had given him. This gave Adam time off to see his family just across the Chattahoochee. One day Marg heard Bubber talking to Matilda. She explained, Matilda was to be ignored. Bubber nodded, understanding perfectly.

The rednecks were pressuring Marg with terrible high bills for gas usage at the hospital. John worked late looking for items to cut in the hospital's budget. Also he'd see that the night porters did a proper cleaning job in the wards. Often when he worked late Marg and Cindy would have a light dinner together, and play dominoes. One early September night when they played, waiting for John, rain came and brought a chill. Marg was about to call Bubber to get him to make a fire, when she saw a dark shadow cross her lawn. It was only John coming home.

"Did you eat, Boy?" she called affectionately, allowing him to kiss her cheek before going to Cindy. "With yo' wife expectin', you too have to stay in top shape. We just had soup. Would you care for a steak?"

"A steak sounds great," said John, sitting at the table. "Is Irene still up?"

Marg threw her hand. "It's after nine. I don't bother her so late. You have to be civil with servants. I'll fry it, John."

"No, Mother, don't trouble yourself," said Cindy pushing her big belly against the table to rise. "I'm his wife." Just then, she and Marg saw a dark figure cross in front of the window. "Who was that?"

"I don't know," said Marg, rising cautiously. "Did you lock up over at yo' house, Cindy?"

"No'm. I didn't think I'd stay long."

"John, go upstairs an' bring my shotgun an' pistol. Hurry!"

As John moved off, a sleepy-eyed Charles came out of the billiard room. "What's wrong, Marg?"

"I think we've got some prowlers. Lower the lights, Charles. And barricade the doors!"

Just as Marg spoke, an Indian-like yell went up outdoors, and several shots rang in the air. Marg ushered her people into Malcolm House's darkened parlor to see what they could see. "It's the Klan!" yelled Cindy, frightened. "They've got on sheets. See!"

Sure enough, it was the Klan. About twenty of them gathered in front of the Muggeridge house. Already a fiery cross was burning savagely on the lawn. If poor Bubber was over there they'd frighten him to death. Marg had already told everybody about the secret room in the chickencoop, and now she wanted John and Cindy to go out there, to avoid the untold danger for them in the house. When John protested she said: "You do as I say! I'm sure I know why they're here. It's you, John!"

"What have I done?"

"It's you and yo' wife, John."

"Oh." Now he understood. The Klan had come because of their interracial marriage. Two years old, and now they were having trouble! At that moment they smelled smoke.

"They're burnin' my house," screamed Cindy, crouching near the window. As John grabbed her arm, ready to lead her to the backdoor and the chickencoop, someone outside yelled:

"Cindy! What you doin' in there with that nigger? Nigger John! Come out, you bastard! You white-faced bum! We'll teach you not to marry a white woman!"

Now there was sound of rocks thrown at both houses, and the crashing of glass. Windows in Malcolm House began to shatter. Irene and the other girl ran into the parlor to be with the family. Then came a frightened Adam Hinds, shaking like a leaf. The only one who didn't show was Bubber, and Marg was really concerned, now that there was steady shooting.

"Charles," she called, handing her husband a shotgun. "If anyone comes through that door, you shoot!" Marg, with another gun and pistol, decided the front door was hers while Charles could handle the rear door. She made everyone get down and away from the windows now lit up from the raging fire next door.

"Nigger John, you bastard! Come out like a man!" There was more crashing. John and Cindy stood in a corner hugging each other.

"You'd better go to the chickencoop," ordered Marg. Her son uttered a slight protest, and she grabbed him cruelly by the ear, then pushed him toward the kitchen. Cindy wobbled up to his side and together they started out the backdoor. Now somebody was jiggering at the frontdoor. Irene's crying turned to gulps while Adam said his prayers loudly.

All of a sudden there was a neying of horses, and a wicked exchange of crossfire outside. Neither Marg nor Charles knew what was going on. The attacks on Malcolm House seemed to stop. When she went to the door and cautiously opened it, she saw a big mob of black people. It was Mr. Wilkins and his firefighters!

"We came as quickly as we could, Mrs. Spence," said a perspiring dark-brown Wilkins. "We really got to rush to save the Muggeridge house."

"Oh, thank you! God bless you, Mr. Wilkins! Can we help?" Marg, still with her weapons, went grabbing Charles and the others, pushing them outside. Now from under the porch came two pointed-head Klansmen in white sheets. One started for Charles with a raised, glittering knife. Marg screamed, and the other grabbed her guns. Charles wrestled with his attacker. They went down on the porch. Marg's two servantgirls and Hinds ran back into the house. She and Charles had to struggle alone. In the bright light from the fire, Wilkins saw them and came again. He came, big and burly, swinging his fists. The two Klansmen quickly got up and scurried off the porch and down the street. Charles was hurt. His clothing was bloody.

***** ***** *****

Next morning, local citizens stared at the broken windows of Malcolm House. The flagpole was lying across the lawn, like a broken mast, among bits of red, white and blue, rippings of the country's flag. Another crowd stood in front of the burnt-out shell next door, all that was left of the Muggeridge house. All windows were gone. All curtains, gone. John and Cindy likewise were gone. At the hospital. She had suffered a miscarriage. Jeb Hunter held his daughter while she cried in his arms, in a bed in the "nigger hospital", as people called it. Clark Memorial also had Charles in another room. He had lost an eye from the cruel slash of a Klansman's knife. Marg was bitter and heartbroken. She had stayed there all night, thankful for the good doctors, for the hospital she had built. Poor Bubber was nowhere to be found. She worried that somebody would come and announce they had found his body.

"I doubt that he'd dead," said a tearful Valerie. "Bubber's too clever for that."

"He'll come home when he's hungry," said a sympathetic Edna Clark, also visiting at the hospital. "Now Marg, if you're ready to go home, I'll see you get in bed there. You need complete rest."

"I must talk to John," Marg told her friend. "He's talkin' crazy, saying he'll quit his job an' leave Georgia."

"Is that so crazy?" asked Edna, bucking her eyes. "Marg, let him go! They have each other. An' they have a whole life before them."

"Now he wants to get back to medical school. Up to Harvard again."

"Let him go! Let him go!"

Marg was tearful now. "H-he says he'll never return here. Never g-go to Muggeridge h-house any more. H-help me. What am I to do!"

Edna talked three days and three nights to John and Cindy. They had made up their mind never to go back to Muggeridge house or Malcolm House. The Klan had frightened them away. Edna had to take them in. She made everything comfortable. She even hired musicians to serenade them with soft quiet string music. It didn't work. A sober John, still in shock, asked her to go to the railroad station and get two tickets to Cambridge. They departed, at night, even before Charles was let out of the hospital.

Marg sat at her breakfast table with empty teacup. She was thinking. Bubber had come back. He said he bravely had followed the Klan that night. He went running in the shadows after they had done their burning. He stuck with them until they disbanded to individual houses. The one he followed home was Brady Innis, the mayor of Maple. Bubber said he waited there until the hooded man went inside his house and took off his white sheet, with lamp burning. There he saw his face. It was Mr. Innis!

Marg thought about this testimony. With crooked whites now running the courthouse again, there was nothing they could do. Maybe the Federal judge would listen. She had heard that Judge McKnight was back in Georgia, over in Augusta. She could write to him. Or she could write to President Grant. But to what purpose? She had to live with these Maple crackers after the Federals were gone. And they'd soon be gone. They couldn't stay forever.

When Charles got better, she talked to him about what action they should take. That nasty Bowman heading the Freedmen's Bureau should have come himself to talk to them. Instead he sent a deputy. He would do nothing. The most sympathetic person had been Sylvia Sharkey Redberry. She had told her minister what Bubber had seen. The minister promised to get a group of respectable whites on the matter. Marg now cautioned Bubber not to go any place alone. While Sylvia had wanted to help, she had marked him forever.

Marg thought he should go now back North, perhaps to live with Larry in New Jersey. Her financing. Meanwhile, she went ahead and had new windowglass put in Malcolm House. The Muggeridge house was too badly damaged by fire. They had to tear it down. The winter weather did not deter Marg in ordering a big, beautiful four-tier bronze fountain tinted white; and soon hers was the only property on Plum Avenue with a giant, park-like spread of grass, flowers and fountain. It was her cemetery. She had lost John and Cindy.

Chapter 45

That winter of 1875-76 was a long dreary one. John and Cindy were happy up North but Marg didn't feel right losing them this way. Poor Jeb Hunter with his little freedom of being a cotton executive in the white under-class, came to Marg with sorrowful face, and gave her back $500 of what he had borrowed eight years earlier, thinking she would need it. He understood Klan hatred; all of his neighbors had it.

Marg persevered, getting her hospital a county designation which meant some public funds coming into its budget. Her days became more relaxing. One frosty morn out at the Wentworth place she and Matilda met at the door, and a quick smile passed through their eyes. Matilda had an expensive sweater at her shoulders. Marg had heard that she was active at Spruce Baptist. If she gave up this business, and adopted some kids, Marg thought she might put her in her will. But now she was letting out the sheriff, which meant collusion with money-hungry whites. *Jesus, save her*!

That same winter, county auditors came to Clark Memorial Hospital checking all the books. They kept asking what John's duties were. Soon they hinted of a shortage of twenty thousand dollars. Marg showed them her personal files, and slowly they began to piece something together. While first going after John, the deeper they got, it couldn't be denied they had to concentrate on Bill Cahill. It seems in concluding contracts, he had put an extra ten per cent on the books for himself. When they arrested him, Marg of course visited him at the jail, that same ugly grey building where Poor Bill had himself come with Mrs. Bowne to visit a dejected imprisoned Marg.

Marg got Cahill a good Atlanta lawyer. It was the least she could do. In a way, she knew that Bill had been stealing from her. But so had all the other white business people she knew! Sending Bubber away, up to New Jersey to live, she knew that even there he'd have to watch out for vicious whites, even in matters of law. An honest colored youth, or a helper like Cahill, could suffer where petty kingdoms got out of control. The country, she felt, could not afford city-rule, county-rule, state-rule and Federal-rule—all corrupt.

In March 1876 Marg got a new $10,000 contract with Mr. Edison. It was her biggest business. Luckily her woodworkers did fine, in spite of indiscreet disturbances from Matilda's hotel. Marg wished she could go next door, plop down ten thousand cash on the counter, and dare Matilda to refuse it. That was the way to get rid of trouble!

Marg relaxed reading about the Belknap scandal in Washington. Sue told her things where the newspapers left off. Marg remembered proud Mrs. Belknap as a cute and dashing Kentucky belle who married the Secretary of War after her own sister, his first wife, had died. Now as queen of the Cabinet, hers was the fashionable Washington set that spent summers at Long Branch where President Grant also summered. However, a House committee was investigating charges a real estate agent made against the Belknaps. An old friend, Mrs. Marsh, turned perky; her husband was to be called up and Mrs. Belknap wanted him to perjure himself. The papers talked about Mrs. Belknap's fantastic wardrobe, with forty pairs of shoes, parasols with coral handles, Worth gowns (they said when the Paris designer got her trousseau order he went to a cave and fasted seven days). Well, now the House voted to impeach her husband! The public still sympathized with her, the beautiful Venus, because they did not know she was ready to corrupt the law Judge Edward, Marg's father, swore by as the strength of America.

One rainy April day Marg entered Broad Street way up, on her way to Malcolm Spanish Court; she stumbled upon a beautiful bronze statue of her father! It startled her so, she injured her ankle on the carriage brake. Daddy with greenish face smiled mischievously at her. It was a good likeness. *Whites had done this without including her*! She didn't exist. A nobody. She imagined the white Malcolm family coming down from Atlanta for the ceremony, proud as peacocks. How could she have missed it in the papers? And nobody mentioned it, not even the servants. Some not-jealous friend should have told her. Yes. Steadfast Family and Friends. *Life, give me these, please*!

Reaching her office building she felt like talking to someone wise. She went to old Uncle Vincent. The clickety-clack of his presses was impressive, as was his white apron and white wallboard where he had clippings of the Maple *Clarion's* great stories. It was a quiet newspaper, never abrasive, never challenging the vindictive bitter whites who ran the town.

"Darling, we've entered a new age," he told her, with trembling voice. "Now, it's slavery of the word. A new crafty plot to control the black man. An' he can't survive unless he knows history to a tee. They won't print it right! An' every new foreigner comin' here will git the abridged story. They'll never know nothin' about people like you and me."

"What are we to do?" Marg asked, accepting his coffee.

"Haven't you noticed in my paper? Always a history lesson. That's it! Clever young people will pick it up an' go to git knowledge an' courage. Progress!"

"Colored people don't stick together, Uncle Vincent. I tried with that Blake woman, but she came at me like a tiger, demandin' things."

"There ain't no *one* simple colored man!"

"Well, I wouldn't come down to her level, an' most of them don't want to reach up to our level. They think it's stiff an' false."

He took a serious face. "It's what the country runs by. Anglo-Saxon. That's part of me. But pure whites'll point you *only to Africa*! Slavery of the Word again! Now I'll tell you about Bonnie Blake. She and most blacks in dis town'll follow Ida Wilkins, yo' Matilda, who got rich off prostitution. Now dat Wilkins woman ain't all bad. Good for politics! Hah! But dat Blake kind, the Devil-judges, think they's Jesus-judges. She hates you for yo' background, yo' looks. They can sit there in St. James Baptist clappin' religion; dey ain't got no sense! I had one dark cousin; first she was stickin' pins in me, but I always talk nice to her. Slowly she began to love an' appreciate me, more than my own sister. An' I took care of her till she died. When you appreciates fully, you *respects* people! We had good times together. Hah! Good times! An' I never saw her as a dark woman, an' she never acted like one!"

A smiling Marg pushed his shoulder. "A judge would say you're prejudiced."

He bucked his eyes. "Dey say anything! So long as he's sittin' on top bein' superior. Did you know our navy was fifty per cent colored when dey was winnin' all dem battles? Naw-suh, nobody tells you! Marg, America can never get rid of us. We *is* America!"

Marg smiled at his drop in English. She understood it. He was being two people. Had always been. And, in two weeks' time he was dead. At seventy-two. A full life.

Marg congratulated her friend Edna Clark for taking over Vincent Simpson's *Clarion* newspaper. Also in the spring of 1876 Edna helped start Meharry Medical College up in Nashville, the first such Negro institution in America. Her son, Ed, would go there in September. Marg continued to welcome white doctors at her hospital, and continued to read the local white paper, Maple *Star-Journal*, in spite of all its evil intent. She balanced it with sane northern publications.

That same glorious spring of 1876, Marg took her gang, Bob Jenkins, Adam Hinds, Mitchell and Albert, all up to Philadelphia, to the Centennial Exposition. This her working force from Spence Enterprises, was her royal entourage. With a smile she'd show them the fabled North. In a dedicated fashion, they built a very impressive booth for Mr. Thomas Alva Edison, and one next to it for Mr. Alexander Graham Bell, who would show the world his new invention called the telephone. Those same northern newspapers who raved about the inventions of Edison and Bell, began to talk about Marg's two handsome booths. They thought she was a stage designer from New York. When they discovered her a Georgian, they wrote about this, to show that the cementing of the country had happened.

While a fashionable Marg stood alone on duty at Edison's booth, she got seven more contracts for convention display work. Mr. Edison was so pleased that he signed her up for something new on his phonograph. In June, he had Larry and Maggie Mae there in Philadelphia. And they brought Bubber with them! Marg was thrilled to see them all again; they really looked fresh and happy. Larry now spoke better English; he was in school, reading difficult things: science and physics. Edison told Marg most any man's mind could be inspired to higher heights, usually upon leaving the path of common men, establishing some spiritual connection with books, dreams and with God. He said the manmade limitations should be broken like shackles. Marg thought he meant something racial, but it was never specifically declared, and she'd never ask, because she knew Mr. Edison shared her own concept that mankind was colorless.

Mr. Densmore came, acting important like the men he was with. It seems the typewriter, now Mr. Remington's, was a great success, making them millionaires. Marg worried because now he acted as if he had never known her. Was she so inferior? Or was recognition so precious it moves a man out of your world? She thought his weak, anti-Christian behavior. Yet, didn't the strength of success bring satisfied joy, and an idea of being superior? Phyllis Korner and Matilda should know. Maybe one day they could talk it over—in Heaven.

The first thing Jason said when they met was: "Who is my real mother?". Marg kissed him and said: "I am, angel!". He seemed convinced. Jason enjoyed taking his mother to his school, so the white boys could see he had a family just as white as theirs. His toughness was a quiet kind, and Marg knew he needed this to survive.

Bountiful pride and joy came in July, when Ted and Beth, John and Cindy visited Marg. Like a glowing mother hen, she took them to the best places. Jesus had made them all so perfect-looking. She prayed that their lives would equally be at an apex.

A great surprise came in August. Angela Baker, looking very pretty, walked up to the booth with a group of distinguished men. Finally, Marg got the chance to meet Mr. Leonard Jerome, Jennie's father. He was pleasant and nice-looking for 58. A blondish young man stood at his side; it was none other than Lord Randolph Churchill, now a member of Parliament. Wearing a handsome grey frock coat, he smiled nicely on Marg, and introduced his traveling companion, Harry Tyrwhitt. They were on their way to Jerome Park in New York where Mr. Jerome was introducing polo to America. Lord Randolph was pleased to meet someone who knew his Jennie. He said she was busy with their baby, Winston, back in London. He showed Marg a photo, saying they would go to Ireland later that year. Marg couldn't help but feel that the attractive popeyed Lord Randolph looked more like a mulatto than a white man. But the British, of course, never had any mulattoes!

At the end of summer Marg sent her group on, back to Georgia. Anthony tried to get her to come to New York. Haney too. But she said no. She had engaged a Philadelphia lawyer to work with her on her case to regain Justine. The firm had sent a lawyer to Washington to talk to Louise. Finally she was willing to let Justine go. She'd get five thousand dollars, as much as Lydia Farley Smith got from Mr. Thaddeus Stevens, and Lydia had worked many more years for him than sour Louise had spent caring for Justine.

Marg was ready to return to Georgia after a brief court appearance in Washington. With the court's decision, a confused Justine frowned and pouted, wondering why this so-called Aunt Margery wanted to take her away. Cousin Sue was better at being explicit, sweet and patient with the child. Her own two were about the same age; she wanted Justine to feel she had relatives. All the cousins!

Reluctantly Justine allowed them to take her to Georgia, her first train ride. A somewhat disfigured Charles met them at the railroad station. No longer dreamy-eyed. But Marg was glad to see him, after four months. She had told him her great secret while he suffered in Clark Memorial, when he admitted being shot at in Savannah, by a girlfriend's Spanish suitor. He said he was a good Christian now. With one eye gone, she felt he could feel no more pain. She had explained to him that Christianity was born of pain. Charles understood. He could accept Justine.

The child was not satisfied with the quick attention he gave her. He got on telling Marg the sad news. Matilda was dead. Shot dead in front of their building. Just like a wild animal. It was some disagreement with Brady Innis. A money matter, people said. The sheriff shot her; said she was resisting arrest.

Marg blinked away a tear. Well, it was done! She told Charles they'd go to Matilda's funeral Tuesday, first sending a blanket of roses. No. It would have to be a blanket of orchids. Something rare! Having digested the sad local news, Marg gave a business smile to Justine who was not impressed by the huge, shiny Spence carriage with its uniformed coachman and footman.

To quiet a restless Justine Marg had explained to her on the train that she was her real mother, that her name was Spence and not Johnson, that a court of law had reaffirmed it, and everybody had to live by the laws of the land. Justine was not convinced. All through the Carolinas Marg had kept shouting: "I'm Mommy. Now love Mommy, Justine." When Justine saw a greying, one-eyed, cashew-colored Charles waiting at the Georgia station, it presented a new problem to figure out. She had never known a father. Mother Louise had told her that her father was dead, that he had been a white man. Justine looked at Charles suspiciously all the way home.

Trying to forget Matilda, Marg ate strawberries. Justine stood there with upturned nose. Marg showed her the beautiful lavender bedroom which would be her very own. It was bigger than two rooms in Louise's house, the best two rooms. Next, there was a whole cupboard full of dolls, including several made by Matilda, now looking too much alive and mischievous like that smiling statue of her father. Then they went out to the refurbished big-as-life dollhouse resting on green grass in the backyard. Next came real china dishes for her dolls, and a look at Charles' three handsome German retrievers. Justine still wasn't impressed.

As they sat down in velvet chairs, servants with food put on a little parade in the dining room. There were lots of tasty things to eat. Justine ate like a bird. Marg, tired from a whole day and a half of urging, decided she'd go up and rest in her room, and let the child find something to interest herself.

As Marg reached the foyer, Justine suddenly appeared, and stood there with hands on her hips. "He's not my father," she shouted at Marg.

"Why do you say that?"

"He's not white enough!"

Marg smiled. "Well, darling, we can go to Sweden and find you a real blond father, then you'll tell me he's not the true one because he has kinky hair. Remember that picture we saw at the museum of the starving black African child? It had light hair. Blondish-white hair. Same as the Swede's kinky hair. Much in coloration is determined by food and how yo' body utilizes food. The starving African child turned blond . . . now, I see you're not listening! Justine, your father could be the man in the moon, but I say he's my Charles."

"Are you telling me the truth?"

"I swear, darling, my Charles is your father."

Justine was snappy now. "Put yo' hand on the Bible an' say it." She was standing right at Marg's huge family Bible on the foyer's original Spence table.

Marg allowed Justine to put her fingers on the thick soft pages of her father's big Bible. She mumbled something as Justine demanded. Now the child looked satisfied. Biting her thin lips, she skipped away, wanting to get another close-up look at Charles, her new father.

Marg stood in the foyer feeling a bit weak. Her chest was paining again. This child would have her in her grave! But she thanked God just the same. She was happy to have Justine home. She knew now she'd have to change her will. Since her real three children probably couldn't stand Maple, Justine perhaps would be the one to love and care for Malcolm House. She'd inherit it, and she was a Malcolm. Maybe Jason too, if he were a Spence. They'd get Cliff and Sylvia as godparents. To conquer the Devil she had thought of leaving it to Matilda, or Phyllis Korner. What would poor, jealous, white Phyllis do with Malcolm House? No, better to let Justine have it. She had the fight, and eventually she'd carry her head proudly. Especially when told the Waverly part of it.

Marg sat down by the fine English walnut lowboy table, allowing her fingers once again to go over the smooth paper of the Bible. It was open to the family page. She saw her mother's name, Alice, then the names of all the children: Paul, Margery, Gregory, Anthony. There were methodical entries of birth dates. All in her father's strong handwriting. Above, next to her mother's name, there was a conspicuous blank line. Practically the only blank line among many names. It was meant for her father's name. But Judge Edward Malcolm had never had it in mind to write his name in this particular family Bible. Marg had once asked him about it when she was young and sassy like Justine. He never answered her. And she never forgave him for that. But neither she nor her dear mother would ever write in his name. The blank line remained conspicuous among all the very correct listings of husbands, marriages, children, and deaths.

She thought of all the fashionable guests who had come to Malcolm House over the years, some surely looking into this giant book of life, the family Bible. Minus a name. Her children had spent their hours absorbing the beautiful colored pictures between its rich Moroccan leather cover of red and gold. Marg knew that the omission of the crucial name was a kind of acceptance of a social system that forbade the thought of it. Her dear father had always said he was from a legal world of truth! Now she believed that all the judges and lawyers reserved a space in their minds to remain uncommitted, where the truth would go against them. *That fear of man.*

Marg left the foyer's sun and started up the cool, sturdy, curving staircase. Malcolm House had truly been her refuge. Thank you, Jesus! Now on with teaching Justine. She heard her screaming somewhere. The little brat thinking herself white was no whiter than her other children, even with her so-called pure white father! *Dear Charles, how is it in Heaven?* Now she remembered the sky's blackness when Charles Waverly died. She understood it. All the Negroes out there, they knew that special tunnel through America, and they would move through the dark, seeing very well, understanding the privilege of darkness, a gift from God, and understanding the water wheel beyond the tunnel, understanding all the busy lawyers and general-like judges very well.

EPILOGUE

Sitting in the warmth of a familiar hearth, through the cold wintry nights, one comes again to spring, to the beauty of flowers, to the natural light of the outside world. 1877 blossomed like the rest, but one thing did happen: Grant left the Executive Mansion, and with him all hope for a long-suffering people. Rutherford B. Hayes did not win the election as President in his place. The Republicans had Blaine, the Halfbreed, the more popular candidate. He had cultivated the money groups who knew that their party could not win forever with bayonets and Negroes. Neither Conkling nor Morton could seriously expect the nomination. Hayes like Bristow was regarded as rather dull. But it is said that his very weakness won him the position. On the Democratic side, Samuel Tilden of New York was to gain through the election of an aggressive temporary chairman, Henry Watterson, and of course with a platform against corruption.

Enough of the people, fed-up with the word Reconstruction, seemed to realize certain superiorities of either Tilden or the Democratic position. On election day, November 7, 1876, the popular vote gave Tilden 4,284,265 and Hayes 4,033,295. However, there was dispute in the southern states, and a certain suzerainty allowing adjustment. Tilden had 184 undisputed electoral votes, and 185 were necessary. Hayes had only 165 undisputed electoral votes. Somehow Zachariah Chandler announced on November 8th that Hayes had won, but the three disputed states in the South became a point of political war. Legal minds felt the Constitution did not offer a solution to the problem. An Electoral Commission was established by the two houses of Congress meeting together on February 1st, 1877. Behind the scenes, the political maneuvering continued right up till March. It is said that Democratic electors yielded to political pressure.

In the end, Hayes was inaugurated President on March 5, 1877. Thirty-six short days later he began withdrawing Federal troops from the South. The Negro people were stunned, and wondered if this were just another Washington deal: a promise to get somebody something. They were to suffer unaided another vicious and bitter Civil War. During this much longer war, localities imposed their stealing, their black codes, their Slavery of the Word, and managed to wipe out practically all freedoms won. The North allowed it. A new century dawned, a new America of foreigners. The Negro still was in bondage. And the half-Negro felt, for the first time, subjugation of caste. All semblance of class, dignity, position and honor was taken from them. What they had given America as individuals—rivers, buildings, history—was no longer theirs to give. They became a race of slaves which they had never been. The starting over was made basic and fictional. Everyone of color could be reduced down to a level of oneness. Inferior oneness. Blackness. Race was really politics.

*****   *****   *****

THE END

*****   *****   *****